"Mar...s of his.........ice, and for most gay read............................more deeply than anything Mann has written since *An American Boy*.
                    —*Edge*

"A beautifully crafted masterpiece of a story."
                    —*Echo* magazine

"Mann's story telling moves us to a world of deeply realistic characters . . ."
                    —*Boston Spirit*

"An excellent summer read."
                    —*OutSmart* magazine

"Reaffirms William J. Mann's reputation as one of gay fiction's major narrative powers."
                    —*Gay Chicago Magazine.com*

Men Who Love Men

"Powerful . . . Mann's most mature and ambitious fiction to date . . . a strong, sexy novel that will stand out."
                    —*Lambda Book Report*

"There is a satisfying sense of completion for the characters and the trilogy."
                    —*The Gay & Lesbian News*

All American Boy

"[Mann's] most complex novel to date . . . fans will be refreshed by his audacious change of pace."
                    —*Publishers Weekly*

Where the Boys Are

"Mann's party boys make a sexy first impression but prove surprisingly deep upon further inspection. The same goes for *Where the Boys Are*."
                    —*Kirkus Reviews*

The Men from the Boys

"One of the most honest and engrossing books in years."
                    —*Out*

"This first novel distinguishes its author as one of gay fiction's most promising writers. Mann eloquently tells a story of mature, but gay, professionals who have shaped their own lives and created their own families."
                    —*Booklist*

Books by William J. Mann

Novels

THE MEN FROM THE BOYS

THE BIOGRAPH GIRL

WHERE THE BOYS ARE

ALL AMERICAN BOY

MEN WHO LOVE MEN

OBJECT OF DESIRE

Nonfiction

WISECRACKER: The Life and Times of William Haines,
Hollywood's First Openly Gay Star

BEHIND THE SCREEN: How Gays and Lesbians Shaped
Hollywood, 1910–1969

EDGE OF MIDNIGHT: The Life of John Schlesinger

KATE: The Woman Who Was Hepburn

HOW TO BE A MOVIE STAR: Elizabeth Taylor in Hollywood

GAY PRIDE: A Celebration of All Things Gay and Lesbian

OBJECT OF DESIRE

WILLIAM J. MANN

KENSINGTON BOOKS
http://www.kensingtonbooks.com

KENSINGTON BOOKS are published by

Kensington Publishing Corp.
119 West 40th Street
New York, NY 10018

All Kensington titles, imprints, and distributed lines are available at special quantity discounts for bulk purchases for sales promotion, premiums, fund-raising, educational, or institutional use.

Special book excerpts or customized printings can also be created to fit specific needs. For details, write or phone the office of the Kensington Special Sales Manager: Attn. Special Sales Department. Kensington Publishing Corp., 119 West 40th Street, New York, NY 10018. Phone: 1-800-221-2647.

Kensington and the K logo Reg. U.S. Pat. & TM Off.

ISBN-13: 978-0-7582-1378-5
ISBN-10: 0-7582-1378-6

First Hardcover Printing: July 2009
First Trade Paperback Printing: July 2010
10 9 8 7 6 5 4 3 2 1

Printed in the United States of America

For Tim

PALM SPRINGS, CALIFORNIA

The first time I saw him, he was nothing more than a face and a pair of hands. Not once did his eyes meet mine. Even as he took my order, his chin was already lifting to greet the man behind me. The first time I saw him, he did not see me.

It was a green night. The mountains were gray and the sand blowing in from the desert was yellow, but the night itself was so green, it was almost emerald. A mirage, I knew. A trick of the setting sun. On a green night, nothing was what it seemed.

"Do you know who he is?" I asked my friend Randall, my eyes fixed on the bartender.

"Who?"

"Him."

Randall shook his head. "Never seen him before."

"He's beautiful."

"You think?"

With much reluctance did I turn my eyes away to focus on my friend. A green cast was coloring his face as the last slanting rays of the sun reflected against the mountains. Night was rushing in to fill up every corner of the bar's outdoor deck, and the busboys were busy lighting the lanterns that hung over our heads. Little flames leapt and hopped as if they were living, breathing creatures, and I was reminded, yet again, of the night my sister disappeared twenty-seven years before, the night when everything in my world changed, the night I came to understand that I would never grow up to be the man I had expected to be.

"He is *beautiful*, Randall," I said, with conviction. "Absolutely beautiful."

"Danny," my friend replied, "I did not come out with you tonight to moon over beautiful bartenders." He glowered at me, his face pinched and unhappy, as if he'd just bitten into a lemon.

I gave him a small smile. "I'm sorry," I said. "I know you want to talk about Ike. Go ahead. I'm listening."

He looked aghast. "I do *not* want to talk about Ike."

"Okay, then, let's not talk about him."

Randall huffed. "Why would I drive all the way out here to the desert if I wanted to ruin your birthday by talking about Ike?"

I managed a small smile. "It wouldn't ruin my birthday, Randall."

He pouted. "Of course, it would. It ruined my entire *life*." He raised his martini to me. "Happy birthday, Danny."

I raised mine to him. "Thank you, Randall."

My birthday. Ever since my teens, the day had felt awkward and peculiar, even inappropriate, fraught with memories tattered and terrible but sometimes freakishly funny as well. After the age of fourteen—the age I turned on the day my sister disappeared—all birthday parties ceased in my house. I never blamed my parents for it. I never thought it unfair. Not until I was twenty did I have another birthday party—given to me, in fact, by Randall, soon after I'd arrived in California. It felt odd, all that singing and merrymaking, not to mention the sex that went on after the party. I felt as if I was being unfaithful—not to my sister, not to my parents, but to me, to the boy I'd left behind in Connecticut. The boy who had done everything he could but still had ultimately failed.

"Talk to me," I said to Randall. "Talk to me about Ike."

He frowned. "It's your *birthday*, Danny. We're out to have *fun* tonight. It's not often you and I get a chance to go out on our own. Usually, there's Frank with us and—"

"And Ike," I finished.

"And Ike." Randall let out a long, dramatic sigh. "Oh, alack and alas. Our happy little foursome is no more."

We were never a happy little foursome, but I didn't say that to Randall. Neither Frank nor I had ever cared all that much for Ike. I didn't say that, either. What I did do was glance back at the bar. I couldn't see the bartender anymore. It was too dark now. Besides, too many men had crowded around his station.

"Did I tell you he wants to take the dog?" Randall asked.

I returned my eyes to Randall's face. "You never liked that dog."

"Still, we got it together. I paid for its shots."

"Now you're being petty, Randall."

"Well, what's *wrong* with being petty? *He's* the one who fell in love with someone else. Someone younger, someone more attractive. Now *that's* being petty."

No, not petty. Cruel. Heartless. Inconvenient. Honest. All those things, maybe, but not petty. Yet none of it did I say to Randall.

Instead, I looked again for the bartender and spotted his face emerging for a moment from the crowd. "How can you say he's not beautiful?" I asked despite myself.

Randall snorted. "Please. They're a dime a dozen, those bartenders. He probably has a crystal meth habit." He took another sip of his martini. "Well, what are you doing standing here if he fascinates you so much? Aren't you going to introduce yourself?"

"Maybe."

Randall leaned in for the kill. "Make sure you tell him you're married. You know how pissed these boys get when you fail to mention that little detail."

Instinctively, my thumb moved inside my palm to feel the titanium band around my left ring finger. Married. Yes, I supposed I was, even if California had yet to consider what Frank and I had done in Canada legal. But what did "married" mean, anyway—especially here, on this green night in the middle of the desert? What did it mean after twenty years—the last four of which had been a string of silent nights, the only sound the tapping of our computer keys, our faces bathed in the blue light of our monitors, each of us waiting for the other to call it a night so that the last one of us awake might be free to jack off, to find some fleeting, puny satisfaction with the boys of online porn?

I looked back over at the bar. All I could see was the top of his head. His thick, dark hair, the sharply cut sideburns. How very much I wanted to see his eyes.

"I know what you're thinking," Randall said. "I should have defined my relationship with Ike the way you've defined yours with Frank. You can't lose someone if that's simply not part of the playbook. That's why you and Frank have held on all these years, despite all the boys who've come between you." He knocked back the last of his martini. "How very *nice* for you."

I smiled, eyes still averted. "Bitter doesn't become you, Randall."

"I'm not bitter."

That was debatable. Randall had always had big dreams, though they weren't anything like my big dreams. My dreams had always been about success; Randall's were about contentment. Once, just starting out in med school, he'd imagined he'd be a great surgeon; he'd ended up as a kids' orthodontist in Century City. Once, when we were young, he'd dreamed of finding a husband with whom he'd grow old. But the only thing that had happened was that Randall himself had grown old.

"I could never have been like you and Frank," he was saying, shaking his head, as if he were reading my mind. "I could never have let Ike sleep around."

I shrugged and finished my vodka.

Once, I had been in love with Randall. We had both been twenty years old—slightly more than half our current ages. We'd been living in West Hollywood, in those exciting months when it first broke away from Los Angeles to become its own city—the first gay city in the world, we liked to say. It was difficult for me to remember the way Randall had looked back then. The eyes were the same, round like buttons and as blue as an August sky. But the glorious black hair had receded over the passing years, and the belly, once trim, had grown thick. I tried to picture him as he was, but I couldn't.

Not that it surprised me. So little of my months in California before Frank remained in my memory. All I could remember now with any real clarity were the Big Weenie hot-dog stands (BIG WEENIES TASTE BETTER) and the NO FAGS sign posted at Barney's Beanery. And the clubs. I remembered more about the clubs than anything else: the smell of piss and beer, the silver strobe lights, the music (Duran Duran, Cyndi Lauper, Yes). I think my strongest memory of those days was doing lines of coke behind the bar as "Owner of a Lonely Heart" played on the sound system.

But not much else remained in my brain from the time before Frank. I'd been a scared, insecure kid just off the bus. I'd lived with Randall in an apartment near Fairfax. I remembered a claw-foot bathtub, a ratty old couch, VHS tapes stacked against the wall almost to the ceiling. There'd been sex, a lot of sex, even though the plague was all around us then: sex with Randall, sex with Edgar, sex with Benny, sex with tons of others, usually on my waterbed, which one time sprang a leak.

But what could never fade from my memory of that time was the ambition, so tightly wound up inside me that it sometimes woke me in the middle of the night, bolting me upright, my hands clenched at my sides, causing me to scream out loud, wak-ing the neighbors. I had traveled all the way across the country on a Peter Pan bus in order to be someone. I had failed back home, failed miserably, and so I had come west, like so many had before me. *To be someone.* And so I did—I became someone on top of a box in a club on Santa Monica Boulevard, wearing a pair of cowboy boots and a yellow thong, twisting my ass to Boy George and "Karma Chameleon."

Oh, yes. A very long time ago.

On nights that were never green.

"I thought it would be *me* who found the lasting relationship," Randall was saying, his voice low, his words beginning to slur from the vodka. "I thought it would be *me* who ended up living happily ever after—not *you,* Danny. You were always so flighty. Al-ways moving from one boy to the next."

I lowered my gaze at him. "You'll *find* someone, Randall. You'll forget Ike, and you'll fall in love again. With someone who is *wor-thy* of you this time. Ike never was."

This mellowed him a bit. "I'm just not sure how many more times I can go through it." He looked so sad standing there. So sad and so old. "Falling in love is *hell,*" he said.

"You're crazy. Everyone wants to be in love."

"Oh, sure, in the beginning." Randall drew up his chin and

looked defiantly at me with his blue eyes. "It's great to be in love in the beginning—when you're giddy and lovesick, and you think about the person all the time, and he thinks about you. You call each other nine, ten times a day. You wish you could be together all the time. You start to miss him even before you say good night. It's the most thrilling feeling in the world, being in love." He paused for dramatic effect. "*In the beginning.*"

I laughed. "What you need is to get laid tonight."

Randall scowled. "Oh, let's just get out of here and have some dinner."

"I'm not hungry," I lied.

"Well, we've got to eat."

"Who says?"

Randall was looking past me, into the crowd. I followed his gaze. A slim, blond young man in blue jeans and a vintage Atari T-shirt.

"He's cute," I said.

Randall's scowl only deepened. "Well, then it's *your* lucky night, Danny, because he's been looking at *you* ever since we got here."

"How do you know that? Maybe he's been looking at you."

Randall narrowed his eyes at me. "No, Danny. Let me give you a visual. Me, chubby and balding. You, muscles and a full head of hair. Need I say more?"

"You're too hard on yourself, Randall."

"He's just a kid, anyway," he said, shrugging. "Why would he look at old men like us?"

I laughed. "You forget that in Palm Springs, even turning forty-one still qualifies us as chicken." I gestured with my drink. "Look around you."

The place was, as usual, packed with fifty- to seventy-somethings. Distinguished-looking men mostly, men who had once been handsome, men who even now retained some awareness of how they should look, even if they were largely held together by buttons and cinched belts and oversize Tommy Bahama floral-print shirts. A noticeable few displayed the plumped lips and shiny foreheads of cosmetic surgery. But the ones who stood out most were the heirs of Liberace, scattered randomly throughout the crowd, wearing red velvet blazers and too much sweet cologne.

"Go ahead," I urged Randall. "Go make a move on blondie over there."

"Oh, please. He wants *you*, Danny. Don't you want a birthday fuck?"

I leveled my eyes at him. "For your information, I had already planned on going home to Frank tonight."

"Oh, really? And will there be a trick waiting to sleep between you?"

"Tonight, my friend," I told him, "it will be *you* who goes home with the trick."

I took hold of Randall's arm and tugged. I owed him this one.

"What are you doing?" he asked, big-eyed.

"Come with me."

I led him across the deck. The curly blond in the Atari T-shirt noticed our approach but continued talking with two older men, pretending he hadn't.

"Hello," I said to the group. "I hate to interrupt. . . ."

"Well, we've been hoping you might do just that all night," said one of the older men. "Or at least, *he* has."

The man's eyes twinkled. He wore a black double-breasted blazer with a pink silk pocket puff. I assumed the "he" being referenced was blondie.

"Great," I said. "Because I want to introduce you to my great friend Randall here. Randall Drew, prominent orthodontist of Century City, collector of East Asian artifacts, and all-around good guy, meet . . ." I gestured around at the three men.

"I'm Thad Urquhart," said the man with the pink puff.

"Jimmy Carlisle," said the second older man.

Our eyes turned to the young blondie.

"Jake Jones," he said. If his eyes were still on me, I didn't know it. I kept mine elusive.

Randall was shaking each of their hands, leaving Jake for last. "I'm sorry for my bold friend," he was telling them. "I hope we didn't intrude."

"Not at all," said Thad Urquhart, apparently the spokesman for the group. "We enjoy meeting new people, don't we, Jake?"

Jake didn't reply. And I refused to look at him to see his expression.

"But we didn't get *your* name," Thad said to me.

"Call me Ishmael," I told them, and before anyone could stop me, I lifted my hand in a gesture of farewell and shouldered my way back into the crowd.

Randall was on his own now.

And I was on my way back to the bar.

Friday night happy hour was always packed, and this night was no exception. A crush of men clustered around the bar, waiting for drinks. It was easy to understand why the line at this station was longer than any of the others. Apparently, much of the crowd agreed with my assessment of the bartender's beauty.

He was young, perhaps very young, but with none of the childish insignificance of Jake Jones. He moved with a determined concentration, mixing drinks with an intense, uncanny focus. Not once did I see his lips, full and pink, stretch into a smile. From his black tank top protruded lean, muscled arms, their lower halves covered with soft dark fuzz. A cleft indented his chin. His hair, almost black, was artfully messy; his cheeks were covered with carefully clipped dark whiskers. At the very base of his neck, a small tattoo of an eagle spread its indigo wings.

But what I couldn't see—and longed for—were his eyes.

"Danny Fortunato?"

I turned. A man was approaching me, a short, slight man of maybe fifty-five. A toothy, eager smile seemed to precede him.

"You *are* Danny Fortunato, right?"

"Yes," I said, studying him. I didn't know his face.

"That's what I thought," the man was saying, extending his hand. "I'm a *huge* fan. I'm staying at one of the resorts in Warm Sands, and the innkeeper told me you often come to happy hour on Fridays. I was *hoping* I'd bump into you, and well, here you are." His smile extended, revealing more teeth. "I'm a *huge* fan."

I shook his hand. "Thank you."

"I just saw the cover of *Palm Springs Life*." His face was reddening. "I'm an artist, too, though certainly not of your caliber. . . ." He was still pumping my hand. "I'm not anywhere as good as you are. I've bought several of your prints, in particular the whole series you did for Disneyland. That was amazing! Hollywood classic!"

"Thank you," I said again.

"Do you still sell your prints in retail? Or is it all now just by commission?"

I wanted to get away, get to the bar, discover the eyes I wanted to see. But this man wouldn't let go of my hand. He was gripping it so hard, I was losing feeling in it.

"Mostly commission now, yes," I told him, hoping the conversation would end there. "Hotel chains and restaurants . . . you know, that sort of thing."

"Oh, if only *I* could ever get to that point," he said, "when I'd be well known and well regarded enough to get commissions and just live off those, and not have to crank out so many prints—and you're so much younger than I am!" He sighed, drawing in closer. "I do mostly giclée prints myself. They're sold in a few galleries in L.A. How did you ever get a commission with Disney?"

"An old friend works for them," I said, moving my fingers deliberately. He finally let go of his grip. I rubbed my hand.

"Connections!" he crowed, nodding. "*That's* what I need. But maybe what I really need is your talent!" He laughed, a loud, honking sound. "I really *am* a fan. Your work is so, so powerful. The print of the Malibu coast with the sun setting—gorgeous!"

And then he literally shivered. Stood there, wrapped his arms around himself, and shook back and forth. I wanted to laugh out loud. That particular print was a joke as far as I was concerned. Sunsets were the cheap and easy way to make a buck. And in the last year, they'd made me a lot of bucks. More bucks than I'd ever made in my whole life. Not bad for a guy who'd never gone to art school, whose higher education consisted of a few part-time community college classes. But what did I need a degree for? I'd take a picture of a sunset, fix it up in Photoshop, and soon prints of it were hanging in doctors' offices and model units of condo developments. They weren't art. They were commodities. Which was fine with me. They served a purpose. They made me some money. They just didn't deserve shivers.

I knew that I was being ungrateful. The man was paying me a compliment, and that was kind of him. I appreciated the recognition. I'd spent too many years driving the smoggy streets of L.A. between auditions not to enjoy my successful second life as a digital illustrator. I had come to L.A. to *be* someone, after all, and finally I was—even if it had taken almost two decades to get there. My work was featured on the cover of magazines. A gallery in downtown Palm Springs had given me a show. I was somebody—even if it was somebody I'd never expected to be.

"Are you working on anything new?" the man asked.

"A few things."

"Can't say for who?"

I shook my head.

"Did I read somewhere that Bette Midler commissioned a piece?"

"Sorry," I said. "Can't divulge."

"I knew it! Bette Midler! How exciting is that!"

Now, in fact, Bette Midler had never commissioned a piece from me. But if this man wanted to think so . . .

I supposed I should have asked him more about his work, or at least asked his name. But just at that moment I saw an opening at the bar. The boy I'd been looking at all night was finally idle, gazing up from under his long dark lashes at the television screen that soundlessly played a video by Mary J. Blige. He wouldn't be idle for long.

"I've got to go," I said hastily. "It was nice meeting you."

"Oh, it was pure joy," the man said, his face reddening, his lips spreading, his teeth glinting in the overhead light. "I'll keep an eye out for more of your work!"

He grabbed my hand once more to give it another hard, hearty pump.

As I feared, that tiny delay meant someone else managed to sidle up to the bar before I could. Quickly, I positioned myself next in line.

Looking back now, I can no longer say for sure what was going through my head that night. After everything that has happened since, it's hard to recall exactly. I'm certain I wasn't hoping to trick with him that night. I had my plan with Frank. I was certainly not going to disrupt that. Probably all I was hoping for was a chance to speak to him—no, even that wasn't necessary. I think all I wanted to do was see his eyes. That was the extent of it. That night, the first time I saw him, my only goal was to see his eyes.

If I saw his eyes, that would mean he had seen me.

There was a boy in eighth grade, during that last halcyon year before my sister disappeared, whose name was Scott Wood. Scott had long, curly dark hair and a mole on the side of his cheek. He was the most beautiful boy I had ever seen in my entire thirteen years, and all the girls seemed to think so, too. Scott played basketball and hockey and was a huge fan of the Eagles. He'd doodled their logo all over his paper bag–covered schoolbooks and was always singing "Plenty of room at the Hotel California" to himself. Scott had stayed back in fourth grade, so he was a more mature fourteen, with a downy, dark mustache on his upper lip. When Scott walked into a room, everyone turned, even our teacher, Miss Waterhouse, a stick of a lady who might have been twenty-nine or forty-nine, so bland and gray were her face and her hands.

Did Miss Waterhouse think about Scott the way I did? Did she hump her mattress at night the way I did, squeezing her eyes together to imagine Scott running around the basketball court or laughing in the caf? Did she go out and buy the Eagles' *Hotel California* album and play it over and over, imagining it was Scott singing to her: "How they dance in the courtyard, sweet summer sweat. Some dance to remember, some dance to forget . . ."

When I sat behind Scott in class, I'd watch the way his thighs moved in his tight polyester pants. He'd idly twirl one of his dark curls around his finger, and I'd sit there, mesmerized. Once, at recess, he removed his shirt while playing basketball, and I stopped playing jump rope with my friend Katie and just sat on the asphalt, watching him. I didn't understand it fully, this fascination I had with him, with the way his back muscles moved when he shot the basketball toward the hoop.

Scott moved away after eighth grade; I never saw him again. But he stayed in my memory. Many nights I'd lie in bed at night, listening to my mother cry for my sister downstairs, and I'd rewrite my past, imagining how I might have become friends with Scott. I might have shown him my comic book collection; maybe he collected, too. Or maybe I should've learned as much as I could have about the Eagles and started talking about them one day. He would have thought I was cool, and then we could have hung out. But it didn't work out that way. Instead, whenever Scott turned around in his seat to pass me a test or a handout, my throat would tighten and no words would form. I don't think he even saw me. I was completely off his radar screen. I think, even now, if someone said my name to him, he wouldn't remember that we had ever been classmates.

It was my turn at the bar.

"Hi," I said.

The bartender turned to face me.

Was it the dimness of the light? The sun had fully set by now, and the patio was lit only by the flickering lanterns. A greenish darkness had settled over the whole place, cheating me of a full glimpse of the bartender's eyes.

"Grey Goose martini," I said. "Up, with a twist."

He nodded and turned away.

The line behind me was growing again. I'd have to act fast. I felt my heart start to quicken.

His back was to me as he shook the martini. I watched as the wings of his eagle tattoo stretched and retracted on his neck.

"Did you say olives?" he asked over his shoulder.

"Yeah, that's fine, great," I said. My brain had no control over my words. "No, actually, I said a—"

But he was already plopping the olives into my glass. He looked up at me.

And I saw them.

His eyes.

Dark, like black mirrors. Behind them burned an intensity that was both fierce and brittle, and barely contained. Some might look into those eyes and call them crazy. But all I saw reflected in them was myself.

"It's okay," I said. "Olives are great."

And then his eyes were gone. I paid him, leaving an enormous tip, and once again missed the opportunity to speak to him. I should have turned the mistake about the olives into a joke. I should have been witty and flirty, and asked him his name. I knew how to play the game. Hell, I was an expert at it. Or at least, I had been, once. The zit-faced kid from eighth grade had blossomed into Danny the Stripper, the boy who drew in customers all down Santa Monica Boulevard, the boy in the yellow thong who shook his ass and flashed his jewels and at the end of the night routinely plucked tens and twenties out of his bulge. But I wasn't wearing a thong anymore. Instead, I was forty-one years old, standing now on the other side of the divide, just one of the anonymous faces in the crowd, waving their cash. Whatever I once might have had, this boy behind the bar didn't know about it. I had come, I supposed, full circle.

It was time for dinner. Looking around for Randall, I couldn't spot him. Had he gone home with Jake Jones? I tried not to be envious. I stood off to the side, sipping my vodka, watching the crowd.

The night was no longer green. It was black. And I was hungry—hungrier than I had been in a very long time. On a black night, all illusions disappeared. Everything was real. And I could no longer deny how hungry I really was.

EAST HARTFORD, CONNECTICUT

Twenty-Seven Years Earlier

If it weren't for Chipper Paguni's underpants, I would have turned around, hurried back along the path, and told my mother that my mission had been a failure. I hadn't wanted to make the trip at all, so fearful was I of the poison ivy that grew along the path to the pond. The ordeal I'd gone through in the seventh grade, when I'd scratched the skin along the entire length of both legs until it was red and bleeding, had left me forever terrified of that vicious weed. But when I spotted the underpants ahead of me, a bright white pair of Fruit of the Looms shimmering in the mid-day sun, I knew I had to go on.

A twig snapped. My eyes darted to the left, where a crumpled pair of black parachute pants had been dropped among a patch of ferns. I took another few steps along the path and discovered a trail of discarded clothing. Reebok sneakers. White socks. A lacy pink bra dangling from a wispy branch of a young maple tree.

Another snap. I paused, sucking in my breath. And then, a voice.

"Come on, Becky."

It was Chipper's voice, somewhere up ahead in the woods, low and unemotional.

"Come on," he said again.

I crouched behind a tall fern. As I did, my knees cracked. Mom was convinced I suffered from a calcium deficiency, and made me drink ten glasses of milk a day. Now I feared my knees had given me away. I held my breath. But around me only a heavy, humid silence filled the woods, broken now and then by the noisy squawk of a blue jay somewhere above me in the trees.

Finally I heard a splash. And then another.

Parting the fronds of the fern ever so carefully, I peered out over the water. Languid dragonflies hovered above the murky green surface. Ripples were just now lapping at the muddy shore, where a pair of brand-new Sergio Valente blue jeans, with the red stitching on the pockets, was rapidly turning wet and brown. I could imagine just how pissed Mom would be when she saw that.

Suddenly the surface of the pond was broken. Becky emerged from the depths, shaking her long, dark hair and sending cascades of droplets from side to side. In an instant Chipper popped up in the water in front of her, his glistening back momentarily obliterating my sister from my view.

They were kissing. My eyes grew wide as I crouched in my hiding place, keeping as still as I could. I watched as Chipper maneuvered Becky through the water toward the old wooden dock that jutted into the pond in a triangle. Lifting her up by her armpits, he sat her along the edge. For a moment I glimpsed my sister's breasts, larger than those of most girls her age, with hard pink nipples that stood up like pencil erasers. I felt my face flush. I watched as Chipper now gripped the dock and hoisted himself up, the muscles in his broad back tensing, his small white buttocks knocking me back onto my heels.

It was my fourteenth birthday. Tomorrow I'd start my first day of high school. All summer long the prospect of my new school had been all I could think about, and as the day had grown nearer, I'd become more and more anxious. When my father, trying to be helpful, had asked me just what it was about high school that frightened me so much, all I could offer was the fact that I'd have to use a locker. I'd spent nine years at St. John's Elementary School, from kindergarten to eighth grade, and I'd always kept my books and papers in a simple, top-lifting desk. Now there would be a code to remember—and a series of clicks to listen for—and I'd have to stand next to some kid I didn't know who'd surely had a locker in his public junior high and would look at me as if I were a dweeb. So Dad had gone out to Sears and bought a combination lock for me to practice on. I'd mastered the lock quickly enough, but still my fear didn't go away.

Behind the fern, I started to shake. I sat on the damp earth and tried to catch my breath. The day was hot and getting hotter. The chattering of the jays had been joined by a chorus of summer beetles, their shrill drone common on scorchers such as this one.

"Come on, Becky," Chipper was cajoling, and I peered through the fronds as he leaned forward over my sister.

Like my sister, Chipper Paguni was going into his junior year. All last year and the year before, I'd watched him from my bedroom window, emerging from the house across the street and heading down to the bus stop at precisely 6:45 a.m. Usually Chipper wore shiny black parachute pants and an untucked white collar shirt. His book bag would be slung over his shoulder. I imagined that rolled up inside the book bag was the necktie that was required by Chipper's all-male Catholic high school. The tie remained unworn and unknotted until the last possible moment, when the bus pulled into the school parking lot.

Now I would be joining Chipper at that same school, wearing my own tie as I trooped in for my first day tomorrow morning as a geeky, green freshman. I had heard the stories of how the upperclassmen taunted the new boys. St. Francis Xavier was a hotbed of testosterone. Its slogan, "Be a man," was enshrined over its front doors and embodied by its strutting, title-holding football team. This year, as a defensive linebacker, Chipper would probably see his first real action on the field, and I'd be required to sit in the bleachers and cheer him on. It was called school spirit. Whether Chipper would turn out to be a tormentor or a friend remained to be seen. I was hoping that his interest in Becky would work in my favor. But one could never count on such things.

Holding my breath, I watched as Chipper's white buttocks rose in the air from on top of my sister.

I leaned in for a better view, but as I did so, my knees cracked again. I let the fronds swing shut but too late. I heard Becky ask, "What was that?"

My armpits suddenly poured sweat. Then I heard a splash.

I bolted. But not before, without even thinking about it, I snatched up Chipper's underpants in my hand.

I was stuffing them up my shirt as I came skidding back into the house, the screen door slamming behind me. Suddenly my mother was two inches from my face, her hair wrapped around huge orange curlers.

"Did you find your sister?"

"No."

"Mother Mary! One simple favor I ask of her and she disappears on me!"

I knew it wasn't one simple favor. It was more like five or six or thirty. Ever since Becky had gotten her driver's license three months ago, she'd been forced to act as Mom's personal chauffeur, driving her to the grocery store, to the hairdresser, to the Wednesday night meetings of the Rosary Altar Society. That was the whole reason Dad had bought that used mustard-colored Vega, so that Becky could drive Mom around on her errands, freeing him from the chore. See, Mom didn't know how to drive a car. "In my day," she explained whenever someone expressed surprise at the fact, "not every lady got her driver's license." The truth was, Mom didn't do well with technology, whether it was driving a car or adjusting the antenna on top of the television set or resetting the clock after a power outage. All those things she left up to my father. Once, when I was eight, Dad had tried to teach Mom how to drive. She'd stepped on the gas instead of the brake and charged straight over the sidewalk into Flo Armstrong's peony garden, tires spitting soil. Never again did Mom get behind the wheel.

Margaret Joan Cronin Fortunato, better known as Peggy. Five feet four, big hands like a man's, and breasts so large they sometimes made her seem as if she'd topple over frontward. It was easy to see where Becky got her measurements.

"She'll remember," I said, assuring my mother of my sister's promise as I pulled off my muddy sneakers on the mat inside the front door. "The party's not until four o'clock."

"Well, it's already twelve thirty and—Danny! Look at that mud! Were you at the pond? I told you not to go up there. Do you want to get poison ivy again?"

"I wasn't at the pond," I said quickly.

"Well, if you were looking for Becky, you *should* have gone to the pond. You know she's always sneaking up there."

I just sighed as my mother made the sign of the cross. She always did this when she was anxious, which meant she was crossing herself a couple hundred times a day. Ever since Becky had turned sixteen, Mom had been even more anxious, it seemed. She'd always doted on Becky. Becky was her little angel, whose annual dancing school recitals had always reduced my mother to a puddle of tears. "Isn't she the most beautiful child ever?" she'd repeat over and over to herself, watching Becky pirouette on the stage. Mom always went easier on Becky than she did on me; on snow days when school was canceled, Becky got to sleep in, but I had to get up and shovel the driveway. "Because you are the boy," Mom would say, and boys shoveled driveways and cut the grass and raked the leaves. Becky just dried the dishes after dinner. I didn't think it was a fair balance.

When Becky turned sixteen, Mom freaked. Her little angel now had ideas of her own. Becky was getting "too serious" with Chipper Paguni, Mom argued. She had quit dancing lessons and spent all her time with Chipper. I always believed that Mom's demands that Becky drive her everywhere were part of a strategy to keep her close at hand. And I suspected Becky thought so, too. Hence their arguments.

But all that was not to say that Mom paid no attention to me. On the contrary. Becky might have been her favorite, but I received my share of Peggy Fortunato's extravagant solicitude. My fourteenth birthday party, for example, had turned into a state occasion. Mom had been up at five, washing the floor, vacuuming the drapes, wrapping Hershey's Kisses in blue tulle, setting—and then resetting—the table. Just so five of my friends, plus Nana and Aunt Patsy, could sit around drinking Kool-Aid and eating chocolate cake.

"Well," Mom said, throwing her hands in the air, "if you don't have any balloons for your birthday party, Danny, you'll know who to blame. Not me!"

She disappeared down the hallway.

From the kitchen I could smell my cake baking—yellow Duncan Hines, my favorite. Peering around the corner, I spied the jar of chocolate frosting waiting on the table, and beside it a bag of

M&M's, with which Mom would spell out my name across the top of the cake. The candles had already been laid out and counted. Fourteen of them.

I was really too old for kiddie parties like this. I'd tried to protest, but Mom had insisted. Only with great effort had I been able to persuade her not to drag out the pin-the-tail-on-the-donkey game. Certainly next year there would be no birthday party like this. High school kids didn't have parties with Hershey's Kisses wrapped in tulle. Next year my birthday party would be very different.

That was, if I survived high school to make it that far.

I dialed a number on the beige phone mounted to the kitchen wall.

"Katie?"

"Danny?"

"What time are you coming? Come early, okay? We can hang out."

The girl on the other end of the line sighed. "I can't. My mom is taking me shopping."

"Tell her you can't go. You can't be late to my party, Katie. My mom is already having a bird. You said you'd help us set up."

"I know, but I'm going clothes shopping for school tomorrow."

"Clothes shopping? You're going to be wearing a uniform!"

Katie Reid, my closest friend since kindergarten. Short, chubby, with a blond Dorothy Hamill wedge cut. The worst thing about high school—worse than having to use a locker, worse than fearing the taunts of upperclassmen—was being separated from Katie. I was being sent one way, and Katie another. She was heading to St. Clare's, the all-girl sister school to St. Francis Xavier. Unlike their male counterparts, whose only dress code was a collar shirt and a necktie of choice, the St. Clare girls wore white blouses and pleated plaid skirts. So what kind of clothes shopping could she possibly do?

"Shoes, socks, sweaters," she told me, as if reading my mind. "And underwear."

I suddenly became conscious of Chipper's underpants bunched up near my armpit. "You can't be late," I told Katie again. "After this who knows when we'll see each other again."

"Don't say that, Danny! We'll see each other every week!"

I grunted. "I hate high school."

"You haven't even started it yet."

"I know, but I still hate it."

"Danny, I have to go. My mom is calling me."

"Okay. Don't be late."

"Good-bye, Danny."

I hung up the phone. The timer over the stove pinged.

"Cake's done," I called to my mother as I ran upstairs to my room, pulling Chipper's underpants out of my armpit and stuffing them into my drawer. I threw myself onto my bed and lay there with my hands behind my head, staring up at the ceiling. On my wall were posters of Lynda Carter as Wonder Woman and *Monty Python and the Holy Grail.* On my floor was a pile of nearly one hundred record albums, which had tipped over, sending Andy Gibb, Hall & Oates, and Peter Frampton sliding across the orange shag carpet. Orange was my favorite color. I'd chosen it because no one ever picked orange.

The window was open, and there was a slight breeze moving the flimsy brown and white checked curtains. I must have fallen asleep, because the next thing I knew a car door was closing, and I could hear my aunt Patsy's voice in the driveway.

I sat up, rubbed my eyes, and headed back downstairs.

Mom was propping an electric fan on the windowsill to cool off the room as Nana and Aunt Patsy came through the front door.

"Danny off the pickle boat," Nana said when she saw me.

It was what she'd always called me. I had no idea what it meant, but ever since I could remember, Nana had been calling me "Danny off the pickle boat"—just before she'd grip my shoulders and leave a big, wet red kiss on my cheek. It was no different today. Her perfume, as ever, was heavy and spicy. Nana's scent would often linger for hours after she left. Mom sometimes had to open a window.

Adele Mary Horgan Fortunato, better known, to me, anyway, as Nana. Stout and silly, a crazy little jingle perpetually on her lips. *Danny off the pickle boat. Here comes Becky in her BVDs. Sing a song of six-packs and a pocket full of beer.* Nana often made no sense at all, but she always made me smile.

Beside her stood Aunt Patsy. Her daughter. Dad's older sister. Patricia Ann Fortunato. Never married. An old maid. And now Aunt Patsy had cancer. When Mom spoke of it to the neighbors, her voice always dropped to a whisper on the word. "Patsy has *cancer.* They had to take one breast and then part of another. It doesn't look good." And she'd make the sign of the cross.

Today Aunt Patsy looked very gray and drawn. She wore a bulky sweater even on hot days so that she could cover up her uneven chest. When she smiled at me, her teeth seemed too big for her face. "Happy birthday, honey," she said. "Are you excited to be starting high school?"

"Yeah," I lied, accepting the shirt box she was offering me, wrapped in green and blue paper. I knew what it was even without opening it. A white collar shirt from Sears. Probably a tie, too, for me to wear to school.

"Where's Becky?" Nana was asking. "Beckadee, Beckadoo?"

"God only knows," Mom said. "I can only hope she's downtown, picking up the balloons I ordered for Danny's party."

"But her car's still in the driveway," Aunt Patsy observed.

"I know, so she must be off with Chipper. Maybe he's driving her down." Mom was unfolding a string of silver paper letters that spelled out HAPPY BIRTHDAY. "I haven't seen her since this morning. I told her not to forget the balloons, and she'd better not! I'll have her *head!*"

"Mom, please don't pin up that HAPPY BIRTHDAY sign," I said.

Mom looked at me as if I were mad. "Why not? It's your birthday."

"It's dweebish."

"You can't have a birthday party without a HAPPY BIRTHDAY sign," Mom declared.

"It's for little kids, Mom."

She sighed dramatically, folding the sign back up. "First, no pin the tail on the donkey. Next thing he won't want a cake."

"Where's Becky?" Nana asked again.

We all looked over at her.

"Mommy, Peggy just told us," Aunt Patsy said gently. I'd always thought it odd that a grown woman still called her mother "Mommy." "Becky's in town, getting the balloons for Danny's party."

"Oh," Nana said. "That's right."

Nana had been getting forgetful. She sometimes confused my father with her late husband, Sebastian. Sometimes she repeated herself several times a day, asking the same questions over and over. Dad remembered his own grandmother, Nana's mother, getting the same way. Eventually, they had to put her in the state hospital, where she died, crazy as a loon. I looked at Nana and felt very sad. I knew she was thinking about her mother, about the state hospital. She wasn't so forgetful that she'd forgotten about that. She knew what was happening. Nana caught me looking at her and seemed startled. Then she winked at me.

It was getting close to three o'clock. I wished that Katie had been able to come over earlier. I headed back upstairs and sat on my bed, my back against the wall.

"This might be the last time we see each other," I'd said to Katie almost every day since the end of eighth grade.

She'd always scold me. "Stop saying that. It's not like we're moving away. We still live in the same town."

Should I have asked Katie to be my girlfriend then? If she were my girlfriend, then we'd have a connection, something to really bind us together. I sensed it would be good insurance to have a girlfriend upon entering high school. It would offer some kind of protection, I suspected, but just what kind, I wasn't sure.

And yet I hadn't asked her. It would have seemed odd after all these years. She probably would have laughed at me. Now, sitting on my bed, I wished I had.

My eye caught movement outside the window.

Chipper Paguni was pulling into his driveway in his rebuilt, re-painted gold metallic 1971 Mustang Mach 1, with the black stripe down the hood. I leaned forward to get a better view. The door on the driver's side popped open, and Chipper emerged in a white T-shirt and shiny black parachute pants. I knew he wasn't wearing underwear, and my cheeks flushed a little as the thought crossed my mind. I waited for the passenger's side door to open and for Becky to get out, but nothing happened. Chipper paused to inspect something on the side of his precious car—a dent? a ding? a scratch?—then headed into the house.

I was scared.

Had he seen me out by the pond?

And what had Chipper thought when he couldn't find his under-wear?

It didn't even cross my mind to wonder where Becky was.

PALM SPRINGS, CALIFORNIA

I headed up our walkway just as the sprinkler system kicked on, a small, insistent hiss under the bushes, a soft spray of mist across the dry purple night.

We weren't meant to be here. Humans weren't designed to live in deserts. But we did, anyway. We pumped in water and planted bougainvillea. We built swimming pools and golf courses and laid out vast stretches of grass. We put up shopping malls. We did it because we *could*. But that didn't change the fact that we were not meant to be here.

In the air hung the fragrance of dry sage. I paused, looking up at the sky, a vast dome of indigo studded with thousands of stars. At night the desert's stillness never lost its power to astonish me. A quarter of a million souls resided under that big sky, but at night I heard only the rustle of dried weeds. From somewhere far away came the crackly, impatient whine of a coyote.

Against the sky, the mountains ringing the valley were a slightly darker shade of purple. I stood there, trying to make out the line that separated mountain from sky. From eighty-five hundred feet above, the bright white eye of the tram winked at me. I took a deep breath, pulling the dry, clean desert air into my lungs. Then I let myself into the house, uncertain of what I might find.

"Frank?" I whispered.

The living room was dark. I flicked on a lamp, sending light spilling throughout the room, illuminating the sleek black-and-white tiled floor and the low-slung midcentury-modern furniture. On the wall hung two of my prints: a giclée of the Chocolate Mountains and a close-up of a sunflower, which Frank called his green daisy. They were images that suited our house, a classic Alexander built in 1955, a butterfly-roofed exemplar of rational design and modernist style, with its exposed beams and gabled spun-glass walls. Back in the day, these houses were built on the cheap, snapped up by postwar California's tail-finned, consumer-happy middle class, eager to snare their own piece of a desert playground popularized by the Rat Pack and other Hollywood elite. Now original Alexander homes fetched millions. From every oblong window, the house offered stunning views of the mountains, and fifty years of stringent municipal policy had ensured that nothing was ever built too high to obscure that scenery. Very few moments in my life were more treasured than my early mornings out by the pool, sitting with my coffee and watching the reflection of a very pink dawn against the blue gray of the mountains.

I set my keys down on the table and stepped through the living room into the dining area. The hallway was dark. No light emanated from the doorway of the bedroom. Might they both have fallen asleep?

I turned and headed through the kitchen. Only then did I notice the light coming from the second bedroom, which we used as an office. I peered around the door.

"Frank?"

He was sitting at the desk, a pile of papers in front of him, his brow creased, his glasses at the end of his nose. He looked up at me.

"Danny. I didn't hear you come in. How was happy hour?"

"The usual." I gave him a confused look. "What are you doing in here?"

"Polishing up my syllabi for the start of classes." He sighed, removing his glasses and rubbing his eyes. "I'll stop if Randall wants to pull out the bed. . . ."

"Randall isn't here. I assume he's tricking."

Frank looked up at me and smiled. "Well, good for him."

"Yeah. If it gets his mind off Ike."

Frank nodded.

"But where's Ollie?" I still couldn't fathom why Frank was in here, poring over papers, when I'd expected to find him engaged in a very different sort of activity.

"He's in the casita." Frank had replaced his glasses and was once more looking down at his desk.

"The casita? What's he doing out there? And why are you in here?"

He didn't look up at me. "I really needed to get these syllabi done. I don't want them hanging over me all weekend. And rather than having Ollie in the living room, watching television, where he'd distract me, I suggested he go out and watch whatever he wanted to in the casita and get comfortable there, and then, when you got home . . ."

I nodded, following his line of thought. "So you want me to go bring him in, then?"

Frank hesitated. He took his glasses off again and looked up at me.

"Danny, why don't you just go out to him? I'm exhausted. I'm going to finish this one syllabus and then head in to bed."

I made a face and folded my arms across my chest. "You don't want to . . . do anything with him, like we planned?"

Frank smiled. "He came down for *your* birthday, Danny. And look, I'm so beat, I'd just end up sitting at the foot of the bed, watching the two of you."

"That's all you've done the last few times, anyway."

That came out harsher than I wanted. Frank ignored it and looked back down at his papers. "Really, Danny, it's fine. I'm exhausted. You go have fun. I'm honestly looking forward to sleeping a good solid nine hours."

I just stood there in the doorway. There was silence.

"Frank," I said finally. "It's my birthday. I don't want to spend the night with Ollie if it means I spend it without you."

"That's very sweet of you to say, baby." He looked up and gave me a genuine smile. "But, of *course*, you want to spend the night with him. He has an ass you can bounce quarters off, remember?"

"I'm serious, Frank."

"Oh, baby."

He stood, placing his hands on my shoulders. We were nose to nose. Once, Frank had been a few inches taller than I, but no longer. Somewhere over the last two decades, he had settled, like the frame of a house. His joints had retracted; his bones had curled inward ever so slightly. I studied him now at close range, observing the dark circles under his eyes, the mosaic of brown spots etched across his high, shiny forehead.

"Are you really too tired?" I asked him.

He nodded. "You can't disappoint him, baby. He drove all the way in from Sherman Oaks."

I leaned in and kissed him lightly on the lips.

Frank smiled. "We'll take a drive up to Joshua Tree tomorrow, go for a hike." He took my chin between his thumb and forefinger. "Just the two of us. Maybe we'll even finally spot a bighorn sheep after all these years."

"Frank—"

"Let me finish this syllabus, Danny. And leave a note in the kitchen for Randall, if he comes back at all, that all he has to do is pull out the bed here in the office. I've already put sheets on for him."

He sat down at his desk again. I remained unmoving in the door frame, watching him.

"Go," he said, not looking up at me. "Skedaddle. Have fun."

I stood there for a moment longer, then turned away.

One of the wonderful things about properties in Palm Springs was the casita—the "little house" on the grounds, which could be used for guests. Ours had a Spanish tile roof and beige stucco walls, accessed by a zigzagging stone path through a garden of cacti and creeping rosemary. Passing the kidney bean–shaped swimming pool, I could see the blue glow of the television from the casita's windows reflected on the water. I looked closely and caught a glimpse of Ollie through the sheer curtains, lying on the bed, shirtless and barefoot and in jeans, the remote in his hands. I think he was watching *America's Next Top Model.* I wasn't sure, because he snapped off the TV as soon as I walked in.

"Hey," he said.

"Hey," I replied.

The California king bed was so massive that it took up nearly the whole casita. There was no room for any other furniture except the flat-screen television hanging on the opposite wall. A small bathroom and medium-sized walk-in closet completed the casita. "Perfect for in-laws," our Realtor had said—or, in our case, our boy toy from L.A.

I leaned over the bed and gave Ollie a quick kiss on the lips.

"Happy birthday," he said.

"Thanks."

"I got you a gift."

Indeed, at the end of the bed sat a small box wrapped in blue- and green-striped paper. A white ribbon was tied around it in a clumsy bow.

"You shouldn't have gotten me anything," I said.

"Well, I saw it at the mall. . . ."

Ollie worked at a Ritz Camera at a mall in Studio City. He'd worked there since he was eighteen. He was twenty-six now.

I opened the gift. It was a cinnamon-scented candle in a glass jar from Yankee Candle.

"I don't know if you like cinnamon," Ollie said. He remained propped against the pillows, turning the remote over and over in his hands.

"Oh, I do. I do like cinnamon." I opened the lid and took a whiff to be polite. "It's very nice. Thank you."

He smiled.

I put the candle aside. There was never much small talk with Ollie. We didn't have much in common, really, other than liking the way my cock felt in his ass. We had met online, on ManHunt, or maybe it was Adam4Adam. Or Connexion. One of them. That first night, he drove all the way down to Palm Springs in his '04 Toyota Corolla, and Frank and I took turns fucking his scrumptious ass. Afterward, he fell asleep between us in our bed. The next morning Frank fried bacon and eggs, while I fucked Ollie one more time. And that, we thought, would be that. Sweet ass not withstanding, Ollie wasn't one of our more memorable tricks. Awkward silences took the place of conversation. Ollie didn't get our jokes and didn't make any of his own. He was either painfully shy or incredibly dull, Frank deduced, and yet, for some reason, I was moved to stay in contact with him, getting his number and his e-mail. In the last year, Ollie had been back down to see us half a dozen more times, and I still didn't know much more about him other than where he lived, where he worked, and that he liked getting plowed.

"Where's Frank?" Ollie asked as I slid in next to him on the bed.

"He's beat. He's got to finish getting ready for his classes. You know they start this coming week. So he's going to bed, and he told us to have fun out here."

"Oh."

I had a feeling Ollie wasn't too disappointed. I knew the reason he kept coming back out to the desert had more to do with me than Frank. I wasn't being arrogant. It was just obvious. Ollie would kiss Frank only if Frank made the first move. He would suck Frank only if Frank maneuvered his cock in the direction of his mouth. On the other hand, he was all over me. Frank and I had never discussed this. But I was sure if I'd noticed, Frank had noticed, too. I felt bad, and a little guilty. But I didn't bring it up. There was, after all, the slightest chance that Frank *hadn't* noticed.

Of course, Ollie's apparent disinterest might have been the reason why Frank, the last few times, had chosen to drop out of the sex and simply play the voyeur. He'd sit at the foot of the bed, watching and wanking as Ollie and I sucked and fucked. I'd try to lure him back up, but he'd resist, staying right where he was, shooting his load before we did. When Ollie and I would shoot soon afterward, Frank would be right there, waiting with a towel, like a dutiful butler offering his young masters a cum rag. It broke my heart.

Frank was fourteen years older than I. In five years, he would be sixty. Once, age had mattered very little between us. But increasingly of late, the disparity in our ages had begun to weigh heavily on me. I saw myself becoming Frank a few years down the road, moving slower, my body settling, shrinking, withering. It frightened me.

I touched Ollie's smooth, unlined face. He was handsome, in an all-American kind of way, with sandy hair and blue eyes. We kissed. His lips tasted like wintergreen breath mints, and his little tongue darted in and out of my mouth. I moved my hands up and down his back and over his arms. His was the typical body of a twentysomething white boy who never went to the gym. Not thin, not fat, though his waist was starting to get a tiny bit squishy. Largely hairless, except for a happy trail leading up from his crotch to his belly button. Too many hours spent laboring inside an air-conditioned shopping mall had left his skin pale and pasty. He tasted like deli meat—bologna, maybe, or a salty ham. Leaning back into the pillows as I kissed my way down his torso, Ollie let out an almost inaudible moan. Talking during sex was not for him. No "Yeah, that's it" or "Fuck, man, that feels good." I only knew he was enjoying himself by the rock-hard six-inch cock that stood straight up in the air, perpendicular to his groin, from start to finish.

I unbuckled Ollie's belt and slid down his jeans. Sure enough, his cock was spearheading his gray Hanes briefs. I got everything off him, jeans and underwear, then flipped him over to showcase his most impressive attribute, that incongruous bubble butt. I was quickly naked myself, dry humping the deep cleavage between those two delectable mounds. And in the process, I caught a glimpse of what we were doing in the mirrored closet doors. Absurd, really. Two grown men, naked, rubbing body parts all over each other like a couple of dogs in heat. I couldn't help but smile.

That was a mistake.

Because in my smile, I saw what I no longer recognized. Myself. The man in the mirror looked nothing like me. I felt as if I were in a *Twilight Zone* episode, where the face looking back from the mirror was someone else's, a doppelgänger from another world. What was it about my appearance that had changed over the last few years? I no longer looked like photographs of myself. I couldn't put my finger on the difference. I hadn't lost any more hair, and Just for Men had kept the gray at bay. There weren't any new wrinkles on my forehead or around my eyes; Botox had taken care of that. So what was it that was different? Why did my face no longer look like me?

Ollie had wriggled out from under me and was now sucking on

my cock. Leaning back into the pillows, I looked down at his body, so white, so soft, so unmarked by time or love or pain. A body not unlike the one I'd once had, before I'd started lifting weights and using creatine and protein and finally testosterone cream to replace what I was losing, a little bit more every year. Hair grew in my ears and fell out from my head, but my body remained hard and toned and supple. The skinny little boy who'd hated taking his shirt off in gym class had buffed up considerably by his late twenties, spending his thirties on the dance floor with friends, reveling in the glances of strangers, if never fully believing they were glancing at him. But, of course, they were: for an intoxicating nanosecond, I had actually been beautiful. And for an equally fleeting moment in time, I had believed it.

Ollie was moving up from my cock to my stomach, licking the outline of my abs. In a moment like that, I could close my eyes and believe that the years hadn't moved so fast, that I still had a couple of decades ahead of me, that time wasn't running out, that like the young man who had danced on the box in his thong, I still had plenty of time for sex, for love, for life. Plenty of time left to savor that necessary fiction of youth—that happiness was one's due. But I didn't close my eyes. Not that time. I kept them open and fixed on Ollie's body, a body that I craved, that I needed, that I kept bringing back into this house even when Frank seemed indifferent to it. I grabbed Ollie's butt with my hands so hard that I'm sure it hurt him. I hoped, in fact, that it did.

I flipped him over. Fumbling for a condom and lube on the floor beside the bed, I felt the blood surge to my cock. This was going to be fast. I felt the heat building up in my body, the pressure growing inside my head. I was going to have him—have every last bit of him—his body, his mind, his soul, his youth, his future. I pushed my cock inside him and clamped my lips over his. Above us the sun shone like a benevolent god, and the waves crashed against the sandy coast of Venice Beach. The brine of the sea was so strong, I tasted it on my tongue. Sand was creeping up my bare legs, scratching its way into my ass, but I didn't care. I loved him—I loved him so much, I felt as if my whole body would explode, arms and legs strewn across the beach. I fucked him right there on the open sand, kissing him the whole time, our bodies entwined, two dogs in the surf. I finally understood what they meant when they talked about falling in love.

"Fuck!"

I pulled out in time to whip off the condom and shoot ropes of semen across Ollie's chest. Breathing heavily, I steadied myself with one hand on the bed, accidentally hitting the remote control. *America's Next Top Model* suddenly flashed once again on the screen behind me.

Ollie came himself then, a paltry dribble compared to my cannon shot. I was already out of bed, flicking off the TV, hunting for a towel in the bathroom.

"That was hot," Ollie said as I returned, settling in beside him, pressing the towel against his chest.

"A quickie," I said. "Maybe we'll go a bit longer in the morning." I smiled. "I'm a little drunk. Three martinis tonight."

Ollie shrugged. "Didn't affect the performance."

"Thanks."

We were quiet, sitting shoulder to shoulder against the pillows. Outside the wind had picked up. The glass in the windows rattled almost imperceptibly, but I could hear it.

I had begun to nod off when Ollie spoke again.

"I'm getting a new job."

I opened my eyes and turned to face him.

"I'm going to be the manager of Spencer's Gifts," he said. "It's in the mall, too."

I didn't know what to say, so I said nothing.

"I figured Ritz Camera was pretty much a dead-end job, you know? How many people still take pictures on film to be developed? Even though we've started selling digital cameras and webcams and stuff, I really think I've gone as far there as I ever can. But people will always need to buy gifts, you know?"

I nodded, closing my eyes again. Yes, people would always need to buy glow-in-the-dark posters of heavy metal bands and mugs made in the shape of women's breasts.

I felt immediately guilty for being judgmental. How different was I, really, from this kid? I'd never gone to college; I'd never had any great-paying job. But I *was* different from him. I'd had one very important thing that he didn't have.

Ambition.

Even if it had almost killed me.

We dozed off, but I woke up quickly; the lights were still on, and Ollie had slumped forward onto my chest. I gently moved him down into a more comfortable sleeping position and got up to switch off the lamp. Climbing back into bed beside him, I lay facing the ceiling, eyes wide open. Ollie began to snore, a nervous little whistle tickling my ear. I turned on my side, willing sleep to come. But even as I tried, I knew it was futile. I wasn't going to fall asleep. Not here. Not tonight.

I waited until Ollie's snoring had reached a steady rhythm. Then I slipped out of the casita, padding naked past the swimming pool, the pungent fragrance of rosemary hanging in the dry night air. Through the glass sliders, I stepped into the dining room. The clock on the mantel was ticking off the seconds with a fierceness undetectable during the day. In the bathroom, I brushed my teeth and washed my hands and applied a hot, wet cloth to my cock. That would have to do for washing up after sex. I was exhausted. In our room, Frank was sound asleep. His own snoring was far deeper, far more profound than Ollie's tremulous whistle. Pulling back the sheet, I climbed in beside him, pressing my chest against his back, my lips against the soft white fur on his shoulders. I snaked an arm around him. He stirred.

"Baby," he mumbled.

"I'm here," I told him.

In moments, we were both asleep.

WEST HOLLYWOOD

Twenty-One Years Earlier

Out of the hundred or so men gathered around me, I noticed him right away. He was an older guy, maybe even thirty. Well preserved for his age, as Randall would say, with big shoulders packed into a tight white T-shirt. Randall liked older men. He said their receding hairlines were more than compensated for by the expanding bulk of their bank accounts. Whether this guy in the tight T-shirt had money or not, I couldn't tell. He wasn't part of the mob pressing in around me, waving their Hamiltons and Jacksons as I gyrated on my box to Kim Wilde's "You Keep Me Hangin' On." Instead, he was leaning against the far wall, sipping a Rolling Rock, watching, but not watching me. I couldn't take my eyes off him.

"Hey, Benny," I said, leaning down, grabbing the barback by the shoulder as he loaded empties onto his tray, "go get Carlos to take over for me for a while."

Benny yanked himself away from my grip. He was still pissed at me for breaking up with him a couple of weeks ago. "Carlos isn't ready yet," he said icily.

I knew what that meant. Carlos wasn't yet high enough to get up on the box. Carlos, a good Catholic boy from Mexico, had to do a couple lines of coke before finding the courage to take off his clothes and dance. So much for hoping I might get a reprieve to hop off my box and introduce myself to Mr. Tight Tee. It was probably just as well. That one was far too put together for me. He wasn't like these guys up front, slobbering all over a skinny kid just because he'd taken his clothes off. No doubt Mr. Tight Tee was here to meet a friend, a friend with a real job, a real life. A friend who was *somebody*.

"Come on, hot stuff, give it to us," someone shouted from the crowd. Kim Wilde was mixing into the Pet Shop Boys' "It's a Sin," and I shook my ass and tightened my abs to prove just how sinful it really was. A large black man with very cold fingers was stuffing several dollars into my thong. By the end of the night, I'd probably bring home about three hundred in tips.

It still boggled my mind to think that guys would pay money to see me naked. Me, the kid Scott Wood had never even noticed in eighth grade, the pimply kid in the back row all through high school who had endured hundreds of paper airplanes bouncing off his head. I didn't exist then, except to be a failure. But here, in West Hollywood, I was a star.

I glanced up, over the heads of the crowd, catching a glimpse of myself in the mirror on the wall. The pulsing red and gold lights distorted my features, but still I could make out the contours of my body. A skinny little blond, barely any muscle, a stick figure in a bright yellow thong. In school I'd always been embarrassed by how thin I was, forever trying to lift weights to build muscle but always giving up after about a week and a half. In gym class I'd been mortified by my twig of a body. But when Edgar, the club manager, was considering whether to hire me, he'd asked me to strip to my underwear, and I'd noticed the tight smile that had slowly stretched across his face. "Perfect," he'd purred, running his hands over my torso. "Not a hair anywhere. You look seventeen."

But in fact I had just turned the ripe old age of twenty. Randall threw me a party for the occasion, my first since I was fourteen. I was in great spirits that night, filled with ambitious plans. I had come to L.A. to be an actor, and nothing was going to discourage me. "This time next year," I'd announced at my birthday party,

"I'll be a regular on a TV series." A few of my friends had laughed skeptically. "You just wait and see," I'd told them. "I'm trying out for a part on *Punky Brewster!*"

I didn't get the *Punky* job, and neither did I land parts on *Who's the Boss?* or *The Facts of Life,* all of which I auditioned for. But I hadn't given up yet. Randall thought working as a go-go boy might hurt my chances of getting on TV, but Randall was a fuddy-duddy when it came to things like that. He was such a *serious* young man—a med student at UCLA. He was always saying things like, "Consider all your options before you take a leap."

Climbing up on my box in my thong three nights a week, I had no idea what Randall was talking about, nor did I really care to know. All I knew was that I was making good money for doing very little—and for this skinny little kid, all that hooting and whistling was kind of fun. Sure, the free booze and free blow that Edgar provided were nice perks, but the best part was simply getting up on the box.

"Hey, baby, give me a wink," the large black man called out.

I obliged, turning around to moon the crowd and flex my butt hole. A scattering of guys up front hooted, and more dollars flew my way. I loved it. Who ever would have *thought?*

It was getting hot up there under the strobe lights. Sweat rolled down my forehead, and even the half-pint of mousse I'd used to spike up my hair wasn't going to last all night. "Benny," I said, leaning down again as he passed, "get me some water, will you?"

"I'm busy."

"Fuck you, Benny."

I glanced around for Randall. He was across the room, chatting up some guy in an oxford shirt and loosened tie. Leave it to Randall to spot the executive types. I motioned to him; he spotted me; I simulated drinking a bottle of water. Actually, it probably looked more as if I was asking to suck his cock, but those days, thank God, were over. Randall turned to Mr. Oxford Shirt and seemed to tell him that he'd be right back, and then he headed over to the bar. What would I do without Randall?

"What would you do without me?" he asked, handing me up the bottle of Evian.

I winked, unscrewed the top, and guzzled down about half the bottle. The rest I poured over my torso, sending a cheer up from the crowd.

"Show-off," Randall said, smirking. He returned to his executive.

Once, I had been in love with Randall. It was right after I'd first arrived in L.A., a scared kid with big dreams. Randall was a native and not nearly as scared as I was, but he had dreams that matched my own. It was a very long time ago. Six months, in fact.

I'd responded to an ad he'd posted on the bulletin board at Pavilions, looking for a roommate. I called him, got his address, and walked the two miles to his place. It was one half of a pink stucco house just below Santa Monica Boulevard, near Fairfax, with a bunch of straggly birds-of-paradise growing out front. When Randall opened the door, he was wearing only a white terry-cloth towel around his waist, with shaving cream carefully applied to his cheeks and chin. As he showed me around the place, his towel kept slipping, and I couldn't take my eyes off his broad, furry chest. By the time we got to the kitchen, the towel was gone and we were kissing over the sink. I found the taste of shaving cream to be surprisingly sweet and arousing.

We fucked on his mattress—Randall believed a bed frame was a waste of money for a struggling student—and after I'd shot three head-splitting loads, I paid him two months' rent. Suddenly not only did I have a place in L.A., but I had a boyfriend as well. Quite the accomplishment—since I'd only stepped off the bus at Union Station that morning. It was far, far easier than I had imagined, far simpler than Dad had warned.

For a couple of weeks, I was head over heels in love with Randall. But then, one night, walking home, I spotted a tall blond in leather pants approaching me. After the classic double take as we passed each other, we circled back around, grins on our faces. Soon we were humping on his mattress—another West Hollywood boy without an actual bed—and I decided then and there that *this* was my true love. After all, Lance shared my passion for *Doctor Who* and *Monty Python,* while Randall's tastes were more highfalutin, what with all his classical music cassette tapes. So I broke up with Randall and started dating Lance. I expected Randall would ask me to move out, but he didn't. "I've gotten used to you," he explained. So I turned the spare room into my bedroom, buying a used waterbed because I'd thought they were sexy ever since Starsky had one on *Starsky & Hutch*. Randall said he always knew when I was having sex with Lance, because it sounded like the coast of Malibu in the next room.

"Ow!"

Some guy had just pinched the shaft of my cock as he stuffed a couple of bills into my thong.

"No touching allowed," I scolded him.

The guy, bald and red, giggled like a girl.

Up there on the box, you could really smell the crowd. The cigarettes, the beer belches, the body odor, the Calvin Klein Obsession cologne. All the smells braided together, wafting up from below, held in place by the thick blue smoke that encircled me like a wreath. At the moment, I couldn't breathe, so I waved my hands in front of me as if swimming through the air, clearing a passage for oxygen to flow. Inhaling deeply, eyes closed, I took a long, deep gulp. When I opened my eyes, I looked around.

Mr. Tight Tee was gone.

"Damn," I mumbled.

But then I spotted him against another far wall, looking bored. He still held his Rolling Rock at his side. He didn't seem to be watching me. Of course, really hot guys never watched the strippers. Instead, we watched them.

My eyes swung back over to Randall, who was once again busy with his executive. After I'd broken up with him, Randall had announced he wanted no more boys, only men. "I want a smart, successful guy who is going places," he'd told me. When I'd replied that I intended to "go places," that I'd moved to L.A. to become a famous actor, Randall had just given me a withering look. Okay, so it had been six months, and nothing had come of any of my auditions, but after each one, I'd been told that I had a good face and a good voice. I was certain stardom awaited. Randall had just smiled and said nothing.

I don't know why Randall's patronizing attitude annoyed me so much. I certainly didn't want to go back with him. Not at all. I was busy with my own string of romantic adventures. After I'd broken up with Lance, I'd fallen in love with Rico, who'd introduced me to Bobby, with whom I'd fallen madly in love after he'd got me this go-go boy job. That was how I'd met Benny, for whom I'd left Bobby and whom, for a couple of weeks, I'd really, really liked. But suddenly up there on my box, I was overwhelmed with attention—a heady experience for a kid who'd never gotten a second look during all his years in Connecticut, who had spent most of his time watching *Doctor Who* reruns and listening to Blondie, except, of course, when he'd had to tag along after his mother through motorcycle bars and strip clubs—like this one, only straight—looking for his sister.

So, compared to that, being up on my box was really fun. *Me,* on a pedestal! I decided to stay single for a while, enjoying the lavish attention a single go-go boy attracted. But, like Randall, I was also biding my time, waiting for Mr. Right.

"Yeah," Randall had scoffed recently, "more like Mr. Right Away."

"Not true."

"Danny, all you're about is one thrill after the other. If you don't watch out, you'll end up dead. You'll get AIDS, or you'll overdose or wind up hacked up by some stranger in some back alley—"

He'd stopped.

He'd crossed a line.

He'd known he might be describing my sister's fate. He'd apologized. We'd dropped the subject.

Across the crowd, I once again laid my eyes on Mr. Tight Tee. And he was looking at me. When our eyes met, he turned away, almost as if embarrassed.

"You have no idea how beautiful you are," Edgar had said to me a few weeks ago, his voice thick with lust, both of us wiping our noses after two lines of coke. "Just give me one night with you, Danny. Just one night."

Edgar was an old guy. Forty, I think. Maybe forty-one. He was balding, with a puckered face and nostrils that were permanently red and distended from too much blow. Rumor had it that he had AIDS, too. I wouldn't let him near me.

"You little bitch," he'd growled after I'd recoiled from his touch, but he didn't hold a grudge. "You know, you could make a lot of money if you'd let me sell that sweet ass of yours. Lots of guys ask about you. We'll split the cash."

"Thanks, anyway," I'd told him. "I make enough in tips."

"Soon it won't be enough," Edgar had replied.

I didn't know what he meant, but it didn't matter. Soon I'd be out of that place, done with stripping, playing a recurring part on *Mr. Belvedere* or *Perfect Strangers*. I was up for parts on both. I was certain one of them would come through.

I glanced back over at Mr. Tight Tee. He was chugging his Rolling Rock now, and even as I thrusted my crotch in some guy's face to the beat of "Never Gonna Give You Up" by Rick Astley, I kept my eyes fixed on him. The object of my desire finished his beer, set down the bottle, and turned with deliberate force, heading for the door.

"Hey!" I shouted.

Without even thinking about it, I hopped off my box and made a beeline after him. The crowd parted, stunned into silence by my sudden action, allowing me to pass.

Mr. Tight Tee was already out on Santa Monica Boulevard when I caught up with him.

"Hey!" I shouted again.

He turned back, surprise on his face.

"Where you going?" I asked.

He seemed flabbergasted that I had followed him. "I'm going home," he said after finding his voice.

"But it's early!" I said. "It's not even midnight!"

His mouth was open, but he didn't speak. No wonder he was flummoxed. There I was, on the sidewalk, standing in front of him, with dollar bills hanging out of my thong.

"I was hoping," I told him, "you'd stick around for my break."

He smiled shyly. "You *noticed* me from up there?"

"Yeah." I laughed. "Come on back in with me. I'll buy you a drink."

"Really, I can't," he said, but I could see that he was flattered. "I have work in the morning. Lesson plans to make out."

"Lesson plans?"

"I'm a teacher," he said.

"Hey, Danny!"

I turned. Benny was in the doorway, pissy as usual.

"What the fuck are you doing?" he snarled. "You've still got ten minutes on the box! Carlos is *still* not ready!"

I gave him the eye. "I'll be right there," I said, turning back to Mr. Tight Tee—Mr. Tight Tee *Teacher,* as it turned out. I was impressed. "Not one quick drink?"

He smiled. Man, was he adorable. Green eyes, freckles, sandy brown hair thinning ever so slightly on top. He might be thirty, but he was still adorable. His well-rounded shoulders and defined pectorals were evidence of many hours in the gym. He was only a couple of inches taller than I was. We'd fit well together in bed.

"One quick drink," I repeated.

He shook his head. "Sorry, but I really have to go. Maybe another time."

"I dance on Saturday, too. Come back then."

Suddenly I realized how pathetic I sounded. The absurdity of it all struck me. What was I thinking, running out onto the street, nearly naked, after a man like this? A man so smart and accomplished—a teacher, for God's sake. A man so far out of my league, he might as well have been another species.

But he just smiled and extended his hand. "I'll try to come by on Saturday night," he said.

I brightened, grasping his hand. "Excellent. I'm Danny. What's your name?"

"Frank," he said.

"Frank," I echoed.

But Frank didn't come on Saturday night. I looked and looked, scanning the crowd all night, but he never showed. It would be some time, in fact, before I would see Frank again.

PALM SPRINGS

I woke early and spent the morning working. Ollie had slipped out sometime during the night, leaving a note, and I felt bad that I hadn't been able to say good-bye. I figured I'd call him later and thank him for coming down. Just for the heck of it, I lit the candle he had given me and took a photo of it, just as a little wisp of smoke rose upward from the glass. I brought the image up on my computer and changed the color to a bright pink. Then I changed it to yellow. Then I dragged it to the trash.

Randall staggered home then and convinced Frank and me to go out for coffee. It was Saturday morning, after all, and the local java hangout would be packed. On the ride over, I got the scoop on the night before. As it turned out, Randall hadn't slept with the young blondie Jake Jones. Instead, he'd had a three-way—with the sixtyish Thad Urquhart and his lover, fiftyish Jimmy Carlisle.

"It was far, far better to go with a couple of experienced pros," Randall told us as we settled into chairs in the courtyard, "who knew what they were doing, who were actually *good* at it, than go with some eager young tyro who would just lay back and make you do all the work."

Both Frank and I laughed out loud. All around us, shirtless men with hairy, distended bellies were sunning themselves, their poodles and Welsh terriers sniffing through the grass. A coterie of boys, probably from WeHo, sat under a tree, sipping lattes and laughing in that high-pitched way coteries of young gay boys always did. The sun was high over our heads, the mountains sparkling gold and copper behind us. In another hour it would be too hot to sit out here, the sun beating down with all its late summer power, sending us scurrying inside like desert rats exposed to the light by overturning a rock.

"Admit it, Randall," Frank said, "this Jake kid just wasn't going to put out. Otherwise, you would've been all over him."

"I'm tired of kids," Randall sniffed, aiming the straw of his mocha freeze at his lips. "All week long my practice is full of them. Screaming, bratty kids who don't want me poking in their mouths. I don't need that when I *date* as well." He paused for emphasis. "I want a *man.*"

He'd been saying exactly that for as long as I'd known him, and that was a long time. Boys had never served Randall well, starting with me. Ike was thirty-one, and since Randall was ten years older, I supposed he still counted as a boy.

"He was cute, though. I'll give him that," Randall said, daydreamy.

"Jake, you mean," I clarified.

Randall nodded. "You saw him, Danny. Didn't you think so?"

Randall seemed to have conveniently forgotten his idea that Jake had been cruising me last night, and I certainly wasn't going to bring it up now. I just shrugged. "He was all right, I guess. I don't usually go for blonds."

Randall nodded. "That's because *you're* blond. We always want what we aren't. What we don't have."

We were silent on that, sipping our iced drinks in the sun, seeming to ruminate on the wisdom of his words, or maybe their absurdity. My eyes wandered over to the boys under the tree. They were goofing around, tickling each other. I couldn't help but smile.

"I think I know Thad Urquhart," Frank said after a bit, stroking the bristles on his chin. He hadn't shaved this morning, and I noticed how very white his whiskers looked in the sunlight. "The name is very familiar."

"He's a big real estate guy," Randall said. "You should see his house. Gorgeous! Right at the foot of the mountain in Las Palmas. He's on the city council, too. A real mover and shaker in town."

The Palm Springs City Council was almost entirely gay, and the mayor was gay, too. The latest estimate was that 60 percent of the population was homo. Anecdotal evidence suggested it could even be higher than that. You couldn't go to a restaurant anywhere in town without seeing several tables full of queens, and sometimes a scattering of dykes. I remembered when Randall and I, all those years ago, had celebrated West Hollywood's independence. A city all our own, we'd declared. Now it was almost commonplace. Palm Springs was even gayer than WeHo now, it seemed.

"Anyway," Randall was saying, "Thad and Jimmy are giving a party next weekend, and I want you guys to come with me."

I raised my eyebrows. "You're coming back to the desert again next weekend?"

Randall smiled. "If it's okay with you guys."

"Of course, Randall," Frank said. "You know you're always welcome."

"I don't know about that," I said, smiling over at my husband. "I might be getting a little tired of all his whoring around."

"Listen, Danny, I'm only coming back for you," said Randall.

"Me?"

"When I told Thad who you were, he was *dying* to meet you. He's a fan of your work." Randall smiled. "I told him a couple of your prints would look simply marvelous over his dining-room table. And this guy has the moola to pay you whatever you want."

"I suppose he's in with the whole Donovan and Penelope Sue crowd," I said.

Randall nodded. "He mentioned their names a couple of times."

"All the big fags here do. If Donovan and Penelope Sue Hunt have accepted you, you've arrived," I noted.

Palm Springs, for all its charms, was the proverbial little pond with lots of big fish. The elite was made up of people who spent their time raising money for charities and then giving themselves awards for doing so. The desert's charities were flush with cash, and that was a wonderful thing—except that sometimes all the self-congratulation became a little wearying. Every season there were more than a dozen black-tie award ceremonies, where the elite rose in unison for one long standing ovation after another. Since moving to Palm Springs, I'd discovered just how much rich people liked to cheer for themselves.

And sometimes they were *very* rich, like Donovan and Penelope Sue Hunt. Penelope Sue was Texas oil money, and her first husband had been head of Columbia or Sony, or something like that. She'd gotten a lot of money—and I mean *a lot*—in the settlement. Donovan had his own money, too, mostly family money, but he'd made quite a bit producing some big blockbusters in the late 1980s, lots of whiz-bang action flicks starring Bruce Willis or Chuck Norris, before turning over a new leaf about ten years ago and funding only serious independent pictures.

Most of the money in Palm Springs came from entertainment-related fields, or else it came from real estate. There was very little old money in Palm Springs. Donovan Hunt, with his connections back East, was a rare exception. Most of the movers and shakers here had come from L.A. or San Francisco, where they'd decided at some point that the big ponds there were too crowded with too many other big fish, and so they'd leapt over to a smaller pond, where they'd have more room to swim. And to raise money. And to receive standing ovations. Except in this case the pond was actually a desert, and the desert was built on the scurrying backs of desert rats, like Frank, who had never received a standing ovation, except for the time he was named Teacher of the Year back in Inglewood about fifteen years earlier.

Frank was born here—well, not *here,* not in Palm Springs, but in Beaumont, a working-class town thirty miles to the west on the 10. His father had owned a small apple orchard in the 1940s, back in the day when Beaumont was called "the land of the big red apple" because of its orchard industry. But then, during the cold war, Lockheed had opened a rocket test site just to the south of the town, spilling toxic chemicals into local streams, which Frank's father believed eventually destroyed his orchard. One year the trees simply failed to produce fruit; the next year they were all dead. Frank's father had to declare bankruptcy. There were no charity fund-raisers to help Frank and his family.

So they moved to Los Angeles, where Frank's dad got a job at a factory and saved enough money to send Frank to Cal State L.A., where he got his bachelor's as an English teacher. When I met him, he was teaching at a high school in Inglewood. Ten years later, after getting his master's, he accepted his current job at the College of the Desert, because he had vowed to himself on the day his family had packed up and left their orchard in Beaumont that someday he'd return to the area. And Frank Wilson was a man who took his vows seriously.

I looked over at him, his face lit by the sun, the mountains reflected in his sunglasses. How he loved it here. When Frank was a boy, his father used to take him out of the cool orchard valley and drive along the dusty road into Palm Springs (Interstate 10 had yet to be built). They'd cheer on the sports car races along the airport tarmac, gravel flying every which way, and then they'd head over to the Saddle and Sirloin for hamburgers, keeping an eye out for Frank Sinatra or Bob Hope or Gene Autry. As a boy, Frank had thought Palm Springs was the most glamorous spot on the planet. "I'd look up at those mountains," he told me, "and in my mind's eye, I'd see Indians hiding behind the rocks, popping up now and then to shoot their arrows, and posses of cowboys riding in across the valley."

My eyes followed the uneven crest of the mountain range in front of me, the subtle transition from brown to purple to gold to blue. The ridges and the canyons, the granite outcrops suddenly jutting into the sky, the serpentine trails worn down by generations of men and coyotes and bighorn sheep. In two thousand years these mountains had never changed. They still looked the same as they had when Frank had come here as a boy, omniscient and indestructible. They still offered the same awesome views once marveled over by pioneers in covered wagons and Elizabeth Taylor in a Cadillac convertible. It was the city around them that had become different. The old dusty roads and the arid valleys studded with cacti and red ocotillo had been replaced with three-lane highways and Fatburger drive-ins, marble mansions and golf courses, man-made lakes and rainbow-hued gay bars. Yet those sturdy granite sentinels enclosing the valley seemed to temper the excess, to contain the ostentation, like stone-faced colossi charged with keeping the peace.

I hadn't always shared Frank's love of the desert. On my first trips out here, for casual weekends of sex and drugs, I'd thought the mountains looked dead. They weren't like the hills of New England, where I'd grown up, lush and rolling and green. Palm Springs might be fun for lazy lounging around swimming pools, or drinking martinis at Lucite bars, or for dancing shirtless at the White Party, allowing yourself to be passed among a hundred different boys in the course of an hour. But beyond that, I'd seen little of value, just Canadian snowbirds in wide-brimmed hats and Bermuda shorts and ticky-tacky T-shirt shops along the palm tree–lined main drive.

All that changed the morning Frank first took me hiking, insisting we get up early and pack a breakfast of trail mix and chocolate chip cookies and oversize canteens of water. Up into Tahquitz Canyon we trudged, deep into the folds of the mountains, where I saw not death but teeming life. The purple lupine and the yellow brittlebush, the beavertail cactus with pink buds, the apricot mallow, the bright orange mariposa lily. And everywhere blue lizards skittering and white-headed woodpeckers clattering. In the sky sharp-shinned hawks soared in great, swooping arcs. Our goal, however, was always to spot that most elusive of all creatures, venerated by the Indians: the bighorn sheep, with its massive curved horns and fleecy white rump. Yet not once in all our time hiking in the mountains—which from that day forward became considerable—did we spot one of the bighorns. Still, I trusted that they were there, pausing to sip from the same stream we waded through as the waterfall crashed behind us.

Ten years had passed since Frank had moved to Palm Springs full time. At first, I came out only on weekends, not wanting to leave L.A., not willing to abandon my dream of making it as an actor. But a decade of walk-on parts and missed opportunities— not to mention a decade of working as a waiter, as a cabbie, and as a housepainter—was wearing thin. The biggest jobs I ever landed were a commercial for Gravy Train dog food and a non-speaking recurring role as a clerk on *Matlock*. And so, on a whim,

I started to take photographs. Faces of friends, the Hollywood sign, palm trees in a windstorm. Then, equally on a whim, I began scanning the photos into my computer. With Photoshop, I altered them, outlined them, fragmented them, turned them into mosaics. No rhyme or reason existed to what I was doing. I was just playing around. When I printed a few of these manipulated photographs, I showed them to a friend who ran a gift shop in Beverly Hills, and she asked me if she could put them on greeting cards. I laughed, but I agreed—and the cards actually sold. I actually made some money. Not a lot, but enough to make me think maybe I could make more if I got serious. And so, four years ago, I moved out here full time, so I could take pictures and play with them on my computer. So I could, finally, become someone. An artist, they say.

What did it mean to be an artist? Did it mean the tortured screams of Jackson Pollock, splattering his paint everywhere? Did it mean Vincent van Gogh cutting off his ear? Did it mean agonizing over your work, pulling out your hair as you tried desperately to express yourself? These were the questions I wondered about as I signed up for a summer photography class at CalArts. There I encountered a woman who considered herself a very serious artist. Her name was Thelma, and she had been an abused child and a battered wife and had spent a few years in a mental hospital. All her work, she told us, was channeled from those experiences. Her photographs of open mouths and dead birds contrasted strikingly to my sunflowers and Marilyn Monroe impersonators. "A searing indictment of the male hegemony of modern life," our teacher called one of Thelma's photos. About mine, she said, "Nice matte finish."

I accepted my limitations. "I'm no artist," I told the teacher. "I just want to make things that look nice."

Only Frank seemed to get it. "Danny," he said, looking at one of my sunflower shots, stripped of its yellows and pumped up with green, "that is probably the craziest-looking flower I've ever seen, but I sure as hell can't stop looking at it." It had hung ever since over our mantel. Frank had dubbed it his "green daisy."

But an artist? No, I wasn't an artist, even though Frank insisted I was. He'd always been very sure of that point. I made art; ergo, I was an artist. I just laughed. Now Becky—*she* might have become an artist. She'd had the passion. She'd had the talent. I remembered the easel that had stood in our backyard—

"Danny."

My thoughts shattered, like glass through which a rock had been thrown. My eyes darted away from the mountains and onto Frank's face.

"You seemed far, far away," he said.

"I'm sorry." I rubbed my forehead. It was damp with sweat from the sun. "I was . . . thinking."

Frank nodded. Twenty years we'd been together. He knew how often I got lost in thought. And he knew where those thoughts usually led. No matter what I began thinking about, they often seemed to come back to one thing. He smiled gently.

I was fortunate to have him. Many men would gladly have traded places with me, sitting there in studied contentment, sipping my coffee with my partner of many years, watching the sunlight dance against the mountains. Frank knew me better than anyone alive, and more than anyone, he had been there for me. For two decades, Frank had believed in me, encouraged me, supported me—even when I was at my nadir, convinced I was a failure. Frank had never bought that line, and consequently, he'd kept me from buying it completely, either. So what if I knew, deep down, that Frank's heart had never been fully mine? What did that matter? He had never left me wanting. Many men indeed would have made the trade.

But not, I suspected, those boys across the way, the ones giggling and wrestling each other in the grass. They wouldn't want to switch places with me. After this, they'd probably go back to their guest resort and fuck in the pool. And then maybe they'd do a line of coke or a hit of E. Tonight they'd dance their asses off at Hunters, and tomorrow they'd head back to West Hollywood, sated and satisfied and happy. No, those boys wouldn't make the trade. The question was, would I?

I looked from them back over to Frank, and then to Randall, who had pulled off his shirt and stretched out on the grass. His face was turned up at the sun. Frank and Randall. The two people who knew me best in the entire world, who understood what my birthday made me think of every year. I looked down at Randall in the grass, the hair on his fleshy torso glistening with perspiration. I knew he shouldn't get too much sun, that it could affect his meds. But not once in more than a decade of living with HIV had Randall developed any opportunistic infection. His T cells remained high, and his daily regimen of pills and potions had rendered the virus undetectable in his body.

Still, I asked, "Do you have sunblock on?"

"It's just for a few minutes," Randall said to me, eyes closed.

We stayed that way for a while more, three silent men occasionally distracted by the laughter drifting across the grass from the boys under the tree. I slurped up the last of my iced cappuccino, making a noise, the way a kid would do.

"Don't you think we ought to get moving?" I whispered, leaning in toward Frank. "I don't want it to get too hot in Joshua Tree to go hiking."

Frank's eyelids flickered. "Danny, you know, it might be too hot at that. Maybe we should plan to do it another day."

"If we leave *now*," I argued, "it won't be too hot. It's not as hot up in the high desert as it is down here."

"Yes, but you know, I'm kind of tired today." Frank's eyes were making an appeal to me. "I'm afraid I'd be a drag on you. . . ."

"Frank," I said, the annoyance tightening my throat. "You said last night we would go hiking for my birthday. Just you and me. Maybe we'd even finally see a bighorn sheep. Those were your words."

"I'm sorry, baby. If you really want to go, we'll go."

I turned away from him. "No. Forget it if you're too tired."

We sat in silence for a moment.

"*I'd* go with you, Danny," Randall said, sitting up and pulling his shirt back on, "but I should be heading back to L.A."

I said nothing. I didn't want to go hiking with Randall. I wanted to go with Frank. I stared at Randall and wondered if—as so often happened—he was reading my mind. If he, too, was remembering what he'd said to me two decades ago, standing in the bar on Santa Monica Boulevard. Frank had just asked me to move in with him.

"I just want you to think long and hard about this, Danny," Randall had said then. "When you're thirty, he'll be forty-four. When you're forty, he'll be fifty-four. When you're fifty . . ."

It hadn't mattered at thirty. But now, at forty-one . . .

It was at that very moment that I looked up, and coming through the courtyard toward us was Jake Jones. His blond hair seemed to glow in the sun, and the flip-flops he wore, barely visible under his long, loose jeans, slapped the pavement in a regular beat as he walked. He seemed in that moment the personification of youth. The lightness to his step. The indifference of his shoulders. He noticed us.

Or rather, he noticed me.

"Hey, Ishmael," he said, approaching. I couldn't tell if he was being ironic or if he really thought that was my name. "Why'd you disappear so fast last night?"

He came to a stop barely a foot from where I was sitting. My eyes were level with his crotch. A black belt with silver studs was half visible from under his semi-tucked white T-shirt, and green checkered boxer shorts bunched up over the waist of his jeans. From the corner of my eye, I could see both Frank and Randall watching our encounter, Frank with curiosity, Randall with envy. Jake had walked right past the two of them and straight up to me. I lifted my eyes to meet the youngster's and smiled.

"Because," I said, "my boyfriend, Frank, was waiting for me at home." I gestured with my head toward Frank.

Jake's eyes turned to look. "Hi," he said, unflappable. "I'm Jake."

"Good to meet you, Jake," Frank said.

He spoke the way fathers do when meeting their sons' friends. The two of them shook hands.

From behind us came a small voice. "Hi, Jake," Randall offered.

The boy finally turned, lifting an eyebrow in my poor, forgotten friend's direction. "Oh, hey," he said. "Did you and Thad and Jimmy go out to dinner last night after I left the bar?"

"We . . . um . . . we ate something back at their house," Randall replied.

I smiled despite myself. *They ate something, all right.* Frank caught my smile, and our eyes met. He chuckled. It broke the tension between us.

"Well," Jake was saying, returning his attention to me, "it was good seeing you again, Ishmael." And then in front of my boyfriend, he took my phone off the table, where I had placed it, and entered his number. "Just in case you ever have a party and want to invite me," he said, handing the phone back to me. "Good meeting you," he said to Frank. To Randall, he said nothing more, just disappeared inside the café.

"What's up with the Ishmael?" Frank asked.

"A silly joke," I said.

"He's cute," Frank noted.

Randall was standing now, brushing off his shorts. "Thad and Jimmy told me to watch out for him. They have done so much for him. They've let him live with them for a while, and they've helped him get a couple of jobs. . . ."

"And what's their problem with him?" I asked. "Is it that he accepts their help but refuses to put out?"

Randall didn't reply. I had my answer.

"Well," Frank said, "I think it's obvious he'd put out for Danny, since he gave him his number."

"Danny isn't interested," I said.

Randall snorted. "Thad says he's a scared little twenty-one-year-old who pretends he's seen it all and done it all. He's got a chip on his shoulder the size of Nevada. He might be cute, but Thad assured me I was better off staying far, far away from him." He gave me a pair of very big eyes. "And I'd suggest the same thing to you, Danny."

I saluted him.

It was time to go. The sun was becoming unbearable. My armpits were wet, and I could feel the bridge of my nose starting to burn. It was time for us humans to retreat into our air-conditioned hiding places and not emerge again until after sunset, when we might wade into our pools or sit under the misters on our decks, gazing up into the purple sky.

"You know," Frank said as we walked to the car, his joints stiff from sitting so long, "maybe I ought to start jogging. I'll get up early in the morning, before it gets too hot."

I gave him a look. "Jogging?"

He nodded. "Yeah. I'm out of shape. I'll firm up a bit, and then we can go hiking again."

"It's okay, Frank."

He stopped walking and looked at me. Randall was ahead of us, rolling down the windows of the car and running the air conditioner full blast so the interior could cool off. I held Frank's eyes. In many ways they barely resembled the eyes I had known for so long. The lashes had gone gray, and the whites of his eyes were perpetually bloodshot. But the color of his eyes had never changed. They were still as green as they'd been that night on Santa Monica Boulevard when I'd run out of the bar, chasing after him, worried I'd never see this beautiful, mysterious stranger again.

"Danny," Frank said, and he was holding my gaze as tenderly as he ever had. "You know that when I look at the mountains, I see Becky, too."

I managed a smile but said nothing. As always, Frank understood.

Yes, Becky was always there—not just in the mountains, but in everything I saw, everything I heard, everything I felt—and Frank, dear Frank, knew this. That was the way it always was this time of year, when August turned into September, when the late summer sun was at its peak, and lesson plans were being made, and schools were opening their doors, and parents worried about sending their children off into the world, and young boys did their best to pretend that they were brave.

EAST HARTFORD

The rattle of the garage door startled me. I was on my bed, engrossed in the latest issue of *Action Comics*—Superman and Green Arrow—when I heard the unmistakable sound of my father's return from work. I slid off the bed and headed into the hallway, pausing at the top of the stairs, my hand resting on the banister.

"Becky isn't with you?" I heard my mother asking from the kitchen.

"No," my father said. "Should she be?"

I began to descend the stairs slowly.

The first thing I noticed was that Mom had gone ahead and hung the HAPPY BIRTHDAY sign, anyway. I sighed. The cake was now frosted, placed in the center of the table, my name spelled out in M&M's. Six places were set around the table, adorned with blue plastic plates, American flag napkins, and the wrapped Hershey's Kisses. By now the curlers were out of Mom's hair, which had flipped up like Mary Tyler Moore's on the old *Dick Van Dyke Show*. She had changed into a pink plaid pantsuit and pink high heels.

"Well," Mom was huffing, "it's almost four! Becky was supposed to be back here by now with the balloons!"

"Maybe the balloons weren't ready," Dad was saying as he set his briefcase down on the counter.

"For crying out loud, the balloons were already paid for! I went down and paid for them myself yesterday! She drove me down there, for God's sake! They were all ready and set to be picked up."

"I don't know, Peggy, she—"

Nana had come into the kitchen, beaming at Dad. "Sebby," she said.

"Mommy, that's Tony," Aunt Patsy corrected, behind her as ever.

"Hello, Ma," Dad said, leaning in to give his mother a kiss.

Anthony Sebastian Fortunato, better known as Tony, except when his mother got him confused with her dead husband and called him Sebby. Dad was a real estate salesman, living on commissions, which were sometimes very good for long stretches of time and sometimes very bad for even longer. His brown tie was loosened and his shirt collar open, his jacket apparently left in the car. Armpit stains showed through his thin yellow poplin short-sleeved shirt.

"Hey, Danny," Dad said. "How's it feel to be fourteen?"

"Same as it did to be thirteen," I lied, and I think my father knew. Dad could read stuff like that, where Mom was simply clueless. He just gave me a smile that seemed to say it all.

"She's got to be with Chipper," Mom was saying. "She's been spending entirely too much time with him."

"I just saw Chipper come home," I said. It felt good to be able to offer some real information. "Becky wasn't with him."

"Then where the hell is she?" The vein on my mother's forehead was pulsing, the way it always did when she got really anxious.

"Peggy, calm down." Dad was unknotting his tie and sliding it out from under his collar. "She's probably with Karen or Pam. She'll be here. Becky's good for her word."

"Well, this place needs balloons," Mom said, the vein still throbbing. "What kind of a birthday party doesn't have balloons?"

"I'm too old for balloons," I said.

"You're not too old! *I'm* too old! You're having balloons, Danny, and that's it!"

"Okay, okay."

The doorbell rang. It was the first of the guests. I hoped it would be Katie, but it was Desmond Drysdale, red haired and freckled, the only boy I'd invited, the only boy I was really friends with, in fact, if anyone could really be friends with Desmond. Desmond was a comic book fanatic, which was where we connected. But while I liked my comics, I just couldn't grasp the depth of Desmond's passion. Over his bed he'd mounted—safely preserved in acetate and held within a plastic container—a rare mint edition of *Silver Surfer* Number 1. Previously, that place of honor had been occupied by a crucifix.

Next to arrive was Theresa Kyrwinski, tall and gangly, followed by Theresa Dudek, with the lazy eye. The phone rang suddenly: Joanne Amenta's mother calling to say that Joanne had a stomach bug and so she wouldn't be coming. Mom breathed fire through her clenched grin as she gave the news to the rest of the party: "What a shame for poor Joanne to get a stomach bug so quickly that they weren't able to call and let me know earlier so I wouldn't have wasted time wrapping Hershey's Kisses for her."

Finally, at exactly one minute to four, came Katie.

"Sorry," she said, trudging up the walk, a present under her arm. "I tried to get here sooner but—"

"Whatever," I said, annoyed.

Katie went on. "My mother took me to the mall after Sears, and we—"

"I said whatever."

But I couldn't stay mad at Katie. This might be the last time I saw her. I took the gift from her hands.

"Shouldn't you wait?" she asked.

"It's a tape. Who is it?"

"Wait until you open the others," Katie protested.

I didn't listen. I tore off the silver wrapping paper and laughed out loud. "Meat Loaf!"

Katie was grinning.

"I want you," I sang.

"I want you," Katie echoed back, the way we did on the bus.

"I need you."

"I need you."

"But there ain't no way," we both chimed in, "I'm ever gonna boink you!"

"Danny!" Mom shouted. "Stop that!"

"Danny off the pickle boat!" Nana called over, laughing.

Across the room Aunt Patsy and the two Theresas were blushing. Desmond seemed oblivious. And Dad was on the phone, talking with the balloon store.

Becky, he was told, had never shown up.

And so the party went on without balloons. And without Mom, who was on the phone, calling every one of Becky's friends.

Aunt Patsy and Nana took over, pouring Kool-Aid and cutting cake. Without Mom to direct the proceedings, I was able to veto any singing, but Aunt Patsy still lit the candles, and I leaned over the cake to blow them out. Scrunching up my face and closing my eyes, I wished that tomorrow morning the headline of the newspaper would report that St. Francis Xavier High School had burned to the ground—but, in case the birthday gods found that just a little too extreme, I offered an alternate wish: that tomorrow would simply go by really, really *fast*.

"Not at Pam's, either," Mom reported to Dad.

The kids around the birthday table sensed the party wasn't destined to last long. They made little conversation, eating their cake in silence, listening to the adults in the other room, dialing phone numbers. Aunt Patsy, looking even more gray than she had earlier, suggested I open my gifts right there in my seat. I agreed, and my self-conscious friends all quickly pushed their offerings across the table. From the first Theresa, I got a St. Francis Xavier sweatshirt (which I knew I'd never wear); from the second Theresa, I got a mug with my name printed on it (which I knew I'd never use); from Desmond, I got a Silver Surfer Versus Captain Marvel board game (which I knew I'd give back to Desmond someday).

The table settled into an awkward silence, broken only by the sound of the rotary dial from the living room and my mother's monotonous questioning of Becky's friends, asking if they had seen her.

Finally, Katie turned to Theresa Kyrwinski and asked her what classes she was in at St. Clare's.

"Do you have Sister Eileen?" Katie wondered. "She's supposed to be really mean."

"No," Theresa said. "I heard that Sister Agnes is even worse."

"I have her for social studies," the other Theresa piped in.

"Agnes or Eileen?"

"Agnes."

"Then we must be in the same class!"

"Cool!"

Katie was suddenly grinning. "Do you want to meet, all three of us, outside the front doors tomorrow morning?"

"Yeah, let's do that!"

"Excellent!"

I looked at them with envy. How apart I felt. How alone, after nine years together, nine years of shared classes, shared teachers, shared experiences: The time in second grade when Katie and Theresa D. and I got locked in the janitor's room and had to crawl out through the window. The time in fifth grade when we put on a variety show, when Katie forgot the lyrics to "Killing Me Softly With His Song," and I had to whisper them to her offstage. The time last year when all of us—me, Katie, both Theresas, Joanne and Desmond—held a séance among the crumbling gravestones of the cemetery behind the school and were scared shitless by the sudden appearance of a squawking crow. For nine years together, we'd endured Fun with Phonics, Reading is Fundamental, and *Davey and Goliath*. We'd survived clumsy slide shows about good nutrition, the dry twang of Miss Waterhouse, the nasal incantations of Father Drummond from the pulpit, and the ruler-wielding of Sister Mary Kathleen.

Now, after all that, I was being ripped out like a flower from its bed, torn from the rest and planted elsewhere, while the others could continue to bloom together and grow ever closer. I had been forcibly separated from my little community because of one fundamental, absurd reason: I had a penis, and the girls didn't. Arm in arm would Katie and the Theresas waltz through the front doors of their new school, while I was forced to trudge on alone. I looked across the table at Desmond, staring mindlessly down at the crumbs on his plate. No hope there. Desmond wasn't going to St. Francis Xavier. His parents couldn't afford it, he'd told us, so off he was heading to the public school, the dreaded East Hartford High.

"Mother of God, where the *hell* could she be?"

Mom's voice cut through the room as she slammed down the phone.

"Maybe I ought to drive you kids home," Aunt Patsy whispered, looking around the table. My friends all nodded gratefully, frightened by Mom's outbursts. Standing dutifully, they dropped their crumpled American flag napkins onto their plates. Only Desmond stuffed the Hershey's Kisses into his pocket; the rest left the little chocolate candies unopened in their tulle.

"Happy birthday, Danny," Theresa Dudek said from across the table. "Have fun at school tomorrow."

I said nothing. I watched as my friends filed out through the door, behind Aunt Patsy.

"Happy birthday, Danny," Katie said, coming up to me.

I looked into her round blue eyes. This was it. The last time I'd see her. Any of them. I just knew it.

I started to cry.

"Danny," Katie said.

"I'm okay. I'm just . . ."

"Worried about Becky?" Katie smiled. "I'm sure she'll be home soon. She's probably just lost track of the time."

"Yeah." I stopped crying.

"Good luck tomorrow."

"Yeah, whatever."

Katie hesitated a moment, then turned to follow the rest.

"Where *is* she?" Mom was screeching from the living room. "I'll throttle her neck for making me so worried! I'll *throttle* her!"

I headed out the back door and sat on the steps. I wiped my eyes, embarrassed that I'd cried in front of Katie. The sun was dropping low in the sky, turning the afternoon red. The backyard was filled with long shadows across the grass. Near the rusted old swing set, unused for years, stood Becky's easel. Becky wanted to be an artist; as a kid, she'd finger paint for hours, and Mom would cover the refrigerator with her creations. I thought finger painting was messy, and wanted nothing to do with it. But Becky lost herself in it, as she did with her crayons and pastels and, finally, oil paints. A little more than a year ago, with money Mom had given her, Becky had gone out and bought the easel and some paints and a whole shitload of brushes. Now, when she wasn't with Chipper, Becky could usually be found at her easel, facing the cornfield behind the house, painting the long rows of corn or the houses up on the hill. After high school, she announced, she would attend the Pratt Institute in New York. Mom asked her how she thought we'd be able to pay for that, and Becky replied she'd get a scholarship. She was pretty serious about her painting. A few nights ago, it had started to rain, and Becky had jumped out of bed, rushing outside to save her precious work of art. She'd replaced it on the easel a few days later, adding a few touches here and there. Her painting of the white house on the hill remained unfinished.

The sun was turning the cornstalks pink. The field stretched on for a mile, all the way to the dark green woods. I could barely make out the trees from where I was sitting, but I could hear the owls. For some reason, this time of day, as the sun started to drop in the sky, the owls always began hooting, long, mournful sounds, like horns on a ship, I thought, even though I'd never heard a ship. I rested my elbows on my knees and my chin in my hands, staring out across the pink cornfield. I tried to tell myself that there was nothing to fear, nothing to worry about, that it was just school. Why did I feel as if everything I had ever known, everything I had ever counted on, was about to disappear? High school was just *school*, and I wasn't a bad student. I'd go to classes and take tests, just like always—even if there were things like lockers, and required intramural sports, and kids from the public schools I'd never met. Not to mention *no girls*—and girls had been pretty much my only friends up until this point. How was I going to survive in a world of only boys?

"Danny."

Nana had come up behind me. She startled me slightly. I turned around and looked up at her. She was holding a small wrapped gift in her hands.

"I had something else I wanted to give you."

I stood, accepting the present.

"Thanks, Nana."

I tore open the blue tissue paper. Inside was a framed black-and-white photograph of several people from the old days.

"Who are they?" I asked.

Nana pointed with her crooked finger, its knuckles enlarged from arthritis. "Those are my grandparents there," she said, indicating a couple of small, white-haired people in dark clothes.

"David and Honora Horgan. They came from County Cork, Ireland." She laughed. "They weren't too happy that I ended up marrying an Eye-talian. Next to them are my parents, Daniel and Emily Horgan. That's who your father named you after. His grandfather."

I nodded. I'd been told that, but I'd never seen a picture of my namesake. Daniel Horgan was a tall man in a dark suit and a vest buttoned nearly up to his chin. He was looking directly into the camera without smiling. He wore a short white beard.

"And finally," Nana said, continuing to point with her finger, "that's your grandfather and me, holding the baby."

Nana looked very young in the photograph, slim, dark haired, wearing a polka-dotted dress. She was holding a baby wrapped in a long white christening robe.

"Who's the baby?" I asked.

"Can't you guess?"

"My Dad?"

Nana smiled. "We took it the day of his christening, to get four generations in the picture. I'm giving it to you so that someday, when you have a baby, we can do the same pose, you and your wife and baby and your parents and me."

I was staring at the photo. I could barely make out Dad's face, so bundled was he in the white robe. It seemed strange that Dad was ever so small. I imagined having a baby like that myself someday. It made me happy to picture it, me and my baby and Mom and Dad and Nana—though the part about a wife just felt too weird. But the baby—a son—that I liked.

"Thanks, Nana." I kissed her on the cheek. She pulled me in to her plump bosom for a quick hug. Her perfume was heavy and sweet.

"Now where's Patsy?" she asked.

"She took my friends home," I reminded her.

"Oh, that's right. And did Becky go with her?"

I sighed. "No, Nana. That's what my mom and dad are having a bird about. Becky hasn't shown up."

"Oh, right."

We headed back into the kitchen. With some difficulty Nana sat at the table, the same place where Katie had been sitting a short time ago. The kids' plates, some with half-eaten slices of cake, were still arranged around the table. I began cleaning up, scraping the cake into the trash and setting the plates in the sink. I knew my mother would want to reuse the plastic plates. In the living room she was still on the phone, talking to someone, her voice alternating between a whisper and a shout.

"Who are they looking for?" Nana asked.

"Becky," I said.

"Oh, that's right."

Mom slammed down the phone. "Carol Fleisher hasn't seen her, either."

"Look, Peggy," came Dad's voice from the other room, "just calm down. There's going to be a rational explanation. Let's not panic—"

"Panic! I'm not panicking! I'm furious!" Mom shouted. "The rational explanation is that girl has gotten high and mighty since she turned sixteen and has been acting all Miss Independent, and I'm going to throttle her! Throttle her!"

"Who's she going to throttle?" Nana whispered.

"Becky," I told her.

I dried my hands on the dish towel hanging from the refrigerator door.

"Nana, I'm going to go across the street for a minute," I said as my mother began dialing another phone number. "I'll be right back, okay?"

"Okay, Danny."

Of course, she'd probably forget, and if Mom or Dad asked where I was, she'd say she didn't know, and then they'd go even more ballistic. But I didn't want to interrupt them, and besides, I would only be gone a moment. I was just going across the street.

To talk to Chipper.

I found him in the garage, working on his car.

The Mach 1's hood was open, and Chipper was leaning inside it, his hands covered in oil. He didn't see or hear me approach. I was able to watch him for a few moments, the way he leaned over the engine, his parachute pants riding low, exposing the dimples at the base of his spine and just the slightest hint of a crack. He wasn't, of course, wearing any underwear.

Did he know I'd been at the pond? Had he and Becky seen me?

"Chipper."

My voice sounded thick and unfamiliar.

Chipper looked up, dark eyes reflecting the red glow of the setting sun.

"Did Becky come home yet?" he asked.

"No. I was just going to ask you if you'd seen her."

Chipper made a face and returned his gaze to the engine of his car. "Like I told your parents—three times now—I have *not* seen Becky. So they can stop calling, and you can stop bugging me."

"You haven't seen her all day?"

"No!"

Chipper pulled his body back away from the car and, with one sweeping move, lifted his T-shirt over his head and threw it to the side of the garage. The gesture made me step back in surprise, and I found I couldn't speak. Chipper stood there in front of me, naked from the waist up, his broad shoulders, sharply defined pectorals and abdominals, sweaty and oil stained, not more than ten inches from my face.

"What is it?" Chipper asked, glowering at me, moving even closer. "You don't believe me?"

He knew. Suddenly I felt certain that Chipper knew I'd been spying on them at the pond. He knew I had stolen his underwear.

"I haven't seen her since yesterday," Chipper insisted, looming over me now. The musky, mingled aromas of boy sweat and engine grease threatened to overpower me. I felt as if I might pass out right there at Chipper's feet. I tried to say something but couldn't.

"What are you looking at?" Chipper asked, pulling back just a bit now.

I opened my mouth to speak, to tell him I wasn't looking at anything, but the words that came out startled me. "Will you be my friend at St. Francis Xavier?" I blurted.

Chipper made a face. "Your *friend?*"

I stood there dumbstruck, like an idiot dweeb.

Chipper laughed. "You're gonna be a freshman. Juniors aren't friends with freshmen."

"But I'm Becky's brother."

Chipper snorted, returning to his car. "When Becky gets home, you have her call me, you understand? Make sure she does."

"Okay. I will." I was backing away now.

"Make sure she calls me!"

"Okay, okay, I will."

I turned and ran.

Back home, Dad was on the phone to the police.

The sun setting had made everything worse.

Aunt Patsy had returned from taking my friends home. As darkness filled the house, she went around turning on lights. She finished cleaning the kitchen of the remnants of my party, though she left the HAPPY BIRTHDAY sign clinging to the wall. Since her surgery, she couldn't lift her arms easily, and so the sign remained, absurdly, a reminder that I'd never again have a birthday like this one.

Nana was getting restless, and her frequent inquiries about just whom Mom and Dad were waiting for made everyone agitated, so finally Aunt Patsy suggested they leave. Mom was obviously relieved. She was far too concerned with running to the front door every time headlights came sweeping down the street to tolerate the mutterings of her forgetful old mother-in-law.

The police car pulled into the driveway just as Aunt Patsy and Nana were backing out. The officer sauntered in, tall and genial, and Mom immediately launched into a physical description of Becky: tall, pretty, brown hair, blue eyes, and a birthmark like a crescent moon on the inside of her upper arm. "Just like mine, see?" Mom offered her arm up for inspection. The officer leaned forward, squinted, but made no comment.

In truth, Mom's birthmark bore only a superficial resemblance to Becky's, less of a crescent moon than a squiggly line. But both were the same purplish brown color, and I'd always felt a little cheated that I didn't get a birthmark, too. It was one more connection between Mom and Becky that I didn't have, and even though Dad had tried to make me feel better by pointing out that he didn't have a birthmark, either, I still wished I'd been born with one.

The cop just smiled, taking none of the information down. He assured Mom and Dad that it was too early to file a missing person report, that Becky was certain to be home soon, that she was probably just acting like a typical teenager, staying out late and getting her parents all upset. "I'm going to throttle her when she gets home," Mom kept saying over and over, and I was beginning to understand that she repeated it so often because it allowed her to cling to the belief that Becky was, indeed, coming home.

For the first time, I wondered where she was.

Becky and I weren't exactly friendly. Oh, we *had* been, as kids, when we'd play house in the backyard with her dolls, or climb the giant maple tree to build a fort out of cardboard. We'd used a green Magic Marker to write BECKY'S AND DANNY'S FORT—DO NOT ENTER on the outside. But ever since she'd started getting breasts and having her period, I'd rarely spoken to her. She was Chipper Paguni's girlfriend. I was just a kid at St. John's School.

Yet it was definitely creepy wondering where she was out there in the night.

Sitting on my bed, my back against the wall, I clamped on my earphones and listened to my new tape. "Now don't be sad, 'cause two out of three ain't bad . . ."

Juniors aren't friends with freshmen.

"Danny." Dad had poked his head in through the door. I slipped off my earphones. "Look," he said, "your mother's too upset to make supper right now. . . ."

"It's okay. I'm not hungry."

Dad seemed at a loss for words. "Well, you should eat something . . . There's some bologna and cheese in the refrigerator."

"I'm really not hungry."

He closed his eyes tightly, then opened them again. "Danny, did Becky say anything to you? Do you have any idea where your sister might have gone?"

Juniors aren't friends with freshmen.

"No," I said.

"None at all?"

"No."

Dad sighed. "Well, make yourself a sandwich if you want." I just nodded as my father closed the door.

Juniors aren't friends with freshmen.

I stared out the window into the darkness, where a light now burned from Chipper's room across the street.

I didn't want to think about Chipper's underpants. I still didn't know why I'd stolen them. What was I going to do with them? What had I been thinking?

The night went on. I turned off my boom box, put on my pajamas, switched off the light, and got into bed. I doubted I would sleep much. Downstairs, I heard the clock on the mantel chime nine times. Mom let out a long wail of anger, terror, despair. It was among the worst things I had ever heard in my life.

I got up to pee. Man, was Becky ever going to be in deep, deep shit when she got home.

After peeing, I stepped out into the hallway and peered down the stairs into the living room. My father was sitting in a chair, with a cigarette lighter in his hands. He kept flicking it on and off, a little flame popping to life in the darkness. He did this over and over, staring straight ahead, the little flame darting in and out like an animal's tongue. I couldn't see my mother, but I could hear her, her voice rising shrilly, then dropping to a whisper, not forming words, just making sounds. Her footsteps came in a steady rhythm—three thumps, then silence; three thumps, then silence—as she paced across the wooden floor.

I turned, heading back to bed, but paused at my dresser. Pulling open my drawer, I lifted out the stolen underpants, setting them down on my dresser and turning on the light to get a closer look. Clean. Probably taken from the dryer and put on for the first time this morning. But that was still enough time for one tiny pubic hair to have found its way into the fabric of the crotch. I stared at that hair lodged there. I dared not touch it, fearful that it might become loose and disappear into the air. Instead, I gently smoothed out the creases of the soft cotton, finding the material curiously exciting against my fingers. In my pajamas, my cock stiffened. My hands trembled, and my throat felt tight. I didn't understand the floaty feeling rising from my belly up to my ears. My cheeks burned as I touched the fly of the underwear, knowing that right there, that very morning, Chipper's boner had grown hard, straining against the cotton, as he and Becky had headed to the pond.

Danny, do you have any idea where your sister might have gone?

Why hadn't I told my father that I'd seen Becky and Chipper at the pond? Because she wasn't supposed to go there. Because she wasn't supposed to be doing what she was doing with Chipper. Because Chipper obviously wasn't telling, and if I *did* tell, then Chipper wouldn't be my friend.

Suddenly all I wanted to do was to lift Chipper's underpants and press them to my face. But I steeled myself, fighting off the urge, and instead thrust them back into my drawer, hiding them among my own underwear and socks.

Then I got back into bed. I willed the morning not to come too quickly. Maybe the gods still had time to take pity on me, and I'd wake up to find the high school had burned to the ground, after all.

But sleep would not come easily. I had to cover my head with my pillow to block out the sound of my mother's sobs.

PALM SPRINGS

The second time I saw him, he was again behind a bar, focused on his work, withholding his eyes from the crowd. For a moment, I could neither speak nor move.

The night was golden, an appropriate hue for this house of affluence set into the mountains, its moveable glass walls obscuring distinctions between interior and exterior. The soft golden glow came from carefully concealed floor lights and artfully recessed ceiling lamps and a crystal chandelier that hung grandly in the marble foyer. From the terraces came the illumination of torches. Everywhere, the night was gold.

And as my beautiful bartender moved behind the bar, the light accentuated the goldness of his skin and left me transfixed.

"Danny?"

Frank was looking around at me, clearly wondering why I had paused in our walk across the room.

"Are you coming?"

"Yes," I managed to say and, with a soft exhalation, resumed my stroll across Thad Urquhart's parlor.

"Danny!" Our host had spotted us and was grabbing my hand with both of his. "Danny Fortunato! And to think I didn't recognize you the other night."

I smiled. Why would he? Who recognized artists? But, then again, I had a name—a name that people were talking about in this town, a name that was supposed to be new and hip and happening, a name that Disney had thought good enough to hire, that *Palm Springs Life* had placed on its cover—and in Palm Springs, names meant something. Palm Springs needed people with names to prove it was more than just a weekend getaway for Angelenos or a nude resort town for flaming queens. And so the people with pull in Palm Springs put me on their local radio shows and the local cable access station, and started inviting me to their parties. In the city's gay rag, my face showed up as a "local artist." The gallery downtown reported people were making inquiries about my prints, even if no one had bought one yet.

Still, I had a name, however meager, and people with names came to Thad Urquhart's house.

People with names—and their spouses.

"This is my partner," I said, gesturing to my side. "Frank Wilson."

Thad gave Frank a warm, pleasant smile, shook his hand briefly, then immediately returned his eyes to me.

"Is it true," he asked in a stagy, conspiratorial whisper, "that Bette Midler has commissioned a piece from you?"

"I don't reveal who's commissioned my work," I said, with a smile.

His eyes danced. Of course, he took my reply as confirmation and giggled. Thad looked the same as he had the other night—short, maybe five-five, with immaculately combed white hair, so white and so even, it was obviously dyed and transplanted. His face was pudgy but smooth, laser blasted, I was sure, at regular intervals in the cosmetic surgeon's chair. He sported a pin-striped, double-breasted charcoal gray blazer and a white shirt without a tie. His large pocket silk was gold, to match the lighting, no doubt. His small hand sported gold and amethyst rings on three fingers.

But I liked him. There was something about Thad Urquhart that seemed comical, ironical, as if he knew all of this was merely a show, and for the night, he was the ringmaster—so why the hell not just have a good time?

Thad was leaning into me, his arm around my shoulder. "Funny," he said, "for a guy with such an Italian last name, you don't look very Italian. You're very fair."

"Only my father's father was Italian," I explained. "His mother was Irish, and so was my mother. A hundred percent."

"But you don't look Irish, either." Thad made a face as he studied my features. "Are you sure you weren't left on your parents' doorstep, in a basket?"

We laughed. But the comment touched a nerve somehow.

Thad took my arm and led me out onto the terrace. Frank followed half a step behind. "Let me get you boys something to drink," our host said.

Of course, it was sheer delight to be called boys at our ages, but in Palm Springs, even for Frank, it wasn't really so far off the mark. Up ahead of us the crowd was mostly gray haired and over sixty, though among the sea of blazers, a handful of buff boys stood out in their tight white T-shirts. And, as always, there were a few stars from the old days—de rigueur for Palm Springs parties, especially *gay* Palm Springs parties. Not the really big stars, of course—they were mostly all gone now—but people with names who added a little gloss to the festivities, who cast a little glow of nostalgic recognition. In the last few weeks, I'd seen Anne Jeffreys and Howard Keel and Kaye Ballard. Tonight I noticed Ruta Lee in a red boa. And Wesley Eure, the former star of one of my favorite shows when I was a kid, *Land of the Lost,* as handsome at fifty as he'd been at twenty.

"What would you like, Danny?" Thad asked me as we approached the bar.

"Vodka martini," I said, drawing my eyes away from the crowd. "Grey Goose if you have it."

Thad nodded. "Of course, we have it. With olives?"

"No," I said. "With a twist."

"And you?" he asked Frank.

"Just a glass of pinot noir, please."

The three of us pressed up against the bar. The bartender turned to face us.

Was I hoping he'd remember me? Was there some crazy notion in my head that our fleeting encounter the previous weekend at happy hour might have stayed in his brain? If I was, I was being silly. Schoolgirlish. Our interaction had lasted only a few seconds.

I'd ordered, he had gotten my drink wrong, giving me olives instead of a twist, and that had been it. There'd been nothing memorable about the moment. Absolutely nothing.

For him, anyway.

I watched as he approached us. The soft hint of a smile was playing across his full lips. But he smiled because he was looking at our host, the man who had hired him, who no doubt was paying him a pretty penny to bartend this private party. He was not smiling at me. I was under no delusions that he might be.

Thad gave him our order. The bartender listened attentively, nodding, then went swiftly about his work. I noticed the head of his eagle tattoo peeking out from below the neckline of his T-shirt. I had to force myself to look away.

"Now, tell me," Thad was saying, leaning against the bar and turning to face Frank and me, "where do you live? How long have you been out here in the desert?"

"We live in Deepwell," I replied. Thad raised his eyebrows and smiled. Deepwell might have been modest compared to the mansions in this part of town, but it was an architecturally rich neighborhood, and Thad seemed to approve. "I've been out here now about four years," I continued, "while Frank's been here for ten."

"*Ten?*" Thad looked wide eyed at my partner. "And we've never met before this?"

"Well, we poor college professors don't often get invited to swanky parties," Frank said.

I had to smile. Frank always called rich people and rich events "swanky." It was a great word. He said his mother had always used *swanky* to describe the movie-star parts of Palm Springs when they'd go sightseeing through the town. "Over there is where Frank Sinatra and Ava Gardner live," Mrs. Wilson used to say, pointing out the house on Alejo. "They give the *swankiest* parties. I've read all about them in *Photoplay.*"

"Well, it's about time that changed," Thad said, giving Frank a warm smile and a clap on the back. "I hope you and Danny visit us often."

I felt he was being genuine. I glanced up and imagined one of my prints hanging over his bar.

The bartender had returned with our drinks. He placed them

on the bar in front of us, and I noticed his hands, the thin line of fine dark hair that crept along the outer edges. I had an over-whelming desire to bend over and lick that line of hair. I actually felt my body moving into position to do so, and I had to stop my-self. My heart was suddenly thumping in my chest. As I looked up from his hands, I came into contact with his eyes—those dark mirrors that suggested a kind of glassy madness. But already he was looking away, indifferent to me, if he had even seen me at all.

For a moment, I couldn't lift my drink. Frank and Thad went on talking, but I just stood there, unable to move or think. My palms were actually wet. What *was* it about this young man that so compelled me? Of course, I had always loved beauty, been partial to it, easily susceptible to its charms. I had worshipped Scott Wood. And as a teenager, I had clipped photographs of beautiful men from magazines and pasted them in a spiral scrapbook on which, in black Magic Marker, I'd written "Beautiful Men." That scrapbook had been kept hidden in my drawer so my mother wouldn't find it—even though I really hadn't needed to worry, since she'd rarely come into my room after Becky disappeared. My bed had never got made; my floors had never been dusted. So, in fact, my Beautiful Men had been safe in their drawer: Robert Redford and Burt Reynolds and David Cassidy had had lit-tle chance of being discovered. Sitting on the edge of my bed, I'd page through that scrapbook, looking at the beautiful men, studying their faces. Then I'd stand in front of my mirror, some-times for hours at a time on a Sunday afternoon, and compare my features to theirs—because, after all, there was nothing else to do except go downstairs and get dragged into one of Mom's schemes to find Becky. So I'd stay in my room, in front of my mir-ror, looking at myself, wondering if I was handsome. I was never sure.

I managed to lift my martini and take a sip. The potency of the alcohol seemed to steady me. I looked around at the men placing their orders. I was sure they found the bartender beautiful, too, yet they were not struck dumb. They went on laughing and talk-ing to their friends. They thanked the bartender and seemed to have no particular urge to connect with his eyes. I couldn't under-stand it. Could they not see the classic structure of his face? The way the golden light caught the dimples in his cheeks? The way the muscles of his back moved under his T-shirt? Why weren't they standing in place, as I was, staring, mouths agape, mute?

"Danny."

I turned abruptly.

"Thad just thanked you for introducing him to Randall," Frank said.

"Oh," I said and managed a smile. "I gather you all had a good time last weekend."

"We did indeed." Thad grinned. "It's not often a couple of sixty-somethings score a young man on a Friday night."

"I'm sure Randall will appreciate the description." I glanced around the terrace. "Where is he, anyway?"

"I introduced him to a friend of mine," Thad said. "I felt it wasn't fair to keep him just for ourselves."

I laughed. "How generous of you."

Thad smiled, then turned his eye to Frank. "So, Professor, I'd like to know where you teach, what you teach, and who you teach."

Frank took a sip of his wine. "College of the Desert, English literature and composition, and my students are a pretty good mix of college-age kids and older people returning to school."

"A rewarding vocation, no?" asked Thad.

Frank nodded. "Yes. Usually."

"My mother was a teacher," Thad said. "My father died in World War II, and she supported four of us kids on her teacher's salary. Wasn't easy."

I looked around at all the spun glass and marble. So Thad Urquhart hadn't come from money. Maybe Jimmy had. But I suspected Thad had worked hard for all this, and I respected him more for that.

"Was it a hard adjustment moving out here, Danny?" Thad asked. "Leaving L.A., coming to Palm Springs?"

"Hard?" I shook my head. "I wouldn't say it was hard. *Excruciating,* maybe. Horrendous and horrible. That gets closer to it than hard."

"Oh, Danny," Frank said, shaking his head.

Thad was laughing. "And why was it so excruciating?"

"Well, I was thirty-six. Practically everybody else out here was retired. All my friends were in L.A., and I missed the social life I had there." I smiled. "But it was important that Frank and I be together full time again."

We exchanged a look. Frank gave me a small smile in return.

"But now you love it?" Thad asked. "Tell me you love it now."

"I love parts of it." I took a sip of the vodka. It felt good going down, its magic spreading through my body, from my throat to my chest to my shoulders and down my arms to my fingertips. "I love the mountains. I love the feeling I get looking at them, being surrounded by them. I love hiking up to the peaks, exploring the canyons. And I love our house and our yard. I create really well out here. I've been far more productive out here than I ever was in L.A. And you sure can't beat the weather—except maybe now, in the summer."

"But at night . . ." Thad gestured around him. "These cool desert nights . . ."

I laughed. "It's still ninety degrees at nine o'clock. That hardly counts as cool."

"But it's dry. Dry heat. Muggy summer nights back East are far worse," Thad noted.

I conceded the point there. As a kid in Connecticut, I'd spent many a hot, humid night spread eagle on my bed, nothing covering me, not even a sheet, a big electric fan pointed directly at me. We never had air-conditioning. I'd lie there, facing the ceiling, tongue out, listening to my mother bang around in the kitchen downstairs at two thirty in the morning. After Becky disappeared, Mom never slept a full night through. She slept in odd patches of the day, like from ten to eleven in the morning and again from five to six in the afternoon, usually on the living-room couch. She rarely made dinner after Becky disappeared. Dad would bring home buckets of chicken from KFC or double cheeseburgers with extra fries from Wendy's. How I remained skinny as a beanpole, I'll never understand.

"But what parts of Palm Springs *don't* you like, Danny?" Thad was asking. "You've described all its natural wonders. What about when you move indoors?"

I made a face. I didn't know this man well enough to say what I really felt. Frank called me judgmental, and maybe I was. Yet parties like this one recycled the same fifty or so people, the same faces that appeared, issue after issue, in the local gay rag. There was the local radio "personality" who carried fake Louis Vuitton bags and billed herself as a Hollywood actress (she'd made a few commercials in the 1960s). There was the local impresario who produced bad—very bad—musical theater, starring such *Love Boat* veterans as Mary Ann Mobley and Ken Berry. There was the self-help guru who self-published her own books and then self-printed promotional postcards declaring they were "critically acclaimed." Yes, if we counted all the self-reviews.

And all that was needed to get a good cross-section of the gay population here was to sign on to ManHunt or Adam4Adam. Very few GoodLookingRedheads or TallNiceGuys. Eighty percent of the Palm Springs profiles had names like CumEatMyMeat or DumpYr-LoadNMe. One drive through the Warm Sands area at 2:00 a.m. was enough to catch dozens of crystal-meth heads sniffing around for sex like mangy dogs hunting through a trash heap for a meal.

"You're being judgmental."

I snapped my head toward Frank. He hadn't actually said the words, but I'd heard them just the same. He was looking at me as Thad awaited my answer.

I smiled. "Let's just say I haven't made many friends here. Most of my friends come in from L.A. on the weekends, like Randall."

Thad put his hand on my shoulder. "Well, I hope that will change. I hope you and Frank will come back soon to have dinner with Jimmy and me."

"We'd like that," Frank said.

I lifted my glass, and we all clinked.

"And you must let me look at your portfolio," Thad said, a little grin playing with his lips. "Don't you think a Danny Fortunato print would look good over the bar?"

"Hmm, now that you say it . . ." I smiled, but I dared not turn around to look where Thad was gesturing. I might see the bartender again, and I didn't think I could bear it.

It was at that moment that I spotted Randall. He was approaching us, waving his hands like an excited teenage girl. I wondered if the man accompanying him might be the cause of his excitement.

"I was wondering when you'd get here," Randall said, bestowing kisses all around. "Doesn't Thad have a marvelous house?"

I nodded in agreement. My eyes were fixed on the man with him, a dark, well-muscled man of Middle Eastern background, with a short-clipped beard.

"Hassan," Thad was saying, "these are two new friends of mine. Danny Fortunato is an artist, and Frank Wilson is a professor of English."

"I am pleased to meet you," Hassan said, with an accent I couldn't quite place. He shook Frank's hand, then mine.

"Hassan is a photographer," Randall told us, and I could see that he was smitten. "That's his work on the wall over there."

"Yes," Thad said, gesturing across the room to a large black-and-white photograph of a naked man, only half visible, against a stark concrete wall. "It's a self-portrait. Taken in Baghdad before the fall of Saddam."

"Are you Iraqi?" Frank asked.

Hassan nodded. "I was born in Basra and lived many years in Baghdad. My family was not religious, and we did well for a time." He smiled tightly. "For a time."

"Hassan was explaining to me that he doesn't take portraits of people to flatter them," Randall said. "He looks at a person and sees the quality that most defines them, and he takes a picture of *that*."

"Oh?" I looked over at the photo on the wall. Hassan had a beautiful body, and he had photographed himself quite provocatively. "And what quality is captured in that picture, might I ask?"

Hassan turned his dark eyes to me. "Faith," he said simply.

"Faith? But I thought you said you weren't religious."

"Faith need not be about religion," he said. "It is faith that has defined me from infancy. Faith in my own destiny, faith that I would go where I needed to go. That I would make it from there to here."

"Fascinating, isn't it?" Randall gushed.

Smitten indeed.

"Go ahead," Randall was saying, nudging Hassan. "Tell them what you see when you look at me. The quality you say defines me."

"Hope," Hassan said plainly.

I sneered. "Clearly, you've just met."

The photographer's eyes hardened. "It is when I just meet a person that I see most clearly."

Randall smirked. "My very good and dear friend Danny is being sarcastic, because I've been a bit, well, *pessimistic* of late."

"That doesn't mean you are not hopeful at your core." Hassan looked from Randall back to me. "At his core, would you say he was hopeful?"

My mind flashed back many years. A night at Randall's house in West Hollywood. A horrible night. It was raining miserably, and there was a leak in the ceiling, and water was pooling in the kitchen. And Randall sat on his couch, his eyes unblinking. "Positive," he said over and over again. "The test came back positive."

"What are we going to do?" I asked, the "we" uttered by instinct. I was terrified.

Randall didn't answer right away, but finally he just shrugged. "Just go on living," he said. "I guess we just go on living."

Just go on living.

"Yeah," I admitted to Hassan. "Hope is a good word for Randall."

"And me?" Frank ventured. "If you were to take a picture of me, what would you be photographing?"

Hassan turned to face him. "Gravity," he said, without a pause.

"Gravity?" I asked.

"Yes. Do you disagree?"

Frank was looking at me.

"No," I said. "Once again, you've hit the nail on its head." I smiled. "Just don't do me, okay? I don't think I want to know."

"Well," Thad said, "I'm sure it would be talent or beauty or artistry or something like that." He was such a good host. "Now, my friends, I must go and mingle. Do enjoy yourselves. Wander around anywhere you like. Have as much to drink as you like. Enjoy this beautiful desert night."

We all nodded as he moved off into the crowd, embracing and kissing the next group of people. The four of us stood awkwardly for a moment.

"Oh, go ahead," I finally said. "Tell me what you see in me, Hassan."

He hesitated. "No, I think when someone is reluctant, it's best not to."

Now I was curious. "No, really. Go ahead. I was just kidding."

"Yeah," Randall said. "What do you see in Danny?"

Frank looked at me uncomfortably over his wineglass as the photographer trained his gaze on me. This time there was no quick pronouncement. He started to say something, then stopped.

"What is it?" I asked. "I feel like I'm with a fortune-teller who doesn't want to give me bad news."

"I don't see anything," Hassan said finally.

I smiled. "So finally someone has stumped you, huh?"

Hassan shook his head. "No. I mean I see nothing. If I took a picture of you, I would be taking a picture of emptiness."

I had no reply to that.

"Well," Frank said, moving in to defend me, placing his arm around my shoulders, "you're wrong about that, Hassan. Danny is hardly empty. He has tremendous passion and great talent—"

"I am sure that he does," Hassan said. "I did not mean to offend. But you asked me what I saw. And when I look at you, my friend, I see a great aching emptiness. Something that is missing. Something that you are always looking for but have never found. If I took a picture of you, that is what would come through on the image."

"Well," I said, trying to lighten the mood, "then maybe I ought to stick to getting my shots done at Olan Mills."

We all smiled.

"Please," Hassan said, "you will not take offense at my words?"

"No," I assured him. "No offense."

But I lied.

I wanted to get away from them. From all of them. From this entire party of powdered and perfumed peacocks. Friends in Los Angeles had told me I'd never make it big, really big, as an artist until I learned to schmooze. But I hated schmoozing. Hated smiling at people I didn't know, making small talk with people I didn't want to talk with, being charming to a room full of phonies when all I really wanted to do was hang out at home, on my couch, the remote control in my hand, flipping back and forth between re-runs of *Doctor Who* and the *E! True Hollywood Story.*

But smile I did, and small talk I did engage in, as we moved in and among the crowd, getting kissed by Ruta Lee and clucked over by queens. I did my best. At least forty percent of the assem-blage would leave that night with my card in their pockets. As Thad dragged me from one of his friends to another, I kept smil-ing and shaking hands, popping breath mints repeatedly into my mouth. Soon enough, I needed another drink, and Jimmy, Thad's less gregarious lover, was dispatched for a refill. I was glad for that, not wanting to approach the bar again myself.

And then, midway through the night, a murmur rippled through the crowd. Donovan and Penelope Sue Hunt had arrived at the front door. Everyone stopped their conversations, whipped their eyes away from their companions, and turned to see.

"Well," Randall purred in my ear, "if it ain't your old boyfriend."

"Donovan," I breathed.

Long before he'd married Penelope Sue, Donovan had carried the torch for me. He was so rich that labels like gay or straight were simply nuisances. Absurd categorizations. Someone as wealthy as Donovan Hunt didn't need to declare one way or the other— though, given the number of beautiful boys he always had on his payroll, his preferences were obvious to everyone. Penelope Sue, at least a decade older than her husband, didn't seem to care one way or another, provided he was on her arm at every function. Tonight she looked her usual shining self, with her big copper hair piled up on top of her head and bright pink lipstick smeared across her face as bold as Joan Crawford had ever worn, outlining and emphasizing her collagen-injected lips. Donovan, at her side, was as tall and handsome as ever, not a fleck of gray at his temples, his cheeks flushed with Juvéderm, wearing a shiny black Prada suit and enormous green Versace sunglasses.

"What's with the shades?" I whispered to Randall.

He looked at me mischievously. "You mean you haven't *heard* what happened to Donovan?"

I shook my head. Truth was, I didn't care what happened to Donovan Hunt, even if everyone else seemed to live vicariously through him. Even at forty-five, Donovan remained the golden boy of the desert, a Peter Pan who refused to grow up, whose toys included a Jaguar; a Bentley; a private jet; homes in the desert, Maui, Highland Park (an exclusive suburb of Dallas), and Nantucket. Some of those homes Penelope Sue shared. Others she most decidedly did not.

"One of his boys beat him up," Randall told me, almost mirthfully. "Stole a bunch of money and credit cards. Donovan had to go to the premiere of his latest picture wearing makeup and dark glasses to hide the bruises." He gave me a look. "Or so I was told." He snickered. "Guess they're not all healed yet."

Thad and Jimmy and a gaggle of others had hurried to embrace the newcomers, bestowing kisses and uttering exclamations of undying love. A few in the crowd around us had returned to their conversations, but most eyes remained fixed on the spectacle that was Penelope Sue and Donovan.

"Which boy did this dastardly deed?" I asked Randall.

"Not sure. I know it wasn't the boy from New York."

"Then it was the Mexican boy," I said.

Randall shook his head. "Oh, no, not Victor. He's a sweetie! He'd never do such a thing. I think this was a new boy, one that none of us had ever met."

I sighed. I was tired of trying to keep track of Donovan's boys. The topic bored me—or rather, I *wanted* it to bore me. But the truth was, I was *dying* to hear about Donovan being beaten up. In detail.

Randall didn't have much to tell, however. "I just heard that he got beaten up right before the premiere, and he wouldn't take off his sunglasses, even in the theater."

"Now, boys," Frank scolded us, easing in. "Don't be so gleeful."

"Gleeful?" I asked. "About Donovan getting beaten up? *Us?*"

"Say what you want about Donovan, but he's made some good movies in the last couple of years," Frank said. "He's using that money he made in the eighties for good purpose now. Few studios would commit to making films like he does. I read a fantastic review of this latest one a few days ago in the *Times*. No matter what you think about him, Donovan really gets behind some worthwhile filmmakers."

I grunted. I knew I was being unfair to Donovan. He really wasn't so bad, and it was true that he was making some good, gay-positive films. I guess he'd made so much money from Bruce and Chuck that he had no idea what to spend it on. Once, years ago, he'd offered to spend it on me. He'd told me if I left Frank, he'd make me a star. He'd finance a movie that I could both star in and direct. It was quite the offer, and I believed he was serious. After all, he'd argued, Frank was going nowhere, but he, Donovan Hunt—one of the biggest independent producers in Hollywood—could do anything he wanted, including make a movie star out of a failed kid from East Hartford, Connecticut. I thought about it overnight, lying there beside Frank, listening to him snore. The next day I went to Donovan and said no thanks.

But our paths continued to cross, especially after Donovan married Penelope Sue and bought a huge estate in nearby Rancho Mirage. Frank and I got invited to every party he threw, with Randall often tagging along. And yet in all that time, his wife had barely spoken three words to me. Even now, I doubted she would recognize me on the street.

"Donovan's last party was pretty fabulous, you have to admit that," Randall was saying, both of us still watching him as he crossed the parlor with Penelope Sue to the bar. "I mean, come on, the champagne fountain. The prime rib. The bubble-butted waiters wearing aprons and nothing else . . ."

I turned on him sharply. "Don't forget that was the party where you met Ike."

That shut Randall up. He frowned and went off in search of Hassan.

Suddenly Thad Urquhart was at my elbow. "Danny," he was saying, "I want to introduce you to two very important people."

Before I had a chance to say anything, he had my forearm in a firm grip. I turned to Frank for help, but he just smiled and held up his hands. "Tell them I said hello," he said, winking. "I've got to make a visit to the boys' room."

"Thanks a lot," I grumbled as Thad tugged me toward the bar.

Penelope Sue was sipping a glass of white wine as we approached her. Donovan wasn't drinking. Thad practically pushed me in front of them. "Darlings," he said, "you have to meet my latest discovery, Danny For—"

He was quickly cut off by Donovan. "No need to sing the praises of Danny Fortunato to me, Thaddeus," he said. "I've been singing them myself for more than a decade." He bent forward to embrace me. "How are you, angel puss?"

"Just ducky," I told him. "What's with the glasses?"

"An eye infection," he said blithely. "Penelope, have you ever seen Danny's art? You need to commission a few pieces."

She smiled. Nothing more. No extended hand, no hello. But I was treated to the sight of that thick, broadly painted pink lipstick curling upward. Not everyone got that much from Penelope Sue. Then she turned to greet someone else.

Donovan was moving away himself, another set of hands eager to touch his shoulder or his arm, hoping some of his wealth and privilege might rub off. But before he was gone completely, he turned back to me. "Danny," he said, "you and Frank *must* come next week to Cinémas Palme d'Or. It's the desert premiere of my movie, and there's a party afterward at the Parker. You *must* come!"

I nodded. He smiled, blew a kiss, and was gone.

"So you know Donovan Hunt," Thad said.

"An old friend," I replied dryly.

His eyebrows lifted knowingly. "A small world, isn't it?"

"When you're gay, very small," I said. "Not that I'm saying Donovan is gay . . ."

Thad laughed. "I'd imagine a boy as good-looking as you must have gotten to know quite a few people on your way up."

It was my turn to laugh. "There's one person I *don't* know, Thad, and I was hoping maybe you could help me with that."

"Of course," he said. "Who do you want to meet next?"

"I'm not sure I want to *meet* him," I said. "Maybe just know his name."

Thad looked at me strangely.

"Your bartender," I said.

A smile slowly stretched across his face. "Ah yes," he said. "Kelly."

"Kelly?"

Thad nodded. "A sweet boy but—"

"But what?"

He laughed. "No buts. He's a sweet boy."

Our eyes moved over to watch him behind the bar. He was shaking a martini, the muscles in his lean arms taut.

"I noticed him at happy hour last Friday night," I said.

"Oh, you won't anymore," Thad told me, shaking his head. "He was fired. So he was quite appreciative when I hired him to bartend here tonight."

"Why was he fired?"

Thad winked. "He tossed one drink too many into a customer's face. You see, the boy has a bit of a temper."

"And what did the customer do to get a drink in his face?"

"Who knows? But whatever it was, Kelly took offense."

I looked back at the bartender. He was handing the martini over to a man who was leaning in to say something. I couldn't hear what was said, of course, but I knew the gist. It was a pickup line, a come-on. The man's face looked as if he considered himself very clever, and no doubt he thought what he'd said was funny and provocative. He probably thought it was something that Kelly hadn't heard before, that he'd found the magic word that would entice the boy into his bed. I laughed to myself. No wonder drinks had been tossed in customers' faces. Kelly was no doubt hit on all the time, always being treated like an object for the amusement of old men's libidos. I remembered that feeling, standing on my box in my yellow thong. I had liked it at first, gotten off on the rush. But it had got old quickly, and by the end I had come to despise the men waving their cash, who thought a Benjamin could buy their way into my life. To this latest idiot, Kelly didn't respond, didn't so much as raise an eyebrow or crack a smile. He just moved on to the next person in line, leaving the humiliated man to slink away back into the crowd.

"I'll bet," I said, turning to Thad, "that the recipients of the drinks in the faces deserved every drop they got."

"Perhaps," Thad said, coming in close, "but I'd suggest, my dear Danny, that you use extreme caution when dealing with this particular boy. Oh, sure, he's pretty to look at and endearingly sweet on first encounter, but beyond that beguiling surface, there is something not quite right."

I said nothing, just gave him a slight nod. I'd let him think I was taking his advice, at least for the time being. I wanted the conversation to end, and that was the best way to achieve my goal. Thad winked at me, then moved back among his guests.

I leaned against the wall and trained my eyes on the bartender. *Kelly*. That was his name. Not a name I would have expected for him. In my mind, he was a Rick or a Tony or a Brad. But now I couldn't imagine any other name for him. *Kelly*. As I watched him, I repeated his name in my mind. *Kelly. Kelly. Kelly.*

I recalled Thad's warning to Randall about that insipid little Jake Jones. I suspected that Thad Urquhart, no matter how much I had started to like him, was a fussy old man made nervous by the unpredictability of youth. Instead of exhilarating, he found it disquieting. Instead of wondrous, worrisome. But what he feared, I *longed* for. Suddenly I realized how much I craved the very volatility that Thad dreaded. Suddenly I was on fire for someone to take my staid, stale routine and turn it around, stand it on its head, shake it up the way Kelly shook his martinis.

I wanted him.

I stood there against the wall and watched him for some time, desiring him more and more with each passing minute, oblivious to everyone in the room but him. Finally—maybe after an hour, or even more—Frank found me and asked me if I was ready to go home. I wasn't, not by a long shot. But I said I was.

That night in bed, I touched a hot hand to Frank's cold leg, made that way by bad circulation. He did not stir. Of course, he'd fallen soundly asleep as soon as the light was switched off, just as he always did. But I lay there wide awake for a very long time, staring up at the ceiling, just as I had on so many nights when I was a boy.

WEST HOLLYWOOD

It was one of those gray June days when the sun never appeared, when the whole city was wrapped in the dismal mist of delusion and disappointment, and the air had the bitter taste of stale coffee. And, to make everything worse, Randall was angry with me—furious, really—because I didn't know who Mary Pickford was.

"How can you claim to want to be an *actor*," he admonished, "to want to be part of the whole great *pantheon* of Hollywood stars, and not even recognize the name of the woman who started it all?"

"I'm sorry," I said. "I've just never heard of her."

We were standing in the forecourt of Mann's Chinese Theatre, although Randall refused to call it by its name and insisted it was—and always would be—*Grauman's* Chinese Theatre, after the man who had built the place in the 1920s. In this, I deferred to Randall's greater wisdom; after all, he was a native Angeleno and surely could impart some wisdom to this wanderer from New England. Pacing across the theater's forecourt, gesturing up grandly at the exotic architecture, he regaled me with descriptions of the golden pagodas which spiked into the murky sky, the temple bells and the Heaven Dogs which had been imported from mainland China in the heyday of silent-movie opulence. But for me, it was the floor of the forecourt that held more interest, those names and footprints imprinted in the cement, dotted with old wads of chewing gum and scuffed by decades of shoes and sneakers. And yet even still, I had to admit that the signature over which I was currently standing, scrawled under especially petite footprints in the cement, meant absolutely nothing to me.

"Mary Pickford was the first true superstar," Randall said. "She was *huge*. The whole world knew her. And then she went on to found United Artists. None of this—none of Hollywood—would be here today if not for her."

"Is she still alive?"

"No." Randall stooped down and brushed away an M&M's wrapper from Pickford's slab. "She died a few years ago. They gave her a special Oscar toward the end. It was the *least* they could do."

He sighed as he stood up.

"This town does not appreciate its history," he said, still acting grand, the way he often did when he tried to pretend he was many years my senior instead of just eleven months. "Look around you. This was once the thriving downtown of the American movie industry. Gala premieres were held here, at this theater. Searchlights swept across the sky, Clark Gable and Marilyn Monroe and Audrey Hepburn all stepping out of limousines."

Not far from where we stood, a homeless man was urinating against the side of the building. The acrid smell quickly permeated the thick, muggy air, and we had to move away. Closer to the road, an Asian prostitute with dyed blond hair was adjusting her fishnet stockings, balancing precariously on stiletto heels, her flat ass barely covered by a faded pair of hip-hugging denim shorts. A couple of times she glanced our way, but she must have pegged us as gay, because she just smirked and went on walking.

Randall shook his head. "Pickford once said, 'What a tawdry monument we left behind.'" He gestured down the street at the tattoo parlors and porn shops and shuddered.

I thought he was being melodramatic. Hollywood Boulevard was seedy, no doubt about that, but it was nothing compared to Times Square. You could get stabbed standing in Times Square. For a while, I'd taken the train in from Connecticut to audition for shows in New York, and I'd always been on my guard walking through Times Square. That was not even considering the seedy neighborhoods Mom had dragged me to in her relentless search for Becky. As tawdry as Miss Pickford might have found all this, I didn't feel I was going to get stabbed in front of Mann's Chinese Theatre.

Glancing down at the cement, I smiled. "Hey, here are some names I recognize," I said to Randall. "Darth Vader and R-two-D-two."

He rolled his eyes. "That was a travesty. Imagine putting mechanical footprints alongside Betty Grable."

"Who's she?"

Randall clenched a fist in front of my face. "You will be lucky to make it home in one piece, you ignoramus."

I laughed. What would I do without Randall?

I'd woken up that morning in a funk, in a gray mood that matched the day. It was the one-year anniversary of my arrival in Hollywood, and I had yet to land one job, one lousy commercial, in all that time. Randall had set about giving me a pep talk, telling me I needed acting lessons and vocal training, that I couldn't just hop off the bus and expect to be "discovered." That might have happened to Lana Turner, who was supposedly spotted sitting on a stool at Schwab's drugstore. But it sure didn't happen that way anymore.

"Who's Lana Turner?" I'd asked.

So that was why he'd dragged me here, to Hollywood Boulevard. It was a crash course in film history. We'd already been to the Paramount gate and were still planning to drive out to Culver City to see what was left of MGM. Randall blathered on and on that if I wanted to be an actor, I needed to see the great films—*Intolerance* and *Greed* and *The Grapes of Wrath* and *Citizen Kane* and *All About Eve*—not waste my time watching crap like *Star Wars* and *Doctor Who* and *Battlestar Galactica*. I smiled and let him rant, for what else was there to do? Otherwise, I'd just be shut up in my room by myself, the remote in my hand, flicking through the channels, or else I'd be jacking off to video porn on the new VCR we had both chipped in to buy.

"Maybe," I ventured as we walked over the footprints of John Wayne, "I'm not meant to be an actor."

Randall spun on me. "Oh, sure. You're just going to give up. Just like that. Why don't you climb up on the Hollywood sign and

end it all? Jump to your death like Peg Entwhistle, the failed star-
let of the thirties."

I sneered. "I'm just saying I've been trying for almost three
years now. First, in New York, and now here. Maybe I should get a
job. Or go back to school."

I was thinking of my father, and that last conversation we'd
had. It wasn't going to be easy, Dad had told me, and he'd been
right about that. He'd been worried about me. Sitting opposite
him in the little reception area of my grandmother's nursing
home, I could see that clearly. I could see his concern for me in
the way he creased his brow and in the lines that formed around
his eyes. Not in a very long time had I seen that look on him, at
least not directed at me. When Becky disappeared, my parents
stopped worrying about me. Sometimes I said things like "I'm
going to learn to skydive" or "I'm going to visit a friend who has
malaria" just to see if they had any reaction. They never did. They
didn't even hear me. But the day I told Dad I was moving to L.A.,
he sat down opposite me and nearly began to cry. From his wallet,
he pulled out a hundred dollars, handing it over to me with trembling hands and telling me to say nothing about it to Mom. It was
money that could have been used in the search for Becky, and I
felt guilty taking it.

I knew what my father feared. I knew why he'd almost cried.
Dad had never understood my being gay. He thought it meant a
life of seedy sex in back rooms—and since arriving in L.A., I'd
done my best to prove him right, to ensure that all his fears would
come true. Eventually, Edgar had worn me down. Many a night
over the last several months, I'd gone home with customers he
brought backstage to meet me, and the money I earned letting
them blow me I split with my pimp sixty-forty. Just as Edgar had
predicted, the tips I pulled out of my thong were no longer
enough. I needed more money because I needed more clothes
and more cigarettes and especially more blow, and Edgar, no
fool, was no longer as generous in offering it. So I ended up having sex with him, too, even though I felt certain he was lying
when he said he didn't have AIDS.

"You need to get serious about what it is you want," Randall was
telling me, for the four thousandth time, as we walked into the

theater's enclosed courtyard. "I want to come here someday and look down and see Danny Fortunato inscribed in this cement."

I shook my head. "I don't have your sense of purpose, Randall."

He just shrugged, but he knew it was true. Randall was a serious medical student. *Very* serious. He'd stay up late at night diagramming molecular theories or some such thing, papers stuck all over the walls with Scotch tape, lines and arrows and words that made no sense to me scrawled everywhere with a blue felt-tip pen. Why he hung around me, vagabond that I was, I was never quite sure. Why he allowed me—a go-go boy with a mounting need to snort prodigious amounts of white powder up his nose—to remain as his roommate had never made sense. "I've gotten used to you," was all he'd say. He promised never to kick me out so long as I never lied to him. But I broke that promise not an hour after I'd made it, when he asked me if I was still doing coke, and I told him no.

"Of *course*, you have my sense of purpose," Randall said, trying to convince himself as much as me. "You got on a bus and traveled three thousand miles to come here. You left behind everything you knew, your entire family and all your friends—because you wanted to follow your dream."

Was that the way it had happened? Sometimes I told the story that way myself, and I believed it, too.

But that wasn't how it had been.

Randall hadn't seen me waiting tables at Friendly's in the south end of Hartford, saving my tips in a glass jar to make train fare into New York. I'd tell my boss I was heading into the city to audition and that, fingers crossed, I might not be coming back, but then, when I got there, I'd just wander around Greenwich Village, not knowing where to go or who to meet. I'd wind up tricking with some guy in a fifth-floor walk-up studio on Bleecker Street with no air-conditioning, slapping away the cockroaches that crawled up my legs in his bed.

Oh, there were a few real auditions from time to time. Occasionally, I'd read about a Broadway casting call and I'd show up, sometimes even getting in to read a line or two. But mostly, I'd just shuffle around outside on the sidewalk, my hands stuffed down into the pockets of my corduroy pants. I'd look at the other actor wannabes and conclude I'd never make it, never get past them, that they were all superior to me.

And that was why eventually I headed to Los Angeles, why I quit my job at Friendly's and decided to board that cross-country bus. Because I came to realize that the ambition that burned so deep and so fierce inside me could never be released so close to home, so near the scene of my failures. It could only be unleashed here, far away from all that, in a world I could make entirely my own. It was as if by stepping off that Peter Pan bus in downtown Los Angeles, I was no longer Danny Fortunato of East Hartford, Connecticut, the son of my parents. I was no longer the boy who'd forgotten he was entitled to dream.

But what were dreams, really? Wisps of smoke. Flickers of imagination that popped up late at night, waking me from sleep. How real they seemed at 2:00 a.m. when I was half awake. In those moments I could really believe I was on the stage, basking in applause, or that I was starring in my own TV show, running up to collect my third Emmy Award—or discovering Becky in the backyard, at her easel, painting the sunset, and calling to Mom that I'd found her, *I'd found Becky*, just as she'd asked me to do.

Dreams. Even three thousand miles, I realized, weren't enough to distance me from the enormity of my failures. Except, of course, when I snorted that wonderful, magical powder up my nose. A dream powder, really. I'd get up on my box and swing my slender hips to the music, really believing that someday I'd be somebody, that someday I'd *matter*, and this—*this!*—was the way to make it happen.

"He's cute."

I lifted my gaze from the pavement. Randall was nodding toward two men standing across the courtyard. I narrowed my eyes to make them out.

I recognized one of them.

"Randall," I whispered. "That guy."

"I know. He's hot. Looks wealthy in that seersucker suit."

"Not him." Randall was, of course, looking at the older of the two, the one with the possibility of a hefty bank account. I was looking at his companion.

It was Mr. Tight Tee. The teacher. The guy who had never shown up again when he said he would.

"It's *Frank*," I said to Randall. I had never forgotten his name.

"Oh, dear." Randall looked at me. "Not the one you were completely obsessed with for three weeks, always looking around to see if he was in the bar?"

"He's so beautiful," I said, staring at him.

And he was. Absolutely beautiful. I watched him as he moved about the courtyard, pointing out to his friend various names and footprints in the cement. His biceps were still as round as melons, stretching the short sleeves of his lime green Izod shirt. His butt was equally as round and hard, framed perfectly in his beige, high-waisted Z. Cavaricci pants. I couldn't help but stare. And then he must have sensed he was being watched. He looked over at me with those bright green eyes.

"Go say hi to him," Randall said.

"No," I said, frozen in place.

"He sees you looking. Go say hi."

"Why should I? I mean, he never came back to see me, so he's clearly not interested."

Randall shrugged. "You don't know that. Maybe something came up."

I took Randall's arm and turned both of us away. "Come *on*," I whispered hard. "It's been six months. If he'd wanted to see me again, he could have come back at some point during all that time."

"Go say hello, Danny," Randall said firmly. "Otherwise, you'll wish you did later."

He was right. I could see myself regretting my inaction, pacing around the apartment, imagining what I might have said and how Frank might have responded. But I hated approaching people. I really did. With the exception of that night running after Frank, I never came on to guys at the bar. I was too nervous. It was odd, really, that I could get up on a box and shake my ass in front of hundreds of slobbering queens. But one-on-one, face-to-face, I was chickenshit.

I also hadn't done a line of coke today.

"*Go*, Danny," Randall urged.

I steeled myself. I turned around and walked across the court-yard. Frank was again pointing out a name to his friend. Halfway there, I wimped out and hurried back over to Randall.

He glared at me. "Okay, Danny, you've given me no choice."

"What? What are you going to do?"

Before I had the chance to stop him, Randall was marching over to Frank and his friend.

"Hello," he called. "So sorry to interrupt."

The two of them lifted their eyes to look at him.

"I'd like to introduce you to my great friend Danny here," Randall said, waving at me to come join them. "Danny Fortunato, up-and-coming actor, soon-to-be gigantic star, collector of rare and vintage first editions, and all-around good guy, meet . . ."

My face was burning. *Rare and vintage first editions?* What the hell was he talking about?

"Gregory Montague," said the older man in the seersucker suit.

Frank's eyes were on me.

"Frank Wilson," he said.

"We've met," I said softly, still several feet away.

He made a face, signaling he didn't remember me. Of course not. Why would someone like *him* remember someone like *me?* This was a big fucking mistake.

"Maybe you don't recall Danny," Randall was saying, "because he's wearing *clothes.*"

I saw Gregory Montague's eyebrows lift on that statement. Suddenly I felt certain he was Frank's lover. Oh, man, was this ever a mistake!

"Oh, right," Frank was saying. "That club on Santa Monica Boulevard . . ."

I laughed, inching just a bit closer. "Yeah, I'm a dancer there."

"Just temporarily," Randall said. "Danny is simply mastering his stage presence. You'll see. He'll be a big star a year from now."

"I see already," Gregory Montague said. A smile played with his lips as he reached inside his jacket and withdrew his wallet. Opening it, he handed me a card. "I'm an agent. Give me a call sometime."

The spark I saw in Montague's eye was the same spark I had seen in dozens of the "clients" Edgar found for me. Montague figured me to be a hooker—or else an actor so desperate, I'd sleep with anyone who called himself an agent. And maybe I was. I felt dirty as I took his card. I caught a glimpse of Frank watching me. No spark in *his* eye. Whether Montague was his lover or not, Frank knew what was going on. He understood the exchange.

"Well, you must come back and see Danny perform sometime," Randall was saying, directing his words at Frank.

I was so humiliated. I just turned away.

"We will," said Gregory Montague.

But Frank said nothing.

I couldn't get away from them fast enough.

"That was horrible!" I shrieked when we were back on the street.

"I'll say," Randall agreed as we quickly made our way down Hollywood Boulevard. "Here I was, doing all the introductions, and oh-so-fancy Mr. Gregory Montague never even once asked *my* name."

"It was a mistake to go over to them. A *big* mistake!"

"Hey, maybe he's a real agent," Randall said. "Maybe he can help you."

I spun on him. "All it did was make me look like a tramp in front of Frank."

"Oh, Danny. At least he knows where he can find you."

I stood in front of him, not letting him pass. "Don't you see? He *isn't* interested in me! Twice now I've made a fool of myself in front of him! He has known where to find me all along and has never come by. Why would he come now—especially when his boyfriend, or whoever the fuck that was, thinks I'm some piece of boy trash he can get into bed with the promise of a part?"

"Hey, maybe it'll be a good part," Randall said.

"Fuck you," I said, turning away, folding my arms across my chest. "And what was all that bullshit about 'rare and vintage editions'?"

"You collect comic books," he said dryly. "I had to pretend you had *some* culture, since you certainly weren't showing any earlier, on our little trip to Grauman's."

"Fuck you," I said again.

There was a moistness to the air now, almost as if it might rain.

"I should never approach a guy I'm interested in," I announced. "No guy that I've ever liked has ever gone for me. It's a fact of my existence."

"That's not true, Danny. You've had lots of boyfriends."

"But they came after me! It's a very real distinction, Randall. If a guy approaches me, it's one thing. But when *I* approach a guy, if *I* really like a guy, it never works out. As soon as I make a move, it's over."

"I think you're acting crazy."

We walked in silence for a while. The day got darker. Rain seemed a very real possibility. When rain loomed in Los Angeles, everyone got a sense of foreboding—like some dark disaster was about to erupt and ruin all our lives. Back East, it could rain in the morning and again at night, and in between the sun could shine, and no one would give it much thought one way or the other. But in Los Angeles when the skies got dark, the threat of rain was an unspoken terror that left everyone anxious and un-settled.

Rain. Yes, I was scared of the rain.

There was a day when I was sixteen. It was early spring, and it was raining really hard, *pouring* really, and my mother and I were walking under a pier on New York's West Side. The stink of the Hudson River was burning my nose. We'd gotten a tip that Becky might be living there, and we were walking up to homeless peo-ple huddled in the shadows, rainwater dripping down from the planks above, and Mom would aim her flashlight right in their faces. Some would yell, some would curse, and others said noth-ing. I kept apologizing for my mother and her flashlight. By the time we got back to our car, we were drenched and freezing.

Yes, I was terrified of the threat of rain.

Up ahead, the Asian prostitute had stopped to talk with one of her colleagues. A dark-haired girl with slumped shoulders, not much older than I was, in a red satin miniskirt and pink vinyl boots. I paused as we neared them. Randall watched as I walked over to the girl and looked her directly in the face. Then, satis-fied, I returned to him, and we resumed our walk down the street. Neither of us said a word.

Certain old habits, I had come to accept, would never go away.

EAST HARTFORD

"I've got your sister tied up in my basement," the boy in front of me whispered as he turned around in his seat to pass me a test.

Oh, how I hated school. Just as I thought I would. I missed Katie and the Theresas terribly. At St. John's, they had formed a protective barrier around me, keeping me safe from too much interaction with the other boys, the boys who played basketball and made lewd comments about the way Jaclyn Smith's breasts bounced on *Charlie's Angels*. It was best that I kept my distance from them, because if they saw how different I was, how essentially unlike them I was in every way, there might be trouble. But here at St. Francis Xavier, there were no girls to protect me. Just me, and the rest of the boys.

Becky's disappearance had proved to be endlessly amusing to these good Catholic young men. Taped to my locker one day, I found a crude drawing of a girl hanging from a tree, with the caption SAVE ME, BIG BROTHER scrawled in purple crayon. It didn't seem to matter that I was the *little* brother, or that there was nothing—*nothing!*—I could do to save her, not even if I found the guts to tell my parents that I had seen her that day at the pond, skinny-dipping with Chipper Paguni. Ripping the drawing off my locker, I heard snickers from the boys behind me. I didn't give them the satisfaction of a reaction.

Just like now, looking at the smirking cretin sitting in front of me. Despite his taunt, I kept my face absolutely stoic. He laughed. Turning around to pass the test to the kid behind me, an elastic band suddenly bounced off the side of my head.

Oh, how I hated school.

"All right, boys," said Brother Finnerty. "You have twenty-five minutes to take the test. Begin . . . now."

The classroom smelled of pencil shavings and mimeograph ink. I took a deep breath and looked at the first exercise. Of course, I'd ace this test. It was language and composition, and for the past eight years, the nuns at St. John's had drilled into me the difference between nouns and verbs and how to diagram sentences and how to build paragraphs. It was the kind of old-fashioned schooling the boys from the public schools hadn't gotten. I finished the entire test in nine minutes flat. Then I sat back in my chair, clasped my hands in front of me, and looked up at the clock over Brother's desk. How slowly the hands turned, how much sixty seconds could feel like a lifetime.

Even as the bell rang, some of the dumb-ass kids were still struggling to finish their tests, but Brother was insisting he collect them all.

"I noticed you finished first, Danny," he said to me as he walked past my desk. Brother Finnerty was a heavyset man, maybe thirty, with a doughy pink face. He was wrapped in the long, flowing brown robes of a monk. "You sure you checked all your work?"

I nodded, gathering my books to head out to lunch.

"I wonder if I could have a moment of your time, Danny," Brother said.

I looked at him as the other boys filed out of the classroom.

"Might I impose on you to befriend a young man who has started classes just today?" Brother asked, not looking at me, straightening the test papers on his desk. "He comes from a very good family. His father's a vice president at Connecticut Bank and Trust, but he's had a hard time of things lately. He could use a good friend, and I think you might be an excellent choice."

I said nothing. Brother finished organizing the papers and looked up at me. There was a certain twinkle in his small blue eyes.

"You've had a tragedy in your family, and so has he." Brother Finnerty gave me a wan smile. "His mother died last year. He's had difficulty dealing with her death, which is why he's started school late. Maybe you and he—"

"Becky's not dead," I said, parroting the phrase my mother used over and over with friends, neighbors, policemen, newspaper reporters. "We'll find her. She'll come home."

"Of course." Brother gave me another smile, broader this time. "But still, you might be able to empathize a bit with his family trauma, what they've been through. His name is Troy Kitchens. He'll be in the cafeteria. May I point him out to you? Perhaps you could sit with each other and eat your lunches together."

No doubt Brother had noticed that since school had started three weeks ago, I always sat alone at lunchtime. I was a loner. I was even excused from having to participate in intramural sports this year, due to the fact that Mom wanted me home every day right after school. That was one good thing to come out of Becky's disappearance: I didn't have to play sports. It meant that I made the acquaintance of very few classmates, however, which was fine by me. So this idea of making a new friend sounded pretty doubtful. The guys at St. Francis Xavier had certainly not proven themselves to be friend material. I had given up, in fact, on ever having friends again. Katie and the Theresas were in their own world at their own school. I rarely heard from them. I had become resigned to spending the next four years on my own. I looked at Brother Finnerty and gave him a noncommittal shrug.

"I would appreciate it if you gave him a chance, Danny," he said. "I know you'll like each other. Troy is a very smart boy, just as you are." He dropped an arm around my shoulders as he led me toward the door. "I'm sure you'll be great friends."

It was not good for me to be seen in the hallway with Brother Finnerty's arm around my shoulders. The boys called him Brother Pop—short for Poppin' Fresh, the annoying little doughboy of television commercials, who was always giggling when ladies poked his gut. Brother shared a certain white, fleshy quality with the dough-boy, even if his laugh wasn't nearly as high pitched, but rather deep throated and raspy, as if in the privacy of the brothers' quarters, he smoked too many packs of cigarettes. As the heavy, robed arm came down around my shoulders, I even thought I caught a whiff of tobacco smoke. I shuddered. It was too late to get away from him now. Walking out into the corridor, I could feel my face redden as every last one of my classmates seemed to turn in unison and stare at me getting cozy with Brother Pop.

The corridor always smelled of a mix of Lemon Pledge and ham-and-cheese sandwiches, especially when the boys were at their lockers, digging through their books and sweaty gym clothes for the paper-bag lunches their mothers had packed for them. They glanced over their shoulders with suspicion as Brother Pop led me to the caf.

"Do you need to stop and get your lunch?" he asked, dangerously close to my ear.

I shook my head. I didn't bring a lunch to school. Back at St. John's, Mom had always made a sandwich for me to take, peanut butter and jelly or liverwurst, carefully trimming the soft brown crust from the Wonder Bread. But now it went without saying that she had more important things to do with her time, like going over police reports or reading through tips that came in the mail or making phone calls to people she didn't know. Now I bought my lunch with the five dollars Dad gave me at the start of every week, and it was nearly always the same: a plate of SpaghettiOs, a bag of State Line potato chips, and a Coke, totaling ninety-five cents. Five dollars actually got me through the week with a quarter to spare, so on Fridays I splurged and got a cheeseburger.

We entered the caf to the sound of trays slamming and soda machines fizzing. Up ahead a boy sat alone at a table, with his back to us. I knew it was Troy Kitchens even before Brother Pop pointed him out to me. He was slouched in his chair, his feet propped up on the table in front of him, his ankles crossed. He had long red hair and wore aviator glasses tinted blue. Shiny avocado-colored parachute pants were topped by a white, neatly pressed shirt and a wide, Windsor-knotted blue and white striped tie. Brother Pop and I walked up to the table and stood at Troy's side, looking down.

"Troy," Brother said.

The kid didn't budge.

"Troy, this is Danny Fortunato. The young man I told you about. I thought the two of you might have lunch together."

"Makes no difference to me," Troy said, still not looking up at us.

Brother gestured for me to go get my lunch. I did, deciding at the last minute to ditch the SpaghettiOs for a cheeseburger even though it wasn't Friday. Somehow it just seemed the right thing to do. Carrying the tray back to the table, careful not to spill my paper cup of Coke, I saw that Brother Pop had left. I sat down opposite Troy Kitchens.

"Not eating anything?" I asked.

"Food here sucks." He lifted his head an inch or so to peer over at what I was eating. "Prefab hamburger. Probably not a whole lot of meat going on in that thing."

The caf's burgers did taste rubbery. I just shrugged.

We sat in silence for about ten minutes. I finished my lunch and was sipping the last of my Coke through the straw, making that slurping sound, when he spoke again.

"So your sister got killed, huh?"

"No. She just went missing." I set my empty cup on the table. "Who told you she got killed?"

"The fat monk."

"Brother Pop?"

"His name is irrelevant to me. I never bothered to learn it because I don't intend on staying in this shit-hole school."

"Well, she's not dead," I said. "She went missing right before school started. The cops have looked everywhere for her. They've followed up like a million leads, but none of them have gone anywhere. It's like she just vanished into thin air."

Troy shrugged. "You oughta just accept the fact that she's dead, then."

"Why?" I was feeling indignant. "There's no evidence she's dead."

"No evidence she's alive, either."

I didn't respond.

"These assholes think I can't accept the fact that my mother died," Troy told me, finally putting his feet on the floor and leaning over toward me across the table. "They're fucked up. Of *course,* I can accept it. I was in the next room the night she blew her head off with my father's gun. I went inside and saw the gray, gooey guts of her brain dripping down the wall. So I've accepted the fact that she's dead. She's dead and she's not coming back and so I've just got to move on."

"I'm sorry," I said in a small voice.

"About what?"

"Your mother."

He scowled. "Why are you sorry? You didn't pull the trigger. She did."

"I just mean—"

"I don't care what you meant. I don't need Brother Fat Ass finding me a little friend. I'm not staying in this lousy excuse for a school. I'm gonna move in with my older brother in New York City. I just gotta convince my father to let me go."

He put his head down on his arms as if he were going to sleep. His eyes remained hidden behind his tinted glasses. I looked at the skin on his arms and neck. It was very pale, with lots of brown and orange freckles. His hair was greasy, as if it hadn't been washed in several days.

There was nothing more to say. I sat back in my chair and waited for the bell to ring. If Brother Pop asked, I'd tell him that Troy Kitchens wasn't looking for a friend.

But for the rest of the day, the image of Troy's mother's brains dripping down the wall stayed with me. I guessed that was a hell of a lot worse than anything I was going through.

After the last bell, I dropped my books into my duffel bag and made my way outside, heading past the line of yellow school buses spewing their stinky white exhaust. I didn't ride the bus home. I could have—my parents thought I did, in fact—but after the first few rides, with paper airplanes continuously bouncing off the side of my head, I decided walking the mile and a half between school and home wasn't really so difficult. The buses would rattle by as I trudged down the street, my duffel bag slung over my shoulder, and a couple of boys usually stuck their heads out of the narrow windows that opened sideways and yelled, "Faggot!" It was just par for the course by now. I barely heard them anymore.

I wasn't sure why I was singled out for abuse. It wasn't Becky: her disappearance was merely something they had on me, a strategy, a course of action they could pursue, rather than a cause. I think their antipathy had more to do with the attitude I seemed to project: that I was different, maybe even better, than they were. I never said as much; in fact, I never said a word. I never raised my hand in class, speaking only if called on. I never started conversations in the corridor or in the cafeteria. I never laughed at any of the dumb jokes my classmates made—and it pissed them off. "Silent Dan" they called me. They hated what my silence implied. That I was on to their silly games, their stupid boy tricks, the hopelessness of their futures. They hated me because I was going to be somebody, and they weren't. I was going to be a politician or an author or a famous movie actor. They were going to punch time cards or work as mechanics or become alcoholics. I'd have hated me, too, if I had been them.

As for my own feelings about my missing sister, I didn't really think much past the idea that she was missing. She'd eventually come home; I took that for granted. In the days following her disappearance, the house had swarmed with people: cops, neighbors, reporters, strangers who'd wander in off the street, attracted by all the commotion. One lady, with silver cat's-eye glasses, had sat in Dad's chair for about an hour, eating the bologna sandwiches that the local deli had sent over, until I'd walked up to her and asked who she was. "A concerned citizen," she'd told me. Mom had had Detective Guthrie, the cop in charge of investigating the case, throw her out.

My mother, too, operated on the belief that Becky's return was imminent. Her room, Mom insisted, should be kept just as it was: "She'll be furious when she comes back if we mess up her things." Outside, Becky's easel, with its unfinished painting of a white house, stood exactly where she had left it, taken in only when it rained and always replaced the next day. Every night Mom still set a plate for Becky at the dinner table—that was, on those nights when she still made dinner. Lately she'd stopped cooking pretty much altogether, I think because Becky's empty plate made her too depressed. Dad had taken up the slack, bringing home pizzas or buckets of chicken, which I ate on my own on the couch, watching *Doctor Who,* or up in my room, reading comic books. On the nights that Dad stayed late at the office—which were getting to be more frequent—I'd just fend for myself. I didn't mind Fluffernutters for dinner. In fact, I kind of liked them.

Mom and I spent hours plastering MISSING signs all over store windows and telephone poles. Becky's name and class photo were printed boldly in purple ink, along with a personal description, including her height, weight, eye and hair color, and the crescent moon birthmark on her arm. Underneath were special phone numbers to call.

In the beginning, right after Becky disappeared, reporters from the *Hartford Courant* had come by to ask us a thousand questions, their pained expressions twisting and stretching their faces so much, I almost wanted to laugh. So far there had been three articles in the newspaper, and another one was promised. The Associated Press had picked up the story last week, and lately we'd been getting calls from friends and cousins in other towns and states, every one of them shocked and horrified, asking what they could do. Mom would say, "Come down and help us look for her" or "Send money." To the best of my knowledge, none of them did either.

Becky's friends were more forthcoming. Carol Fleisher organized a rally at St. Clare's, and they raised six hundred dollars to help in the search. The Rebecca Fortunato Fund was set up at Connecticut Bank and Trust, and lots of people, many of whom we didn't even know, contributed money to it. Soon we were up to several thousand dollars—more money, Dad said, than he'd ever had in his own bank account at one time.

Two weeks ago, Channel 3 had shown up in our driveway, their mobile broadcasting equipment towering over our roof. Mom decided she'd be the one to go on the air that night; Dad declined. The television lights were so bright, they turned our living room white. Mom sat on the couch and described Becky for the cameras, showing tons of photos of her. The photo from last Halloween made me sad. I had teased Becky about dressing up as

Fonzie from *Happy Days,* with her slicked-back hair and leather jacket; I'd told her she looked better as a boy than she did as a girl. I think I hurt her feelings, and I regretted that now, wishing there was some magical way I could take my words back. That night, all the neighbors came over to watch the six o'clock broadcast, and afterward, they told Mom she'd been so heartfelt, so *compelling,* as she pleaded for information about Becky that they were certain someone would come forward.

Did they ever. As the tips poured in, Mom turned the living room into a command post, with three telephones, stacks of notepads, and cups of sharp pencils. It was my job to check regularly to see if any of the pencils needed sharpening. After Mom went on TV, the phones rang nonstop for the next two days. Neighbors came over to help staff the phones. Then, by the third day, they fell silent for a while, but periodically they'd start up again, especially late at night. Some of the calls came from psychics, who said they were seeing visions of Becky being held in a warehouse, maybe in New York City, or waiting tables on a Caribbean island, maybe Aruba. All of it was dutifully written down by Mom, who passed it on to Detective Guthrie. Some of the calls were cranks. "Becky's in my freezer!" some kid would chortle, hanging up. And then there would be these kinds of calls: "If you accept Jesus as your personal Savior, He will bring your daughter home." (You could hear the capital *H*.) I'd lay in bed at night, wide awake, listening to the phone ring downstairs, Flo Armstrong from next door answering with, "Find Becky Fortunato now! May I get your name?"

Yet even with the cranks, we got quite a few leads. Becky had been spotted working at Macy's in New Haven, or riding on the back of a motorcycle in Springfield, Massachusetts, or walking Forty-second Street in Manhattan in fishnets and high heels. Mom and the neighbor ladies dutifully wrote all the information down. They were supposed to refer all callers to the police, but Detective Guthrie had agreed that some people might have a fear of calling the cops, so he'd consented to Mom's phone bank. But none of the leads that came in over the phones had panned out. The cops assured us they'd looked into every one we'd given them, but so far, not a trace of Becky had been found.

I was passing one of the parked school buses, thinking about

Becky in Aruba, when one kid, whose face I had never seen before, slid open a window on the bus and shouted at me, "Hey, Silent Dan, did you suck off Brother Pop?"

I ignored him as always. I just went on walking.

"Hey, your sister's in the back of the bus, giving us all blow jobs!"

Something snapped inside me. I suddenly stopped walking. I threw down my duffel bag and turned to face the kid. What I was going to do or say, I had no idea.

I'd never find out, either.

Because someone else had beaten me to the punch—if indeed, a punch was what I had planned to throw. Someone *else* had reached up and grabbed the punk's throat and yanked him out of the bus so that his wiry little body was now wedged by its shoulders in the window frame.

Chipper Paguni.

"You fucking asshole!" Chipper was seething. "You say that again and I will fucking wipe the parking lot with your fucking faggot ass!"

My eyes were fixed on Chipper's arm, the one that held the kid in a death grip. He'd rolled up his white shirtsleeves, and I could see the tendons tensing in his forearm. They were pulsing with rage, with passion. I couldn't look away.

Chipper shoved the kid back into the bus. "I fucking mean it, you asshole!"

The bus driver had stepped out onto the pavement, glaring at Chipper.

"Its okay," Chipper told him, with a smile. "I'm just keeping some underclassmen in line."

The driver sneered but said nothing. He turned around and got back into the bus.

I stood staring at Chipper.

"You want a ride home?" he asked me.

I nodded, unable to speak.

He gestured for me to follow him.

My heart was in my throat as I hurried across the parking lot, keeping several feet behind Chipper. He was undoing his tie, sliding it out from under his collar. The sound of silk against the starched shirt excited me for some strange reason. Chipper pulled his keys from his pocket and unlocked the driver's side door of his golden car. Becky used to go on and on about this car, about how much power it had, about the sculptured door panels, the simulated wood, the high-back bucket seats. Chipper popped open the passenger's side door, and I slid in, taking the spot that had once been Becky's. I stuffed my duffel bag down on the floor between my legs. My shoulder rubbed against Chipper's, and I felt my dick get hard in my pants.

"Those guys are assholes," he said to me. "You can't just ignore them. You gotta kick their ass, or they will say that shit for the rest of your four years here."

"But Becky won't be gone for four years," I told him. "They'll quit when she comes home."

Chipper didn't reply, just started the ignition. The car roared into life.

We squealed out of the parking lot. From the corner of my eye—because I didn't dare look at him directly—I watched Chipper drive. He steered with his right arm, resting his left out the window. His arms were covered with a soft dark fuzz, which I couldn't ever imagine having on my own arms. His hair, so dark it was almost black, was long and feathered back against the sides of his face. His nose was large but not unattractive, the kind of nose most Italians in town had, except for me. I supposed I took after Mom's Irish side, with my small nose and nondescript features. But Chipper had a strong jaw and a cleft chin, like Superman's and Batman's, in fact like all the superheroes whose adventures I kept preserved in mold-resistant plastic bags under my bed.

We drove on, yellow cornfields stretching for miles on either side of us. The air smelled of cut grass and burning leaves. I thought about Chipper's underpants, stuffed in the back of my drawer. I'd been too embarrassed to take them out and look at them again, but every day, coming into my room after school, I knew they were there. A part of him, inside a part of me. I felt my face get warm and worried that he somehow knew.

"Your mom doing okay?" he asked.

"Well, she's following up lots of leads."

Chipper grunted. "Yeah, I know. She came over my house again last weekend, with a whole new theory."

"The one about the Hare Krishnas?"

He nodded. We had come to a red light. He looked over at me.

"Apparently, there was this busload of Hare Krishnas parked in front of the balloon shop on Main Street for most of the morning," he said, telling me nothing I hadn't already heard, several times. "Your mom says maybe Becky thought they were cool, or maybe they lured her in. For whatever reason, maybe she got on that bus. So your mom is asking me, yet again, when the last time was that I saw Becky that day. She wants to be able to rule out whether or not she could have gotten on that bus."

His eyes were burning holes in me. At least, I felt as if they were.

"The bus left at eleven thirty," I said, repeating what Mom had told me.

The light turned green. Chipper started to drive again.

"Yeah, and like I've told your mother, again and again, I didn't see Becky *at all* that day." He was no longer looking at me. "The last time I saw her was the night before. So sure, maybe she did get on that bus filled with a bunch of crazy Hare Krishnas— though for the life of me, I can't figure out *why* she'd do such a thing."

He was lying, and I knew it.

He *had* seen Becky that day.

At the pond.

At noon.

So she could *not* have gotten on that Hare Krishna bus.

I knew that.

Chipper knew that.

But did he know that I knew?

We drove in silence for another minute or two.

"Thanks for sticking up for me," I finally said.

Chipper laughed. He switched on the radio. A sudden loud burst of Aerosmith. "Schoolgirl sweetie with a classy kinda sassy, little skirt's climbin' way up her knee . . ."

Becky had loved Aerosmith. I wondered if she'd ever listened to this very same song in this very same seat in this very same car. I felt very odd, a kind of tingly odd, being in her place.

Chipper and Becky had gotten very close in the last few months.

I understood why Chipper was so anxious talking to Mom. Because when the police had interviewed him, he'd had to admit that he and Becky had smoked pot together, and that they'd cut class a few times to hang out and eat pizza and watch television at his older sister's apartment. But he had no idea why Becky might want to run away, if run away was what she did. He had no idea of anything dangerous she might have been involved in, of any bad crowd she might have been hanging with. He had told them all he knew, so help him God!

The police had stopped questioning Chipper, and he didn't want them coming back. His revelations of smoking pot and skipping school had knocked Mom and Dad for a loop, but the cops saw nothing incriminating there. Mom wasn't so sure. She'd never liked Chipper's influence on Becky, and to learn these things—her little girl using wacky weed!—had simply hardened her against him. So if Chipper ever admitted to this—that he had lied about the last time he'd seen Becky—Mom would surely turn the police back on him so fast, he wouldn't know what hit him. And I knew that the last person to see a missing or murdered person was always considered the prime suspect.

"Listen, kid," Chipper said, adjusting the volume of the radio down, "you gotta start taking care of yourself." He looked over at me with eyes so dark and so deep, they seemed like holes in his face. "After next year, I won't be around. You've got three more years of this shit."

"But Becky—"

"Whether Becky comes back or not," Chipper said, interrupting me, "these assholes will find a reason to pick on you. That's just the way it is. That's just a lesson of life. Fight 'em off or get beaten down. Your choice."

We had turned onto our street. Chipper pulled into his driveway and turned off his car. I thanked him and stepped out.

And turned to see an ambulance in front of my house.

"Jesus," Chipper said as he saw it, too. We both hurried across the street, getting there just as Aunt Patsy was being carried out the front door on a stretcher. Nana followed, like a wandering ghost.

"Where are they taking her?" Nana asked me.

"I don't know," I said.

Aunt Patsy was awake. She looked up at me from the stretcher. "Danny, I'm so sorry. Tell your mother I'm so sorry."

"What's going on?" I asked.

"Where are they taking Patsy?" Nana asked.

I left her standing there on the grass and rushed up the front steps. In the living room, Mom was seated on a folding chair at a table. Three different phone lines had been installed so that if anyone called with a tip on Becky, they'd never get a busy signal. At the moment Mom was on one of the phones, listening intently. With her free hand, she was covering her other ear to drown out the commotion of the ambulance.

"Mom," I asked, "what's wrong with Aunt Patsy?"

She waved me away irritably. I looked out the picture window and saw the ambulance guys slam the doors, having secured Aunt Patsy in back. Then the lights started flashing and the siren sounding, and they took off down the street. Nana stood in the grass in her big black old lady shoes, watching them go. Chipper came up behind her and said something to her, gesturing back toward the house, but she didn't move. She just kept standing there, looking down the street in the direction the ambulance had gone, like a little kid waiting for the ice-cream truck.

"*Mom,*" I said again, more insistent this time.

"Okay, look," she said into the phone, "I'll have to call you back. This has all been very interesting. I will definitely look into it. Thank you. Thank you *so* much."

She hung up the phone.

"Mom, what happened?"

"This could be it," she said, her eyes wide. "This could be the lead we were praying for!"

"What happened to Aunt Patsy?"

She was up, out of her chair, scrambling for a notepad. "I've got to write this stuff down! This could be it! This could be the answer!"

"Mom!" My voice grew higher. "What happened to Aunt Patsy?"

She spun on me, rage suddenly filling up her bloodshot eyes. "She had to go to the hospital! Don't bother me with that! I know how to find Becky!"

My mind was like a merry-go-round. "You . . . do?"

She was scribbling in her notepad, her hand like a cramped claw holding the pen. "Call your father," she was telling me. "He has to come home. We have to follow this up."

I heard the squeak of the screen door behind me and turned. Chipper was helping Nana up the front steps and holding the door open for her. Mom ignored them. She just continued to write in her notepad, her front two teeth chewing on her bottom lip.

"There you go, Mrs. Fortunato," Chipper was saying.

"Is Patsy in here?" Nana asked.

"No," I told her, taking her hand and leading her to the couch. "She had to go to the hospital."

"Why?" Nana asked, big, round blue eyes looking up at me as she sat down.

"That's what I'm wondering myself." I knew better than to ask my mother again. "I'm gonna call my dad."

"Tell him to get home *now*," Mom said, not looking up.

Chipper stood there awkwardly, shifting his weight from one foot to the other. He was wearing neon blue sneakers with yellow stripes.

"Mom knows where Becky is," I told him.

He turned sharply to look at her. "Where?" he asked.

"Danny, *call your father!*"

"Okay, okay," I said.

"Is Patsy here?" Nana asked from the couch.

"No," I told her again. "She went to the hospital."

"Why?"

"We don't know," Chipper told her softly.

I picked up the phone that hung on the wall between the living room and the kitchen and dialed Dad's work number. I got Phyllis, the secretary for the real estate office. Whenever I went in to see Dad at the office, Phyllis was always sucking on orange hard candies, snapping them around with her tongue so much you could actually smell the fragrance of orange. Now, on the phone, I could hear the candy in her mouth as she spoke. She told me my father was out showing a house, but she'd have him call home as soon as he got in.

"Damn it!" Mom shouted when I hung up the phone. "How can he go to work when his daughter is missing? God *damn* it!"

"Mom," I said. "What did the person on the phone tell you about Becky?"

"He *saw* her!" Her eyes were still big and wet and wild. "He saw her on Cape Cod! Near where the Kennedys live!"

"You mean Hyannis Port?" Chipper asked.

"No! I said *Cape Cod!* Weren't you listening?" Mom's face was really red. She looked down at her notes and began reading them off. "This man—he said his name was Warren—saw her on Cape Cod on Sunday, and she was with a man who had a bald head and a beard and who was wearing a Led Zeppelin T-shirt."

I didn't think my mother knew what Led Zeppelin was, but she must have asked the guy how to spell it, because she pronounced it correctly.

"But how did he know it was Becky?" Chipper asked.

Mom looked at him as if he were crazy. "Because he'd seen her pictures! In the newspapers! On all the telephone poles I've stuck them on!" She looked again at her notes. "This man—Warren—is a motorcycle rider. There was some kind of motorcycle rally on Cape Cod on Sunday, near where the Kennedys live. On Sunday afternoon on the main street of the town, he saw a couple get off a motorcycle. The girl had long dark hair, and she was arguing with the bald-headed man, and he grabbed her arm and told her to do what he said and not to argue anymore." Mom looked as if she might cry at that moment. I felt horrible for her. I wanted to cry myself. "The bald man forced the girl to cross the street, and that's when Warren lost sight of them."

"What's Warren's last name?" Chipper asked.

Mom shook her head. "He didn't want to give me his last name. He says the bald-headed guy is in some rival motorcycle gang, and he doesn't want retribution." She shuddered. "But he *had* to call me, he said. He was shocked by the way the man treated the girl. And when he got back home here to Connecticut, he began seeing Becky's photo everywhere, and he recognized her!"

"Where does he live?" Chipper asked.

Mom shrugged. "I don't know that, either. But this is good information. It's a real lead."

Chipper seemed dubious. "Lots of people have called saying they've seen Becky. What makes you think this Warren guy is for real? Did he talk to her—"

"Get out of the way," Mom said, pushing past us to get to the phone herself. "I need to call Peter Guthrie. He's got to get on this *right away* and get in touch with the Cape Cod police." She began dialing.

"Is she calling Patsy?" Nana asked, a little voice from the couch.

I looked over at her. She seemed so small sitting there. As always, Nana was wearing stockings and those big black shoes and a bright floral-print dress, which Aunt Patsy had probably picked out for her this morning. I still didn't know why Aunt Patsy had been taken away by ambulance. I just knew that *whatever* had happened, it had no doubt irritated Mom, and, most likely, my aunt had had to call the ambulance herself. I walked over to Nana and sat down beside her. She looked at me with those tired, old, confused eyes.

"Remember this, Nana?" On the side table I had placed the photo she had given me. I lifted it now and showed it to her. "Tell me who these people are again."

She seemed to calm down when she saw faces from her past. "Well, those are my grandparents, Nana and Papa Horgan," she said, pointing with her arthritic forefinger. "They came from Ballyhooley, in County Cork. And those are my parents."

"I was named after your father, right?" I asked.

Nana looked at me oddly for a moment, and then something seemed to click. "Oh yes, that's right." She smiled. "*Danny.*" Her eyes brightened. "Danny off the pickle boat."

I laughed.

"And that's your father," she continued, "in the christening robe."

"Four generations," I said.

She was nodding. "And someday, when you have children, we'll take another picture—"

"I need to talk to him *noooooow!*"

Mom's voice startled all of us.

"I don't *care* if he's on another call," she screamed into the phone. "I need to talk to him *right away!* He is the detective in charge of investigating the disappearance of my daughter, and I have information for him! I need to talk to him right this *fucking* minute!"

I had never, in my entire life, heard my mother, good Catholic that she was, use the *F* word. We were all stunned into silence, even Nana.

"I gotta be getting home," Chipper finally said, approaching us. I nodded.

"But, you know, if you find out anything . . ."

"I'll call you. Thanks for the ride."

He nodded uncomfortably. "See ya later, Mrs. Fortunato."

Nana's eyes flickered up at him. She was confused again.

"And Danny . . ." His words trailed off as he looked at me with those big dark eyes of his, so deep you could just topple over into them. "Remember. You gotta take care of yourself. I'll take care of you while I'm still here, but after that . . ." His words trailed off.

I looked at him. Chipper Paguni. Offering to take care of *me*.

Chipper shuffled around uncomfortably in front of us for a few moments, then turned and hurried out the front door.

"I am *still* waiting for Detective Guthrie," Mom spit into the phone.

"Where's Patsy?" Nana asked me in a whisper.

"She's just taking a rest," I told her. "She's fine."

This seemed to soothe Nana a bit, and she sat back, folding her hands in her lap.

Chipper Paguni had said he'd take care of me. *I'll take care of you while I'm still here.*

In that moment, despite everything that was going on around me, I was the happiest boy in the world.

That night, for the first time, I took Chipper's underpants out of my drawer and held them in my hands all night as I slept.

PALM SPRINGS

Randall called them the Gods of Palm Springs. Many of the guys filing out of the movie theater, where we had just seen Donovan's latest opus, were huge and hulking. Massive shoulders, ropes for veins, big, hard protruding bellies. *Gods,* Randall called them. Gays On Disability and Steroids.

"Remember when people with AIDS were skinny and wasted?" he whispered in my ear.

"Not anymore," I said.

"The hulking look has been fetishized," Hassan said, with a photographer's observant eye. "Among the HIV community, I have discovered, the big veins and the prominent gut are considered erotic."

"I would never want to look like that," Randall said. We were heading across the theater's parking lot toward my car. The various Gods had dispersed in different directions, after noisily kissing each other on the lips. "I just would never, *ever* take steroids."

"You would if you had wasting," I said, opening the door of my topless Jeep Wrangler and sliding in behind the wheel. "I know you, Randall. If your face or your arms suddenly started going all hollow on you, you'd be shooting up faster than Courtney Love with an unlimited supply of heroin."

Randall took the passenger seat beside me as Hassan climbed

over the side and into the back. "Yes," my old friend admitted, "I would probably take something for facial wasting, but not to look like *that*." He looked around to make sure they all were gone. "I mean, come on. They actually think they look *good*. Have you seen them strutting around the gym?"

I started the ignition and steered the Jeep onto the street. "Well," I said, "as Hassan points out, that very disproportion in body shape is now eroticized by the men who have it. And good for them. I mean, if you've got a big gut and enormous veins, it's better to have them considered sexy than unattractive." I took a right onto Highway 111, back toward Palm Springs. "I spent way too long beating myself up for not making it as an actor, never recognizing that I could, in fact, do something else better. So I've learned my lesson. You need to make the best of what you've got. It's either that or spend your life being miserable."

"You are wiser than I first thought, Danny," Hassan told me.

I laughed a little, embarrassed.

"It's true," Randall said. "He's becoming quite the sage. Sometimes I barely recognize him. Since moving out here, he's become Danny the Serene, Fortunato the Unflappable."

"Then the desert has been very good to him," Hassan observed.

I just laughed again.

We were quiet for a while. I was pleased that Randall and Hassan seemed to be connecting. Randall had made a couple of trips down to the desert already to see him, heading out of L.A. as soon as the last kid had run screaming from his dentist's chair. I hoped this latest romance would last a while. Too many boyfriends came and went for Randall in rapid succession. He needed somebody to stick around a little longer this time.

I glanced in the rearview mirror. Hassan was sitting with his hands behind his head, looking up at the sky. It was a flat, dull black, without any stars that I could see. The night was hot; summer wasn't releasing its grip on the desert any time soon.

I wondered if Randall's reaction to the Gods of Palm Springs reflected his own fear of what might become of him. So far, he'd avoided any major physical complications from the virus or the meds. He was lucky. I imagined he must worry sometimes that one morning he'd wake up to discover a hump on his back or deep hollows in his cheeks. He rarely spoke of such things. He hardly ever made mention of his HIV.

We stopped for the light in Cathedral City, almost on the border of Palm Springs. I noticed Hassan sit forward and take Randall's hand, holding it down by the stick shift. I smiled.

"So what did you guys think of Donovan's movie?" I asked as the light turned green. "You've been curiously silent on the topic."

"I did not mean to be silent," Hassan said. "I thought it was wonderful. I thought the actress you call Posey was quite marvelous."

"I love Parker Posey," Randall said.

"It was a great cast," I admitted. "Judith Light was terrific."

"I love Judith Light," Randall agreed.

"And that other girl?" Hassan asked. "From the TV show . . ."

"Tori Spelling," I said.

"I love Tori Spelling," Randall said.

I laughed. "But did you love the movie?"

Randall looked over at me, with a sly grin. "Did you?"

I groaned. "I hate that I always love Donovan's movies."

"Me, too," Randall said.

"Why is it that you two have such antipathy for this man Donovan Hunt?" Hassan asked. "He produces fine movies and invites you to the premiere parties, even allows you to bring guests like me. I would think you would *adore* him."

"That's the problem," I said, turning right on Cherokee and into the driveway of Le Parker Méridien. "He's completely adorable, and therefore, everyone adores Donovan. I guess Randall and I just prefer not to follow the crowd."

"Here's the thing," Randall explained. "Donovan has everything. Fabulous homes, expensive cars, and boys hanging from every chandelier."

"Then your antipathy would seem to be rooted in envy," Hassan said.

"Yeah, it would seem so, wouldn't it?" I laughed, pulling the Jeep up to the front door. "But I also can never forget that he's married to a woman, and he uses that status to move through conservative society in places like Dallas and Nantucket, where having a boyfriend just wouldn't do." I turned and faced Hassan, a man from a world where arranged marriages were common and boyfriends among men were unimaginable. "You see, it didn't have to be that way for Donovan. I knew him when he was young, when we *both* were young, living in West Hollywood. He could have chosen a different life. But he didn't."

I switched off the ignition. A handsome young man in a pink jacket was immediately opening the door for me. "Welcome to the Parker," he said. "Are you here for Mr. Hunt's party?"

"That we are," I replied, sliding out of the Jeep, leaving the keys for him. The young man handed me a tag, which I slipped into my back pocket. The three of us made our way inside.

"I never know if I'm supposed to tip before or after," I whispered.

"*Before*, you idiot," Randall said. "Go back. Give him a five. Otherwise, he'll scrape up the car."

"No," Hassan said. "Tipping is for a job well done. You give a tip when the job is completed."

"Oh, well, too late now," I said.

We walked into the foyer. To our left stood a shiny suit of armor. Above us exotic tapestries fell in random patterns like in the great hall of a medieval castle. Neon pink pillows competed with bright yellow curtains for attention. From the ceiling hung gold chains, which tinkled in the slight breeze.

"Rather eccentric this place is," Hassan said, looking around.

I laughed. "Wait till you meet our hosts."

We turned and ambled into the dining room. Donovan was standing right beyond the curtain as we entered, wearing a double-breasted black blazer with gold buttons and a big white peony in his lapel. No sunglasses tonight. His eye had healed, though I detected a lingering puffiness. Suddenly I wondered if maybe he'd deliberately spread that whole story about getting beaten up; it was certainly a far more exotic scenario than admitting to yet another eye lift. Because, believe me, Donovan Hunt had had almost as many eye lifts, cheek implants, and chin tucks as Joan Rivers, and everyone knew it. It was a wonder he could still smile at all.

But smile he did when he saw us. "Danny! Randy!" he exclaimed.

His arms opened wide to embrace us, but I saw his eyes had latched onto Hassan like lasers. But of course. Hassan was new meat—and a well-packaged slab at that.

"Donovan, your movie was absolutely fabulous," Randall was saying. "I *loved* Parker Posey!"

"And Judith Light," I said.

"And Toni Spelling," Hassan added.

I saw Donovan's eyes sparkle. "It's *Tori*, darling, but *you* can call her anything you like." He extended his hand. "I don't think we've met."

"Donovan Hunt," Randall said, and I could hear the reluctance and trepidation in his voice, "Hassan Masawi."

They shook hands. "I am most pleased to meet such a talented filmmaker," Hassan said, infuriatingly polite and obsequious.

"Oh, *please*, sweetheart, I'm just the moneyman." Donovan did not immediately release Hassan's hand. "The director is the true artist. I just write the checks."

"Well, Mr. Moneyman," I said, anxious to break up their little tête-à-tête, "are any of the stars here?"

Donovan finally let go of Hassan's hand and looked over at me. "Sorry, angel puss. It's just us desert rats here tonight. I thought maybe I could get Judith to come down, but everyone was busy."

That was usually Palm Springs' luck. Once in a while, like during the big, glitzy film festival in January, the town was able to lure a bunch of A-list stars. But most often we were left with our own homegrown celebrities, like Penelope Sue. I glanced around the room. I was right. Donovan had made sure his wife was in attendance. She was surrounded, as usual, by a gaggle of queens, all wearing black blazers and white peonies in their lapels. Must've been the theme for the night. Nobody had told me.

"So where's *Frank?*" Donovan asked, placing an arm around my shoulder. "Don't tell me you're a single boy tonight."

"That I am," I said as we headed into the party. "Frank had a faculty meeting. The semester's just started, you know, and he just couldn't get out of it."

Frank had, in fact, wanted to attend the premiere even more than I had. He'd heard good things about the movie, and he didn't share my—what had Hassan called it?—*antipathy* for Donovan.

But, in fact, right about now I felt guilty for being so hard on him. With his arm around my shoulder, it was hard to feel negatively toward Donovan. Hassan was right to say that I was envious. That was where the hostility came from. I'd be fooling myself to deny it.

In truth, Donovan wasn't so bad. He could have iced me out after I'd rejected him, but he kept inviting me to his soirees, making sure I was on the guest lists for his parties and premieres. The little devil who sat on my shoulder, with his cloven hooves and pointy little pitchfork, was forever whispering in my ear that Donovan did all that merely to show off and rub my nose in the kind of life that could have been mine if I hadn't turned him down. But if that was true in the beginning, it certainly couldn't be true anymore. I was far too old to still be on Donovan's radar: his boys were all youngsters, occasionally wide eyed and innocent but usually hard edged and shrewd. Boys who had not only been around the block a few times but around the globe—often in Donovan's private plane—and who understood the terms of the deal very well. They were required to look pretty, to put out when required to do so, to be charming at parties, and to never, ever upstage Penelope Sue. If they did all that, their reward was the good life.

Oh, and one other thing. They had to be gracious when their time was up. Those who dared to resist the end by putting up a fight were coldly cut out of Donovan's life. But those boys who accepted their exits gracefully were rewarded with BMWs or something else equally as shiny and flashy. Suddenly I felt resentful that I couldn't buy Ollie—my trick who drove all the way down from Sherman Oaks in his rusty old Toyota Corolla whenever I snapped my fingers—a brand-new snazzy car.

"I didn't realize this was dinner," Randall said as we approached the table.

"But of course," Donovan replied. "I presumed no one had had a chance to eat."

On our way to the theater, the three of us had wolfed down burritos at Baja Fresh, but now we were confronted with a large, round table, dominated by an enormous spray of magnificently aromatic white peonies. At least twenty chairs were arranged around the table, and busboys in black aprons were depositing leafy green salads at each place setting. Across from me I watched as Penelope Sue took her seat, Donovan holding out her chair for her. He sat to her left. A slim, doe-eyed, freckled redhead—Donovan's latest boy, I assumed—was sitting beside him.

"We cannot refuse," Hassan declared. "To decline dinner would be an affront."

I nodded. The three of us pulled out our chairs to sit, Randall in the middle. Unfolding my white linen napkin, I settled it in my lap.

That was when I looked up and saw him.

"Danny," Randall said, leaning in to me, seeing him at the same time, "isn't that—"

"Kelly," I said.

Randall looked at me. "You know his name? The bartender from happy hour?"

I couldn't speak. Kelly. Was he working *here* now, at the Parker? He wore a black sweater over a blue collared shirt, hiding his exquisite arms. For once he didn't seem confident and controlled, the master of his surroundings. Rather, he seemed adrift, unsure, at a loss as to what to do. Awkwardly, he stood there at the side of the table, shifting his weight from one leg to the other, glancing around at those of us who were seated. I assumed he was waiting to take our drink orders.

But then, from across the table, Donovan spoke—and changed my life forever.

"Kelly," he said, "why don't you sit over there, next to Danny?"

I felt the blood drain from my face.

"Do you two know each other?" Donovan asked.

Kelly looked at me. It was the first time his beautiful dark eyes had ever fully turned to look at me. It was the first time, I was certain, that he had ever seen me.

"No," I managed to say.

He extended his hand. "I'm Kelly," he said.

"Danny." I took his hand briefly. Our eyes held for the slenderest of moments. Then he sat down to my left.

I couldn't say a word. In my lap I clasped my hands to keep them from trembling. I didn't dare lift my water glass to my lips, because I feared I'd spill its contents. When the waiter came to ask us what we wanted to drink, my throat was so tight I just said, "The same," indicating I'd have what Randall had just ordered, a Ketel One martini, up, with three olives. Kelly ordered a Sauza margarita with salt. I realized that tonight, somebody would be making *him* a drink for a change.

Around the table, conversation was bubbling from chair to chair. I heard voices, including Penelope Sue's syrupy Texas drawl, but I couldn't see past my plate. Carefully, I forked some radicchio into my mouth. Out of the corner of my eye, I noticed Kelly wasn't saying much to anyone, and he was eating just as slowly as I was. Neither of us looked at the other. My mind was like a box with the lid taped shut.

"Aren't you going to talk to him?" Randall asked under his breath.

"Shut up," I replied in the same way.

I took a deep breath and let my eyes move around the table. Donovan was deep in conversation with his redheaded boy toy. Penelope Sue was talking to the woman to her right, making sweeping gestures with her hands, her big collagen lips flapping like a duck's. The rest of the guests were all unknown to me. Everyone was chatting away. Only Kelly and I were silent. Finally, I let my gaze sweep past him. It was almost as if he had been waiting for me to do so. Our eyes caught, and he lifted his eyebrows at me.

He lifted his eyebrows.

My heart sped up all at once, and I quickly looked away.

Had he just—*flirted*—with me?

No, no, I told myself. *Don't be absurd.* He wasn't flirting. He just raised his eyebrows. That was all. Just a simple acknowledgment. *It's what one does when eyes meet. It's just a silent hello. No, not even a hello, not really. It's just an acknowledgment.*

Still, it was more than I'd ever gotten from him when I'd seen him behind the bar.

"Talk to him," Randall was urging again, his lips not moving.

"Shut up," I repeated.

Randall looked at me oddly. "What has come over you, Danny?"

I said nothing. I was still. Completely frozen.

Across the table my eyes were drawn to a heavyset woman who had stopped by to pay court to Donovan and Penelope Sue. She was complimenting Donovan's jacket and gushing over Penelope Sue's hair. There were smiles all around, and a couple of air kisses deposited somewhere northeast of Donovan's forehead. And as the woman departed, I saw Penelope Sue roll her eyes.

At my left, Kelly broke into laughter.

I couldn't help but turn. His black eyes caught mine.

"Sorry," he said.

I couldn't say anything. He laughed again.

My voice surprised me. "Care to share the joke?" I managed to ask.

He shook his head. "No. I shouldn't even be here, let alone laughing at your friends."

"They're not really my friends," I told him.

He lifted an eyebrow at me. "You're not a fop?"

"Fop?"

"Friend of Penelope?"

I smiled slightly. "Not really. I doubt she even remembers my name."

"Well, she does that all the time," he said.

"Does what?"

Kelly looked across the table at her to make sure we weren't being overheard. Then he leaned into me, our shoulders nearly touching. I felt as if I were on fire.

"She rolls her eyes," Kelly said. "Did you see it?"

I nodded.

"People pay her a compliment, and she *rolls her eyes.*" He shook his head. "I was sitting here, waiting for it, because I've seen her do it before. And then, bang, she rolls on cue." He laughed again.

"Why does she do that?"

"Because that's what rich people do. They roll their eyes. They cannot abide sincerity in any form. Everything must have a degree of irony, or they can't filter it." He paused. "Sorry. Don't mean to offend you if you're rich."

"I'm not."

He narrowed his eyes as if to study me. "Then why are you here?"

"I'm an old friend of Donovan's. From way back."

He gave a small laugh. "Oh." He averted his eyes. "Same here."

That was when it hit. That was when I figured out their connection.

Kelly had been one of Donovan's boys. Donovan had had him— had had him, done him, discarded him—long before I'd ever laid eyes on him. Of *course,* he had. I should have *known* he had.

Damn Donovan Hunt.

We fell into an awkward silence. The waiter placed our drinks in front of us. I took a sip immediately. Kelly did the same.

"I'm fascinated by rich people," he said finally. If he hadn't spoken again, I'm not sure I would have had the courage to restart our conversation. I turned to face him and watched his mouth as he talked. "How they act. How they talk. How they behave."

"You sound like an anthropologist," I said.

He smiled, a broad, childlike grin that pushed up his cheeks and showed off his dimples. "That would be fun, wouldn't it? To go on an expedition among the rich. To chart out their movements and their habits like Jane Goodall did for apes."

"It might be amusing," I conceded.

"It would make a fabulous documentary for the BBC. I could crouch down behind their sofas and observe them in their parlors, being snooty to their butlers and rolling their eyes behind their friends' backs." He laughed out loud, a sharp, quick sound. I sensed he often amused himself in this way, chuckling at his own imagined scenarios.

I wanted to keep the dialogue going, to say something he would find witty. "Maybe you could secretly videotape their mating habits at the country clubs of Bel Air," I suggested. "Or go undercover at a posh prep school back East."

"Like Miss Porter's," he said. He seemed to like my comment, and I was relieved. "Jackie Bouvier went to Miss Porter's, you know. I love Jackie. *Adore* her. That's who I wanted to be when I grew up, Jacqueline Bouvier Kennedy Onassis."

I smiled, relaxing a little into the conversation. "I wouldn't think you'd be old enough to remember her."

"*Please.* Everybody knows Jackie O. She's the patron saint of America. I worship her. I was a teenager when she died, and it was a terrible blow to me. I was depressed for months. You see, when I was ten, I had wallpapered my room with pictures of her."

I laughed. "I suppose that gave your parents a clue."

He looked at me. "A clue about what?"

"Oh, maybe that you were, I don't know . . . *gay*?"

His face was blank. "I didn't have parents," he said.

I wasn't prepared for that answer. I had no response.

But it didn't matter, because suddenly the waiter was between us, asking for our orders. I hadn't yet looked at my menu. Kelly, clearly more familiar with the restaurant's offerings, ordered the prime rib. I imagined Donovan had taken him here often. I glanced fast at the choices on the menu and asked for the broiled duck.

Someone was standing now, making a toast to Donovan and his movie. We all lifted our drinks and offered the requisite clinks and a chorus of "Hear! Hear!" From my right, Randall was leaning into me, his breath on my neck.

"You seem to have broken the ice," he said.

"*Shut up,*" I whispered yet again.

It was vital that Kelly did not hear, vital that he not know that I'd ever noticed him before tonight. Why that was so vital, I wasn't yet sure. I had no sense, not then, of what he might mean to me, or what I might want from him. All I knew was that his nearness bewitched me, that the very heat of him left me dizzy. I needed to find my balance. I did not want Kelly to view me as yet another of those men who lined up around his bar, waiting to woo, to flirt, to pay homage to him as the most beautiful man ever to walk the face of the planet. Oh yes, I was enthralled, way over my head, and even then I knew that much—which was the reason I struggled to maintain a semblance of power. Kelly could not be allowed to grasp the depth of my fascination for him.

It was completely absurd. I knew nothing about this young man who sat beside me—only that he had a temper and a checkered employment history. Oh yes—and I knew that he was beautiful. I knew that all too well. He was as gorgeous as the men I'd once kept hidden in my secret scrapbook, to whom I'd turn on bleak Sunday afternoons, when the rain beat against my windows and my mother paced the floor downstairs, yelling into the phone at some police detective or some newspaper reporter or some crank who'd called to say he'd spotted Becky at Disney World. Paging through my scrapbook, I could push all of that far away. I'd stare into the eyes of Rick Springfield and Rex Smith and Richard Gere, marveling at the shape of their chins, the curl of their eyelashes. My body would fill up with a terrible ache, a hard, desolate longing to know how they smelled, how they tasted, how their bodies would feel pressed up against mine. But sitting there on my bed, my scrapbook in my lap, I felt certain that I'd never find out, that such beauty as theirs would remain forever elusive to me, always just out of reach.

And Kelly was even more beautiful than any of them.

For weeks I'd watched him. No, not just watched. I'd *hungered* for him. I'd stood, immobile, watching him work. My mind had been a blank. Kelly was no casual trick, the kind I'd spot in a bar and take home, sometimes sharing with Frank and sometimes not. Kelly didn't stimulate my thoughts; he shut them down. When I looked at him, I became mute. My mind ceased. I was again a thirteen-year-old boy, sitting behind Scott Wood in eighth grade, praying that he'd turn around and notice me. But he never did. The hard, cold fact of my life was that nobody I had ever really wanted had ever really wanted *me*.

And that included Frank, a fact with which I'd had to live for twenty years.

Sitting there next to Kelly, I inhaled his sweet cologne, getting high on it. I watched him make indentations along the tablecloth with his fork. My scalp began to tingle. He was more effeminate than I'd imagined. No, not effeminate. That wasn't the word. He was *animated*—which surprised me, given how severe and taciturn he'd always seemed behind the bar. He was animated and expressive and forthright—like a kid, I realized. And I found him, up close, to be even more fascinating than I had from afar.

He was looking at me when I turned my face toward him. He smiled and once again raised his eyebrows.

He *was* flirting with me.

My brain couldn't wrap itself around the thought. I had to be mistaken. He was just bored. He didn't like these parties filled with rich people. He probably hadn't wanted to come. But for some reason, he had felt obligated to do so. I wanted to ask him what he owed Donovan Hunt—what he'd gotten when Donovan had broken it off with him. Was it a car, a Rolex, a Prada suit? Clearly, it had ended well, for Donovan didn't routinely include his discarded boys at intimate gatherings such as this. But another part of me didn't want to know the details. I didn't want to think too long about Kelly in Donovan's arms.

How crazy was this? There I was, being jealous over a guy I'd just met, whose last name I didn't even know, with whom I'd exchanged no more than a handful of sentences. What was going on here? Why was I feeling this way? Well might Randall ask what had come over me. I had no idea.

Our meals were served. "Any good?" Kelly asked.

"Pretty tasty," I told him.

"I do love eating out," he said, gesturing to the waiter to bring him another margarita. "It's one of my favorite things to do."

"Mine too," I said, and I wasn't lying. Frank said we ate out far too often for our budget, arguing that we'd save thousands every year if we ate home more. No doubt he was correct about that. Dinners out in Palm Springs were rarely less than a hundred dollars per couple. But I hated to cook, and so did Frank, and so we ended up eating in restaurants four, five, sometimes six times a week. "Maybe it's because I rarely ate out as a kid," I mused, as much to myself as to Kelly. "It still feels like a great, big, happy occasion whenever I go into a restaurant."

"Me too!" Kelly declared. "I can be miserable all day, but the moment I walk into a restaurant, I cheer right up."

I smiled. "So you didn't go out to eat a lot as a kid, either?"

He shook his head. "Never. Hardly even McDonald's. Let me tell you. I was dirt poor. Not just poor. *Dirt* poor."

My heart swelled like a blowfish in my chest. It always did for working-class boys. "Well, I wouldn't call my family dirt poor," I said, "but we certainly had our struggles."

Kelly seemed to be lost in thought, a forkful of steak suspended in midair. I waited for a comment, but none was forthcoming. His eyes seemed far, far away, a small smile playing with the corners of his mouth. Finally, he looked over at me, as if he'd just had a brilliant idea.

"What if," he said, "all of a sudden that lady over there stood up and took out an Uzi and started mowing all of us down?" His eyes were wide and black and shining. "Do you think you'd be quick enough to make it under the table?"

The question was wild, unexpected, and I laughed awkwardly. I stuttered for a few moments, trying to think of a response. "I'm not sure the table would be adequate protection from an Uzi," I said finally.

He laughed in that sharp, sudden way of his. "I'm always on the alert for stuff like that." He took a sip of his drink. "Hope I didn't freak you out. Don't worry. I'm not a psycho. I just like thinking of weird things."

I looked at him. Should his question have set bells ringing in my head? Should it have made me wary of him? Should it have made me wonder what went on in the mind of this beautiful young man?

Well, it didn't. It was, to me, a question a kid would have asked, a kid who hadn't yet conditioned himself to say only certain things in certain company. A kid who still took chances, who lived life as it came, who hadn't given up on possibilities and dreams. A kid who gave in to his impulses, who lived for spontaneity and incongruity. No, the question didn't make me wary. It only made me like Kelly even more.

When we finished our meals and the waiter came and cleared away our plates, Kelly reached around to his back pocket and produced a small spiral-bound tablet. He flipped it open and, with a felt-tip marker, began to draw. It was bizarre behavior, no doubt about that; a man across from us lifted an eyebrow in a curious glance. But I said nothing; I just watched Kelly draw. The waiter came around to fill our coffees and ask if we wanted dessert. I demurred, as did Randall and Hassan, but Kelly made no reply. He was hunched over the table, absorbed in his task. I watched his hands—in particular, the sexy line of fine dark hair along the edges. Once again, I wanted to lean down and lick it.

"May I ask what you're doing?" I finally ventured, my voice tight.

He gave me one eye. I saw myself reflected in its blackness.

"When I see something that intrigues me," he explained, "I just have to draw it, right then and there, no matter where I am." He held up the tablet so that only I could see. It was a sketch of a woman—of Penelope Sue, I realized—and she was rolling her eyes. "Didn't you see?" he whispered. "She did it again. She rolled her eyes when someone came up to her. And I just *had* to draw it."

"You're quite good," I told him honestly. With just a few deft strokes, he had caricatured her brilliantly.

He suddenly seemed embarrassed. He flipped the tablet shut and stuck it back into his pocket. "I don't usually show anyone my drawings," he said.

I felt honored. "Well, thanks for showing me."

He was standing. "Donovan," he called across the table, "thanks for dinner. I have to go. Bartending at Blame it on Midnight now."

"Okay, babe." Donovan blew a kiss. "Thanks for coming. Good to see you."

Kelly made no other good-byes to anyone at the table. He looked down at me. "What was your name again?" he asked.

"Danny. Danny Fortunato."

"Good meeting you, Danny."

"Yeah." I was suddenly desperate to keep him from leaving. "Listen, I'm an artist. I'd love to see more of your sketches—"

"What kind of an artist?"

"A photographer-illustrator. I produce digital lithographic prints."

"Are you famous?"

I laughed. "I wouldn't quite say—"

"Then you are. If you weren't famous at all, you would have just said no. I'm sorry I didn't know who you were."

"Oh, don't be. I'm not—"

"Sure, I'll get together with you and show you my sketches." He whipped out his tablet and flipped it open, scrawling his number on a blank sheet and tearing it out. He handed it over to me. "Text me so I'll have your number as well."

I took the paper and nodded my head, not quite believing all this was happening.

And then he was gone.

"Nice to see you haven't lost it, Romeo," Randall said, leaning into me.

I stared down at Kelly's number. The sevens were written European style, with lines struck through them. Below the number he'd written "Kelly" in a bold script, rendering his *y* with a big, happy loop—which was exactly the way I was feeling at the moment. Happy, and more than a little bit loopy.

I took out my phone. I texted Kelly a brief message. GOOD TO MEET YOU. Then I used the arrow to go back and add an adverb. VERY GOOD TO MEET YOU.

Still a masterpiece of understatement.

And I could not deny what I did next. Onto the seat he had just vacated, I placed my hand, soaking up the last lingering remnants of the warmth he had left behind.

EAST HARTFORD

Mom insisted on putting up a Christmas tree because if we didn't, it would be like admitting Becky wasn't coming home.

Nana sat on the couch, watching as Dad and I stuck the artificial branches into the plastic tree trunk. Nobody was saying much. In silence, I handed Dad branches in order of increasing size, starting with the small ones up near the top, finishing with the big ones that filled out the bottom of the tree. Then came the lights, three strands wrapped around the tree, and when we plugged them in, we discovered the middle set didn't light up. Dad groaned and said he'd go down to Genovese Drug to get replacements. After he left, I sat down next to Nana to look up at the unfinished tree.

"Where's Patsy?" she whispered.

She asked this five or six times a day. It drove Mom crazy. Nana knew that the question had become irksome, but still, she was heartbreakingly unable to retain its answer. So when she asked it, she tended to whisper it, and usually she directed it to me.

"She's at St. Luke's," I replied.

When she heard this, Nana would always nod, as if she recalled everything. And maybe she did, at least for that fleeting moment. Maybe she remembered that Aunt Patsy's cancer had spread throughout her body, stunning her doctors with its swiftness, and that she was now wasted down to about eighty-five pounds, living at the hospice run by the Catholic church. But even if the memory had come flickering back to her, in a short while she'd be asking again where her daughter was, the daughter who had taken care of her for the last decade, the daughter from whom she'd rarely ever been separated for the last forty-five years.

The phone rang on the table set against the far wall. The phones there hadn't been as busy over the last few weeks as they had in the beginning. Becky's disappearance had become old news, no longer featured in the papers or on the local newscasts. The police had followed up on lots of leads, like that one about Becky being with some motorcycle guy on Cape Cod. For some reason, Mom had really thought that one was going to pan out. Maybe because the cops told her that they'd followed a couple of suspicious motorcyclists on Main Street on the very morning Becky disappeared. Of course, she'd also been convinced that the Hare Krishnas had taken Becky, because *they'd* been in town that morning, too. But it didn't matter. For a good two weeks, Mom remained *certain* that Becky had been kidnapped by bikers and was now on Cape Cod—until, that was, an exhaustive search by police turned up no one on the Cape who looked like Becky or the bald-headed guy with the Led Zeppelin shirt. And so now we were back at the beginning, without any real leads that might explain what had happened to my sister.

Mom was undaunted. She kept her command post staffed with friends and neighbors, but as the holidays drew closer, fewer people came by to help out, so she hooked up an answering machine to the main line whenever she couldn't be there herself. This was one of those times. Mom was at Mass. She went to Mass every morning. Because she couldn't drive, a local taxicab driver had volunteered to pick her up and bring her back every day. It was his contribution to the Rebecca Fortunato Fund, he said. At church Mom would grip her hands so hard in prayer that she left bruises on her knuckles.

But now, while she was at prayer, the phone was ringing. On the fourth ring, the answering machine clicked on.

Nana and I listened. "This is Peggy Fortunato. If you are calling about my daughter, Rebecca Ann Fortunato, please leave a message and please, please, *please* leave a phone number. Thank you and God bless you." Then came the beep.

"Hello," a voice said. I couldn't tell if it was male or female. "I'm calling about Becky." The voice was shaking, as if the speaker was frightened. "We have her. She's right here. And you can get her back if you give us ten thousand—"

I bolted from the couch and lifted the phone. "Who is this?" I shouted.

The caller seemed startled into silence. Finally the voice resumed. "We have Becky. Pay us ten thousand dollars and we'll let her go."

"Who are you? Where are you?"

I heard another voice in the background. "Oh yeah," the caller said. "If you contact the police, we'll know. And we will kill her."

"Where are you?" I asked again.

"Bring the money by twelve o'clock noon to the Caldor's Plaza on West Main Street. Drop it into the Dumpster in the back. Then drive away." The voice in the background said something else. "And no cops," the caller repeated. "If we see anything out of the ordinary, we will slit Becky's throat."

"Okay," I said, my heart racing. "I'll tell my parents."

"Twelve o'clock," the caller said again.

"Okay," I said.

And the caller hung up.

I didn't know what to do. My mind was in shambles. Twelve o'clock. That was less than two hours from now. I looked over at Nana.

"They said they have Becky," I said.

"Becka dee, Becka doo," Nana said.

I looked out the picture window, hoping to see either Mom or Dad pulling into the driveway. It had snowed the night before, and a couple of icicles hung from the roof. Across the street Chipper was shoveling his driveway. I ran to the front door and threw it open. "Chipper!" I called. "Come over here, please! Come over!"

Chipper looked up at me. He wore a red and white striped

wool cap on his head. He hesitated, then stuck his shovel into the snow and walked slowly across the street.

"What's going on?" he asked, trudging up our walk, making deep footprints in the snow.

I stood in the doorway. Behind me, Nana was hugging herself against the cold air I was letting inside.

"Somebody just called and said they had Becky," I told him.

He made a face as if he didn't believe it.

"They said they wanted ten thousand dollars, or they'd slit her throat."

"They're lying," he said.

"What if they're telling the truth?"

"Where are your parents?"

"Mom's at church. Dad's at the store." I felt suddenly as if I was going to cry. "They said to bring the money to the Dumpster behind Caldor's. At twelve o'clock."

Chipper scoffed. "How you gonna get that kind of cash on a Saturday?"

Just then I saw the yellow taxicab pull into the driveway. I ran outside in my socks, waving furiously as Mom got out on the passenger side. She could see from my face that something was up. I blurted out the whole story to her.

"But where *is* she?" Mom asked. "If we give them the money, where and when and how *do we get Becky?*"

I was at a loss. "I don't know. They didn't tell me that."

"And you didn't *ask?*" Mom shouted.

"I didn't think to ask—"

She slapped me hard across the face. "You idiot!"

I pulled back, my hand flying to my stinging cheek. The cold air only made it hurt worse. Mom was enraged. She looked up at the sky and screamed, her coat falling open, her big breasts heaving. She seemed like an animal, a bear or a wolf. I was stunned. I couldn't move. Chipper came up behind me and rested a gloved hand on my shoulder.

"Mrs. Fortunato," he said, "take it easy."

"*Take it easy?*" she said. "These goons are threatening to slit my daughter's throat, and you say take it easy!"

"Peggy," came the voice of the cabdriver. "You want me to wait here?"

He was a heavyset man with big jowls and wavy steel gray hair. He had stepped out of the cab and was leaning against the open door.

Mom's eyes darted into the open garage. "Where's your father?" she shouted. "Where is your goddamn father?"

"At the store," I told her, my hand still on my cheek. "Getting more Christmas lights."

Mom's eyes were wild. "How long has he been gone?"

"I don't know. Maybe a half hour."

She made an ugly sound in her throat. "He's not getting Christmas lights." I didn't know what she meant. She turned to the cabdriver. "Oh, Bud, yes, please wait! I'm going to go in and make some calls!"

"Okay, Peggy." The driver got back into the cab.

Mom pushed past Chipper and me to head into the house. We followed. Chipper paused first to take off his boots on the front step. I pulled off my wet socks, too. My feet were freezing. But it was my cheek that stung the most. My mother had spanked me when I was a kid. But she had never, ever slapped me across the face.

And she had never called me an idiot before.

"Okay, we've got to think here," Mom was saying as we came inside. The vein on her forehead was pulsing and she made the sign of the cross. Nana shrunk down a little on the couch at the sound of Mom's shrill voice.

"Look," Chipper reasoned. "Whoever called you is just looking for money. They don't have Becky."

"And how would *you* know, Chipper?" Mom asked. Accusation was in her eyes.

He sighed. "I just think . . . if they really had Becky, they would have contacted you before now. Becky's been gone for almost four months. If somebody had kidnapped her for ransom, they wouldn't have waited this long to contact you."

"Maybe we *should* call the police," I said. The pain had not faded from my cheek. Mom had big hands, and she was strong.

"The police have been one hundred percent completely useless so far," Mom said. "They've given up on Becky. They think she ran away. No, we're not calling the police. Until we know for sure, I have to take what that caller said to be true. They have Becky, and they'll kill her if we get the cops involved. I will not take the chance of jeopardizing my daughter's life. So we've got to get that money out of the fund and drop it off as they said by twelve o'clock."

"Banks are closed on Saturday," Chipper said. "And I'm not sure you can withdraw that much cash, anyway."

"Well, we've *got* to!" Mom shrieked.

"There's only eight thousand four hundred in the fund," I said. Mom turned to look at me with wide eyes. She'd assigned me to keep track of the money that came in. I pulled open a drawer in the kitchen and withdrew the passbook, handing it to her. "See?"

She looked, shaking her head. "Then we'll have to take the rest out of our own savings."

"But the banks are closed," Chipper said again.

Mom spun on him. "Then we've got to get them to open up for us, *don't* we, Chipper?"

Chipper made no reply.

"I can call my friend," I said, anxious to regain my mother's trust and affection. My cheek was still painful. "His father is a vice president at the bank."

"What friend?" Mom asked.

"His name is Troy Kitchens. We sit together at lunch." That was, in fact, the extent of my "friendship" with Troy. We sat together because no one else wanted to sit with us. We were *de facto* friends. We said very little to each other, but lately we'd been exchanging a few laughs at Brother Pop's expense, commenting on his cigarette breath and pasty, doughy hands. I felt certain Troy would do what I asked.

I was wrong.

"You want me to do *what?*" he replied after I'd gotten him on the phone and asked if his father could open the bank for us. The woman who'd answered the phone, probably the housekeeper, had seemed surprised that someone was calling for Troy. When he'd come to the phone, his hello had dripped with suspicion and wonder. But when he'd heard it was me, there'd been a little rise to his voice, as if he were glad that I'd called. Still, when I made my request, he froze.

"No way," he said. "My father doesn't do any shit that I ask him."

"Please, Troy. We need to get money out of the bank *today*. It's about my sister."

"Sorry," Troy said.

"But we really need to—"

"Give me that phone!" My mother grabbed the receiver from my hand. "Listen," she barked at Troy. "We have no other choice! Let me speak to your father!"

Mom was more persuasive than I was. When Mr. Kitchens came to the phone, Mom babbled out the whole story for him. She even cried a little. Finally, he told her to meet him at the bank in half an hour. That didn't leave us much time; it was 10:45. Still, Mom hung up the phone flushed with happiness, as if she had found Becky already and had her in her arms.

"Should we go down to Genovese and try to find Dad?" I asked.

"He's not at the drugstore," Mom said, pulling her coat back on.

"Where is he?" I was genuinely befuddled.

"Chipper," Mom said, ignoring me, "I'll go in the cab, but I want you to follow us when I go to deliver the money. Park at the far end of the parking lot, and just keep an eye."

"You should call the police," Chipper said.

"No!" Mom shouted. "I'm going to do as they say. I'm going to drop the money in the Dumpster. But then I'm going to hide and wait. And whoever comes to pick it up is going to take me to Becky."

Chipper just shook his head. "I can't do what you ask, Mrs. Fortunato. My parents don't want me to have anything more to do with you, or with the search to find Becky. I'm sorry, but I shouldn't even be over here right now. They think you're scapegoating me, and they said I should keep my distance from you."

Mom's eyes went cold. She stared at Chipper for a long time. He grew uncomfortable under her stare, shuffling his feet, looking down at the floor. But he didn't leave or change his mind. Finally, Mom said quietly, "Get out of my house."

"I hope you find her," Chipper said. "I really do."

I watched him go. The screen door swung shut behind him, and through the glass, I saw him bend down, pulling on his boots.

Mom just stood in the center of the kitchen, seething.

"Where's Patsy?"

Nana was in the door frame of the living room.

Mom exploded. *"She's dying!* Okay? She's *dying!"*

Nana blinked.

"I've got to get out of here," Mom grumbled in a low voice, pushing past her confused mother-in-law and heading back outside. In a few seconds I heard the door to the cab slam shut and the tires crunch over the snow in the driveway.

Nana just looked at me. Her eyes were moist, and her chin was trembling. "Where's Patsy?" she whispered again.

"She's just resting for a while at St. Luke's," I told her, and she nodded, like she always did, as if she remembered everything.

We both returned to the living room, where we sat on the couch and looked at the Christmas tree. I had no idea what my mother had meant when she'd said my father wasn't at the drugstore, but neither did I have any idea what could be taking him so long. Mom should have gone looking for him. He should be informed about this latest news of Becky. Because maybe, in fact, by the end of the day, my sister would be back home, telling us all about how she'd been kidnapped. The newspapers would run stories about it for several days, and Becky and Mom would be featured on the local news. And then everything would get back to normal—except, of course, that Aunt Patsy would still probably die, and we'd have to deal with that.

We sat there for quite a while. Dad didn't return. Neither did Mom. She must have gone straight from the bank to Caldor's. I looked at the clock. Eleven thirty-five. Twenty-five minutes before twelve, before the money was due to be dropped off. Nana had dozed off, her chin on her chest.

I stood up when I heard a car pull into the driveway, but it wasn't a car I recognized. It was big and black, with a silver hood ornament that looked like an animal. A Jaguar. That was what it was. Dad had always commented on Jaguars, wishing he had one.

And its driver was Troy Kitchens.

"Hey," he said, coming to the front door.

"Since when can you drive?" I asked, opening the door a crack.

He shrugged. "I've known how to drive since I was twelve."

"But you're too young to have your license."

He shrugged again. "Maybe. But I'm not too young to drive."

I studied him, all wrapped up in a shiny down parka trimmed with fur. His red hair stuck out from under the hood. His eyes were hidden, as usual, by his blue aviator glasses. He wore no gloves and rubbed his bare hands together to keep them warm.

"Why are you here?" I asked.

"'Cause my father told me you were about to find your sister. He went down to meet your mother at the bank and give her the money. So I came here to get you."

"To get me?"

Troy nodded. "Don't you want to see what happens?"

I didn't know what he meant.

"Don't you want to go and see your sister get rescued? We could hide and wait and see what happens."

"My mom is going to hide," I told him.

He gave me a face. "You're gonna let your mom take that chance? What if these guys have guns? What if they shoot her?"

"Oh," I said in a little voice, suddenly terrified.

I hadn't thought of that. I supposed it could happen. Mom could get killed. And I had just let her run off without even trying to stop her, or to offer any help. She had wanted Chipper to follow her for protection, but he'd refused. And that old guy Bud the cabdriver didn't seem like he'd be much protection. He'd probably have a heart attack if he tried to save her. I suddenly felt horrible. I should have insisted to Mom that I go with her. What kind of son was I? If something happened to her, it would be all *my* fault.

Troy took off his glasses. His pupils were wide, and the whites of his eyes were flecked with red. I knew what his eyes were saying to me. *I saw my mother with her brains blown out. Do you want to see the same?*

No, I didn't. No, I wanted my mother safe and protected. To lose your mother had to be the worst thing ever, in the whole entire world. Look what it had done to Troy.

"Okay," I said. "Take me down there."

I turned and saw Nana. I couldn't leave her alone. I opened the door again and called back out to Troy. "My grandmother's got to come, too." He just shrugged and got into the car to wait.

"Nana," I said, "find your coat. We're going for a ride."

"Where are we going?"

"Just for a ride with my friend Troy. You'll like him. He's nice." Troy wasn't nice, but that didn't matter at the moment. Neither did the nagging feeling in my gut that Mom would be very, very pissed that I had taken Nana out for a ride with a kid who didn't even have his driver's license yet. But Mom would certainly forgive me if I could save her from getting shot.

Just how I was going to do that was unclear. All I knew was that I needed to be with her. I couldn't let her do this alone. That day, worrying about my mother, was the worst day so far in the whole ordeal of Becky's disappearance. That worry was by far the worst I'd felt. I had let my mother go off on her own, possibly to get killed. I hadn't tried to stop her. My own mother. The mother who had always been there for me, worrying if I got sick and making sure I wore my boots and making me drink extra glasses of milk because she thought I had a calcium deficiency. In third grade, when I was having a hard time with math, she was waiting for me every day when I get off the bus, with a pack of flash cards to drill the times table into my head. Even though I'd hated it at the time, I'd known she was doing it for my own good, because she cared about me, because she *loved* me, because she wanted me to grow up to be successful. And I learned my times table, backward and forward, all because of Mom.

And now she was out there, all alone. All I could think about was Troy's mother, her brains dripping down the wall.

I helped Nana over the ice and snow and into the backseat of Troy's Jaguar. She was silent. The car smelled like leather and cigarettes.

"Park at the far end of the lot," I told Troy, "so we can keep an eye."

He shook his head. "You should hide in the Dumpster. You should be in there so you can see who reaches in to get the money."

I looked at him as if he were crazy.

"No, really, man. You should climb inside the Dumpster."

"No," I said. "We can keep a lookout from the car. . . ."

"Don't you care about your *mom*, Danny?"

Troy had taken off his glasses and was rubbing his eyes. They were tearing. I thought maybe he was emotional because all this made him think about his own mother.

"What if they have guns and shoot me in there?" I asked, my heart thudding.

Troy looked at me with his red, watery eyes. "Better you than your mother."

He was right. I should get into the Dumpster. Kind of a stake-out for my mother's protection. I steeled myself. Troy started the car, and we headed down the street. He drove erratically, slamming on the brakes at stop signs, causing us all to bolt forward. Nana didn't seem to mind. "Wheeee!" she said, her eyes lighting up. Her worries over Aunt Patsy were far from her mind. At least she was having a good time.

I saw the Caldor's sign from a distance, and I began to shudder. It was ten to twelve. The taxicab was nowhere in sight. Mom was probably going to arrive just on the dot of twelve, like they said. Troy pulled around to the back of the store and parked at the complete other end from the Dumpster.

"Go on," he told me. "Get out and hop in there."

"Yeah," I said, though I didn't move right away.

"Get going, Danny. Time's wasting. Any minute now your mother could get here, and they could shoot her head off."

"Where's Patsy?" Nana asked from the backseat, her mood no longer so carefree.

I turned around to her. "Everything's gonna be okay, Nana."

She gave me a smile but said nothing.

I turned to Troy. "Watch out for my grandmother," I told him. "Don't let her get out of the car or anything."

He grunted. He withdrew a cigarette from his coat pocket. "Does she mind if I smoke?"

"No, I guess not. Nana used to smoke. Just keep the windows open."

He nodded, lighting up. It was an odd-looking cigarette, un-evenly wrapped, like nothing I'd seen before.

"Keep an eye," I said. "If somebody starts shooting, I'm gonna make a mad dash back here. So keep the motor running."

Troy nodded. He didn't seem so interested anymore. He was more intent on lighting his cigarette than anything else.

I hopped out of the car. I didn't dare look around. I just ran as fast as I could across the lot to the Dumpster. It was big and green and smelly, with dirty snow piled up behind it. I used the snow, pushed there by plows, to reach the top of the Dumpster. I slipped once but caught myself. Throwing myself over the top, I landed on some wet cardboard boxes.

The thing stank of rotting bananas and spoiled milk. I tried to remain perfectly still, but the cardboard boxes beneath me were collapsing, and my ass was getting wet. I placed my hands down to steady myself and found myself sinking into a thick, sticky mess. Broken eggshells and celery stalks bubbled to the surface of the black water. Another smell was released, more foul than before. I closed my eyes and prayed to God not to get shot.

I didn't wear a watch, so I didn't know what time it was. But it had to be close to twelve. In a few minutes, I knew, I'd see a box of money tossed over the top by Mom. I couldn't let her find out I was in there. I was still sinking into the muck, so I looked around for something to steady myself with. That was when I spotted the blue bag with the Connecticut Bank and Trust logo on front. Carefully, I pulled it close and peered inside. Wads of money, held together with brown wrappers.

Mom had already been there.

I waited. Overhead I could see heavy gray clouds moving in to obscure the blue sky. What if it started to snow again? My ass and legs were soaking wet and freezing cold by now, and the smell was starting to make me gag.

Then I heard the sirens.

A screech of tires, a slamming of car doors. "Come out of the Dumpster now," a voice boomed through a megaphone. I froze. "Show yourself, with your hands up."

It was the police. Maybe they'd caught the kidnappers. Maybe . . .

A rush of running footsteps surrounded the dumpster. There

was a loud clanging of metal. *Guns,* I thought. Rifles hitting the Dumpster.

"Don't shoot!" I screamed, standing up as quickly as I could, but I lost my footing, sliding down into the scummy water of the Dumpster. I looked up. A policeman's face peered over the top, looking down. It was Detective Guthrie. I recognized him. And he was, indeed, holding a gun.

"Please don't shoot me!" I cried again, terrified.

Guthrie's face disappeared. I managed to stand, wet and cold, and climb my way back to the top. I exited the way I'd come, over the pile of hardened snow. I was covered with eggshells and green, oily slime. Three police cars had blocked all access to the Dumpster. I turned toward Troy's car at the other end of the lot and saw another police car parked over there. A cop had Troy up against the car and was frisking him. And then I saw my mother.

"Holy Mary, Mother of God!" she screamed. "It's Danny! It's my *son!*"

"Mom," I said in a little voice.

"What the hell are you *doing?*" she shrieked.

I started to cry. "I just . . . I just wanted to make sure nobody shot you."

Mom was so flabbergasted, she couldn't speak. Detective Guthrie put his hand on my shoulder. "Why did you think somebody might shoot your mother?" he asked in a low, calm voice.

"Because . . . because she was going to hide and wait for them, and I wanted to make sure they didn't hurt her."

Guthrie looked from me to my mother. She was crying now, too, heaving. Her hands covered her face. She turned and walked away.

"No one's going to hurt your mother," Guthrie said to me. He was a thin man, with a narrow face, and his voice was kind. "We caught the guys who called your house. It was a prank. A couple of drifters who'd seen the publicity and thought they could make some easy money. Sickos." He gave me a sad smile. "They don't have Becky."

"They . . . don't?" I asked, hiccuping now through my tears.

"No. I'm sorry." Detective Guthrie removed his hand from my shoulder. "They'll be punished, you can be sure of that, for causing your family such distress."

My mind was spinning. "How did you know I was in there?"

"We were watching from inside the store. There's a monitor here. We had already apprehended the punks. They were loitering around here, and when we took them in, they admitted to making the call. But we were keeping an eye on the Dumpster to see if they had any accomplices. When we saw a kid get out of a car and hop into the thing, we thought we had one." He smiled wanly. "But turns out it was you."

I wiped my eyes with my sticky, stinky hands. "So Mom called you, after all?"

He looked over at my mother and sighed. She was leaning, with her head down, against a cruiser, sobbing into the backs of her arms. The other cops were keeping their distance from her.

"No," Guthrie told me. "Mr. Kitchens called us after he gave your mother the money. He was worried about her, too, just like you were. We came down here and found your mom in the woods." He nodded toward Troy's car. "And then we found Mr. Kitchens's own kid in the car over *there*."

I thought of Nana. "My grandmother's in the car, too. She's getting kind of senile, so we should go get her."

Guthrie nodded. "Oh, we got her out." He cocked his head to look at me. "Were you smoking pot, too, Danny?"

I didn't know what he was asking, but then it hit me. So *that* was the funny cigarette Troy had been smoking, and that was why his eyes had looked so red. "I didn't know," I said. "I didn't know that's what it was." I felt like an idiot.

Mom had been right to call me that after all.

Detective Guthrie believed me. "We could charge Troy with a lot of things," he told me. "Drug possession, underage driving, endangering the health of an elderly person. Not sure how your grandma would've responded to breathing in all that second-hand marijuana smoke if we hadn't gotten her out in time."

I felt sick. Troy hadn't endangered Nana. *I* had.

"Next time, buddy," the detective was saying, looking at me, "call us, okay?"

He replaced his hand on my shoulder. I nodded.

He led me to a police car, and I slid in back. In seconds Mom was inside as well. She was still sobbing into her hands, big, heaving sobs. She didn't look at me.

"Your son was trying to help, Mrs. Fortunato," Guthrie said, getting into the front seat. "He's kind of wet and smelly, but he's fine. He knows now not to try to do things on his own. I hope you realize that now, too, Mrs. Fortunato."

She didn't reply, just sobbed all the harder into her hands.

I understood why. All this commotion—and in the end, Becky still wasn't coming home.

I looked out the window. I saw a couple of officers retrieving the bag of money from the Dumpster. I saw Troy being put into one cruiser and Nana into another. I felt sick again, as if it were all my fault.

And it was. Just *how* it was my fault, I wasn't quite sure anymore, but I knew it was. It was me who had gotten the call this morning, who hadn't asked the questions I should have asked. It was me who'd let Mom go off on her own. Now all I had to do was look over at her to see how bad a decision that was, how utterly disappointed she'd turned out to be. So completely crushed. *I* had let that happen. *Me.* It was my fault.

I had let her down in so many ways. I'd never told her what I'd seen the morning of Becky's disappearance. Now it was too late to tell. Mom would hate me forever if I told her now. But would that matter, really? She hated me already. I could see that. I could see from how she cried that she wished it had been me who'd gone missing—*me,* not Becky, not her precious daughter. Despite all the fighting and arguing they'd done, Becky was still her favorite child. I was just the stupid idiot son who'd let her down. That was why Mom cried as hard as she did.

I rested my forehead against the glass of the police car as we were driven home. The sky got grayer, and finally it began to sleet. I knew then that Becky was never coming back. And I knew that for the rest of my life, I would carry the blame.

WEST HOLLYWOOD

The house, as I knew it would be, was magnificent. A marble gate opened electronically when the driver of the car tapped a button on some kind of car phone. Out of the tinted car windows, I discerned the last pink rays of the sun illuminating the city, the spires of downtown L.A. glowing in the far distance. Ahead of us was the house, perched on a hill, with its orange tile roof and marble columns, a curving staircase leading up to a pair of antique-looking mesquite doors. The driver stopped the car. I popped a breath mint into my mouth.

"Jesus, Danny," Randall had gushed, not twenty minutes earlier, as he'd looked out at the car Gregory Montague had sent to pick me up. "Look at that car!"

"What kind is it?" I'd asked, too nervous myself to peer outside. "A Jaguar?"

"Not a chance," Randall had replied, looking at me with eyes like poached eggs. "That's a goddamn Aston Martin."

I had no idea what an Aston Martin was, but from Randall's stunned expression, I knew I should be impressed. I took one last glance in the mirror. I spiked my hair with a bit more gel and made sure my tiny crucifix earring was in place in my right ear. My bolo tie with the turquoise gemstone hung straight down from my collar. My black jeans were skintight, showing off my butt to the best possible advantage. My black leather boots were buffed to a high gloss, with silver caps on the pointy toes.

The doorbell rang and I jumped. "Do you want me to get it?" Randall called. I told him no, hurrying myself to open the door. A Mexican man in a black pin-striped suit stood there. "Danny Fortunato?" he asked. I nodded. "I've been sent by Mr. Montague," he said. I nodded again, yelling good-bye to Randall. The driver held open the door of the shiny silver car for me. I slid into the backseat, nearly overcome by the pungent scent of leather. I settled in for the ride up Laurel Canyon and into the Hollywood Hills. The whole time I didn't speak a word.

Mulholland Drive followed the jagged ridgeline of the hills that led into the Santa Monica Mountains. The many twists and turns left me just the slightest bit nauseous. I closed my eyes. How had I gotten to this point? I remembered gathering my nerve, after nearly a month, to call the number on the card Gregory Montague had given me. And why the hell *not* call? He was an agent, after all, and I was an actor. I needed work. I certainly wasn't getting any on my own. So I'd picked up the card, which had been sitting on my bureau all those weeks, and dialed his number. It was obvious now I stood no chance with Frank, his hunky friend. I ought to at least get something out of that disastrous meeting on Hollywood Boulevard.

Montague remembered me. Yes, indeed, he was very interested in talking with me. Would I be willing to come to his house the next night? He'd send a car.

"Are you sure you want to do this?" Randall had asked.

I'd made a face. "You're the one who got me into this! Why are you second-guessing now?"

"Just want to make sure you're sure."

I'd nodded. I was sure.

"Welcome to Mulholland Pines," the driver said as he opened the car door for me. I stepped outside into the fading sunlight. Enormous, fragrant pine trees spiked into the air all around me, tinted with the same pink glow that bathed the Los Angeles basin below. I mumbled my thanks to the driver and looked up at the house. I swallowed hard—downing my breath mint in the process—and began the long ascent up the stairs.

There was no doorman, no butler, no housekeeper, as I'd expected. Gregory Montague himself opened the door. He was wearing a gold satin smoking jacket with a paisley design, a white shirt with an open collar, and blue jeans. He was barefoot.

"Well, Danny, it is good to see you again," he said. "Welcome."

He gestured me inside. I stepped in, looking up at the vaulted ceiling, the chandelier of colored glass. There were white lilies everywhere, and their perfume was nearly intoxicating. The floor was high-gloss parquetry.

"Can I get you something to drink?" Gregory asked. I saw his eyes drop from my face to my crotch. I was pleased I'd worn tight jeans.

"Not right now," I said.

"Fine." He gestured for me to follow. "Let's talk in here."

He led me down a short hallway to a study. It was lined with bookshelves, though most were empty. In the middle of the room, a curved pink sofa sat in front of an enormous television set. Plaid pillows were scattered randomly across the floor. It was the kind of room I imagined rich people to have, the kind of room I'd always wished for myself. On the wall were dozens of photos. I glanced quickly at some of them. Gregory Montague with President and Mrs. Reagan. Farrah Fawcett-Majors. Ron Howard. Bill Murray. Jennifer Jason Leigh. Cher. I wondered if they were all Gregory's clients. The photos seemed recent. In all of them, he had the same beaming white smile and bushy white eyebrows and surprisingly thick shock of white hair.

"Please," he said. "Sit down."

I took a seat at one end of the curved sofa as he pulled shut the sliding wood door of the study. I folded my hands in my lap.

"Any auditions lately?" he asked.

I shook my head no. "Nothing I could get into."

He sat at the other end of the sofa, appraising me with his cold blue eyes from under those enormous eyebrows. I pegged him to be about fifty. He wasn't unattractive. Indeed, in his day, he might have been quite handsome. He had a strong jaw and very high cheekbones. If Katharine Hepburn had ever done herself in male drag with a white wig and fake white eyebrows, she might have looked very much like Gregory Montague.

"So that's why you decided to give me a try," he said to me.

I shrugged. "Anyone just starting out who is serious about making it in this business would be a fool not to respond when a well-known agent gives out his card."

Whether or not Gregory Montague was well known or not was a matter of some discussion. Yes, he was listed in the directories of agents I'd looked at, with an address and a phone number, but no one I'd asked had ever heard of him. He didn't appear to be affiliated with William Morris, CAA, or ICM. But the photos on his wall seemed to suggest he knew some big names. After all, President and Mrs. Reagan!

"Well, I'd certainly like to do what I can for you, Danny," Gregory said, leaning back into the cushions of the sofa now. The sash of his smoking jacket had come undone, and he patted his round, white-shirted belly as if he'd just had a good meal. "But you know, I can't just sign someone with no experience."

"I've heard that song before," I said. No way was he getting off that easy. My months in West Hollywood had hardened me. Emboldened me. No longer was I the hick who'd just stepped off the bus. I knew how the game was played. That was why I was there, after all.

I narrowed my eyes as I looked at him. "Every agent I've spoken to has said the same thing. You can't get a job in this town without an agent, but you can't get an agent if you've never had a job. So how come the acting pool doesn't just dry up? Sooner or later, you're gonna run out of people, and then, when you guys come looking for me, maybe my price is gonna be a lot higher."

My little rant made Gregory laugh, as it was intended to do. "You have spunk, Danny," he said.

I gave him an eye and a smirk. "That's what Lou Grant told Mary Richards just before adding that he hated spunk."

Gregory's eyes twinkled. "Oh, I can assure you, I *adore* spunk."

"Lucky me."

He rose. "If I can't offer you a drink, might I offer you something else?"

"Whatcha got?"

He walked over to a small bar at the far end of the study. "Around here, liquid refreshment is never quite as effective for doing business." He withdrew a small, thin silver case from a drawer.

I cocked my head at him. "But, we *will* do business, won't we?"

"Oh, indeed, Danny. Indeed we will."

I smiled.

On the bar, Gregory was arranging two lines of cocaine. My heart beat a little faster, and I felt my mouth actually begin to water. It had been a couple weeks since I'd snorted coke, and suddenly I was starved for it. Two weeks of being good, of staying as close to Randall as I could and as far away from Edgar as possible, had made me only want that magic white powder even more. I stood from the sofa and tried to appear casual as I sauntered toward the bar.

"I find it helps the conversation," Gregory was saying, offering me a little straw. "And helps get to the heart of one's talent."

"Yeah, funny how it does that," I said, accepting the straw. In seconds both lines were gone. Gregory was laying out more. They might have been intended for him, but I snorted them myself, faster than any Hoover vacuum cleaner. My host simply smiled.

"Oh yes," Gregory said, finally doing a line himself, "there are many, many opportunities for a beautiful boy like you."

I laughed. The rush was spreading through my body. I could taste some of the powder at the back of my throat. I felt happy and confident and, yes, beautiful. I stood back, leaning against a bar stool, my pelvis thrust forward, allowing Gregory to inspect the merchandise. It was the same cocksure feeling I had up on my box at the bar.

Gregory drew close. He ran a hand up my leg and over my ass. "Very beautiful indeed," he purred in my ear.

"Do you really think so?" I asked in a little voice. Even high, even cocksure, there was still a little part of me that was afraid of the answer.

"Could there be any doubt?" he replied. He took my hand and placed it on his crotch. I felt a hardness there. I smiled.

I wriggled away from him. "Now I'd like a drink," I said.

"Certainly. What can I get you?"

"Dewar's. On the rocks." I thought that seemed like a classy choice. "So if we're gonna do business, let's get down to it. Tell me what you can do for me. I want to be *big*." I moved in a little closer to him. "I'm serious, Gregory. This isn't just a lark for me. I want to be a huge star."

Gregory was fixing my drink. "Movies or television?"

"I don't care."

"Well, you should. Aim high, Danny. Don't you want to be Harrison Ford or Richard Gere more than you want to be Ted Danson or Michael Landon?"

I considered it. "I suppose. But a top-rated TV show would suffice. Like I could do *Family Ties* if Michael J. Fox decides to split permanently for movies."

Gregory handed me my drink. I took a sip.

"Are these your clients?" I asked, gesturing to the wall. "Why don't you have Ron Howard put me in his next picture?"

"We need to start with getting some photos, Danny," he said, ignoring the question and the suggestion. "A sexy portfolio of head shots and body shots."

"Sure."

He smiled. "Mind showing me what you've got?"

I held his smile for a few moments with one of my own.

"Of course," I said and began undoing my bolo tie.

Gregory sat on the arm of the sofa and watched. I unbuttoned my shirt, exposing my slender, smooth, tanned chest. I pushed the shirt open just enough to allow for a glimpse of my nipples, hard little cones that revealed my anxiety. I hooked my thumbs in my jeans and posed, imagining a photographer aiming at me with his camera.

"Well, go on," Gregory said.

I looked at him. "Maybe we ought to keep a little mystery."

He laughed at me. "Come on, Danny. I could go down to Santa Monica Boulevard some night and see more of you than this."

I moved in close. "I'm serious about wanting to be an actor."

"I know you are, sweetmeat." His big white eyebrows twitched, and his blue eyes twinkled. "And I'm just as serious. Believe me."

I placed my hands on his shoulders and held his gaze. "I just don't want to . . . you know, do something for nothing."

He laughed. "I doubt a boy like you ever does something for nothing."

"I'm not a whore," I said, feeling suddenly indignant. "I dance. I strip. But I'm not a hustler."

Gregory slipped his arms around my waist and kissed my nose. "But you've been paid for it. Can you tell me you've never been paid to have sex?"

I couldn't tell him that. I just looked away.

"Oh, maybe you're not leaning up against the wall at Numbers, but if a man wants you, he can find a way to have you." He ran his hands up and down my exposed chest. "And who wouldn't want you? You're beautiful, Danny. Simply stunning."

"Stop it," I said, uncomfortable. "I am not."

"But you are. Those beautiful, perky nipples. Those tight, little boy abs. Those saucy blue eyes."

"Please stop." I felt weird. Maybe it was the coke. But suddenly I felt faint. I would've fallen down if Gregory wasn't holding me up.

"You knew what coming over here meant, didn't you, Danny? You knew what you were doing when you agreed?"

"Yes," I answered, dizzy. "Yes, I knew. But I'm still serious about being an actor. Still serious about wanting your help."

"And you shall get my help." He popped open the top button of my jeans and pulled down my zipper, grinning up at me with that toothy Katharine Hepburn smile. "We help each other, Danny boy. That's how we do things in Hollywood."

He knelt down in front of me. Out of my white briefs, he pulled my cock, gobbling it up as quickly as a kid going down on an ice-cream cone.

I leaned my head back and closed my eyes. Good thing I got hard easily. All a guy had to do was look at my cock, and I got a big, old raging hard-on. It didn't matter if the guy was hot or sexy. Just looking at my cock and wanting it in his mouth were enough to give me a boner. That was the reason I was so popular with Edgar's customers, why they came back for more. I just closed my eyes and let my cock do all the work.

Gregory was making quite the slobbering sound when I heard

the sliding wood door of the study start to open. I turned, not inclined to move or pull out of Gregory's mouth. *So let his housekeeper see,* I thought. I didn't care.

And then my eyes met those of Frank.

"Oh, Jesus," Frank said, quickly sliding the door shut.

Gregory pulled off my cock long enough to gripe. "I told him I was doing an interview. Sorry about that." Then he resumed his slobbering.

I looked down. A glob of his saliva dropped from his chin onto my shiny black boot. And then another. And another.

"Okay," I said. "I can't do this."

Gregory looked up at me, spittle all over his lips.

I was zipping up. "I'm sorry. I just can't."

"What is the matter?"

"I can't do this!" My voice was louder than it needed to be. "He *saw.* I just can't do this. Sorry." I buttoned my shirt.

Gregory got to his feet, wiping his mouth with the back of his hand. "It doesn't matter, Danny. He's just a friend. He doesn't care."

"Well, I do." I stuffed my bolo tie down into the pocket of my jeans. "I'm sorry. I need to leave."

He arched a bushy eyebrow at me. "I thought you were serious about becoming an actor."

"Guess not *that* serious." I let out a long breath. "Thanks for the blow. It was good. But I have to go."

He shrugged. "Fine. Your choice." He picked up the receiver of a phone on the bar. "I'll call my driver—"

"No," I said. "No driver. I don't mean to be rude. But no driver. Nothing."

Gregory laughed. "But how will you get home?"

"God gave me two feet. I'll use them." It was a line my mother had always said.

It only made Gregory laugh harder. "I have news for you. It's a long way down that mountain—"

"I know," I said. "So I'd better start now."

I slid open the wood door and hurried out into the hallway. I saw Frank at the far other end of the house, in what appeared to be the kitchen. He watched me as I walked briskly toward the front door, my boots clicking on the parquetry floor. From the study behind me, Gregory emerged.

"Danny, wait!" he called. "You can't walk all the way back—"

"Yes, I can," I said, heading out the front door. "I don't care how long it takes. I'm walking home." Outside, I broke into a jog, taking the steps down the hill two at a time. I didn't want them to see that I had started to cry.

The night was dark. And Mulholland Drive was very long and very twisty. Even when I got to the end of it, I knew I had steep, winding Laurel Canyon to deal with. How long would it take me to get home? Ninety minutes? Two hours? Four? My heart was racing in my chest. The cocaine was making the anxiety even worse. In the darkness, I began the long trudge down the road, one foot in front of the other, barely seeing two feet in front of me. Every once in a while, through the trees, I'd catch a glimpse of the lights of West Hollywood far below. Cars raced past, their headlights swinging across me. A couple of drivers honked at me when they were startled to see a figure moving on the side of the road. I tried to stay on the grass as much as I could, but the road was so dark, and sometimes I wasn't sure where the pavement ended and the grass began. I was also scared of losing my footing if I walked too close to the precipitous drop; then I'd go tumbling down the rocky edges of the Hollywood Hills.

I may as well just toss myself over the side, I thought, like that girl Randall had told me about who'd jumped off the Hollywood sign to her death when she realized she'd never be a star. *I may as well just jump.*

More headlights swung across me, causing me to squint into their glare. A car slowed down and pulled alongside me. From what I could make out, it was an old Plymouth Duster. The driver was leaning across the front seat and rolling down the passenger window.

"Danny," came a voice from inside the car. "Get in."

I stopped walking. It was so dark that I couldn't make out who the driver was at first. Then I recognized him. It was Frank.

"No, thanks," I said and resumed walking.

He got out of the car. I heard the door slam in the darkness behind me. "You'll get killed out here," he called after me. "Please. Let me drive you home."

I stopped walking. The headlights of an oncoming car momentarily blinded me, and I felt the rush of air as it zoomed past. I turned around and walked back to Frank's car.

"Where do you live?" he asked.

"Just drop me off at Santa Monica and Fairfax."

We both got into the car. It smelled of bananas and coffee. I left the window open to keep the fresh air flowing. My head was really starting to spin. Frank didn't say anything right away. He just put the car into drive and steered it back onto the road.

"Look," I finally said, "about what happened back there . . ."

"None of my business," Frank replied.

"I'm not a hustler."

"None of my business."

We drove in silence for a while.

"Yes, I knew what I was getting into," I said, unable to bear the quiet. "But I just couldn't go through with it after you walked in."

"It's okay, Danny."

I leaned my head against the side of the door, breathing in the night air. "I'm not a hustler."

"So you've said."

"But you don't believe me."

"I believe you."

I turned and looked at him. "It's just that I really need an agent! I came out here to make it as an actor. You think I want to keep dancing on a nasty old box in a skanky old bar for the rest of my life?"

Frank laughed. "I doubt they'd let you do it that long. Usually strippers get forcibly retired at the ripe old age of twenty-five."

"I'm not a stripper, either. I'm a dancer."

"Danny, it's okay. Really."

I started to cry again. My tears were an embarrassment, but I couldn't help them. They just came. Gushing down my cheeks like waterfalls.

"Hey," Frank said. "Baby, don't cry."

He reached over and touched my cheek with his fingers.

"I'm sorry," I said.

"It's okay."

We were heading down the mountain. "Just drop me off on Santa Monica," I said. "I'll walk home from there. I need to clear my head." It was pounding actually, and I could still taste the coke in my throat. My nostrils itched. I kept wiping my nose, and Frank must have figured things out.

"You need something to eat," he said.

"I'm not hungry."

"Okay."

We drove in silence again for a while. There was a backup of cars ahead of us, a constellation of red taillights clustered at the bottom of the hill.

"I hate this road," Frank said.

"Where do you live?" I asked.

"Venice Beach."

"I've never been there."

"Never been to Venice Beach?" he asked. "How long have you lived in L.A.?"

"Little over a year."

"You should check it out sometime. It's like a small town in the midst of a big city. Great beach, too."

I looked over at him. "How do you know Gregory?"

"Long story," he said.

The traffic was moving again. "You can just drop me off . . . oh, I don't know. Maybe at the bar. I can't go home yet. My room-mate is like a mother hen, and he'll start asking all sorts of questions."

Frank looked over at me kindly. "Might I suggest a bar is the last place you should go when you're feeling like this?"

I sneered. "Then what would you suggest?"

"Come with me. I'll show you Venice Beach."

I said nothing.

"Okay?" he asked.

"You don't have to take care of me."

"I'm not. I'm just offering to show you a part of town you've never seen."

"Why?"

"Well, if you don't want to go with me—"

"I do." I looked at him. "I do want to go with you."

So we headed through West Hollywood, down La Cienega and onto Venice Boulevard. I couldn't quite believe the way the night was turning out. I'd thought I'd be planning my future as an actor with Gregory Montague, and here I was instead, heading to Venice Beach in a beat-up old Duster with Frank Wilson. That was his last name, I learned. I also learned that he was born out near Palm Springs, and that he taught English at a high school in Inglewood, and that he was in the process of getting his master's, and that he hoped someday to teach at the college level. Frank reminded me a little of Randall: he had that ambition to become something serious. It wasn't ambition like mine, which was to become something frivolous.

When we got to the beach, I was struck by how fierce it was. Nothing like the soft, gradual beaches of the East Coast. Here the Pacific slapped the coast with big, pounding waves, ridden by surfers whose long golden hair reflected the moonlight. We headed down the boardwalk, the neon of the shops and cafés burning through the darkness. A Rastafarian in dreadlocks and a colorful knit cap played a reggae guitar; Asian girls roller-skated down the boardwalk, holding hands. Off to our left, adjacent to the sand, was Muscle Beach, an outdoor gym. Bodybuilders so big they seemed ready to explode hunched over benches, curling dumbbells, wearing nothing more than Speedos.

"I used to see Arnold Schwarzenegger here all the time when I first moved to Venice," Frank told me. "That was way before *Conan.*"

I smiled, looking around at the people on the boardwalk. A couple of sixties leftovers, a man and a woman, with exactly the same long, straight gray hair, sat ahead of us on the curb, passing a doobie back and forth.

"This is *so* not West Hollywood," I said.

Frank laughed. He gestured to a pizza joint, and I followed him inside. We ordered a large hamburger and pepperoni. I was suddenly famished. Digging in, I momentarily forgot I was with the man of my dreams. I blocked out, for the moment, just how beautiful Frank was, how green his eyes were. He had tucked a napkin into the front of his shirt, a gesture that I'd always found rather dorky. My father used to do it. But when Frank reached over with his napkin to wipe tomato sauce from my chin, I remembered exactly how I felt about him. I was smitten.

And suddenly jealous.

"Is Gregory your boyfriend?" I asked.

Frank sighed. "No."

"You don't sound convincing."

"He's not my boyfriend."

"Then what is he?"

"Long story."

"So you've said."

Frank looked past me, his eyes seeming to rest on the steaming pizza ovens behind us, as if they were far more interesting to consider.

"I'm sorry if I'm prying," I said.

"It's okay." He looked back at me. "Gregory was very good to me when I was young. When I was your age, in fact. Back then, I was a poor kid just trying to make my way through school, and he . . . he helped me."

I smiled. "So then we're not all that different, are we?"

He shrugged. He seemed a little defensive.

"I didn't mean to offend you," I told him.

"It's okay," he said, for something like the hundredth time. "I fell in love with Gregory. I can't deny that. He was a glamorous older man who seemed to have everything. And I had nothing." He smiled. "I'll always be grateful to Gregory. He gave me the confidence I needed to stay in school. He believed in me when nobody else did."

"So you were boyfriends?"

"For a while."

"Then what happened?"

Frank smiled. "Well, as you may have noticed, Gregory likes younger guys. And eventually, I was no longer a college kid."

I sat back in my chair. "You're still in love with him, aren't you?"

"No," Frank said.

But I didn't believe him.

"We've stayed friends," Frank went on. "Underneath all his swagger and airs, Gregory's a good guy. I know you probably don't feel that way right now, but . . ."

"I guess I was a fool," I said.

"Why?"

"For backing out. If I'd gone ahead and given Gregory what he wanted, maybe he would've been as good and helpful to me as he was to you."

This seemed to stir something within Frank. He sat forward and leaned across the little table we shared. "No," he said. "You did the right thing, Danny. Gregory couldn't have helped you. Not the way you're imagining."

"Hey, I saw the pictures on his wall—"

Frank shook his head. "Everyone in Hollywood has pictures like that. You go to an event, you pose with a celebrity, and you put it up on your wall."

"He doesn't represent them?"

"No. This agent stuff—it's just an idea that's gotten into his head this past year. The only people he represents so far are a couple of soap actors and a guy who writes jingles for television commercials. Gregory's from money. He doesn't need to work. He just decided he'd try being an agent because he was bored and it sounded like fun."

"And maybe a way of getting young boys to take their clothes off for him."

Frank didn't have a response to that. Because it was true.

I was certain, sitting there, that he was still in love with Gregory. I imagined that ten years ago Gregory had been quite the debonair lover, and in Frank's eyes, he had remained that way. In fact, I felt positive that they'd still be together if Gregory hadn't had a roving eye, always on the lookout for fresher meat.

"I'm glad you said no to him," Frank said.

I nodded. I thought I understood why.

A father with two little boys sat at the table next to us. The boys were making a mess, throwing paper plates, spilling their paper cups of Coke. A slice of pizza landed cheese-side down on the floor.

"I'm glad I don't have kids," Frank said.

I looked at one of the little boys. He had dark hair and a pug nose. He looked like the kid I'd once imagined I'd have, the son with whom I would pose with Mom and Dad and Nana for our four-generation picture. I used to call the son of my imagination Joey. Not sure why. The name just came to me. I hadn't thought of Joey for some time, but I guessed he was still there, in my mind.

Frank asked if I wanted to see his place before he drove me home, and I said okay. We walked over a couple of blocks to a small, second-floor studio apartment, where the wallpaper was starting to peel from the salty air and the water in the toilet kept running. The centerpiece of the room was a desk overflowing with papers and books. We sat together on his futon, which unfolded at night to become his bed, and watched Joan Rivers sitting in for Johnny Carson on a black-and-white television. We made sure our thighs never touched. Afterward, we switched off the TV and talked in the dark. I told him about Becky. He listened in a way that made it clear he was listening, even though he didn't say a word. I told him about my mother and my father and Nana and how I'd got on that bus and ridden three thousand miles across the country. He listened; he nodded; he took it all in. Still, for that entire time, we made sure our thighs never touched.

When I finally fell silent, Frank said he'd drive me home. But he asked if maybe I'd like to go for ice cream first. I said yes. At two o'clock in the morning, we were slurping strawberry and pistachio ice cream out of sugar cones, strolling once more along the boardwalk. Frank's ice cream fell out of his cone and onto his shoe, and we laughed so hard, harder than I had laughed in a long time. Maybe ever.

Then, as we neared the car, Frank suggested we take a walk on the beach. I agreed. I wasn't so high that I didn't realize that neither of us wanted the night to end. We walked quite a ways down the beach, where the coastline darkened. We were the only people we could see. The waves crashed at our feet, like the sound of breaking glass. Our shadows stretched through the moonlight far ahead of us on the sand.

We were quiet now. The cocaine had worn off, and I felt sleepy.

Frank reached down and took my hand.

Overhead, I heard a gull call out, though I couldn't see it.

And then we were kissing. I didn't even realize he was bending down to press his lips against mine, but suddenly there they were, warm and moist. I responded instinctively, my tongue thrusting into his mouth. Wrapping my arms around him, I felt the strength of his shoulders and back. He was taller than I was, bigger, and stronger. It excited me. We stood there kissing, stumbling around in the sand, for a long time. Then he pulled me under a wooden pier, where we sat in the sand, resting against a pile. I snuggled in between his legs, his arms around me, his lips on the nape of my neck. And we fell asleep that way, lulled by the steady sound of the surf.

We woke with the sun. There were no words, just Frank's breath on my neck. I felt his hands slide up under my shirt, removing it. There was a jingling of belt buckles and the displacement of sand, and before I knew it, I was underneath him. I felt his cock press against my hole. Above us the sun rose like a benevolent god, wrapping us in its pink and golden arms. The brine of the sea was so strong, I tasted it on my tongue. Sand crept up my bare legs, scratching its way into my ass, but I didn't care. I loved him—I loved him with every part of myself, even if I knew he was still in love with someone else. I loved him so much that I felt as if my whole body would explode, arms and legs strewn across the beach. Right there, on the open sand, Frank made love to me, kissing me the whole time, our bodies entwined, two dogs in the surf.

I finally understood what they meant when they talked about falling in love.

PALM SPRINGS

Frank was out of breath, a bag of groceries in his arms, when I opened the front door to find him trudging up the walk.

"What are you doing home?" I asked.

He had told me this morning that he needed to stay at the college late tonight for a departmental meeting. The keys to my Jeep were in my hand. My shirt smelled of cologne.

He was wiping his forehead with his hand. "Still so hot," he said. His light blue oxford shirt was stained with sweat under his arms and above his belt. "Here we are, almost at the end of September, and it's still one hundred degrees at six o'clock. Can't wait for next month, when things start to cool down."

I stepped aside to let him enter, watching him as he huffed and puffed his way to the kitchen. I followed, conscious of how floral I smelled. He set the bag of groceries down on the table. A loaf of French bread stuck out of the top.

"They were having a sale on pork chops over at Jensen's," he said, bracing himself and resting against the kitchen counter. Beads of sweat dripped down his forehead. "Thought we might grill them out on the deck. Whad'ya think?"

"I thought you had a meeting," I said.

He stood there, catching his breath. "I really need to start jogging and get back into shape. This heat just makes everything worse." He let out a sigh and moved over to the table. He began unpacking the groceries. "I said to hell with the meeting. Every night it's something. I told them we needed to reschedule. So what do you think, Danny? Fire up the grill? Damn. I forgot applesauce. Do we have any?"

"Frank," I said, "I . . . have plans."

His green eyes, bloodshot, met mine. I felt exposed. My cologne seemed overpowering.

"Oh," he said. "Where are you going?"

"I didn't know you'd be coming home. I thought you were out for the night."

"Where are you going?" he asked again.

"I'm meeting Hassan." The words came easily, quickly, without any thought. I hadn't anticipated the need to lie. I'd made the date early so that I could be home before Frank returned. These departmental meetings rarely ended before nine thirty. "I'm sorry," I said. "If I had known you were going to be home . . ."

He waved me away. "Danny, it's okay. We'll save the pork chops for tomorrow."

"Good," I said, smiling to cover the horrendous feeling of guilt that was rising up from my stomach, like acid reflux. "Because we *don't,* in fact, have any applesauce. I'll pick some up, and we can grill the chops tomorrow."

He smiled, opening the refrigerator to put the food away. "I'm glad you're making friends out here finally. For so long all you've had is Randall, coming in from L.A. And I like Hassan."

I smiled back awkwardly.

"I guess I'll just make an omelet for dinner, then," Frank said, taking two eggs in his hand and shutting the refrigerator door. "When will you be back, do you think?"

"Oh, not late." I was growing increasingly anxious.

"Where are you going?"

"Not sure."

He shrugged, trusting me completely. "Well, tell him I said hello."

"I will."

Frank made his way over to the stove. With a creak in his knees, he bent down to withdraw a frying pan. He set it on the burner. I just stood there, watching him.

"Okay, then," I said.

He turned and smiled. "Okay, baby. Have a good time."

I despised myself.

Outside, starting the ignition of the Jeep, I tried to remember if I'd ever lied to Frank before. No, I didn't think I had.

I was not sure why I'd felt the need to lie to Frank about where I was going and who I was seeing. We had an open relationship. It wasn't that I was cheating on him. I had no idea if the meeting with Kelly would even lead to sex. It was just a get-together with someone who had intrigued me. Frank wanted me to make more friends in Palm Springs. I could have just told him that I'd had a conversation with one of Donovan's friends who was a young artist and that we were going to have dinner. It would have been no big deal. Frank would have been glad to hear it.

But I couldn't tell him.

Because I knew I wasn't just meeting a friend of Donovan's who happened to be an artist. I was meeting a young man who had obsessed me for weeks. Whose face stopped my breath. Whose eyes made my heart freeze. And, of course, I wanted the meeting to lead to sex. I wanted it to lead right back to his bedroom, where I'd strip him of his clothes and feel his body all over, where I'd kiss the soft hair on his arms and lick the eagle tattoo on his neck.

Even then, I could have told Frank. Our relationship allowed such freedoms. Many times I'd told him about a particular boy I fancied, and he'd say, "Great, Danny. Sounds great. Bring him home. Let's meet him. Maybe we can have some fun." But not this boy. I didn't want to tell Frank about this boy.

Because, I realized, I wanted Kelly all to myself.

The sky was a pale orange. The sun was gone, having dropped behind the mountains an hour earlier, but its light remained, hazy and muted. I looked at my phone to see the time and realized the unexpected interaction with Frank in the kitchen had made me a few minutes late. I had told Kelly I would meet him at six thirty, and it was almost that now.

He'd been insistent that he meet me at the restaurant, that I not come by to pick him up at his place. I didn't really know why. Meeting at the restaurant, I feared, might eliminate any chance of the night ending in sex. But, I reasoned, if the ostensible reason for this get-together was to look at his sketches, then I'd need to go back to his apartment at some point, since I doubted he was going to show up at Spencer's with his portfolio. Then again, he carried around that little sketch pad. Maybe he was planning on bringing the whole Kelly collection under his arm.

He did not. When I got to the restaurant, I saw him standing outside, his hands thrust in his pockets. I pulled up to the valet and handed him my keys. I remembered Hassan's admonition that the tip came afterward. And in my mind, I made a mental note to call Hassan later and make up some excuse for why I would tell Frank I was with him tonight, in case Frank ever mentioned it.

"Hi," Kelly said as I met him on the steps.

He was, as always, beautiful. Standing there in that pastel orange light, he appeared like a figure out of a painting, a dark-eyed, pouty-lipped Caravaggio boy. He wore almost exactly the same outfit I'd seen him in last week, brown corduroys and a black sweater, except instead of blue this time, his shirt was green. Its collar barely surfaced past the neckline of his sweater. On his feet he wore bright white running shoes with a red stripe.

"Hope I'm dressed okay," he said.

I smiled. "You look fine," I told him.

"This is a pretty fancy place," he said.

"No fancier than the Parker."

He smiled. "And I was dressed the same then."

"Were you?" I asked, pretending I hadn't noticed, that I didn't keep such details about him stored away in my head. "You look fine."

I wasn't dressed up, either, really. I wore a black open-collar shirt over a pair of dark blue Dolce & Gabbana jeans, with the pointy-toed black shoes I'd bought a couple of weeks ago at the Beverly Center. The pointy look was starting to become the rage in L.A., and I figured on introducing it to the desert. And cologne. I was wearing cologne. Too much of it, I was now beginning to worry. I thought of my father then but pushed the thought out of my mind.

We headed inside. The maître d' found my reservation and escorted us to our table. We sat, neither of us quite knowing how to begin the conversation. I ordered a bottle of wine, a red pinot. We both looked down at our menus.

"You've been here before," I said.

"Yes," he replied. "Once with Donovan and Penelope Sue. It was her birthday."

Part of me wanted to know how that little ménage had been managed; another part hoped fervently that the name Donovan Hunt never again surfaced in our dialogue. So I changed the subject, to the professed reason I had asked him out this evening.

"So where are your sketches?" I leaned forward on the table, clasping my hands together over my plate. "Are we going back to your place afterward so I can see them?"

He looked up at me with those glossy black eyes. "I'm not sure I want to show them to you, after all," he said. "I hope you understand."

The waiter came by to uncork the wine. We went through the whole rigmarole: he poured a bit into the glass, I sniffed and I sipped and I nodded my head, and then he poured us each a full glass. When it was all done, I looked back over at Kelly and frowned.

"Not show your sketches to me? Why?"

"I Googled you. You're famous."

"No, I'm not. I'm *so* not famous."

"You had a show of your work downtown."

I made a face. "Kelly, I make prints for hotels. I'm not famous."

"High-end hotels. And you did that poster series for Disneyland."

"Yeah." I took a sip of the wine. "I did do that."

"I can't show you my work. You're a big-time artist."

I laughed. "Kelly. Please. Stop saying that."

"Well," he said, sitting back in his chair. "Maybe someday. But not tonight."

I shrugged. "Okay. Your call."

The waiter was hovering. We gave him our attention.

He smiled. He was bald, with a long, aquiline nose and a studied air of sincerity. He clasped his hands and looked from me to Kelly and then back again. "Good evening, gentlemen. Have you had a chance to look at the menus?"

"No," I said. "Actually, if you could just give us a couple—"

"Can I ask a question?" Kelly's black eyes were wide. He motioned for the waiter to bend down a bit, as if he were about to let us all in on a secret. The waiter did so. "Whad'ya got on the menu that's not too pricey? You got maybe some hot dogs or macaroni and cheese? See, we're kind of on a budget here tonight."

The waiter's eyebrows went up; his jaw went down. There was a moment of silence.

"He's joking," I said quickly.

Kelly sat back in his chair, hunching his shoulders, his chin on his chest, giggling.

"Ah," the waiter said. An odd little grin twisted his lips. "Well, I'll give you a moment to look at the menu."

"I love doing that," Kelly said after the waiter was gone.

I couldn't help but smile. "I should be totally embarrassed, but I'm not."

"That's because you're not like most of the people in Palm Springs. Since moving out here, I've discovered there are two types of people that live in this town. Rich and trash. There's no middle."

"Well, I wouldn't go so far as to say trash . . ."

"Hey, where I'm from, *trash* is a compliment. In my hometown, the laundromat doubled as the local day-care center."

I laughed, which seemed to encourage him. He leaned forward to tell me more.

"Halloween pumpkins had more teeth than the people in my family. My mother thought Hamburger Helper was one of the major food groups. My father said having more than one toothbrush in the house was a waste of money."

I laughed out loud. A woman at the next table glanced my way.

"I thought you didn't have parents," I said.

He opened his menu. "They were foster parents."

"So you grew up in a foster home?"

"Several. Hey, do you like squid?"

"Not really."

"Me either. Eating squid in the desert just feels weird to me. Any kind of fish, actually. I mean, it's a *desert*. So where do they get the fish?"

"Maybe they catch it up in the mountains and bring it down."

"Squid?" He made a face at me. "Danny, there's no squid in the San Jacinto Mountains."

I laughed again. "I didn't mean squid. I meant—"

"Hey, what did the fish say when he swam into the wall?"

I was grinning. "I don't know."

"Dam."

It took me about ten seconds; then I laughed out loud again. Kelly was poker-faced, studying his menu.

"I think I'll get the chicken," he said.

"Get whatever you want. This is on me."

He lifted one eye over his menu. "Why?"

"Because I asked you to dinner."

"Okay, fine." He looked back at the menu. "So the chicken looks good. Hey, what's chicken teriyaki?"

"It's Japanese—"

"No, you're wrong. It's the name of the world's oldest living kamikaze pilot." He gave me crazy eyes. "Get it? A chicken kamikaze pilot? You know what kamikaze pilots do, right?"

"Yes, I do," I groaned. "Yes, I get it."

His was on a roll, looking straight at me. "Okay. If fruit comes from a fruit tree, what kind of tree does a chicken come from?"

"I think this one might hurt," I said.

"A poultry."

"Oh, man, it hurt bad."

He smiled, closing his menu. "I think I'll get the fried chicken. Usually, I like to eat fried chicken with my fingers, but since we're in a fancy restaurant, I'll eat my fingers separately."

The waiter had returned. I was laughing so hard, I couldn't give him my order.

"He gets like this," Kelly said, referring to me and shaking his head. "I think they're gonna have to adjust his meds."

The waiter gave an awkward little laugh.

"So I'll start with the heirloom tomato salad with the shaved fennel," Kelly said, his voice dropping into seriousness, "and then the Dijon-coated rack of lamb au jus with the sautéed forest mushrooms and glazed baby carrots."

I looked over at him.

He shrugged. "It's what I always get."

I smiled, then ordered an iceberg wedge and the grilled chicken.

"Have you ever gone bungee jumping?" Kelly asked as the waiter was collecting our menus.

"No," I replied. "Can't say I ever—"

"Don't bother," Kelly said. "It's like getting a blow job from your grandmother."

I thought the waiter heard. He moved away quickly.

"Feels great," Kelly continued, "but for God's sake, don't look down."

I burst out laughing.

It went on like that for a while.

Eating our salads, he had me in stitches. "What came first, the chicken or the egg? Neither. The rooster." One-liners like that. "What do you call a lesbian Eskimo? A Klondike."

Here we were, in one of the most elegant restaurants in town, and he was talking about macaroni and cheese and lesbian Eskimos. Last time I'd been to this place, I'd sat between the owner of the gallery that was showing my work and a couple of his snooty customers. The gallery owner had hoped they'd commission a piece from me, but all night long, all they'd talked about was real estate. How the market had shot up, up, *up* here in the desert, and how there was new construction everywhere. But could the boom sustain itself? How long before everything went bust? I had been bored out of my mind. And no, neither of the two dead-beats ever commissioned a piece. Guess they'd been too busy buying up condos before the housing bubble burst.

But tonight . . . my cheeks were hurting from smiling so much.

Suddenly Kelly spotted a woman at the next table and pulled out his sketch pad. "Just a quick one," he said.

He was scratching away with his pencil when the waiter brought our meals. He didn't move, forcing the waiter to place the lamb in the middle of the table.

"Let me see," I said.

"Almost done."

When he slid the pad over to me, I marveled at what he had accomplished. He had captured her perfectly. Just a few squiggly lines—but there she was, with her oversize ears, the diagonal slash of a mouth, the slightly asymmetrical eyes.

"Brilliant," I said. "You've got to let me see your sketches."

"Someday."

We ordered another bottle of wine.

"So tell me more about you," I said. "Ten minutes of serious talk. Then you can go back to your jokes."

"What do you want to know?"

"I don't even know your last name."

"Nelson."

"Scandinavian?"

"I have no idea."

"Well, you sure don't look Scandinavian."

"I think my birth parents were probably Italian."

"Do you know your birth name?"

He shook his head. "No clue. Kelly was given to me by my first set of foster parents. Nelson was their last name. The state just let it stick."

"Where were you born?"

"San Francisco."

Another surprise. "San Francisco? The way you were talking, I thought you were going to say the hills of Alabama or something."

"Hey, you can find trash anywhere."

I smiled. "When were you put in a foster home?"

"When I was five."

"So you remember your birth parents?"

"Not my father. My mother only a little. I have a bad memory."

I had a feeling he actually had a very good memory, but that there were things he wanted pretty badly to forget.

"And so you were never officially adopted?"

"Nope."

"Why not?"

He sighed. "I think because my birth mother kept trying to get me back. But they never let me go back to her, because she was a drug addict. They just kept moving me from family to family."

"What was the longest you stayed with any one family?"

"Five years. That was at the end, before I went off on my own."

He fixed me with his eyes and seemed, for the first time, to offer some real sincerity. "My last foster mother agreed to take care of me because she'd been forced to give up twin boys she'd given birth to when she was an unmarried teenager."

"Oh, I see. So you kind of filled that emotional space for her."

He looked sad. "I wish I'd been able to do that. She always missed those boys. They were *hers,* you know? And I wasn't. Not really. And she always made sure to remind me that I wasn't one of her darling twins."

I looked across the table and saw a little flicker of something in his eyes. My heart went out to him. "That must have been hard," I said.

He nodded, biting his lip. "She was always looking for her twins. Finally, she found out that the boys had been separated before they were adopted. One went to an Arab family, who named him Amal, and the other went to a Mexican family, who named him Juan. Then one day, she got a photo of Juan in the mail from the adoptive family, and she got all choked up. She showed me his picture and said, 'I wish I had a photo of Amal as well.' Well, I just looked at her and said, 'But they're *twins,* bitch. If you've seen Juan, you've seen Amal.'"

"Oh, man," I groaned, realizing I'd been had.

Kelly let out a whoop of a laugh.

"You had me going there for a while," I told him.

He poured himself some more wine. "You know, speaking of Alabama, do you know what they consider a bisexual down there?"

I rested my chin in my hand, my elbow on the table. "Tell me."

"Someone who likes sheep *and* goats."

I shook my head. "You can't stay serious for long, can you?"

"Ten minutes were up."

"No, they weren't," I said.

He laughed. "What's so good about being serious?"

He had me there. Suddenly I realized how *serious* I'd become. How I'd stand at a bar with Randall and we'd talk about his breakup with Ike, or what I needed to do to get my work more noticed, or how Frank and I were putting new tile in the pool. When did we stop going out just to have a good time? When did we start being so *serious?* At home, Frank and I talked about his retirement plan, or how in a few more years he'd get a nice annuity. Should we buy

a new place? Or should we just fix this one up? We really needed a
new roof. Had I seen the new clay roof the neighbors had installed
down the street? It was really nice. Had I seen how nice it was?

Sitting across from Kelly, I felt alive.

He made me laugh. Not only with his dumb jokes, but with his
boyish enthusiasm for everything. His tomato salad was "out of
this world." His lamb was "the tastiest treat" he'd had in a long
time. He even raved over the glazed baby carrots. "Here, try one,"
he insisted, stabbing a carrot with his fork and presenting it to me
across the table. I plucked the carrot off the tines and laughed at
his exuberance.

"Tasty, huh?" he asked.

"Sure is," I told him, locked onto his eyes.

He told me how, after turning eighteen, he'd left his foster
family in San Francisco and taken the bus, just like me, to Los Angeles. He couldn't stay in San Francisco, he explained. The city
represented his old life, and he needed to start fresh. He had to
get out of his hometown if he was going to start over and become
something new. And so . . . one more thing he shared with that
boy from East Hartford.

He told me about the jobs he'd found in bars, again just like
me, though he'd never taken off his clothes and danced on a
box. When I told him about that little fact of my history, Kelly
grinned wide and asked if I had pictures. Of course, I did. I
promised I'd show him sometime.

"Well, that encourages me," he said, cutting his lamb.

"What does?"

"That you could go from being a stripper in a club to a big, famous artist." He looked at me intently. "I don't want to be a bartender all my life."

I let the "big, famous artist" description pass by for the moment. My heart was jumping out of my chest at him. I wanted to
fill him up with encouragement. I wanted to change his life, right
there and then, right there at that very table. I wanted to jump-
start his future for him, to send him off on his way to success, an
accomplishment he would always trace back to this very moment,
when I had said the words that changed his life.

"You just have to believe you can do it," I told him.

He made a face. "I never went to college."

I leaned in toward him. "Neither did I."

He seemed to consider whether I was telling him the truth.

"I'm not bullshitting you. I barely got out of high school alive."

"But you seem so . . ." He gestured as he tried to think of a word. "I don't know. Educated."

"Well, when I was very young, I liked school. I was a good student. But my high school years were . . ." My voice trailed off. How much should I tell? "I had a lot of distractions in high school," I finally said. "But still, after a couple of years of this, I had a sense that I was missing out on something. So I started reading everything I could, even if it wasn't assigned in class. I'd go to the library and take out the classics. Hawthorne. Mark Twain. Jane Austen. It was a way of occupying my mind."

"But then why didn't you go on to college?"

"My parents couldn't afford it. Besides, I wanted to be an actor. So after high school, I took jobs at Bob's Big Boy and Friendly's Ice Cream to finance my trips into New York to audition."

"Did you get any parts?"

"A few. Nothing much. And certainly nothing ever came of them." Suddenly my life—usually just a string of broken dreams in my own mind—seemed like a trailblazing path to glory. "But you know, I never gave up. Oh, sure, yes, I gave up on the idea of being an actor, but only because I'd found something else. Somewhere in the back of my mind, I knew I'd find my way. I came close to giving up lots of times, but deep down, I always believed that I'd make it."

That wasn't entirely true. I was romanticizing quite a bit. I didn't talk about the hustling, or the jobs waiting tables, or the key fact that for much of the time, I'd had Frank at my side, always cheering me on and paying the bills when I had no money. Right then, I didn't want to think about Frank. The guilt would just kick in again, and I was having too much fun.

"Well, all that sounds great," Kelly was saying, "but I don't have your talent."

I scowled. "That's *so* not true. You have more talent than I do. I don't sketch, remember. I take pictures with a camera, and then I digitize them."

"Yeah, but that takes talent. A lot more than I have."

"I've seen what you do. You're good. When did you start sketching?"

He smirked. "When I saw Jackie O on the cover of a magazine."

"Ah yes," I said. "The cult of Jackie."

"It just came over me. I felt like I had to draw her. Pretty soon my walls were covered not only with photos of her but my drawings of her as well." He batted his long, beautiful eyelashes. "Jackie was a huge influence on my creativity."

I smiled. Our waiter came by to check on us. After he left, I looked over at Kelly and said, "Draw him."

"The waiter?" Kelly scrunched up his face, revealing his deep dimples. "He's no Jackie O. He's a tight ass."

"So? Show me what you can do."

He shrugged, then arched an eyebrow as he checked out his subject from across the room. Finally, he nodded, took out his pad again, and began to sketch.

"We can leave it with the tip," I said.

He was silent as he drew.

"Hey," I said, racking my brain for a joke, determined to play his game. "Why do demons and ghouls hang out together?"

"Don't talk to me when I'm drawing."

"Oh." I sat back in my chair. "Sorry."

He finished. He held up the sketch so I could see. Another masterpiece. He'd nailed it perfectly. The round head, the long nose, the snooty expression.

"Fantastic," I said.

"Everyone knows demons are a ghoul's best friend."

I laughed. "No fair. You know all the jokes."

"It's true. I long for the day someone can tell me a joke I haven't heard."

"I'll keep trying." I paused, long enough so that it would be significant. "That is, if you'll let me."

Our eyes held a moment; then he broke the gaze.

"Your Web site mentions a person named Frank," Kelly said. "Who's he?"

"Frank's my husband," I admitted.

"You're married?"

I nodded. I couldn't hold up my hand to show him the ring, because I'd taken it off. I always took it off when I went to the gym. The ring hurt sometimes when I did crossovers. But usually I slipped it back on after I showered. Tonight I had left it in my gym bag.

"We got married in Canada a couple years ago," I said. "Not that it's legal or anything down here."

"But you must have a domestic partnership thing, too."

"We do. Everything's all taken care of that way. Frank is a teacher. He's very organized. He's very . . . serious."

A smile barely revealed itself on Kelly's lips.

"I don't believe in marriage," he said. "Oh, I mean, it's great for people who want it. I just could never do it. I look at marriages like Donovan's with Penelope Sue—"

I cut in. "Believe me, that's not a marriage most people would ever want to emulate."

He gave me a look. "I wasn't going to say anything bad about it. In fact, I was going to say that was one of the few styles of marriage I could ever tolerate. Where there's complete freedom and complete individuality."

"You know, I can't help but wonder . . . when you and Donovan . . ."

Kelly's eyebrows came together. "When me and Donovan what?"

"Well, I assume the two of you—"

"Don't assume anything." He seemed indignant. For a second I saw a flash of anger in those dark mirrors of his—the anger that had apparently led to him being fired from his job. But then it dissipated, and he was laughing. "Donovan and I are just friends. It was never anything more than that."

"Okay." I sat back as the busboy came by to clear away our plates. "But if that's the case, knowing Donovan, he certainly *wanted* it to be something more."

"You'll have to ask him. I don't know."

"Have you ever had a boyfriend?"

Kelly laughed. "God, no."

"Never?"

"I can barely deal with myself than have to deal with someone else, too."

"How old are you?"

"Twenty-six."

"And no boyfriend, ever?"

He shook his head.

"Have you ever been in love?"

"I've asked myself that. Truth is, I don't know."

I smiled. "Then you haven't been. If you had, you'd know."

He shrugged. "Then I suppose I haven't."

With that, I let my inquisition drop.

Neither of us wanted dessert. I paid the check, leaving Kelly's sketch along with my signed credit card slip. I told him he ought to sign it for the waiter. He just scoffed.

Outside, the night sky was a purple star-studded dome. The air was a little bit cool, a sign that the long, hot summer was coming to an end. I asked Kelly if he wanted a ride back to his place. He told me he didn't live far. He could walk.

"Please," I said. "Let me see your sketches."

"Tell you what," he said. "I'll race you there. If you beat me, then you can see them."

"But I don't know here you live," I protested.

He laughed. "So follow me!" And he took off running down the street.

This was absurd. He was running away from me. We hadn't even said good night. The valet stood at my elbow, waiting for my call slip so he could go get my Jeep and receive his tip. I didn't know what to say.

I turned to the valet. "I guess I should go after him."

He was an older Mexican man. "Better leave now, or you'll lose him."

"I'll be back for my car," I said.

And then I took off. Kelly was quite a ways down Arenas Road by now, a small figure far off in the distance. Once again, he had an unfair advantage over me. He was wearing running shoes. I had on pointy Kenneth Coles. But I did my best. Just because he was twenty-six and I was forty-one, I was not about to concede this race.

I passed him as we neared Cahuilla. "Slowpoke!" I shouted.

He hooted and caught up with me. "You're gonna have blisters, running in those shoes!"

"And it will be your fault!"

"Weeee-hooo!" he yelled.

I yelled back. Our voices seemed to echo off the mountains behind us.

He came to a sudden stop in front of a pink stucco apartment complex. A shingle out front read HAPPY PALMS.

"I won!" he crowed.

"No fair," I said. "I didn't know where to stop."

"Doesn't matter. I got here first."

I jogged over to him. My heart was thudding in my chest, and my face was flushed. My shirt was wet, and my feet hurt. But I was giddy.

"I didn't run all this way not to come in and see your sketches," I told him.

"Sorry. Guess you did."

I got up close. We were quiet for several seconds.

"You smell good," Kelly finally said.

"What? My sweat?"

"No. Your cologne. It's nice."

I kissed him.

When I pulled back, he was looking at me with those big black eyes.

"Thank you for dinner," he said.

I didn't speak.

"I had fun," he said.

"So did I," I told him.

And I kissed him again.

Did he kiss me back? It's hard to say now. I thought he did. I thought I felt his lips move, a hint of his tongue in my mouth. But I don't know. I don't know now if he kissed me back.

But it didn't matter. Standing there, under the purple sky, the neighborhood as still and quiet as an empty church, I tasted the wine from dinner on his lips. I tasted his laughter, his conversation, his silly little jokes.

"What do you call a monkey in a minefield?" I asked him softly in his ear.

He moved around so he could answer me the same way. His

lips tickled. "A baboom," he whispered. "Sorry. Told ya I know them all."

I nudged his face back around and kissed him a third time, bringing my hands up to his hair. How soft it was. How thick. I remembered my own hair being that thick once. My fingers got lost in it as my lips pressed against his. My heart was beating so fast and so strong that I was sure he must have heard it. I felt alive. My blood was zooming through all my veins; my lungs were puffed up with air. *Alive.* I had forgotten how good it felt.

"Let me see your sketches," I murmured.

"Some other time," he said in reply.

He moved away then, slipping out of my arms and leaping onto the concrete stairs. I made a move to catch him, but he was too fast. He turned and looked down at me.

"Thank you again," he said.

"Yeah," I managed to say.

Then he hurried up the steps. I heard his running shoes slap against the concrete. Somewhere overhead, in the shadows of a second-floor terrace, I heard a door open, then clank shut, a bolt sliding into its lock.

I turned and began walking back down the street. My heart was still laboring in my chest, thumping so hard, it almost hurt. I had to stop, place my hands on my knees, and take a few deep breaths to calm it down. Yet all the while, I was laughing.

It didn't matter that I hadn't been invited upstairs. Those lovely pheromones had been released by my brain and were now flooding my body, filling up my head and my torso and swimming down into my limbs. It seemed as if I could actually feel them, little tickles of electricity pulsing through my body. How good I felt.

How alive.

EAST HARTFORD

The way the altar boys were lighting the candles, with the tiny flames blown this way and that by whatever little breezes had been caught in the nave of the church, reminded me of the night Becky had disappeared, when Dad had sat in his chair, flicking his cigarette lighter on and off, and I'd watched from my room upstairs. Now Dad sat next to me in the pew, smelling of too much cologne. It was so strong that it made me cough. I had begun to understand why my father wore so much cologne these days, but I didn't admit it, not even to myself.

The pallbearers were carrying Aunt Patsy's casket down the aisle. Nana sat at the end of the pew, not saying anything. She wasn't crying. She just sat there in the dress Mom had picked out for her, dark green with a paisley print. She had insisted on applying her own lipstick, taking it out of Mom's hand and doing it herself. I looked over at Nana now and felt sad that she'd messed up on her bottom lip. A line of pink pointed down to her chin. But she hadn't let anyone fix it. "Leave me alone," she'd said.

I was not sure she fully understood why were in the church. But she did understand that Aunt Patsy was gone. She used to ask all the time where she was, but from the moment Aunt Patsy died, Nana had stopped asking about her. So many facts no longer stuck in her mind. But this one apparently did.

Mom sat on my other side. I didn't think she wanted to sit next to Dad. She didn't like all the cologne, either, though we never talked about it. Mom seemed to resent being there at the funeral at all. She was resentful whenever she had to do anything that didn't involve looking for Becky. She had gotten dressed hastily herself, pulling on a dark blue dress that didn't seem to fit her right anymore. She'd lost a lot of weight since Becky disappeared. Her shoulder blades stuck up through the top of her dress. She sat there next to me, twisting her Rosary beads in her lap with her big, man-size hands.

I adjusted my clip-on necktie. It was the one I usually wore to school. I'd wanted to get a real necktie, one that I actually tied, but Mom never went clothes shopping anymore, and the ones Dad owned were the really narrow ones from the sixties. So I just made sure my pathetic little tie was clipped tightly to my collar.

It had been a while since I'd been in this church. In the old days, we used to attend every Sunday as a family. Yet while Mom had started attending daily Mass since Becky's disappearance, she no longer insisted I go at all. Once upon a time, she would have warned me that I'd go straight to hell if I deliberately skipped Mass. Now it seemed she had too much else on her mind to worry about my eternal salvation.

The heat was way too high in the church, and I was starting to sweat in my blue polyester suit from Sears. I'd never been to a funeral before. I had no idea what to expect. All I knew was they were *not* going to open Aunt Patsy's coffin, and I was glad of that. Dad said Aunt Patsy had lost so much weight while she was in the hospice that no one would've recognized her. I had never seen a dead person, and I wanted to keep it that way. In my mind, Aunt Patsy was always talking, always asking me how school was going, always carrying in cherry pies for Thanksgiving or Christmas or Easter. Now she'd just be lying there dead in her casket, all skinny and wasted away. I didn't want to see that.

Father McKenna was walking up the aisle now, in a long white robe, swinging an urn of incense. The scent mingled with Dad's cologne, and I was suddenly overwhelmed by the thick, smoky sweetness and began to cough again. As the priest passed us, we stood, and the organ behind us in the choir loft began pumping out its deep, mournful music. I recognized the hymn, "I Am the

Bread of Life." John 6:35. Back at St. John's, we'd had to memorize it. Mom and Dad were mumbling some of the words, so I moved my mouth a little, too, ending with, "And I will ray-ay-se him uh-uh-up on the la-ah-ah-ast day."

Dad started to cry on that. I wasn't sure whom he was crying about. Aunt Patsy, who was his only sister, or Becky, who was his only daughter.

We sat back down after the hymn was finished. The church was quiet. Father McKenna stood in front of the altar and stretched out his hands. "Dearly beloved—"

Suddenly his words were cut off by the sound of a motorcycle outside in the parking lot. Even though it was February, the windows were open a little to let air into the small, stuffy church. The sound was unmistakable. The engine roared like a machine gun, then suddenly cut off, punctuated by a short squeal of tires. Father McKenna stopped only for a moment, his eyes glancing toward the windows; then he resumed.

"We are gathered here today to remember our sister Patricia Ann," he intoned.

"Danny." Mom was leaning down, whispering in my ear. "Danny, tell your father I'll meet you all at the cemetery. Tell him I'm sorry, but it can't be helped."

I didn't move. I didn't know what to say. Mom slid out of the pew. I assumed she walked to the back of the church, but I didn't look around. Then I heard the clack of the church door opening and closing.

Father McKenna was continuing to drone on. I leaned into Dad.

"Mom said she'd meet us at the cemetery," I said softly.

Dad made no reply.

"She said she was sorry, but it couldn't be helped."

He just closed his eyes.

Outside the motorcycle roared back to life. It was really a horrible sound. So loud, so shrill. I heard its tires burn rubber on the pavement.

Only after a few minutes had passed did I consider the possibility that my mother might have gotten on that thing. She couldn't have taken our car. It wasn't there. The funeral director had picked us up in a limousine.

Did Mom get on the back of a motorcycle?

The image was absurd. Ridiculous. Comical. And also terrifying. All through the funeral, it was all I could think about. Why would she do it? Who was driving the motorcycle? Where was she going? At Communion time, when we went up to the altar and took the Host, I slowed down alongside the wall of windows and peered outside. Nothing to see. Mom was gone.

The funeral was boring. It was just like a regular Mass for the most part. In his sermon, Father McKenna said that Aunt Patsy was now accepted into God's embrace and would be living for all eternity with Jesus and all the saints. Except he always referred to her as Patricia. It was like he was talking about somebody I didn't know.

I closed my eyes. I pictured a room in the house I was going to live in when I grew up. It was going to be a big house with an in-ground pool right next to Mom and Dad's, and my favorite room would have a giant television and pillows scattered all over the floor. That's where I'd hang out, watching *Doctor Who* with my son Joey. I was wishing I was there now, far away from this church and Aunt Patsy's casket up front.

Finally, the funeral was over, and we all headed back down the aisle, past the thirty or so people who had shown up. Aunt Patsy hadn't had too many friends. All her life had been spent taking care of Nana. I scanned the faces. Not too many people I knew.

But then—way in back—I saw Chipper Paguni. He sat there by himself, slunk down in the pew. He was wearing a big, bulky black sweater. His eyes met mine briefly, then looked away.

My heart started beating faster. Chipper. I wasn't sure why he'd come. He'd been keeping his distance the last few months. His parents were angry with us. My parents—well, Mom more than Dad—blamed Chipper, believing he knew more about Becky's disappearance than he'd let on. So I wasn't sure why he'd come to Aunt Patsy's funeral. He'd known her, of course, but not well.

We were outside the church when I considered the possibility that Chipper had come because of me.

I'll take care of you while I'm still here.

He had promised that—even if there hadn't been much cause for him to defend me lately. At school I'd fallen into a routine. In

class and in the corridors, I kept to myself; at lunch I sat with
Troy, and we'd make fun of our idiotic classmates under our breath.
No one had much to do with us. There hadn't been any major harassment in some time—partly, I was sure, because Chipper had
let it be known ever since that day last fall that I shouldn't be
messed with. And I remained grateful to him for that.

The funeral director, a tall man with ice blue eyes and thick snow-
white hair, was waiting for us as we emerged from the church. He
gestured silently for us to slip into the limousine. He moved with
a stiffness that reminded me of one of the creepy automatons
outside the Spook House at Coleman's Carnival, the ones that
turned and moved their wooden arms and beckoned you to enter.
Sliding into the limo, I settled in on one side, with Dad and Nana
facing me on the other. No one said a word about Mom.

The funeral procession began. The limo followed slowly as the
hearse bearing Aunt Patsy's coffin led the way. Resting my head
against the back of the seat, I closed my eyes. I thought about
Chipper. It made me happy that he had been there. *He is looking
out for me,* I told myself. I felt special. I imagined that I was in his
car instead of in this dreary old limousine, Aerosmith playing on
the eight-track. Chipper was reaching across, placing his hand on
my knee, and I was placing my hand over his. I could smell him as
we drove along in his car—that sweet, slightly tangy but clean
smell that suffused his underpants. I'd started holding them every
night under my pillow, occasionally bringing them to my face. I'd
kiss them and let the soft white cotton caress my cheeks. In my
mind, riding in Chipper's car, his hand on my knee, I imagined
him leaning over to me and saying, ever so softly—

"Danny."

I opened my eyes.

My father was speaking to me.

"It's time to get out," he said.

We were at the cemetery. I stepped out of the limo and had to
blink a few times. The sun was really bright, reflecting off the snow.
The few people who'd followed us from the church were getting
out of their cars, and we all trudged over to a small stone chapel.
I still didn't know where Mom was, and no one asked about her.
Dad was holding on to Nana's arm as she made her way across the

snow. I looked around, hoping to spot Chipper, but he apparently hadn't come.

Inside the chapel, Father McKenna said a few more prayers. There would be no graveside service since the snow was too deep. Dad had explained that Aunt Patsy would be stashed in the mausoleum for now and buried later, when the snow had melted a little. I fet sad that there wouldn't be anybody here then, just her and the grave digger.

"Danny," my father said when it was all over and we were heading back to the limo. I looked up at him. His eyes were bloodshot. "Your friend is over there."

"Chipper?" I asked, my voice betraying my feelings.

"No," Dad said. "Whatshisname."

I looked in the direction Dad was nodding.

It was Troy.

I approached him.

"What are you doing here?" I asked.

The sunlight brought out the golden highlights in his red hair and had turned his tinted aviator glasses a dark blue. I couldn't see his eyes.

"I saw in the newspaper that your aunt's funeral was ending up here," he said. "And I live just down the street."

"Oh." I paused. "Thanks for coming."

"Want to come over?" he asked.

"I can't. We're going back to my house now for cake and casseroles."

"Come on. Ask your father."

Part of me hoped that Chipper might show up back at our house, since he'd been at the funeral. But I knew he wouldn't. There was too much bad blood for him to show up. So I told Troy to hold on, and I crunched back through the snow to Dad.

"Dad, can I go over to Troy's house?"

He just looked at me with those bloodshot eyes. "The ladies from the church have made lunch for us back home."

"I'm not hungry. Do I really have to go? Can I stay with Troy? I can get his father to drive me home later."

Normally, Dad would say, "Ask your mother" in these situations. But since Mom was AWOL, he just shrugged. "Be back before it gets dark," he said. "And don't mess up your suit. Your mother will raise holy hell if you do."

I hurried back to Troy. We didn't say a word, just clomped through the snow toward the street. My suit pants were soon completely drenched below my knees, and my feet were freezing in my shoes. Troy's house was about a block away. We remained mum the whole time. I looked up at the house when we got to the front. It was made of red brick, with a two-car garage attached. It was a lot bigger than my own house. At the end of the driveway, its head and arm sticking out of the snow, was one of those ceramic black guys holding a lantern. I recognized the Jaguar parked in front of the garage. I hoped Troy wasn't going to suggest we go for a ride.

I felt weird walking into his house. Somewhere inside here, his mother had blown her brains out. This was a day all about death, it seemed.

It was Saturday, so Troy's father was seated in the living room, in his La-Z-Boy, his feet up. Mr. Kitchens was wearing black socks, no shoes. He was a large man, with a white shirt stretched across a very round belly, with an indentation that revealed his belly button. He didn't look like a rich man stretched out in that chair. He looked kind of sloppy, in fact. There was a half-eaten sandwich on the table next to the chair, and a glass of milk. He was watching television. *Some kind of cop movie,* I thought, with a really loud, squealing car chase. He looked over at us as we came in.

"We're just gonna go upstairs and listen to tapes," Troy said.

Mr. Kitchens nodded and went back to watching TV. We climbed the stairs to Troy's room.

I'd never been to Troy's house before. His room was pretty cool. There were posters covering practically every inch of every wall. Patti Smith. Blondie. Troy had turned me on to punk music, giving me tapes at school. His bed was unmade. Against the far wall was a big blue beanbag chair. On the top of his dresser sat a glow-in-the-dark skull, and next to it, a plastic model of a red Corvette.

"I want a Corvette when I get old enough to drive," I said, picking up the model and examining it.

"My dad's gonna get me one." Troy was standing in front of a massive stereo system with enormous speakers. I put the Corvette down and joined him.

"Very cool," I said, indicating the stereo.

"Wait'll you hear it," he promised me. He took off his glasses and began rummaging through a box of eight-tracks. "What do you want me to play?"

"I dunno. Whatever."

"This is really brilliant." He popped a tape into the stereo. "It's from England. All the really cool music comes from England."

A series of discordant notes screeched out of the speakers. "Who is it?" I asked.

"Ian Dury and the Blockheads." He got into the beat and began singing along. "Hit me, hit me, hit me with your rhythm stick!"

I sat down on the edge of his bed. As I moved his pillow, I revealed a box of Cheez-Its, tipped on its side and spilling crumbs onto the sheet. Troy sat beside me and thrust his hand down into the box, withdrawing a handful of the crackers and bringing them to his mouth.

"Hit me slowly, hit me quick," he sang as he chewed. "Hit me! Hit me! Hit me!"

"This is cool," I said. I wasn't entirely sure it was, but it was definitely different. And I liked English stuff. I loved *Doctor Who* and *Monty Python,* after all, which I watched on public television. And I kind of liked the Sex Pistols, too, even though I'd never bought any of their albums, because Mom would've had a bird.

"Want some?" Troy asked, handing me the Cheez-Its.

"Thanks," I said, reaching in for some of those cheesy little squares myself. With my other hand, I unhooked my tie and stuffed it down into my jacket pocket.

Troy was reaching under his mattress. He pulled out a wad of Saran Wrap and began unfolding it.

"Wanta smoke?" he asked.

I figured it was pot. I had no idea where he got the stuff. I'd thought the fact that the cops had caught him and let him go would've scared him straight—as they said on TV. But apparently not. I didn't answer right away, just watched him remove the funny little white cigarette from the plastic. He dug down into his pocket and produced a lighter.

"Want to?" he asked again.

"Okay," I said.

He lit up and inhaled deep. The tip of the cigarette pulsed a deep orange as he sucked in, then faded as he handed it over to me. He kept the smoke in his mouth, his cheeks puffed out. I accepted the cigarette and put it between my lips.

Troy let the smoke out over his shoulder in a long, languid kind of way. "Come on," he said to me. "Take a good long hit."

"I've never smoked before," I admitted.

He made a face. "Duh. That's obvious. Give me the joint."

I presumed *joint* meant *cigarette.* I handed it back to him.

"Watch me." He replaced the joint between his lips and sucked in. He handed it back to me after exhaling. "Like that. Suck it in deep."

I gave it my best shot. Breathing inward, I got a mouth full of smoke. It burned my throat. Instantly, I began hacking and gagging. Troy laughed.

"Try again," he said.

I took another hit. This time I felt the smoke go down. I held it inside me as long as I could, just as Troy had done, then let it out.

"See?" Troy said. "It's easy."

"When do I feel something?"

"Soon."

We sat there in silence, passing the joint back and forth, listening to that strange, up-and-down music. I felt nothing. Troy was rocking his head back and forth, singing. I felt as if I was slipping off the bed, but when I checked, I wasn't.

After a few minutes, Troy pushed himself backward on his bed to lean against his wall. I moved back and sat beside him. Our shoulders were touching.

"Aren't you afraid your dad will come in? Or smell the smoke?"

He shook his head. "He never comes upstairs. Hasn't since my mother."

I inhaled again, passing the joint back to him. "Where did she do it?" I asked after letting out the smoke.

"Right behind us," he said, taking another hit. "Right behind this wall."

It creeped me out, but I said nothing. I was feeling light and airy, as if I was moving forward, even kind of floating forward, but in fact I was perfectly still. I put my head back against the wall to steady myself. The joint was pretty small by now, and I could hardly hold it to my lips.

"I'll get my roach clip if you want," Troy said.

"What's that?"

He took the stub back from me and managed one last hit. "Never mind," he said and rubbed the joint out between his fingers, wincing a little. I imagined that must have hurt, but I was suddenly too lazy to make a comment. I just closed my eyes.

For a long time we sat that way. I noticed the sun in the sky had moved lower. Shadows crept into the room. All the while, the music got weirder. I wasn't sure if the band was just weird or if the pot was doing something to my hearing. But I liked how I felt. It was definitely cool. I felt kind of floaty and happy and safe. That was it. I felt *safe*. Really safe. Safer than I had since Becky had disappeared.

There was a weight on my thigh. I looked down. It took a couple of seconds to register, but I saw that Troy's hand was resting on my leg. I didn't say anything. Neither did I move.

Another span of time elapsed. A minute? Two? Twenty?

"Actually," Troy said at last, kind of startling me, "let's not waste this."

I had no idea what he was talking about. He got up, knocking the box of Cheez-Its to the floor, spilling them everywhere. He pulled open his top drawer, felt around inside, found something, then returned and sat next to me on the bed. In his hand was a little clip, into which he stuck the tiny stub of the joint.

"*Roaches,*" I said, the explanation of the term dawning on me. I felt proud of myself. "Little joints are called roaches."

Troy nodded, snapping his lighter back to life. "There's probably just one hit left on this, so we're gonna do something really cool. It really gives you an amazing high."

I said nothing, just listened.

"I'm gonna take a hit and hold it in. Then you're gonna open your mouth, and I'm gonna exhale into you."

"Okay." My heart was suddenly racing. "What do I have to do?"

"Like I said. Just open your mouth."

"Okay."

He took the hit. I watched his eyes kind of glass over. They were a strange color, kind of gray, kind of green. They turned to look at me.

I opened my mouth.

Troy's breath smelled like Cheez-Its. I felt his lips touch mine, then the sudden infusion of hot, tangy smoke. I breathed in, surprised that I didn't start to cough. Troy didn't remove his lips. We stayed like that, open mouth to open mouth, for several seconds. Then he pulled away, resting his head back against the wall. I did the same.

"Cool, huh?" he asked.

"Yeah," I said.

Again, time passed. I didn't know how long. The room was getting darker.

Something was about to happen. I just didn't know what. Maybe it was the pot, but everything was heightened. My breathing. My heartbeat. Still, I was calm. Extremely calm. I was expectant but not nervous.

"Can you make milk yet?" Troy asked me finally.

I didn't understand. I just looked at him.

"You know. From your prick." He reached down and grabbed the crotch of his parachute pants. "Make the white milk come out."

"I thought only girls made milk."

"No. Boys can, too. Wanta try?"

I said nothing.

"Come on," he said, unzipping his fly.

A bush of red pubic hair appeared. I barely had any hair down there myself, so I was fascinated. And a bit repulsed, too. Troy took his penis, small and pink and fat, in his hands.

"Come on, try," he insisted.

"I don't know . . ."

"Come on." He reached over and grabbed at my suit pants. "Pull down your zipper."

I obeyed.

"Yeah," he said and reached inside my pants. He pulled out my tiny penis. "You're still a baby."

"Yeah," I said weakly.

"I've done this before," he said. "Lots of times. Last summer at camp."

"Done what?"

He didn't reply. He just bent down and put his mouth on my penis. His tongue felt hot, almost scalding. I was shocked. I didn't know what to do. I made a little sound in my throat. What he was doing with his tongue felt good. *Very* good. Almost like those dreams I sometimes had, where I'd wake up and my heart would be pounding and my pajama bottoms would be all sticky and moist. Somehow I knew I couldn't ever let Mom see them that way, so I'd bury them deep under my sweaters in my closet. Troy's tongue felt even better than those dreams. I had never known anything like this. It was new. It was *sharp*. That was the best word to describe it. It was so sharp, it felt like a knife was being stuck into my groin, but instead of being painful, it felt good.

Really good.

"Oh," I moaned.

I felt the warm liquid fill up Troy's mouth. He kept on going, sucking it all down. I had no idea what had just happened. My heart was in my ears.

Troy pulled off my penis and sat back up.

"Now you do me," he said.

My heart was still pounding. I couldn't move.

"Come on."

All at once I stood up. "I gotta go," I said.

Troy just looked at me.

"It's getting dark," I added. "I gotta go."

I bolted out of his room and down the stairs, not waiting for Troy to respond, zipping up as I ran along. Mr. Kitchens was still plopped in front of the TV set, but now he was sound asleep and snoring. The car chase was still screeching along.

I'd have to walk home. I figured it was not really that much farther than walking home from school, and I did that all the time. Except then I was wearing boots and a winter coat. Now, with the sun setting, it was getting very cold, and my thin polyester suit didn't do much to protect me. My shoes and socks were still damp from the walk over. But there was no other option. I just trudged down the road.

I didn't know what to think. Except that Troy was a homosexual. That much seemed clear. Only a homosexual would do what he'd done.

But I'd liked it. Liked it a lot. Even if, at the moment, I was feeling a combination of both euphoria and nausea. Part of the muzziness was likely the pot. Part of it was something else entirely.

I thought of Chipper, of how disgusted he'd be. How much he'd hate me if he knew what had happened up in Troy's room. With a mounting sadness, I realized that what I'd done with Troy made me different, very different, from Chipper. I thought of Chipper's underwear, the ones I held at night when I slept. I felt ashamed.

I pushed on, walking through snowbanks, grateful when I discovered a stretch of sidewalk that had been shoveled. I was starting to shiver. The wind was whipping up the flaps of my suit jacket. My cheeks and hands were getting hard and numb. The sun had nearly set now, the sky a cold slate gray. I got a little lost at one point, not really sure if I should have gone left instead of right on Burnside Avenue; the buildings here didn't seem familiar. But then I recognized a yellow house on the corner and knew I was going the right way. Home was only a few more blocks.

It was then that I heard the motorcycle behind me. It was so loud, it sounded like an airplane coming in for a landing. It zipped past me, rattling to a halt at the stop sign at the end of the block. The driver was a big guy in black leather. And holding on to him, clinging to him so she wouldn't fall off, was my mother, still in her church dress.

I stopped in my tracks. As I watched, Mom got off the bike. The driver revved his engine, and Mom leaned in to say something to him. Then he roared off.

My mind was overloading. With everything that had just happened, I couldn't quite process this new information—my mother riding on the back of a motorcycle with some guy I didn't know.

She turned and saw me.

"Danny!"

I wanted to run. That was my first instinct. I wanted to run away from her. Run away from my own mother. But instead, slowly, I began walking toward her. Her eyes were wide, and I grew anxious. I was worried that she'd yell at me for being outside without an overcoat, for mucking up my suit with snow and mud. But that would have meant she was the old mom, and not the woman she had become. As I neared her, I saw it wasn't anger that energized her eyes. Instead, she glowed with excitement. Her skin was flushed red with adrenaline.

"Oh, Danny!" she exclaimed, grabbing me by the shoulders with her big hands. Our eyes were level. For the first time, I realized I was now as tall as my mother. When had that happened? "Our prayers have been answered!" she cried.

"Mom, why were you on a motorcycle?"

"That man," she said, near tears, "is an angel. An angel sent by God to bring Becky home to us."

I didn't know what she was talking about.

"Danny, that was Warren! Do you remember Warren? He called months ago and said he'd seen Becky with a man on Cape Cod."

"Yeah, I remember. . . ."

"That was *him!* He called again this morning! I told him I had to go to the funeral, but I'd meet with him afterward. He came to the church, anyway, because he thought if we left *right then,* we could maybe catch up with Becky!"

My eyes widened. "Did you? Did you find Becky?"

"No," Mom said, and she tried to cover her disappointment. "But we spoke with several people who told me they'd seen her, too."

"Are you going to call Detective Guthrie?"

"No." Mom's eyes hardened. "Listen to me, Danny. I need your help in this. We can't call the cops. Out of the question."

"Why?"

"Because if the bikers get a clue that we're on to them, they'll split. They'll take Becky and split."

"Split?"

"Yeah, you know. Leave town. Every biker I spoke with today told me the same thing. They said I should do this on my own. That I mustn't involve the cops."

"But—"

"Danny, listen to me!" Mom's eyes were wild. Her hands were still on my shoulders, and they gripped me so hard, it hurt. "I need your help! You've got to help me with this!"

"Okay," I said in a small voice.

"Your father can't know, either." She looked at me sternly. "You know why, don't you, Danny? I think you do."

I thought of my father, stinking of cologne, his eyes bloodshot and distant. I thought of how he went to work in the morning in a daze and sometimes didn't come home until late at night. "Yeah," I said. "I think I know why."

"Good. So it's got to be just me and you, Danny. You understand that?" She had started to cry. "Will you help me, Danny? Will you help me find Becky?"

"Yes," I said.

She pulled me into her, hugging me tight, pressing me into those big, cushiony breasts of hers. For one second, I closed my eyes and felt her warmth. I wondered if now, with her arms around me, she'd notice how wet my suit was and wonder why I was out in the cold without a coat.

She broke the embrace to look me straight in the eyes.

"Danny," she said, her voice firm, "we will both need to be brave if we do this. Do you feel brave?"

"Yes."

But I was lying.

"Oh, Danny," Mom said, "I'll love you forever if you find Becky for me."

Then, with her arm around my waist, we walked back to our house.

PALM SPRINGS

For a week, I'd been unable to sleep. I'd get into bed and then lie there for hours, wide awake, staring at the ceiling, listening to Frank snore, playing out erotic scenarios involving Kelly in my mind. I'd imagine taking him on a trip—to Mexico or the Caribbean—conjuring up images of the two of us strolling along a beach, moonlit of course, hand in hand, heart to heart. A thousand times I relived those moments when I kissed him, tasting his lips, breathing the fragrance of his hair. Against the linen of my pillowcase, I'd rub my cheek, imagining it to be Kelly.

And then Frank would turn, his arm reaching out for me, and I'd feel guilty.

That was why I couldn't lie to him. Not again.

"His name is Kelly," I said. "He's a bartender at Blame it on Midnight. I met him through Donovan."

"Oh," Frank said, hunched, as usual, over his desk, reading a student essay. "That's fine, Danny. What time are you thinking?"

"I told him to be here at eight."

"Fine, fine." He was barely listening to me.

"Frank."

"Mmm?"

I paused. "Maybe we might . . . well, I'm thinking that . . . he's very attractive and—"

That got Frank to look up at me. "Oh," he said. A small smile crossed his face. "I see. That's why you invited him to dinner."

"Well," I said, "that's not the only reason."

And it wasn't. My fantasies of Kelly didn't always involve sex. And when they did, the sex usually came long after our moonlit strolls, our whispered confidences, our tender caresses. Many a boy there was that I'd see at clubs and imagine taking home to fuck. But from the very first time I'd laid eyes on him, my fascination with Kelly hadn't been sexual. It had been something much, much more than that. My fantasies about him were never masturbatory. That would have felt wrong. *Dirty,* even. I didn't want to fuck Kelly. I wanted to make love to him like no one had ever made love to him before.

Frank was still smiling. "Let's see if I'm in the mood. If I'm not, you can take him out to the casita, like you did Ollie."

That was what I was counting on: Frank being too tired—and giving me the freedom to have Kelly all to myself.

I turned away. I didn't like how I was thinking. This whole dinner was manipulative on my part. Ever since the other night, I had wanted desperately to see Kelly again. But I couldn't sneak out the way I had last time. I hated myself for lying to Frank. Just what a scoundrel I had become was made very clear when I called Hassan and asked him to cover for me in case Frank ever mentioned our so-called dinner date the other night. "Are you asking me to lie, Danny?" Hassan had replied. "Because I cannot do that." I'd argued that it was because I'd been out buying Frank a gift for his birthday—which was months away, and yet another lie layered on top of the first. Only reluctantly had Hassan agreed to the ruse.

So there I was, contriving a dinner engagement that could include Frank and would thereby forestall any guilt. But I couldn't deny that I was hoping the night would end with Frank excusing himself and heading into our room to sleep alone. It was a Sunday night, after all: he had school in the morning. And then Kelly and I would have time to sit by ourselves, maybe take a swim in the pool, and yes, maybe wind up in the casita.

Heading into the kitchen, taking the chicken out of the refrigerator, I felt just as guilty as I had on my first date with Kelly.

It was crazy. Frank and I had been nonmonogamous for our entire twenty years. In the past, there had been plenty of occasions where I'd tell him that I was interested in some guy, and he'd ask which one, and together we'd cruise him at the gym or at the Abbey. We'd find a way to meet him, to size him up, and possibly bring him home. But that hadn't happened in quite some time now, I realized. Instead, the way it usually went these days was the way it had gone with Ollie: I'd chat with some guy online, and we'd make plans to meet. Sometimes Frank would join us; other times, he'd take a pass—the more likely scenario of late. Frank usually excused himself by claiming he was tired. I wondered if that was the whole reason. But I never asked Frank about it. I guess I didn't really want to know.

I set my mind on preparing the dinner. Not only did I dislike cooking, but I wasn't very good at it: it was one gay gene that I was missing. Frank wasn't all that fond of kitchen duty himself, but he was better than I was. Back in the old days, when Frank was still teaching high school and I was still auditioning my ass off for jobs that never materialized, I'd come home all depressed, and Frank would be there, cooking away. He knew all my favorites—fried chicken, baked macaroni and cheese, his mother's meat loaf recipe—white-trash comfort food all around—and I'd often come home to find him whipping up one of them. Those were bleak days for me, when all my great plans for success as an actor suddenly began to feel foolish. I'd look in the mirror before an audition and trace the small lines that had begun webbing outward from my eyes, and I'd whisper, "Danny Fortunato, what were you thinking? Who were you trying to impress? Kids from East Hartford don't become television stars."

And yet, looking back, those days didn't seem quite so bleak anymore. Funny what the rosy glow of nostalgia can do for the past. After dinner, Frank and I would sometimes take a run on the beach. We'd race each other. On warm days we'd run in the surf, laughing as the waves crashed against us, knocking us down. We had a dog in those days, too. Her name was Pixie. She was a pure white bichon frise, a little curlicue of a dog, with black button eyes and a tail that was always wagging. Other guys would laugh at us for having such a sissy dog instead of a big butch shepherd or setter. But Pixie was perfect for us. She'd run with us on the beach and stare in uncomprehending wonder whenever a bigger dog would bark at her, as if she were thinking, *What's the problem? Why can't we all get along?* At home, Pixie would run around in manic circles, ending with a giddy collapse onto her back, at which time Frank and I would both pounce, faces first, to nuzzle her silky stomach.

Pixie lived a good long life. We got her as a puppy, and she was with us for eleven years. Like a lot of older bichons, she got cancer, and Frank and I made the decision to put her down. We went together to the vet. Poor old Pixie had gotten so thin, so frail. She was almost blind. No more running in crazy circles in the living room. Frank held her in his arms as the vet readied the syringe. At the exact moment the needle pierced her skin, the tiny spark of life was extinguished in her button eyes. We both saw her go. Frank began to sob, and the heartless vet looked at me and asked if I could step into the next room and make payment. When he offered to "dispose of" the body for us, we recoiled. Instead, we wrapped Pixie in a blanket and carried her home, talking and singing to her lifeless little body. We buried her in our backyard in West Hollywood. When we left that place, how I hated knowing we had to leave her little dog skeleton behind.

Every once in a while, Frank and I would talk about getting another dog, but we never made the move. We told ourselves that when I finally moved out to Palm Springs full time, we'd go to the kennel and pick out another bichon. But it had been four years now since I'd been in the desert, and we'd made no addition to our family. We'd stopped talking about it, in fact. We hardly ever mentioned Pixie anymore, and that made me sad. When she died, I was so bereft, crying for days. I never wanted to stop grieving, because it would mean I'd forgotten what she felt like, how she smelled, how she sounded. But indeed weeks—months—now went by when Pixie never passed through my thoughts. I supposed that was called healing. But when suddenly I would flash on her, when something would remind me of her and that little white face would pop into my mind, I'd hate the fact that I hadn't thought of her in so long. Mom had never done that. She'd always said that if we stopped expecting Becky to come through the front door, she never would.

The chicken was marinating; the vegetables were cut; the salad was made. Now all that was left was to fire up the grill. I wasn't much of a cook, but barbecues I could handle. Frank came out of his office and told me he was going to have a run. I was surprised; he hadn't been running in a few years. But the nights were a little cooler now, and he said he wanted to start getting back into shape. I wondered if Kelly's imminent arrival had anything to do with his motivation. I told him not to overdo it and headed into the bathroom to take a shower.

He didn't listen to me. When he came back about forty minutes later, he was panting, and his face was all red. He stood behind me as I shaved at the mirror. He was chugging a bottle of water.

"Frank," I scolded, "you can't get dehydrated like that."

"I know, I know, baby," he said. He came up behind me, planting a kiss on the back of my neck. He was warm and moist, and I could hear his heart beating. "But it felt good, nonetheless." We exchanged a small smile in the foggy mirror.

I wasn't sure what to wear. I'd been somewhat dressy for dinner at Spencer's. Tonight I thought I'd wear something that showed off my body a little more. I'd been to the gym that afternoon, and I figured I was still pumped up enough to pull off a tight black tee and a pair of low-rise Levi's. I glanced in the full-length mirror behind the door to the bedroom and admired my shape. I'd come a long way since that skinny kid in a thong dancing on top of a box. Taking out some Brylcreem, I slicked my hair back, hoping to look hip. It made my hairline seem even more receded than it was, but it was too late to wash out the gunk now. I paused as I studied myself in the mirror. Once again, the face staring back at me seemed to be someone else's. When had my face changed? I ran a finger along my jaw. Whoever's face it was, it would have to do.

Kelly arrived exactly on time. As soon as I opened the door, my heart was again pounding in my ears. He was holding a bottle of wine.

"I told you not to bring anything," I said, stepping aside to let him enter. "But thank you." I took the bottle from him. He had left the price sticker on. Nine ninety-nine. My heart broke with affection.

"Nice place," he said, looking around.

He was even more beautiful than I remembered. Just what made him more so, I couldn't quite pinpoint. But he was. He was dressed almost the same as he was the other night, with his brown corduroys and white running shoes. His sweater was navy blue this time, and there was no shirt apparent underneath. Maybe it was the stubble, heavier than usual, that made his golden skin stand out even more tonight.

I showed him around the house. The kitchen, the backyard, the pool, the spa. Then we peeked into the office. On one side was Frank's desk, with all his papers and books. On the other was my work station, taken up by my Power Mac G5 Quad and its two thirty-inch monitors, as well as my HP laser printer, which was, at the moment, spitting out gallery-quality photos, thirteen by nineteen inches. I'd set it to print about fifteen minutes earlier so that when Kelly walked in, the office would look all high tech. I wanted him to see my office humming and be impressed with my work.

Be impressed with me.

He was. "Wow," he said, lifting a photo from the printer tray. "This is gorgeous. It looks more like a painting than it does a photo. Who are they?"

"They were with me that night at the Parker," I said. "That's my friend Randall, there, and this is the guy he's dating, Hassan."

I had posed them the other morning at the top of the North Lykken Trail at the end of Ramon Road. The sky was pink, the mountains were blue, and their faces were an odd mix of gold and purple. I had jacked up the color on the computer and obliterated many of the lines and speckles on their faces, turning them almost into statues. I was pretty pleased with the piece. I was planning on giving it to Randall for Christmas.

"Wow," Kelly said again, still looking down at the image. "You see, *this* is why I can't show you my sketches."

"You're being silly," I told him.

"Danny, you're a real artist. I just do it as a hobby."

I beamed. I liked hearing Kelly call me an artist. "You sell your-self short," I said, echoing what Frank had said to me for so many years. I took a step closer to Kelly and looked deep into those shiny black eyes of his. "Here's an idea. Someday we ought to scan one of your sketches into the computer, and then I can play around with it. Might turn out pretty cool."

"Really?" he asked. "You'd really do that?"

"Sure," I said. "In fact, we could—"

"Hello?"

We both turned. Frank stood in the doorway, freshly showered, smelling like lavender skin lotion. The first thing I noticed when I looked at him was his hair, so thin and lightweight, it was kind of sticking up. Then I realized he'd gelled it that way, maybe to look a little younger, a little more hip. My heart broke. He'd also nicked himself shaving his chin, and the brown spots that pa-raded across his high forehead seemed more pronounced than usual.

"Oh," I said. "Frank, this is Kelly Nelson. Kelly, Frank Wilson."

They shook hands.

"Welcome," Frank said. "I see you're getting the tour."

"Yeah," Kelly replied. "These are some amazing pictures."

He gestured around the room. Other examples of my work hung on the walls. There were cacti, palm trees, the Grand Canyon, Maui's Haleakala volcano, the Seattle Space Needle, the London Eye, all looking like something other than what they were. I thrust my hands down into my pockets and grinned.

"Danny's quite the artist, isn't he?" Frank asked, looking from me to Kelly. "They look almost like paintings, don't they?"

"That's what I just said," Kelly replied.

We moved out into the dining area.

"I remember when Danny first started playing with his photos on the computer," Frank was saying. "He was like a kid who'd found a new toy. He'd be up all night, printing out images, and I'd say, 'Baby, come to bed.' But he'd be up until dawn some-times, playing with images. I knew then he'd make it big."

Frank smiled at both of us. His little speech had made me oddly uncomfortable, but I smiled back at him.

"Can I get you a drink?" he asked Kelly.

"Maybe some wine."

Frank nodded. "Excellent. Danny's barbecuing chicken, and he's always heavy with the sauce, so how about if we break tradition and go with a red? A nice Shiraz?"

"Sounds good to me," Kelly said.

The conversation went as well as could be expected. Frank got the basics from Kelly—San Francisco, the foster homes, the bus ride to L.A. Kelly gave a quick rundown of the various bars and restaurants he'd worked at in the desert, without explaining what had ended his time at each. He hadn't shared those details with me, either. I knew only what Thad had told me.

"But Kelly's not going to be a bartender forever," I said. "He's an artist, too." I lifted my glass of wine in his direction.

Kelly seared me with his eyes. "Don't say that."

"But he is," I told Frank. "You should see his sketches. He's—"

"Please *stop*," Kelly said in a voice that would have slit my throat had he been any closer. His black eyes blazed. I just lifted my hand in a gesture of "okay."

A couple moments of awkward silence ensued. We were sitting in the living room, Frank and Kelly on the sofa and me across the room, on the ottoman. Finally, Frank broke the tension by saying, "That's another one of Danny's," and indicating the sunflower hanging over the mantel. "I call it my green daisy."

"It's beautiful," Kelly said, looking up at it.

I stood. "Well, how about if I put the chicken on the grill? Frank, the salad's in the refrigerator. Will you get it?"

"All righty," Frank said, standing and following me out of the room.

"Can I do anything to help?" Kelly asked.

"Nope," I told him, carrying the marinated chicken out onto the deck. "You'll see. When I cook, it's definitely no frills."

"I don't like frills, anyway," he said.

Our eyes caught. He smiled at me. I nearly dropped the platter of chicken.

We sat outside to eat, under the stars. Once again, Kelly delighted me with his enthusiasm, tearing away at his chicken, getting barbecue sauce on his chin and his nose. I couldn't help laughing.

"I'm glad you like my cooking," I told him.

"It's delicious," he said.

Frank was eating more neatly, cutting his chicken into small pieces. Into the front of his shirt, he'd tucked a napkin. "Yes, indeed, Danny," he echoed. "It's delicious."

The conversation was banal. There were no jokes, as there had been last time, no silly humor. I missed that. Instead, we talked some more about restaurants, which ones we liked, which ones we didn't care for. We talked about Thad Urquhart and the rumors that he might run for mayor. Kelly liked Thad; he told us he'd paid him very well for his private party. We talked about Donovan and Penelope Sue. Kelly made sure only to say the most complimentary things about them, especially Penelope Sue. She was so generous to the community, he said, always giving money to every cause. He made no mention this time of her eye rolling. And after the look I'd gotten earlier in the living room, I wasn't about to bring up anything again unless Kelly brought it up first.

Dessert was lime sorbet and wafer cookies. For this, we moved back into the living room. I refilled everyone's wineglass. I noticed as Kelly's eye caught something in the bookcase on the side of the mantel.

"Are those photo albums?" he asked.

"Yes," I said. "From back in the days when we actually had photos to put in albums. Nowadays they're all on my laptop or my phone."

Kelly was smirking. "You said you'd show me pictures of your stripper days."

"Oh, God."

This made Frank laugh. "Do you know that's how we met?" He looked over at me, but I chose not to make eye contact. Instead, I stood to fetch the photo album from the bookcase. "Danny was dancing at some club in West Hollywood," Frank began explaining. "And when I left to go home, he came running out after me onto the street. 'Where you going? Where you going?'" He laughed. "He was frantic. I couldn't believe he did that. Right, Danny? I was practically speechless. Wasn't I, Danny?"

I didn't look at him.

"Wow, that's kind of romantic," Kelly said.

"Yeah," Frank said, sipping his wine and smiling. "I suppose it kind of is."

I made no comment. I sat down on the floor, at Kelly's feet, and opened the photo album. "Let's see," I said. "Those pictures should be in here."

Kelly moved forward so he could look over my shoulder. Frank slid over on the couch so he could get a look himself. I was busy flipping pages.

"Here," I said, tapping the page. "That's me."

Kelly leaned in.

Under the Mylar plastic cover, a skinny blond kid stood on a box, his yellow thong stuffed with tens and twenties. And all of a sudden, I missed that kid terribly. I missed his energy and his freedom, the way he stayed up until four in the morning and slept in past noon. I missed the way he could swing his hips up on his box and excite an entire room of men. I missed the sex with strangers. I even missed the drugs.

"Hot," was Kelly's verdict.

"Yeah, he was, wasn't he?" Frank echoed.

"Was," I said, staring at the photo. "The operative word."

"Oh, come on now, Danny," Frank said.

I flipped the page. "And here," I said, "is Randall and me at Disneyland."

It was from the same time period. Randall and I were grinning stupidly as we posed with Snow White in front of the entrance to Tomorrowland. I was wearing a tight little Bundeswehr tank top, and my hair was spiked up eighties style. Maybe that was the look Frank had been trying for tonight. I'd feel terribly sad if that was the case. His hair gel had troubled me all through dinner.

"Hey," Kelly asked, leaning in. "That's the guy from the pic in your office, isn't it? The one you worked over on the computer?"

"Yep."

"That's cool that you're still friends."

I could feel his breath on my neck as he looked over my shoulder. My skin tingled with his electricity. Every once in a while, his knees brushed against my shoulders. I was getting a hard-on and shifted my legs to make it less obvious.

I continued flipping pages.

"Hey," Kelly said. "Was that you, Frank?"

"Where?"

Kelly reached down over my shoulder to point, his arm grazing my chest. I got a whiff of his cologne. In my pants, my dick got harder.

"Yes," Frank said, laughing. "That's me. A little more hair back then."

"You were good-looking," Kelly said.

"As Danny would say, *were* is the operative word," Frank noted.

I responded perfunctorily. "And as you would say, 'Come now, Frank.'"

"I didn't mean it that way," Kelly said. "You're still very good-looking."

I realized he hadn't said that about me.

"Do you remember that night, Danny?" Frank was asking, indicating the photo.

I gazed down at it. There we were, holding up glasses of champagne, staring into the camera. Frank had set the camera on an empty box and pushed the timer, hurrying around to huddle with me on the floor. Pixie had sat between us. We'd raised our glasses, and the camera had flashed. A moment preserved for posterity.

"Of course, I do," I said, still not looking around at him. "It was the night we moved in together for the first time."

"Yeah," Frank said, and I could hear his smile in his voice. "It was a great apartment. We had a little view out of the bathroom window. You could see down onto Santa Monica Boulevard if you craned your neck." He laughed.

"Where was it?" Kelly asked.

"Holloway," Frank said. I recognized the tone in his voice. It was his nostalgic voice, the one he always got when we looked at old photos. I could predict what he'd say next, and I was right. "That first night, Danny wanted to make dinner. Said it wouldn't be a home until he'd made dinner for the first time for us. Well, neither of us is a cook, but he had his grandmother's recipe for baked macaroni and cheese. Well, he whipped it up and put it in the oven and—"

"And the baking dish shattered, and the fucking cheese went

everywhere," I finished, cutting him off. "You *do* love to tell that story, don't you, Frank?"

"We've laughed about it for years."

I snorted. "Maybe you have." I turned around to look over my left shoulder. That way I could make eye contact with Kelly while avoiding Frank. "Apparently, the baking dish wasn't Pyrex. How would I know? I was just a kid."

"The smoke was *everywhere*," Frank continued. "The smoke alarms all went off. We were scraping cheese out of that oven for weeks."

Kelly was smiling. "Guess you had to send out for Chinese."

"That's exactly what we did!" Frank clapped Kelly on the back. "Did he tell you this story already?"

"No. I just know what I would have done."

I was ready to close the photo album, but now Kelly wanted to see more pictures of Pixie. I flipped a couple more pages ahead and found one.

"She's so cute," Kelly said. "Who's the other guy?"

In the photo, I was holding Pixie. Flanking me were Frank and Gregory Montague.

Frank paused a moment when he saw Gregory. "Oh, that's an old friend of mine," he said softly.

"Frank's one true love," I said brightly, slamming the album shut.

Behind me, I felt rather than saw the look Frank gave to Kelly. "He always says that," he said, sounding a bit exasperated.

I stood, handing the photo album to Kelly. "Have a look if you like," I said. "Does anyone want more wine? I do."

"I'll have a little," Kelly said.

"Not for me, thanks, Danny," Frank said.

When I came back in the room, carrying the bottle, I found that Kelly had indeed begun perusing the pages of the album again. He was showing a photo to Frank, who sat close to him now on the couch.

"Is that the same guy?" he was asking.

Frank nodded. "Yes. That's Gregory."

"He looks sick."

Frank just continued to nod, staring down at the photo. "He was. That was taken a few weeks before he died."

I sat down on Kelly's other side, refilling his glass. "Frank took care of Gregory in his last months," I said. "He was always going up to his place on Mulholland Drive. Sometimes he wouldn't be home for days. None of Gregory's other friends could deal with it. Frank was the only one who remained devoted. He was a real angel to Gregory."

I hoped my words sounded sincere. I meant them to be.

Kelly turned the page. "Who's this with him?" he asked, pointing to a shirtless youth with stringy blond hair.

"That's Christopher, Gregory's last boyfriend," Frank told him, his voice still far away. He gave a little laugh. "Gregory always liked them young."

I laughed, too, but louder and more obviously. "You're telling me. At least Christopher never knew what it was like to get discarded when he got too old."

Once the words were out, I realized they may have come across way too harsh. I regretted what I'd said, and tried to soften it.

"But I think Christopher cared about Gregory, and I know he felt bad that he couldn't handle Gregory's illness. But he was so young, after all. What was he? Twenty-two? Twenty-three?" I took a sip of wine. "Christopher did try to make amends years later, when he got a job at Disney. I know when he hired me to do those images for Disneyland, it was a way of making it up to Gregory, or at least to Frank."

"Danny," Frank said, "Christopher hired you because you do good work."

"Yeah." I laughed. "Work he never would have seen without a call from you, asking him to look at my portfolio."

"Be that as it may," Frank said.

I took another sip of wine. I took it as kind of a consolation prize that something had finally come out of that horrible night with Gregory twenty years ago. At long last, Gregory Montague had helped me to get ahead—albeit indirectly, and several years after he was dead.

We sat in silence. The only sound was the ticking of the clock on the mantel. Kelly continued to quietly flip through the pages of the album. I think he'd decided that he'd asked enough questions for one night.

I stood suddenly, almost spilling the glass of wine in my hand. "How about a dip in the pool?" I asked. "It's a beautiful night."

"I *think*," Frank said, standing himself, "that I am going to hit the hay. I'm exhausted from that run I took earlier. But you boys should go in." He gave me a twinkle, as if to say, "It's fine. Do what you like."

I'd arranged it perfectly. Like clockwork.

There was an awkward hug between Frank and Kelly, and a kiss for me on my cheek. Then Frank headed down the hall to our room.

"Shall we?" I asked Kelly.

"I don't have a bathing suit," he said.

I laughed. "Did you think I was going to wear one?"

He seemed unsure but followed me outside, anyway. In one hand I carried my glass of wine; in the other, the bottle. Setting them down on a table on the deck, I refilled my glass and indicated Kelly should give me his. We clinked a nonverbal toast. From the cabana I produced towels, then pulled off my shirt. I thought I looked pretty good. I tightened my abs just to be sure.

I was feeling cocky. Stripping out of my pants, I executed a perfect dive into the water, slicing the surface with hardly a splash. When I came up, I shook my hair, water spraying all around me, the faint aroma of chlorine in my nose. Kelly was still removing his sweater, then slowly unbuckling his belt. He was unbelievably beautiful. Not as tight and lean as I'd expected; there was a little bit of extra flesh around the middle. But when he pulled down his pants, I saw one monster of a cock, thick and uncut. He seemed embarrassed to be naked. He gripped the aluminum handrails of the ladder and climbed down into the pool, with more than a little self-consciousness.

"Hey," I called over to him. "What do you call cows with a sense of humor?"

He moved toward me through the water. "You know, Danny, I probably should apologize for the other night."

I was treading water with my feet. "Apologize? Why?"

"All those jokes and stuff." He gave me a weak smile. "I was pretty manic."

"You were fine. I had fun."

"I did, too." He looked up at the moon. "But I was nervous to meet you. So I did a line of coke before going to the restaurant."

"You *did?*" I didn't quite know what to say. "Why were you nervous to meet me?"

"Because you're so . . . you know. Successful."

I laughed. The irony was too much. I'd thought I'd been the one who'd been anxious before dinner, that I'd been the one who'd been nervous about meeting him.

"Kelly," I said, "I hope you realize now there was no need to be nervous."

The moonlight reflected in those big black eyes. "I don't get asked out to dinner by guys like you very often."

"Oh, come on," I said. "You're fucking gorgeous. You're a bartender. You must get hit on all the time."

"I don't know if I'm all that attractive, but sure, I get hit on." He moved closer to me. I was now leaning against the side of the pool, my arms stretched out on either side. "But that was the thing. You didn't hit on me. You said you wanted to see my drawings."

I smiled a little.

"You're out of my league," he said to me.

I could barely reply. "You've got to be joking," I finally said.

"No, I'm not. I look around at you and your house and Frank and the life you guys have, and I think, 'Will I ever have that?' I just can't imagine it. I'm going to be twenty-seven next year. *Twenty-seven!* And I still don't have a clue as to what I'm doing with my life, or where I want it to go."

"Twenty-seven is nothing," I said. "You've got plenty of time."

"Yeah, keep saying that and I'll be fucking thirty!" His voice was louder now. "I mean, it's so frustrating! I get a job, and then I get fired. I start to save money, and then I get laid off. I mean, I was supposed to be Jacqueline Fucking Onassis! And here I am, still bartending at dives in the desert, with nothing to show for myself. Nothing."

"Oh, I don't know about that."

"Why do you think I didn't want you to come to my apartment? Because it's a pit. A studio with a mattress. I don't have any furniture. I'm twenty-fucking-six and nothing to show for it!"

His face was a mask of despair. I touched his cheek. "You've got plenty of time, baby."

"No. Not plenty of time."

"Sure you do."

His eyes were wild. "When did you meet Frank?"

I hesitated. "Twenty-one."

"Right. And by my age, you had a whole life going for you. Don't tell me you didn't. I saw it in those pictures. You were younger than I was, and you had Frank and a real home and even a dog!"

"Yes," I said, "but, Kelly, it was a long, long time before I figured out I wasn't going to make it as an actor. It took me until I was in my *thirties* to wake up and decide to do something else. This art stuff is still relatively new."

He was floating away from me. "So what?" he called over his shoulder. "You had a *life*. You had Frank. I wonder if I'll ever have that. If I'll ever fall in love and have somebody in my life. I envy what you guys have. I can see it. Not only in the pictures, but in the way you talk to each other. I can see all the history between you. There's a real commitment there."

My commitment to Frank was definitely not what I wanted to be talking about at that particular moment. I started to say something to get us back on track—the track that led out to the casita. But Kelly took a deep breath and, lifting his shoulders and pushing himself forward, slipped headfirst under the water to swim across the length of the pool. I watched his body move under the surface, transfixed. When he emerged at the other end, his body, strong and solid, glistened in the moonlight. He stretched his arms out at his sides, the eagle tattoo above his shoulders spreading its wings in unison. If he'd asked me a question at the moment, I would have been unable to answer. I was too overcome.

"Laughing stock," he said, turning to face me.

I stared at him across the pool, not understanding

He smiled. "Cows with a sense of humor."

"Damn," I managed to say. "You just can't be stumped, can you?"

"Nope."

Our eyes held.

Then I copied his swim. Dropping down under the water, I swam close to the bottom of the pool until I saw his feet. Rising past his legs and his cock and his stomach, I emerged from the water directly in front of him. We stood nose to nose.

"You are so incredibly beautiful," I said, shaking water from my hair.

He said nothing, so I kissed him.

He was like stone.

I pulled back. He was looking at me.

"I can't," he said.

"Can't what?"

"Frank is inside."

I smiled. "It's okay. Frank is cool about this. We have one of those marriages you so admire. With all that freedom and individuality."

He lifted his eyebrows.

"It's why we've lasted so long," I explained. "We give each other freedom. We play together and we play separately. It's cool. I wouldn't have kissed you if it needed to be a secret."

"I still can't," he said.

"Why?"

He shrugged. "I just feel odd about it. I mean, he's right inside. Only a few yards away."

"We can go to the casita," I said.

"No," he said. "I can't. Not after all those pictures."

"It's not an issue—"

"*No*," he said sharply, moving aside and hoisting himself out of the pool.

I followed. "Hey, look. I didn't mean to—"

"It's totally cool," he said. His wet feet slapped against the concrete. We both left trails of water as we headed for the towels hanging on the chairs. Kelly was quick to cover his nakedness.

"I'm sorry," I said. "It's just that . . . I'm very attracted to you. More than to anyone in a very long time."

He was discreetly drying himself off. "I'm flattered. You're a great guy."

"And I want to help you."

His eyes flickered over to me.

"Hey," I said. "I know what it's like. To leave home, to head someplace and try to make something of yourself. There were lots of times I was just as frustrated as you are right now. And you're right. I was lucky. I had Frank to believe in me." I drew closer to him. "Maybe you just need someone to believe in you."

He was silent.

"Can I kiss you good night?" I asked.

He nodded. I kissed him. This time, to my great satisfaction, he kissed me back a little.

Then he got dressed. He must have thanked me a dozen times for dinner. I walked him out to his car, an old Mercedes C-Class model, probably 1995 or so. Its white exterior was a little rusted, and the backseat was loaded with bags and magazines. I imagined at one time it was a beautiful car. I wondered how he'd gotten it. My guess was Donovan Hunt. So Kelly hadn't rated a brand-new car.

We hugged; he thanked me again; then he drove off. I went back inside. I was filled up with the thought and the scent of him. I couldn't go to bed just yet, slide in next to Frank and listen to him snore. So I headed into my office and sat down at my desk, staring at the photos on my wall.

But instead of any of my own images, I was drawn to the tiny little frame off to my right. Lifting it from its hook, I brought it close to my face. I knew who those people were. I'd memorized them long ago. From person to person, I moved my finger. David and Honora Horgan, white haired and shriveled, my great-great-grandparents from Ballyhooley, County Cork, Ireland. Daniel Horgan, buttoned up and somber faced, my great-grandfather and namesake. His wife, Emily, and their daughter, Adele, who became Nana to me.

Finally, there was my grandfather, Sebastian Fortunato, the first Eye-talian to crash the Horgan family, and in Nana's arms, my father, in a bundle of white lace.

And someday I was supposed to take another picture of Dad and Mom and Nana and me and Joey . . .

"Danny?"

I turned.

Frank was in the doorway.

"Everything okay?"

"Yes," I said softly.

"Come to bed," he whispered.

I waited a few moments, still staring down at the photo; then I replaced it on the wall and followed Frank into our room.

EAST HARTFORD

It was the last day of my freshman year. I had made it. I had made it through an entire year at that hated place. Brother Pop stood in front of my last class of the day, admonishing us all to spend our summers as good Christian young men. I heard snickering from the back row. A straw wrapper shot past my ear. Then the bell rang.

"Thank God that's over," Troy said as we headed down the hill on our walk home.

"Two and a half months of freedom!" I shouted.

Since it was our last day, we'd been permitted to doff the shirts and ties for once. I'd worn a T-shirt emblazoned with the enormous face of Deborah Harry. Troy's shirt read THE KNACK in big white letters. Free of books, we bolted down the hill as fast as we could run.

"Pussy," Troy called, "I'll beat your ass!"

"Oh, no, you won't!"

I was a fast runner. There wasn't an athletic bone in my body, but I could probably outrun an elk. I arrived at the crossroads a full thirty seconds before Troy did. I stuck my tongue out at him.

"Don't stick that tongue out unless you plan on using it," Troy said.

I smirked. "That's for later."

Ever since that day at his house, we'd been sucking each other off whenever we had the chance. Once we even did it in the stalls of the boys' room at school, during rehearsals for the school play. The two months of rehearsing for that play were the best time of the whole year. We'd put on *How to Succeed in Business Without Really Trying* in conjunction with the girls at St. Clare's. Katie and the Theresas were in the chorus, too, but time had moved on, and we weren't really friends anymore. I hung out only with Troy. The play was the one extracurricular school activity I'd participated in all year, and I'd only signed up at the last minute because Troy had encouraged me.

Boy, was I glad he had. I'd loved, loved, *loved* opening night, made up with all that pancake and rushing out from behind the wings into the glare of the spotlights. I loved singing as loudly as I could, no matter if I was off-key. I loved parading around in costume in front of all those people in the auditorium, the smell of wood polish and floor wax filling my nostrils. Then and there, I'd decided that I wanted to be an actor. Next year, I'd vowed, I'd land a real part in the play. They were doing *Oliver!* next year, and even though the leads always went to juniors and seniors, I hoped I could snag a few lines in some small role. Already I'd checked out the play from the school library and decided I would try out for Mr. Brownlow, the guy who adopts Oliver. Mr. Brownlow didn't have to sing anything, which was good, because my singing voice was shit, but he had a whole mess of lines. I couldn't wait. Maybe even Mom and Dad would come this time.

"I got some really smooth weed," Troy was telling me, slightly out of breath.

"Excellento!"

I couldn't wait to get to Troy's house. I knew the routine. We'd say hello to the maid, grab a Coke from the refrigerator, then head upstairs to his room. We'd smoke a doobie and then start sucking face, which quickly moved to sucking cock. I no longer cared what it meant. So what if I was bisexual? David Bowie was, too, and David Bowie was very cool. And in an article I'd read in a *Rolling Stone* magazine that I found at Troy's house, Elton John said everyone was a little bit bisexual.

Everyone.

We were getting ready to cross the street when a gold Mustang Mach 1 pulled up alongside of us.

"Yo, Danny," Chipper said, leaning out the window. He was wearing a white T-shirt, and I noticed the way his bicep splayed against the car door. "You want a ride?"

"I'm going over to Troy's," I told him.

Chipper's eyes moved over to my friend. I didn't think Chipper liked Troy all that much. He never said anything about him, but sometimes when he saw us together, he kind of made a face. But Chipper had kept good on his promise to watch out for me. A few months ago, he'd had to intercede once again when he saw a bunch of idiots picking on me; he'd told them he'd crack their skulls together if he caught them being assholes to me ever again. After that, the harassment dropped into low key. The occasional paper airplane still bounced off my head, but word got around that I was friends with Chipper Paguni, and most of the kids backed off.

Friends with Chipper Paguni. That made me very pleased indeed.

Chipper moved his eyes back to me. "I can give you a ride to his house if you want," he said.

"Cool," I said, and we hopped into the car, Troy in back, me up front.

Once again, Aersomith was on the eight-track. Chipper lit up a cigarette as he steered the car back onto the road.

"So how's your mother?" he asked.

"Well, you know, the same."

He exhaled smoke. "Oh yeah, I do. She had some FBI guy come over and talk to me. Did you know that?"

"No."

"Man, my parents flipped. I mean, the fucking FBI!"

"What did they want?"

He took another drag on his cigarette, then let it out. "Same old shit. When did I last see Becky? Was I sure I'd never heard from her since? All that crap."

I shook my head. "I'm sorry."

"It's okay. I mean, your mom's just never gonna give up, huh?"

"No."

I looked out the window. It had been almost ten months now since Becky had disappeared, but Mom still got up every morning and went to her desk in the living room, like it was a job. She'd review her notes, pore over police reports, make phone calls. I knew she'd gone to the FBI, even if I was unaware that they'd paid a call on Chipper. Mom had had Bud the taxi driver haul her all the way down to the FBI office in New Haven. Armed with maps and signed statements from that guy Warren and his biker friends, she'd reported how a girl matching Becky's description had been seen on Cape Cod in the company of a biker known as Bruno. Bruno was "one mean son of a bitch," Warren had told Mom, and was part of a New England motorcycle gang. And since it would appear that Bruno had taken Becky across state lines, the responsibility of locating her now fell to the FBI. The agents had listened to her story politely and promised to look into it.

I didn't know if Mom was aware that they'd gone to see Chipper. She didn't talk much about her investigations these days, since they were the source of major tension between her and Dad. Some real doozies of fights had taken place lately. There was so much crying and so much shouting in our house that Father McKenna, the pastor of our church, suggested that Mom and Dad talk to a counselor. He found one for them, a lady named Dr. Page, and they went a few times. Once, they even dragged me along. "This affects you, too, Danny," Mom had insisted.

Dr. Page's office was downtown in one of those new, modern medical arts buildings with skylights and fake rubber tree plants. She wore hardly any makeup and said very little, just sat there and nodded as Mom ranted and raved. Dad would try to say a few words; then Mom would shout over him, and he'd sigh and retreat into silence. Dr. Page asked me how I felt about my sister being missing, and I told her I didn't know. Mom told me to stop being so stubborn. "He misses her terribly," she said. "You can see it. They were *very* close."

Dr. Page did explain that if Becky *had* been kidnapped, she might be suffering from something called Stockholm syndrome. She told us that a few years before, four hostages had been taken by bank robbers in Sweden, and eventually they became so brainwashed, so entranced with their captors, they didn't want to leave them. "Kind of like Patty Hearst," I said. Dr. Page smiled wide at me and replied, "Exactly, Danny." I felt proud of myself that I could contribute to the discussion.

But the visits to Dr. Page didn't end the strife between Mom and Dad. Dad thought Mom should just trust that the police were doing everything they could to find Becky. Mom disagreed, vehemently.

"The *police!*" she shrieked. "The fucking East Hartford police!" She had started swearing a lot. No one was surprised by it anymore. "I expected a hell of a lot more than what they've been doing. I expected helicopters with searchlights! I expected an all-points national bulletin!"

"Peggy, what the hell does that mean?" Dad asked.

"I don't know," Mom said. "But I expected it. And you should have, too! Becky is your daughter, too! You don't care about her like I do!"

I heard Dad slam the door and head down into the basement. He'd been going down there a lot in the last few months.

I was upstairs, listening. In this, I sided with Mom. Peter Guthrie, the detective in charge of finding Becky, just didn't get it. To him, Becky was just a picture on a xeroxed sheet stuck to a telephone pole. He didn't wake up from a sound sleep like Mom did, screaming that Becky was being raped in some abandoned warehouse. I'd hear her scream out in the middle of the night, and I'd lie there in bed, desperate and distressed, unable to bear the idea of my mother in such pain. When I was a boy and I'd get sick in the middle of the night, Mom had always been there with a bucket and cold damp cloth for my forehead. But there was nothing I could do for her in return. I hated the police for not making my mother's pain go away. They didn't even want to take her phone calls anymore.

"Don't tell me to trust the police!" Mom shouted from the top of the basement stairs down at my father. "That goddamn Guthrie didn't even take fingerprints from Becky's room until *three weeks ago!* He keeps telling me she's a runaway, that she'll come home when she's ready. He says I should just accept that! My Becky! A runaway! There's no reason in the world that she would've run away from home!"

Mom seemed to have forgotten the fights she and Becky had had in those last few weeks. They had fought over stupid stuff, like Becky being pissed at being Mom's personal chauffeur, and bigger stuff, like Mom insisting Chipper was a bad influence. But if Becky had run away, she would've come home sooner or later. I mean, she was just sixteen years old—okay, seventeen soon. But a teenage girl couldn't just leave home and get a job somewhere and start a new life.

Could she?

My whole freshman year in high school was now complete— and the whole time, Becky had been gone. It felt so strange. I mean, all last summer Becky had known how nervous I was and how unready I was to leave St. John's and all my friends. And she'd say, "Oh, Danny, don't be such a dweeb." It seemed so bizarre that she wasn't around now to look at me with that face she always gave me—the one that was so superior and condescending—and say, "Didn't I tell you that you'd get through it okay?"

That was when I started to agree with Mom. If Becky had run away, she'd have been home by now. She *must* have been kidnapped. It was the only explanation for why she'd been gone so long. And of all the leads that had come in, only Warren and his biker friends had ever come through with any kind of real description of Becky. Only Warren, out of all the leads we'd gotten, had mentioned the crescent moon birthmark on her arm. Dad countered that the descriptions of Becky that had been distributed everywhere had contained that bit of information, so it wasn't like Warren was telling us something he couldn't have known otherwise. Still, Mom was convinced he was the real deal.

I felt sad, sitting there in Becky's seat in Chipper's car, listening to Becky's favorite band. I remembered the cardboard fort we'd built in the giant maple tree in our yard when she was ten and I was eight. We'd sit up there on the branches and read comic books all day. I'd read *Green Lantern,* and she'd read *Betty and Veronica.* Mom would come out, pretending not to know where we were, and call our names. We'd giggle behind the pages of our comics. It all seemed so long ago now.

"Take this left up there," Troy said from the backseat, indicating his street.

Chipper grunted in reply.

He'd worn jeans to school. I'd thought about doing the same but wondered if that would be pushing the "dress down" rules too far. Chipper didn't worry about things like that. He just did what he wanted. I looked over at him, at his denim legs in the leather bucket seat. There was something about his thighs that made it hard for me to breathe. His legs really filled out his jeans. When I wore jeans, they just hung on me. I was such a beanpole, but Chipper worked out. He wasn't as big as a lot of the football players were, but you could see just by looking at him that he was strong. I wished I'd gotten to see Chipper play this year, but back during football season, Mom had never let me go out of the house except to go to school. It was right after Becky had disappeared, and she was paranoid that someone would snatch me, too. Now she didn't seem to notice when I was home or not, so consumed was she in her search.

I could see Troy's house up ahead. Suddenly I didn't want to get out of the car and leave Chipper. Without even thinking about it, I turned to him and blurted, "Do you want to come with us and smoke some pot?"

I knew Chipper liked marijuana. He'd admitted to smoking it with Becky. Of course, it wasn't my pot to offer. I didn't dare look around to see Troy's face.

Chipper stopped the car in front of the house. "You guys got pot?"

I nodded. "Yeah, up in Troy's room."

Chipper looked into the backseat.

"If you're thinking of being a narc," Troy said to him icily, "I will just deny it. There's no way to prove it."

"I could get kicked off the team," Chipper said. "I almost did once already." His eyes returned to me. Big brown eyes, which I fell into, headfirst. "So you guys gotta swear you'll never tell."

"Never!" I promised.

"Man, I'm not a narc," Troy told him.

The maid called a cheery greeting as the three of us clomped up the stairs. Only I responded, as usual.

With the door safely locked behind us, Chipper stood examining the plastic Corvette and the glow-in-the-dark skull as Troy lit the bong. We'd been using a bong lately. It was much more cool and far more effective than just passing around a joint. I'd never asked Troy where and how he got his pot. So much of his world was still a mystery to me. He was a year older than I was, having stayed back in fourth grade, but still, fifteen-year-old kids with their own personal drug dealers? There was so much that I never knew about. Before Becky's disappearance, I'd lived such a sheltered life.

"Good stuff," Chipper pronounced, taking a hit and passing the bong to me. "Very smooth."

"Yeah," I agreed, though I didn't know the difference between smooth marijuana and what? Rough marijuana?

We sat there, getting increasingly stoned, listening to the Patti Smith Group's *Easter* album. Troy was up on his bed, where, if Chipper hadn't been around, I would have been next to him. And by this point, we probably would have been sucking face. But instead, I was in the beanbag chair with Chipper, pressing my left thigh up against his right. I could sense that Troy was a little pissed that I wasn't up on the bed with him.

"Good tunes, man," Chipper was saying, taking another hit, then singing along. "Because the night belongs to lovers, because the night belongs to us . . ."

The warmth of his leg against mine felt incredible. I was getting hard. I could actually feel my cock moving in my pants.

Okay, so I could no longer deny why I'd stolen Chipper's underwear, why lately I'd begun to masturbate as I pressed the soft white cotton briefs to my face. I was bisexual. I liked guys *and* girls. Troy had taught me how to jerk off. Now I was obsessed with doing it. Sometimes I shot four or five loads a day, and usually Chipper's underpants were somewhere close by—though I made sure never to get them stained.

"Mmm," Chipper was moaning. He rested his head against the wall behind us and closed his eyes. Suddenly my heart was thudding in my chest. Did pot make boys horny? Was what I had done with Troy possible with *Chipper?*

The thought was staggering. I moved my hand so that it rested against Chipper's thigh. He didn't stir.

"Danny."

I looked over at Troy on the bed.

"Do you want to stay over for supper? The maid is making pot roast."

I didn't reply.

"But I think there's only enough for you," Troy said.

Still I said nothing. I just pressed the back of my hand into Chipper's thigh.

He opened his eyes. "Shit," he said all of a sudden.

"What?" I asked.

Chipper looked around, narrowing his eyes at the glowing red numerals of Troy's digital clock. "Shit, it's almost four o'clock. I gotta get home."

He stood up. I did so as well.

"You don't have to go, too, do you, Danny?" Troy asked. "Don't you want to stay for supper?"

I looked at him. He was sitting on his bed in exactly the way he always sat when I sat next to him, his legs stretched out in front of him. I thought of his smelly penis and red pubic hair, hidden behind the crotch of his green parachute pants. I was revolted.

"I should go with Chipper," I said, "since he lives just across the street from me."

"Well then, come on, man," Chipper said. "We gotta hustle." He flung open Troy's door and bolted from the room. He didn't offer any thanks for the weed. I thought he should've. But at the moment I just wanted to get away from Troy, too, as fast and as far as possible. I followed Chipper without saying another word to Troy.

The maid called good-bye from the kitchen. This time I didn't answer.

We hopped into the Mach 1. "Damn, that's one mighty fine buzz," Chipper said as he started the ignition. He turned to me and smiled. "You're all right, you know that, Danny? You are fuck-ing *all right.*"

I nearly burst into tears, I was so happy.

Chipper screeched out onto the road, blasting all the way down Burnside Avenue. I loved the sound of the Mach 1. The rumble of the engine, the squeal of the tires. All the way home I rode with a raging hard-on in my pants.

Turning onto our street, both of us saw the motorcycles at the same time. My driveway was filled with them. Six, seven, eight big black bikes.

"What the fuck?" Chipper asked.

"Oh, man," I groaned.

Chipper pulled up in front, and I stepped out of the car.

"Must be a meeting of the Finding Becky Society," I said, leaning back in through the window toward Chipper.

"Good luck," he said and steered the car across the street, to his own driveway.

I trudged up the walk. I didn't relish going into my house with all those bikers inside. I'd seen bikers tearing through town before, and I didn't think they were going to be very nice people. But I took a deep breath and pulled open the door.

The sight in my living room was not to be believed. I was still high, so it seemed even more like a hallucination. There were eight men, with long beards and black leather jackets, sitting everywhere. They filled up the chairs and the couch, and one was sitting on the arm of the couch. Another one was on the floor. Each of them had a can of beer in his hand, and most of them were smoking. A blue cigarette haze hung between their heads and the ceiling. Three women, also in leather, stood among the men, their hair long and stringy. But the most incongruous sight of all was Nana, sitting on the couch between two big, bearded bikers. She looked so small next to them, and her eyes were terrified.

Mom was standing in the middle of the room, a notepad and pen in her hands. "Danny!" she said when she saw me. "Come in! I want you to meet Warren!"

I took a step forward nervously. Mom was gesturing toward the man on Nana's right. His eyes were barely slits in his face. Long black hair was tied back in a ponytail, and a black and gray beard came down to his collar. He wore a black T-shirt and a black leather vest, dirty jeans, and black boots. I just glared at him.

"This is my son, Danny," Mom said in the cheery voice she might use to introduce me to a neighbor or a priest at church.

Warren didn't rise or move to shake my hand. He barely lifted his bushy eyebrows over his hooded eyes to look at me. There was a hint of a smile. I noticed teeth were missing.

"Warren brought his friends to see me," Mom was explaining, "because each of them has seen Becky at one time or another."

"You *have?*" I asked, staring straight at Warren.

"Yup," he said, taking a sip of his beer. "We all seen her. Question is, how do we find her now?"

"Exactly," Mom said. "Now you've told me that you believe this man, this creature you call Bruno, has left Cape Cod and taken her to New York."

"That I do," said Warren. "Now you gotta remember, Peg, that Bruno is not one of us anymore. He's no longer a Skulls man. So he don't trust us, and we don't trust him."

It was then that I noticed they all wore skull pendants around their necks. Tiny silver skulls hung from black leather strings. The women had skulls dangling from their ears. I felt as if I were in a bad horror movie. I glanced from Warren over to Nana. She was moving her lips, maybe praying, maybe talking silently to herself, and turning a handkerchief in her hands over and over in her lap.

"You got another beer?" one of the other guys asked behind me.

"Yes, sure," Mom said. "Help yourself from the refrigerator."

"So if Becky's in New York," I said, "maybe the police should—"

"Danny!" Mom cut me off. "There's no talk of the police here. I've given Warren my word."

 I looked over at him. His eyes opened wide for the first time. He scared the shit out of me.

"There's only one guy that Bruno still talks to that I think we can trust," Warren said after a pause. "He lives outside Holyoke, Massachusetts, and I think he's our only hope of getting to Bruno. But if he thinks the police are anywhere near this operation . . ."

Mom jumped in. "He needs to know that I'm not the heat."

The *heat?* Had she been watching too much *Starsky & Hutch?*

"Can you take me home?"

All heads turned. It was Nana. She was looking up at the big, bearded guy sitting beside her, asking him plaintively if he could take her home.

"*Adele,*" Mom said, louder than necessary, "you *are* home." Addressing the bikers, she added, "Ignore her. She's a little confused."

I watched as Nana's eyes flickered back down to her lap. She began once again to turn the handkerchief over in her hands. My heart broke for her.

"So what is this man's name?" Mom asked impatiently, holding her pen to the pad. "The one in Holyoke?"

"He's called the Rubberman."

Mom blinked. I sat down on the floor. I couldn't believe any of this. My head was no longer spinning just from the pot.

"He's had a lot of surgeries," Warren explained. "Cracked up lots of bikes, been in lots of fights. I think nearly every bone in his face has been broken at one time or another. So his face—it looks like rubber. He's kind of earned the right to be on his own. He's not affiliated with any group."

"So how do I contact him?" asked Mom.

Warren poked his chest with his thumb. "Through *me*, Peg. Nobody else is gonna get to the Rubberman."

"Okay, so *how?*"

"Well, he's gonna need some persuasion if he's gonna talk."

Mom made a face. "You told me this would cost money. How much?"

"Let's say we start with a grand."

"Fine," she said, writing it down on her pad without blinking an eye.

Warren finally smiled at that point. His mouth looked like a jack-o'-lantern's. "Now, you know it's not for us, Peg. None of us Skulls want to take any of your money. We just want to see your daughter home safe with you."

"Why?" I asked. All heads turned to look at me. I couldn't believe I had the guts. The word just came out of my mouth without me even thinking about it. Maybe it was the pot. I was staring straight at Warren's face.

His smile disappeared. "For one thing, little boy, we hate Bruno's filthy, stinking ass, and we want to take what's his." His hooded eyes moved from me across the room to one of the women standing a few feet away. "But go ahead, Lee Ann. You tell him the rest of the reason why."

"Oh, do I gotta, Warren?"

"Yes, you fucking bitch."

I couldn't believe what he had just called her. And Mom just stood there, not batting an eye.

Lee Ann looked over at me. I couldn't tell how old she was. Maybe twenty-five. But her face was lined, and dark circles shadowed her eyes. Her hair was dyed platinum blond like Suzanne Somers, but her black roots were showing.

"When I was seventeen, I was kidnapped," Lee Ann said in a low, halting voice. "I was hanging out with these guys who were bikers, and we went to a party one night. This was back in Ohio, where I come from. And I got pretty wasted, and the next thing I know, I'm with this guy and he tells me I belong to him. I'd never seen the guy. But he took me and never let me go home. I was with him for four and a half years, and he beat me and raped me." She paused. "His name was Bruno."

"Dear God," Mom said and made the sign of the cross.

Lee Ann went on. "About a year ago he dumped me for another girl. Now we got word he's taken two bitches for himself. And one of them, I'm sure, is your daughter. I seen them together at a rally up in Albany. The word was they were heading down to Manhattan."

Mom looked as if she might cry. "Do your parents know you're okay?" she asked.

"I ain't going home now," Lee Ann said. "Too much shit has happened. My mother's a big, old, drunk Jesus freak. She don't care where I am. Besides, I found my man now. Warren is my man now. He's all I need, huh, Warren?"

"Thatta girl, Lee Ann," Warren said.

Mom shuddered. "Well, then, if this monster has my baby, he's probably hurt her very bad. So we need to act fast."

"Get us the money. I'll pass it on to the Rubberman and see if we can find out where Bruno is," Warren asserted.

Mom nodded.

"Okay, I'll—"

"Who the hell are these people?"

The voice startled everyone in the room. We looked up. It was my father, coming in through the kitchen. We hadn't heard his car, and I immediately understood why. All the bikes were in the driveway. He'd had to park in the street and had come in through the back door. Now he stood in the passage leading to the kitchen, with his mouth open and eyes wide. And there was one other thing I noticed about him. He hadn't spritzed himself with cologne. He stank of alcohol.

"Tony," Mom said. "What are you doing here?"

"I live here, in case you forgot," Dad returned. His words were slurring a little.

"These people are helping us find Becky," Mom told him.

"Jesus Christ," Dad said and strode off through the kitchen. I heard him banging chairs and cabinet doors.

Warren was standing. "It's time for us to leave." The rest of the bikers stood as well.

"I'll get the money tomorrow," Mom was saying. "Will you come by here?"

Warren nodded.

Mom began to cry. "May I hug you?"

Warren looked at her with surprise.

She didn't wait for permission. She threw her arms around him and sobbed on his massive barrel chest. "Thank you, Warren! Thank you for helping me find my baby!"

Warren said nothing, just stood there, looking uncomfortable. Finally, he took Mom's arms and gently moved her away from him. The bikers filed out of the house.

I watched from the window as the women climbed on the backs of the bikes, gripping their men tightly. The roar of the engines was deafening. The bikers revved their machines a few times in the driveway, then tore off down the road, one following the other. The sound was louder than any thunderstorm I'd ever heard.

Dad was immediately back in the room. "Jesus Christ, Peggy! You invite these degenerates into our house, let them drink my beer—"

"These degenerates are doing more to find your daughter than you are!" Mom shrieked. "And as for your beer, I think you've had quite enough liquor for a while!"

"Can you take me home?" Nana's little voice piped up in the

middle of the argument. She was still sitting on the couch, turning that handkerchief over and over in her hands. "Can you take me home, please?"

"Oh, Jesus Christ," Mom screamed, her big hands in her hair. "All day long I have to put up with this! I can't take her anymore!"

"Oh, Ma," Dad said, his voice ripped with sadness. "We shouldn't have been yelling. It's okay."

"Can you take me home?" Nana repeated.

Mom started to cry and rushed out of the room. Dad attempted to reach down and touch Nana's hand, but he was so drunk that he lost his balance a little. He steadied himself and then turned away. He headed down into the basement, where he had set up a chair and a television set. He'd probably sleep down there, too. He did that a lot lately.

In the air, the cigarette smoke still lingered. Nana's eyes were watering. I propped open the front door and began gathering up the dirty ashtrays and beer cans.

"Can you take me home?" Nana asked again.

I set down the trash in my hands. I walked over and sat beside my grandmother.

"Nana," I said, "this is home now. I know it doesn't seem that way. It doesn't seem that way to me, either. But it is."

She just looked at me with those sad, vacant eyes.

"You remember who I am, don't you, Nana? Danny. Danny off the pickle boat."

"Danny," she repeated.

I smiled.

"Danny," she said, "can you take me home?"

I thought of Nana's home, the big white house in Manchester, where my father and Aunt Patsy had grown up. How I used to love to go there when I was a kid. Nana was the best babysitter. She'd make her homemade macaroni and cheese and her cinnamon streusel cake. Becky and I would play in the big field out behind her house, catching fireflies in jars. And when we'd sleep over, Nana would tuck me into bed in Dad's old room, which had a big bay window overlooking the field. In the mornings, I used to like to sit there and listen to the crows and watch the sun come up. The room would turn all pink and gold. I loved Nana's house. And at the moment I missed it very badly.

"Will you take me home?" Nana asked again, in barely a whisper.

I put my arms around her. "Nana," I said, "we're just gonna have to make the best of this one for now."

We sat that way for a long time. She didn't ask again if I could take her home.

PALM SPRINGS

"**I** told you it was a pit," Kelly said, stepping aside so I could enter his apartment.

The last slanting rays of the sun sliced through his half-closed venetian blinds, striping the room with orange. A mattress sat on the floor, wrapped tightly in a sheet and covered with a Mexican falsa blanket. Three milk crates placed on their sides held papers and drawing pads. An old door held up by four cinder blocks served as a table. There was a single straight-back chair. The walls were bare except for one spot over his bed, where a black-and-white glossy photo of Jackie O in sunglasses was secured with Scotch tape.

"You should hang some of your sketches," I said. "It'd brighten up the place."

"My landlady won't let me put holes in the walls."

From what I could see, it would hardly matter: the plaster was already cracked and peeling enough as it was. I turned to Kelly and smiled.

"It's not a pit. It's cozy. It's a roof over your head. Now bring out the work. I'm here to see some Nelson originals."

Kelly laughed. "There's not much to show."

It had taken quite a bit of persuasion to get in here. Over the last week, we'd been texting back and forth. I'd ask for a look at his portfolio; he'd say no. I'd ask again. He'd reply with a joke.

DOES A DUCK PAY FOR HIS DRINKS AT A BAR? This time I figured it out, and with glee, I texted back, NO. HE JUST PUTS THEM ON HIS BILL.

That was what got me in here, I think.

That, and the fact that I'd told Kelly that I'd spoken with a teacher at CalArts about him. The teacher was a guy I'd met when I was taking classes there, and I'd read that he was offering a course on illustration next semester for the general public. I had him send me the description, and I handed it to Kelly now.

"If you like the class," I told him as he looked over the papers, "maybe you should think about applying to the school. I mean, you could maybe get a scholarship."

He looked up at me with scorn. "Oh, please. You haven't even seen all my work."

"From the little I've seen, you're damn good." I smiled. "So show me the rest."

He sighed. He sat down on his mattress and reached into one of the milk crates, withdrawing two sketch pads. "Okay," he said, patting the place next to him on the mattress. "Sit down."

I obeyed. He flipped open the first pad. There was a series of doodles and crossed-out images. The next page was more of the same. When he turned to the third page, however, I saw a more complete sketch, a caricature of a woman with a big nose. After that came several more sketches, some more finished than others. Most of them were done in pen, but others were in pencil, with attempts at shading.

I said nothing as he flipped through.

"See?" he said. "I told you that you wouldn't be impressed."

"They're fine, Kelly. Let me see the other pad."

It was here that I recognized the sparkle I'd seen in the drawings he'd done in my presence. It was here that he'd started drawing Jackie O. Jackie in a pillbox hat. Jackie with Caroline and John-John, watching the funeral procession. Jackie with sunglasses and a scarf around her neck. Jackie with Aristotle Onassis. They were brilliant renderings.

But most of the rest were doodles and scratches.

"You have real talent," I told him. "You just need to finish some of these. Give them the same passion you give when you're drawing Jackie."

He laughed, flopping backward onto the bed. His shirt inched up, revealing his belly button and the little tuft of black hair that grew up from his groin.

"Finish them?" he asked. "There's the problem. I don't have the discipline to finish them."

"Draw me," I said.

His black eyes looked up at me. "I thought we were going for pizza."

"Not until you draw me."

He sat up. Our thighs were touching. So were our shoulders. He looked me straight in the face, not two inches away.

"I can't draw you," he said quietly.

My heart was thudding. I could smell him. His soap, his shampoo.

"Why not?" I asked, my throat tight.

He smiled. Oh, those dimples. "Because you're too nice to me," he said.

"Too nice?"

He stood, breaking the electricity that had connected us, and walked across the room. "Yes. Too nice. Nobody has ever talked to me about my sketches as if they mattered before." He turned to face me. "And here you are, telling me I ought to go to CalArts!"

"You said you don't want to remain a bartender all your life."

"Why do you *care?*"

I stood now, too. "Because I was like you once. I see myself in you."

He tilted his head and looked at me. "No other reason?"

That was the question. I'd asked myself exactly that on my way over to his apartment. Why was I so insistent I see his work? Why did I feel such a compulsion to encourage him? Was it just a crass strategy to finally get him into bed—something I'd now been frustrated out of twice?

But even as I asked myself the question, I already knew the answer. My fixation on Kelly these last couple of months had never been solely about sex. I wanted something more from him. Something much more. I wasn't quite sure what it was that I wanted, but I knew it was far more than sex.

"I have no ulterior motive," I assured him.

His eyes didn't let go of mine.

"So draw me," I said again.

He walked over to the makeshift table. A small grin stretched across his face. "I need inspiration if I'm going to draw. Is that okay?"

"Is what okay?"

A small wooden box sat on the table. Kelly picked it up. "Maybe you'd like to get inspired with me."

I still didn't know what he meant. He opened the lid on the box and withdrew a small plastic bag with white powder inside.

"Oh," I said. "That kind of inspiration."

"Are you passing judgment?"

"No," I said. "But I suspect your inspiration might be more lasting if it came from somewhere else."

"Will you join me?"

I hesitated.

"I'm always happier when I do a little blow," Kelly said. "You've seen me. Happier . . . and friendlier."

There was the slightest emphasis on the last word. Was he promising me something?

"How do you afford it?" I asked.

He shrugged. "I don't buy furniture." Then he laughed.

I suspected he saved very little of the tips he made. He used them to buy his blow. I knew how it worked. I'd done the same once.

"It's been a long time since I've done coke," I told him.

He was already opening the plastic bag and using his driver's license to arrange a couple of lines on a small handheld mirror. "Did you like it?" he asked.

"I did. A lot." I paused. "Too much."

"Do you have a crisp new twenty?"

I hesitated but opened my wallet and handed him one. "In my day, we only used hundreds."

Kelly flashed his smile at me. Those dimples again. It was hopeless. He had me.

"Well," he said, "I know you're a big, successful artist and all, but I didn't think you were *so* successful, you walked around with hundred-dollar bills in your wallet."

"Not yet," I told him.

He rolled the twenty tightly into a little tube. "You're gonna join me, aren't you?"

"Why? You coming apart?"

He scrunched up his face and laughed. Then he bent down and snorted one line off the mirror. Wiping his nose and licking his finger, he handed me the twenty.

I stalled for the slightest second—he wouldn't even have noticed—and then accepted. I blocked everything else out of my mind and placed the tube in my nostril, inhaling the powder. It was just like old times. My heart was beating in my ears.

"Just a little," Kelly said. "Just a little to start. Maybe more later."

I sat back down on the mattress. In seconds my head was light, and I was happy. I'd forgotten how good a little white powder could make me feel.

"Okay," Kelly was saying. "Now I *will* draw you. Sit there."

He sat on top of one of the milk crates and opened his pad, getting busy with his pencil. He studied my face, then made a few scratches on the paper. He looked at me again, considering my eyes, my nose, my mouth, my ears. Kelly was looking at me—*seeing me*—noticing me. I was, in that moment, his entire focus, his whole world. I couldn't stop smiling.

"Look serious," he chided, but it was impossible. I was just feeling way too happy, way too lighthearted, to stop smiling.

"Well, if you're going to stay that way," Kelly said, "you're going to end up looking like a big old Cheshire cat."

"However you draw me is going to be transcendent, I am sure," I told him.

I couldn't remember when I'd last felt this happy. A long time ago. A very long time.

And there was one other thing I'd forgotten about coke.

How fucking horny it made me.

"Hold on one more minute," Kelly said, making a few last adjustments to his sketch.

"I can't hold on much longer," I said.

His black eyes flickered up at me. "Why so impatient?"

"Because I can't stand it anymore," I said.

He grinned. "Stand what?"

"I've got to make love to you, Kelly. I can't leave this place tonight without making love to you."

His grin turned into a smirk. "Oh, is that so?"

"Yes. That's so."

He turned the drawing around to face me. "Well, what do you think?"

It was pretty damn good. Awesome, actually. In those few minutes, he'd captured me. There I was, smiling away, my happiness caught by his pencil. And the drawing sure looked a whole hell of a lot more like me than my own mirror image did these days. It looked like the young man I once had been—or anyway, the young man I liked to believe I had been.

Kelly came over and sat down beside me on the mattress.

"So you like it?" he asked.

I answered by kissing him.

"Look," he said, pulling away from my lips. "We can have sex. But I'm not big into kissing. Is that okay?"

I made a little laughing sound, but it was hardly a laugh. "You're kidding."

"No, I'm not."

It was as if someone had just dropped a brick on my foot. The happy feeling didn't completely evaporate; I was too high up to come down that fast. But his statement shook me off my pedestal.

"No *kissing?*" I asked in disbelief.

"Well, okay, just a little. I'm just not that into it." He closed the sketch pad and set it on the floor. "All that foreplay business. It's not really for me."

I didn't know how to respond. I dropped a few pegs down from my high.

"Just fuck me," Kelly whispered, leaning into my ear. "Fuck me hard."

This wasn't how I'd imagined it. I'd imagined a quiet conversation, whispered words in each other's ears. I'd imagined soft kisses on his neck, Kelly throwing his head back, allowing me to undress him. This was not at all how I'd imagined it.

But what was there to do? It was now, perhaps, or never. I did what he asked. I pushed him down on the bed. The Mexican blanket was scratchy, so I pulled it off, revealing his blue and white striped sheets. If he didn't want it slow and easy and sweet, I'd give him what he wanted. Off came his shirt, his pants. I unbuttoned my own shirt, unbuckled my pants. My cock was raging. I popped it out of my underwear and straddled Kelly's chest, plunging it into his mouth. He sucked eagerly.

"Yeah," he said between mouthfuls, "fuck my face."

I complied. But after a few moments I bent down, bringing my lips to his.

"I'm sorry," I said, "but I need to kiss you just a little bit, okay?"

He didn't stop me. But it was like kissing a mannequin.

"Kissing is very important to me," I whispered in his ear.

"Oh, Danny, fuck me," he groaned. "I need your big cock up my ass."

Down a couple more notches I dropped from my high.

But still I wasn't going to give up. I pulled off my clothes, grabbed hold of his thighs, and pushed his legs into the air, his big, uncut cock flopping against his stomach like a Polish kielbasa. Reaching into my pants on the floor, I pulled a condom from the pocket. I'd placed it there earlier this evening, with just this moment in mind. But this moment was supposed to come after a long night biting ears and licking skin. I didn't expect this—*this!*—would be the first thing I did.

"Fuck me, Danny," Kelly breathed.

I fell still farther down.

"Lube?" I asked.

His arm flailed off the mattress, and he felt around on the floor. His fingers closed around a small tube.

"Thanks," I said as he handed it to me. After I'd rolled the condom onto my cock, I squeezed out some lube, using my forefinger to lubricate Kelly's hole a little as well. He moaned as I did so.

"Give it to me, Danny."

I aimed at his hole. But despite the lube, my cock was getting soft. I could almost see it shrivel. I tried pumping it with my hand, closing my eyes and imagining Kelly's smile. His dimples. His astonishing black eyes.

But the more I imagined, the softer I got.

"Sorry," I said, rolling over onto my back.

"Oh, man," Kelly said. "Finger me then."

I did as he asked. He was jacking his own cock now. Pretty soon he came, a frothy bubble of white erupting over his fist.

I was completely down now.

I stood and found a small towel in his bathroom. I wiped up the cum from his abdomen, then tossed the towel onto the floor.

"I should get going," I said.

He sat up quickly, as if he were on a spring. "Don't you want to come?"

"No . . . I'm . . . I guess I'm too high." That was one extremely ironic lie.

"Well, aren't we going for pizza?" he asked.

"You know, the coke seems to have dried up my appetite." I was pulling on my pants. "Thanks for drawing the picture of me."

"Danny, is everything okay?"

I faced him. "That's not what I call making love."

He flopped back down. "I know. I'm sorry. I'm terrible in bed."

"Yeah," I said. "You are." I didn't care if it hurt him.

"I'm sorry," he said again.

I didn't answer.

He sat up, his knees pulled to his chest. "Well, thanks for bringing me the brochure about the illustration class," he said, watching me as I buttoned my shirt. "I really appreciate it. I'll look at it and let you know what I think."

"Sure," I said.

The room fell quiet. I wanted very badly to get out of there.

"Danny," Kelly said, moving up behind me as I sat down on the mattress to put on my shoes. "I'm sorry. It's just the way I am."

I sighed. "It's not a big deal. Forget it."

"I think it is a big deal for you. And I'm *sorry*. I don't know how many times I can say it."

I turned to look at him. "When you deny me a chance to kiss you, to really kiss you, that's like serving me prime rib but only allowing me to lick the gravy off of it."

He smiled a little at the metaphor.

I stood up. "Without kissing, without some sense of the person, sex is just the manipulation of body parts. And I just don't have any interest in that anymore."

"It's all I'm interested in," he said flatly.

I shook my head. "How can you say that?"

He shrugged. "Beyond that, sex is way too dangerous."

"Well," I said, "you can't go through life avoiding danger all the time."

He looked at me with hard eyes. "I can."

I started to say that I felt sorry for him, but then closed my mouth and turned to leave. Kelly got up and walked me to the door.

"I like you a lot," he said.

"It's fine, Kelly. Like I said, it's no big deal. Don't worry about it." I paused, my hand on the doorknob. "Oh. Was the drawing for me to keep?"

"Yes!" He turned quickly and retrieved the sketch pad, tearing the page out. "Here."

I took it. I wanted something to take home from there tonight.

"Thank you," I said and tried to sound sincere.

Then I opened the door and left.

On the way home, all the traffic lights seemed out of sync. I had to stop at every one. And the reds took forever to change to green, so finally I just drove on through, taking a chance that I would be safe.

EAST HARTFORD

Iloved being in Chipper's room. I loved the smell of aftershave and dirty socks. I loved how warm it was, like an animal's den, with its big red shag carpet and oversize cushions strewn everywhere. His window shades were kept drawn almost to a close, with only the tiniest slits of sunshine permitted entry. And in that darkened sanctuary, we'd talk, sitting on the carpet, our backs against opposite walls, our feet stretched out in front of us, almost touching.

"I think when school starts again, I should go out for cross-country," I told him.

"Yeah, you definitely should." We were eating string cheese, passing it back and forth. "You should have some kind of sport. Otherwise, when the yearbook comes out, all you'll have listed after your name is the faggy play."

"I know." I sighed. "I'm a really fast runner. I think I could be really good at cross-country."

Chipper handed the cheese back to me. "Well, now that I'm a senior, the coach is going to use me a lot." I knew he'd been bummed that he'd sat on the bench for most of last season. "I can't wait until I score my first touchdown. And you better be there!"

I peeled off a strip of cheese and put it in my mouth. "Of *course,* I will be."

I was fully aware that my feelings toward Chipper had blossomed into a kind of crush. How could I deny them after what I'd been doing with Troy? At home, I'd play Becky's old Partridge Family album, listening to "I Think I Love You" over and over. It was uncanny how David Cassidy had nailed exactly how I was feeling about Chipper. *This morning, I woke up with this feeling I didn't know how to deal with. . . .* I'd stand in front of the mirror, mouthing the words to my reflection as the chipped little 45 record spun on Becky's old turntable. *I think I love you. So what am I so afraid of? I'm afraid that I'm not sure of a love there is no cure for. . . .*

I'd looked *bisexual* up in the dictionary. I knew what it was, and I accepted it about myself. But Chipper couldn't know the truth about me. No way could he know. He wouldn't let me hang out in his room with him if he did. He wouldn't get high with me, sitting there, facing me on his floor, his toes almost touching mine. He wouldn't be my friend at school next year—and if I'd thought having a junior as a friend and protector had been great, then how awesome would it be to have a senior and the star of the football team looking out for me?

Yet, in a way we never articulated, Chipper seemed to know precisely how I felt about him. And, deep down, I think he liked it. A hint of a smile would betray itself on his lips when I'd say things like of course, I'd be there when he scored his first touchdown. There was a cocky set to his shoulders when I'd tell him how cool I thought his car was, or how much I wished I had biceps as big as his. Once he asked me to walk on his back, the way George Jefferson was always doing for Mr. Bentley on TV. He'd hurt himself throwing a football, Chipper explained, and this could help him. I complied eagerly. It was the most extraordinary sensation, feeling his strong, hard back under my white athletic-socked feet.

I think I love you. Isn't that what life is made of?

Chipper looked up and caught me staring at him. He threw a pillow at me.

I caught it and laughed. "I've got to get going," I told him reluctantly. "Mom wants me back by noon so we can go up to Massachusetts."

Chipper laughed. "So she really thinks a guy called Rubberman can help her find Becky?"

"It's not Rubberman like Superman or Spider-Man. It's *the* Rubberman like *the* Flash or *the* Hulk."

Chipper rolled his eyes. "Whatever."

I was quiet for a moment. "Hey, Chipper, can I ask you something?"

"Sure."

"Do you ever miss Becky?"

"Sure."

"Is that why you haven't gotten another girlfriend?"

He stood up abruptly. "Well, I didn't want to date anyone and get Becky pissed off at me. You know, if she came back."

"I don't think she's coming back," I said in a small voice. It was the first time I'd voiced out loud how I felt.

"When school starts," Chipper said, ignoring my comment and fiddling with his football helmet, "I think I'll ask Mary Kay Suwicki to go out. You know, as a senior, I should have a girlfriend."

I got to my feet. "Yeah," I agreed.

I headed for the door.

"Good luck with Rubberman," Chipper said.

"*The* Rubberman," I corrected him.

He laughed. "Call me tomorrow."

I smiled. "I will."

Call me tomorrow. I loved those words.

Of course, Mom couldn't know I had been at Chipper's. She would've had a bird. So I left Chipper's house by the back door, walking through other people's backyards and crossing the street a block past our house. That way, I could come back down on our side of the street, and it would look like I'd come from entirely the opposite direction of Chipper's house. It sure made for a long walk home, especially since Chipper lived right across the street, but it was a necessary tactic. Mom was waiting at the front door, as usual, her eagle eyes scanning the neighborhood for me. She made the sign of the cross when I came up the walk.

"Danny, get in here! Jesus Christ, where have you been?"

She held the door open for me to enter. "Mom," I said, "it's not noon yet. You said to be back by noon."

"Don't you know how I worry?" She drew in close to me, so that our noses were almost touching, the way she used to do when I was a kid. She'd say "See the owl!" and make googly eyes at me. It always made me laugh. I missed my mother's googly eyes.

"I'm sorry," I said. "But I wasn't late."

"It's just that we're in a jam!" Mom made the sign of the cross again. "Bud is sick. He's in the hospital. He can't drive us to Mass-achusetts!"

Bud. The taxicab driver. "What's wrong with him?" I asked.

"*I don't know.*" Mom's tone was clear: the nature of Bud's illness was irrelevant. It was the burden it placed on her getting to see the Rubberman that mattered. "His wife called to say he's been taken by ambulance to the hospital. Jesus! And on the day War-ren finally got the Rubberman to agree to see us."

I knew better than to suggest calling Dad. First of all, if Dad knew about this meeting, he'd be against it. Secondly, he'd been missing a lot of work lately. Drinking too much, I suspected, and sleeping late in the basement, missing appointments. His bosses at the real estate company weren't happy. Dad's secretary, Phyllis, would call us, asking very sweetly if Tony had left for work yet. Mom would open the basement door and scream down at him. Today, for once, he'd made it to the office on time. No way could we call him now.

"I've tried everyone," Mom was saying, her face flushed red. "I even called Father McKenna, but he's out of town for a diocesan meeting. I can't ask Flo Armstrong, because she's coming over to watch your grandmother—and besides, she's a blabbermouth. She can't know where we're going. I can't trust anyone, because they might call the police, and then everything would collapse." The vein on her forehead was throbbing. "I wish we hadn't had to sell Becky's car. I'd try to drive myself."

It dawned on me to suggest Chipper. But I knew he'd refuse to get involved, and Mom would probably balk at asking him, any-way, since she hated him so much. Then another idea came to me.

"I can call Troy," I suggested.

Mom looked at me. "That pot smoker? Danny, he's not even old enough to drive!"

"But he knows how," I said. "And he drives everywhere. The only time he ever got caught was that time at the Dumpster. And that's only because the cops were there. He drives everywhere, and his father knows it and is fine with it. He has Troy go to the grocery store and the post office and everything. Besides, he's *almost* sixteen."

"No," Mom snarled. "There's got to be someone else."

"Well, then, maybe the Rubberman could see us another day."

"No!" Mom shrieked. "It's got to be *today!* I want to go to sleep tonight knowing where Becky is!"

She was pacing. Literally pacing. Walking around the living room in circles, over and over again. She looked like a cartoon. Nana was sitting on the couch, like she always did, her hands in her lap, watching Mom go round and round. Finally Mom stopped, mid-rotation, and looked at me with enormous eyes.

"Goddamn it then! Call Troy!"

He was glad to hear from me. I hadn't seen him in a few days, preferring to spend my afternoons hunkered down on Chipper's shag carpet, smoking the weed he bought from his own connections—far harsher than what I was used to smoking with Troy. I finally understood why some pot was called smooth.

Troy was eager to help. He'd be at our house in twenty minutes, he said, and he made it in fifteen. In the driveway, with Flo Armstrong safely inside with Nana, Mom gave Troy the obligatory lecture as he sat behind the wheel of the Jaguar.

"I'm only doing this because it's an emergency," she said, wagging her finger at him through the driver's window. "You shouldn't be driving, Troy. You're too young. I'll clear it with your father later."

"My father doesn't care if I drive, Mrs. Fortunato," Troy told her.

She narrowed her eyes at him. "You haven't been smoking any of that wacky weed, have you?"

"No, Mrs. Fortunato. I gave that up."

I suppressed a smile.

Mom got up front, and I slid into the back. We didn't talk much as we headed up Interstate 91, past Hartford and through Bloomfield and Windsor. I think Mom was embarrassed and horrified at what she was doing: allowing an underage driver to take her to see a motorcycle gang leader who was no doubt a convicted felon. And, to make matters worse, she was taking her fourteen-year-old son along for the ride. But she was desperate. Everything Mom did these days was driven by her desperation.

Once we'd crossed the state line into Massachusetts, she finally spoke. "We're to meet Warren and his friends at a rest stop right after Springfield." She looked at her watch. "We're right on time."

"And where do we go from there?" Troy asked.

"That I don't know," Mom said. "Warren said to meet him there, and he'd lead us to the Rubberman."

When we pulled off at the rest stop, I saw two motorcyclists waiting for us. It was Warren and one of the other guys who'd been in our living room. Mom greeted Warren with a hug. Troy and I waited in the car as she spoke with them. I saw her nod, then open her purse and hand Warren an envelope. More money, I assumed. Now I knew where the money went from the sale of Becky's car.

Mom came back and leaned her head through the passenger window. "I'm going with them. You boys wait here for me. They'll drop me back here after I speak to the Rubberman."

"No!" I shouted from the backseat. "I'm not letting you go alone with them!"

"Danny, just sit there and wait for me!"

"No!" I pushed open the door and stood facing her. "I'm not letting you go alone!"

"Danny! Stop this!"

Warren had sauntered up to us. "Peg, it's okay. The boy can come."

Mom shook her head. "He most certainly cannot. I shouldn't even have brought him. He's—"

"He's a brave boy, ain't you, Danny?" Warren asked, fixing me with those hooded eyes of his. "You ever been on a hog, Danny?"

"What's a hog?"

"A bike."

"I've been on a bike, but not a motorcycle," I told him.

Warren flashed his gap-toothed grin. "Well, today's your lucky day, then."

"Oh, no," Mom protested.

"He'll be fine, Peg." Warren motioned for his friend to join us. "Lenny here will let him wear his helmet, just like I got a helmet for you, Peg."

Lenny smiled down at me. He was huge man, probably six-five, with shoulders so wide that when he stepped in front of me, he completely blotted out the sun. It was like standing in the shade of a tall tree. From head to toe, he was clad in leather: a leather cap, a leather jacket, leather chaps over dirty dungarees, and enormous leather boots. He wasn't as old as Warren; there was no gray in his beard, and the face behind the whiskers was unlined. And—for some reason this reassured me—he had all his teeth.

Mom made no further protest. I think she was worried that if we were late, the Rubberman would change his mind about giving us information. She placed the helmet on her head and instructed me to do the same.

"Can I come?" Troy called from the car.

"No!" Mom shot back.

"Next time, buckaroo," Lenny called cheerily to him. He had a Boston accent. "We don't got enough helmets or bikes to go around."

"Wait here for us," I told Troy. "Don't leave or nothing."

"I won't leave you, Danny," Troy promised.

I stuck the helmet on my head. It was way too big. Lenny leaned in to tighten it with the straps under my chin. I felt his rough fingers brush against my skin.

Mom was already up on Warren's bike, gripping his body the way I'd seen her do that time on the street. Lenny lifted his long leg and mounted his own bike, patting the soft quilted leather seat behind him. "Hop up here, kid," he said.

I obeyed, nearly falling off the other side of the bike. Lenny laughed and settled me where I was supposed to be.

"Danny!" Mom shouted, "make sure you hang on tight!"

I ignored her. She was embarrassing me.

"Your momma's right," Lenny said over his shoulder. "Get your arms around me and hold on real tight."

There I was, wearing khakis, red Converse sneakers, a sweatshirt with the words ST. FRANCIS XAVIER emblazoned across the front, and a motorcycle helmet way too big for my head. Gingerly, I reached around Lenny's enormous leather body, my hands barely reaching each other in front. As he revved the bike, the sound sent trembles through my body, and when he took off, the force sent me backward a little bit. I grabbed on to Lenny's jacket for dear life. As we picked up speed, I held on to his solid frame as tightly as I could, my face pressed up against his leather. The wind rushed at us, and I could do nothing but press my face against Lenny's back as we flew down the highway. The smell of his leather was intoxicating. My lips even picked up its taste.

The day was bright, with an unbroken blue sky. On either side of us, rolling green hills stretched for miles. But I couldn't see where we were going. My face remained pressed into Lenny's back. I could tell when we got off the highway, however, since Lenny took a hard left and the entire bike leaned on its side. I was terrified that we'd fall over and go spinning across the road, so I instinctively tried to counter Lenny's weight with my own, leaning to the right. "Just hold on to me, kid," Lenny shouted over his shoulder. "Don't move around." I did what he said, gripping him as fiercely as I could, my eyes once again closed against his back.

Then finally we started slowing down. I opened my eyes and looked up. We were on a road that led through some deep green woods. Warren and Mom were ahead of us. We followed them down a bumpy dirt road. The bikers had to go real slow since there were so many ruts. Clouds of chalky dust were stirred up as we went along. My eyes watered, and I started to cough.

Up ahead there was a small house made out of cement blocks. Several motorcycles were parked out front. Four Dobermans came bounding toward us, barking furiously. Warren slowed his bike to a stop and called out to the dogs, who seemed to know him. They ceased barking and gathered around his bike.

Lenny stopped a few feet away. "Don't let the dogs scare you, buckaroo," he said. "They're not as mean as they sound."

I was immediately embarrassed by the fact that my arms were still around him. The break of my embrace was jarring. I didn't want to look at him. I kept my eyes lowered as I slipped off the helmet.

The Dobermans were growling as we approached. "Hey, King," Lenny called. "How's it going, King?"

The lead dog sniffed at him but growled at me.

"He's okay, King," Lenny said. "He's okay."

Out beyond the house, I spied the carcasses of old cars, their engines gutted. Overhead the trees were so thick, only scattered patches of sun managed to break through. The ground was covered with ferns and jack-in-the-pulpits and lilies of the valley, but the smell of the place was unlike any woods I'd been in before. Everywhere was the aroma of motor oil.

Walking up to the house, Warren called through the windows, announcing our arrival. There was no response. Warren gestured for us to follow him. Mom told me to wait outside, but I ignored her again, keeping close behind her.

The interior of the house smelled of motor oil, too, but mingled with the smells of cigarette smoke and wet dog. Through a filthy kitchen, we filed past a sink loaded with dirty dishes. Beer cans were stacked high on the counter. Off to our right was a small living room, where a gray-haired man sat in a large recliner, watching television. His back was to us. The rabbit ears on the set were twisted oddly, and the picture on the tube was all snowy. Some soap opera. I recognized Susan Lucci and knew it was *All My Children.*

"Rub," Warren called. "This is Peg, the lady I've been telling you about."

We came around in front of his chair. I almost gasped out loud. The Rubberman was unquestionably the ugliest man I had ever seen. His eyes were crooked, one pushed upward by an enormous scar that sliced through the right side of his face. His nose had been broken so many times that it looked as if it had been removed and pasted back on. He had no teeth, and the corners of his mouth were distended by more scars that ran across his cheeks. I knew immediately what had happened. Someone had used a knife to cut a hideous smile into his face, like the Joker in *Batman.* His body was misshapen as well, with one shoulder higher than the other, scrawny bones jutting out of his white tank top. His shriveled arms and sunken chest were covered with a mosaic of blue and red tattoos.

The Rubberman did not move his eyes from his soap opera. He just reached over to the table at his side and lifted a can of beer to his lips.

Mom spoke up. "We're not the heat. I can assure you of that."

I cringed. I wished she would stop saying "the heat."

"Please, sir," Mom said, "if you can help me find my daughter, I am prepared to be very generous."

He still said nothing, keeping his deformed eyes riveted on the TV. I glanced over. Susan Lucci as Erica Kane was arguing with Tom Cudahy. Not until the scene faded to a commercial did the Rubberman finally turn his attention to us.

"How generous?" he asked in a low voice.

"Extremely," Mom said, and she opened her purse. She withdrew a thick envelope, which I figured to be stuffed with cash. It was even thicker than the envelope she'd handed to Warren. So much money being thrown around when we hardly had any.

The Rubberman took the envelope, peered briefly inside, then placed it on the table.

Warren stepped up. "Her daughter's the bitch that Bruno's taken on," he said, oblivious to any disrespect he might be showing. "We've all seen her."

"Lots of bitches look alike," the Rubberman mumbled.

"*Please*," Mom said. "Please, sir. I need you to help us find this Bruno."

"He's like a son to me," the old biker said, not looking at her. He was lighting a cigarette, taking a long drag. "Why should I help you take away his bitch?"

"That bitch, as you call her, is my little girl!" Mom cried.

My heart cracked in two. Suddenly the outrageousness of our situation overwhelmed me. Here we were, in the middle of the woods, and Mom was handing over what was probably the last of the money we'd raised to some filthy derelict and actually calling him sir. Peggy Fortunato was a proud woman. I'd seen the way she ran the church bazaars held by the Rosary Altar Society, clapping her hands and directing her ladies on how to best hang the crepe paper and set up the microphones. This was a woman who had once taken pride in her appearance, getting her hair done every Saturday, and in her spotlessly clean house, which had always smelled of Lemon Pledge. Not anymore. The visits to the hairdresser had stopped, and the dust was half an inch thick on the end tables in our living room. And now here was Peggy Fortunato, groveling in front of a man who didn't even have the courtesy to shake her hand or look her in the eye.

"Bruno's in New York," the Rubberman said, seemingly unmoved by Mom's outburst.

"Where in New York?" Mom asked.

"I think the city."

"Will you talk to him for us?"

"I have no phone here. How can I reach him?"

"When's he next due for a visit?" Warren asked.

The Rubberman shushed him. The commercial was over. *All My Children* was back on. Erica and Tom were still arguing.

"No!" I said, surprising myself with my suddenness. I reached over and switched off the TV. "Talk to my mother about finding my sister, or we take the money back!"

"Danny!" Mom shouted.

"Little boy," Warren growled, "you shouldn'ta done that."

I saw Lenny's eyebrows rise in disbelief.

The Rubberman had me fixed in his crooked gaze. "You put that television back on now," he said in a low, threatening voice.

"Okay," I said, starting to tremble, "but please, you gotta help us."

"I'll help you," he said impatiently. "Now put the fucking television back on."

I obeyed. The Rubberman watched for a few minutes without saying anything. We were all quiet, waiting.

"All right," he said finally, not waiting for a commercial this time. "Bruno is due up to see me this week. I'll find out what I can about his bitch."

"Here's Becky's picture," Mom said, handing him a photograph she'd removed from the family album. He didn't take it from her, so she placed it on the table beside him, next to his beer. The Rubberman gave the photo a sidelong glance.

"Looks like her," he said. "But I can't be sure."

"She has a birthmark that resembles a crescent moon on the inside of her upper arm," Mom said. "It looks like mine. See?"

She pulled up her sleeve to show it. The Rubberman barely glanced over.

"You'll be able to see the birthmark if she raises her arms and she's wearing a sleeveless shirt," Mom said.

"She may be wearing less than that," the Rubberman told her cruelly.

I wanted to punch him. I saw the pained look that crossed Mom's face. No doubt Bruno lived in a hovel as filthy as the Rubberman's. Looking around, I realized that if Becky was with Bruno, this was the kind of life she was now living. The little girl who less than a year ago was still watching Saturday morning cartoons with me was now living as a biker's bitch. It seemed too outrageous to be real. But maybe it was.

Yet even as the Rubberman waved us away, agreeing to contact Warren through some bar they both patronized, I was filled with doubt. The story Warren's girlfriend Lee Ann had told, about falling in with Bruno and being lured into his world, just didn't seem to fit for my sister. Never once had Becky exhibited the slightest interest in bikers. She didn't hang out with a rough crowd. She was a girl who wanted to be an artist, who had stood in our backyard at her easel, painting houses and sunsets and apple trees. She had a boyfriend she was crazy about, covering her notebooks with squiggly letters that spelled out "Chipper." If she was with Bruno now, she was being held against her will; that was the only way to understand it.

Maybe the Stockholm syndrome explained why she had never tried to contact us. But how had Bruno gotten her? Had he just snatched her off the street? Warren said that sometimes happened. But it had been the middle of the day! Sometime after noon, probably while she was walking back from the pond. It wasn't a dangerous walk. Becky would have walked through the woods and then along a quiet suburban street. It was a route both Becky and I and lots of other kids had walked many times. How had Bruno got her? Had he just pulled up alongside her and grabbed her? She would have screamed. The houses were dense along that street. Somebody would have seen or heard. But in none of the hundreds of leads had there been any such description. It just didn't make any sense to me.

Straddling Lenny's bike yet again, slipping on the helmet and wrapping my arms once more around his big torso, I couldn't shake my doubts. This was all too surreal. I thought of the envelope of money sitting on the Rubberman's table, and in my mind,

I heard the arguments between Mom and Dad over the bills that were going unpaid. Lenny revved his engine. Carefully, we took off down the dirt road. I knew my doubts merely echoed the arguments of the police, who had told Mom that they doubted Becky had been kidnapped by bikers. For a while, I'd been swayed by Mom's utter confidence in the theory, but now, coming here, riding around on the back of a motorcycle, everything just seemed far too absurd to be real. This wasn't my life. It was somebody else's.

Troy was waiting for us at the rest stop. I slid off Lenny's bike and removed the helmet from my head, handing it to him. "Thanks for taking me," I said.

"Hey, buckaroo," Lenny said. "You showed guts, standing up to the Rubberman."

I shrugged. "He's just an old, skinny guy."

"He's killed men with his bare hands."

That scared me. But I was determined not to show it.

"You're okay, kid," Lenny said and tousled my hair.

I watched him walk away. I kind of liked the fact that the smell of his leather seemed to cling to me.

Mom was conferring with Warren. From behind me, I heard Troy calling.

"Danny, what happened?"

I approached the car. "Nothing much. Some freak in the woods said he'd try to help us find Becky."

"I was worried about you," Troy said.

I looked at his face peering up at me from the car window. A couple of shiny red zits had broken out on his chin. My face was reflected in his tinted aviator glasses.

"Well, you didn't need to be," I said harshly. "I was with Lenny. He's cool."

Chipper would have liked Lenny, I thought. I couldn't wait to tell Chipper all about the ride on the motorcycle, about the Dobermans, about how I'd turned the TV off on the Rubberman. Chipper would love hearing that.

But to Troy I gave no such information. We were utterly silent driving home. When we pulled into our driveway, Mom thanked Troy for the ride and told him never to drive again until he got his license. She'd square it with his father, she said, but Troy said again not to worry about it. His father didn't care what he did.

"You wanta hang out tomorrow?" Troy asked as I got out of the car. Mom had already rushed up the driveway to tell Flo Armstrong she could go home.

"I can't," I said. "Chipper and I are hanging out."

"Oh."

I didn't say any more to him. I was worried Chipper was watching from his window across the street, and I didn't want him to see me with Troy. I slammed the car door and headed up the driveway. Troy sat there for a few moments. I could feel his eyes on the back of my head, burning me like laser beams. Then he backed the car out and sped off down the street.

In my room, I pulled my Beautiful Men scrapbook out of my drawer and paged through the photos. The trip to see the Rubberman had disturbed me. I felt anxious and dirty. Looking through my scrapbook, I found some small comfort in the way John Travolta's cheeks dimpled when he smiled.

WEST HOLLYWOOD

"So what makes you think you're in love with him?"
Randall was playing devil's advocate. I was backstage, peeling off my jeans and strapping on my yellow thong. Aretha Franklin was pumping through the speakers. *We goin' ridin' on the freeway of love in my pink Cadillac. . . .*

"Because when I'm away from him," I said, "I just can't wait to get back to him." I was adjusting my cock and balls in the pouch. "And because he makes me laugh. And because he's the sweetest, nicest, most considerate man I've ever met." I looked at my image in the mirror, buck naked under the strobe lights. "And he wants me to quit this."

Randall took a sip of his sloe gin fizz. "Really? What will you do for money?"

I squirted some gel into my hands and rubbed it into my hair. "Maybe get serious about acting. It's time, don't you think? Stripping has been a huge distraction."

"In other words, he said he'd support you." Randall made a face. "He'll be your sugar daddy. Okay, *now* I understand the attraction."

"You are being *such* a bitch." I rinsed my hands off in the sink. "Frank is no sugar daddy. He is not rich by any means. He's just a doll. You'll see. He'll be here tonight, and I want you to meet him."

"Guess I just didn't see you ending up with a schoolteacher." Randall sighed and took another sip of his drink. "That seems more *my* league."

It was then that I understood Randall's reaction to my announcement that Frank and I were moving in together. Randall had always been more serious than I was, dating guys he thought would make good husbands. I was just turning tricks. No doubt he'd expected to land a steady, reliable boyfriend long before I did, but all he'd managed was a string of duds. I suspected he'd begun to worry, at the ripe old age of twenty-two, that he'd never find someone. That was certainly in character for Randall.

"Hey, Danny," Benny called, peeking his head around the door. "You're on in five minutes. Carlos is exhausted."

"I'm all set," I told him.

"I just worry," Randall said, once Benny had closed the door, "that in a few years the age difference will really start to matter."

I made a face. "You're crazy. He's in perfect shape. Better shape than I am. He doesn't look his age at all."

"But he's *thirty-five*."

"So?"

"Danny, that's *fourteen* years older than you are. When you're thirty, he'll be forty-four."

"Big deal."

"And when you're forty, he'll be—"

"Randall!" I grabbed his ears. "I know how to add! Besides, that's almost two decades from now! We haven't even moved in together yet."

He smiled. "Sorry. Just wanted you to think it through."

"I have." I took one last glance in the mirror. "Frank is the first thing I think of in the morning and the last thing I think of before I fall asleep."

"Okay, so you're in love," Randall said. "But is he in love with you in the same way?"

I was glad I didn't have to answer the question. Benny came barging through the door at that moment. "Okay, Danny, you're on!"

I hurried out front and hopped up onto my box. Randall followed, leaning against the bar and watching me as he sipped his drink. Chaka Khan was playing. *Baby, baby, when I look at you, I get a warm feeling inside.* I began to swing my hips to the music. Men gathered around, waving their tens and twenties. *I feel for you. I think I love you. . . .*

I spotted Frank coming into the bar and saw right away that Gregory Montague, in sweater vest and oxford shirt, was with him. He was smiling his toothy Katharine Hepburn smile, glancing around the bar, careful not to look at me. That took some effort, since I was in the middle of everything, up on a box, with a spotlight shining on me. But Frank made eye contact immediately. His face creased into a wide smile, which I didn't return right away. Why had he brought that man with him? I had no desire to ever see Gregory Montague again after what had happened at his house.

I stopped dancing. I just stood there, shifting my weight from foot to foot. I heard a hiss from below. "What's the matter with you?" It was Edgar, standing behind me. "You can't be tired already. You just got up there."

"Sorry," I said and began dancing again.

Edgar gestured for me to lean down. "You need a little pick-me-up?" he whispered in my ear, his breath stinking of tobacco and gin.

Right about then, a line of coke would have been absolutely fantastic. But I didn't want to do it with Frank around. And I also knew that Edgar never offered any blow without a price. "What do I have to do for it?" I asked.

"See that guy who just came in? The one in the sweater vest?"

I looked from him over to Gregory.

"Yeah," I said.

"He wants you. Came in here a couple days ago asking about you."

I laughed, straightening up and continuing to dance. "No kidding," I said.

"Yeah. He'll pay us well."

"Oh, I'm sure he would," I said. "But no sale."

"Danny, don't be a prick."

"Fuck off," I told him. "I gotta dance."

What an asshole Gregory Montague was. So I was still just a

whore to him. I knew that Frank had told him that we were dating. But obviously, Gregory didn't care. Or maybe he cared too much. Maybe there really *were* feelings still lingering between him and Frank. Maybe Gregory was jealous. Maybe he was trying to break us up. Or maybe he was testing me to see if I was good enough for Frank.

I watched them. Frank had bought a beer for himself and a cocktail for Gregory. They leaned up against the wall, in exactly the place I had first noticed Frank months before. Frank gave me a little wave. I finally acknowledged him with a smile. Gregory still didn't look over at me. He was clearly waiting to see what message he'd get back from Edgar.

I began bouncing in place, catching the rhythm of the music. *One night in Bangkok and the world's your oyster. The bars are temples but the pearls ain't free.*

"Come on, baby, show me the family jewels," one old man, with curly dyed black hair, called. He was standing right in front of me, his head level with my stomach. He flashed a twenty at me and licked his dry, chapped lips.

I peeled down the thong just enough to expose my pubes and offer him a glimpse of my cock tucked inside. I didn't often do that; he might have been a cop, waiting to charge Edgar with illegal nudity. But he was just a horny old geezer, and for the peek at my pubes, he tucked the twenty into my pouch, copping a little feel as he did so.

I looked up. For the first time, Gregory was watching me directly. He had seen the whole little interaction.

I felt dirty. His eyes appraised me, glassy and hard. A twist of a smile played with the corners of his lips. My face burned. I couldn't bring myself to look at Frank.

Why did it matter? Stripping was what I did. This was who I was. A stripper in a bar who showed his cock and balls for tips. And sometimes I went home with men who paid me money to have sex with them. *This was who I was.* Gregory knew this. Frank knew this. It was no secret.

But suddenly I stopped dancing again. Murray Head went on without me. *One night in Bangkok makes a hard man humble. Not much between despair and ecstasy . . .*

It was strange. It had been a full year now that I'd been dancing at the club, and not once in all that time had I thought about
the place I went to with my mother when I was fifteen. But standing now on my box, with Frank and Gregory watching me, I suddenly remembered that place. It was a stripper bar, much like this
one, except it was grimier. And the dancers weren't boys; they
were girls. And the men watching them weren't as lively as the
men here, but rather sullen, hostile, and hunched over. Mom
and I were following a lead the Rubberman had given us. Becky,
he'd said, might be dancing there, using the name Heather. The
place was called Les Chats, and it was up in Yonkers, New York,
just off the Saw Mill River Parkway.

Troy drove us, as he usually did in those days. It took us about
three hours to get there, because we got lost and ended up in
New Jersey before winding our way back. The building was a plain
concrete rectangle, with a giant neon blue electric sign that flashed
XXX. No longer did Mom make any pretense of trying to shield
me, or even Troy; we just walked into the place behind her, all of
us nearly knocked over by the smell of stale beer and piss. On the
stage, three topless girls danced, wearing fringed boots and thongs—
not so different from the thong I was wearing now. Two of the
girls were obviously not Becky. They were short and plump and
far too old. But the third might have been—if Becky had dyed
her hair blond and gotten a tattoo of a leaping tiger on her thigh.
The men hunched over their beers turned to look at us as we came
in. We were hardly the type of clientele they were used to. We
gathered around the girl who might have been Becky and looked
up at her closely. She ignored us and just kept on dancing. My
mother didn't seem to care that Troy and I were gazing up at this
naked girl. Suddenly Mom just broke down in tears, big, heaving
sobs, her breasts rising and falling. The girl wasn't Becky. But she
might have been. Mom was crying out of both relief and disappointment. The men looked at us strangely. The bartender came
over to us and asked us to leave.

"She's in a place like this," Mom said when we returned to the
car. "She's taking her clothes off in front of men like those inside." She heaved deeply with her sobs, so deeply that I had to
grip her arm to keep her from losing her balance and falling

down. "My baby. In a place like this. Men looking at her body. Touching her body. Her little body, which I once diapered . . ." She dissolved into sobs in my arms. I held her, stroking her hair.

"Mom," I said. "I will go into every bar in every state and look for Becky. Please don't cry."

She looked up at me with bloodshot, swollen eyes. "My poor little Danny. My poor little boy. What have our lives become?"

It was the first time she had ever voiced such sadness, such regret. I continued to stroke her hair as if she were a little girl. If I could have, I would have held her forever. I loved her that much.

And now I never spoke to her. Now I kept her far, far down in my memory. When she did occasionally surface in my thoughts, I became quite adept at pushing her away.

And now here I was, taking my clothes off in a place not so different from Les Chats, allowing men to look at my body, touch my body, the same little body my mother once had diapered . . .

The same life she had so despaired of that day in Yonkers.

"Hey, sugar meat," the old man was saying to me, waving another twenty. "Flash me those family jewels again." He licked his lips like a lizard.

I couldn't. My eyes moved from him to Frank to Gregory. Gregory was grinning.

I hopped off my box and ran backstage.

Edgar was right on my heels. "What the fuck you doing? You've still got fifteen minutes out there."

I pulled off my thong and stood stark naked in front of him. "Fuck you," I said. "I'm done."

"You little bitch. You can't walk out on me. You owe me money!"

"Fuck you I do."

Edgar got up into my face, his drawn yellow skin stretched tightly over his wasting muscles, his cheekbones sticking out like knobs. "I've been keeping track. The last four guys I fixed you up with. You didn't give me my share."

"Fuck you," I said again. I could feel my face getting hot.

"You little bitch!" Edgar shouted again and raised his hand to strike me.

And just like in the movies, Frank was behind him to catch it.

"Don't even think about hitting him, you asshole," Frank growled, shoving Edgar away so hard that he fell on the floor. He turned to look at me. "You okay, Danny?"

"I'm quitting," I told him. I was still naked.

"Good," Frank said.

Edgar was getting to his feet. "You walk out of here, Danny, and don't expect to come groveling back to me."

Frank's eyes were burning. "Don't worry. He never will. He won't need to."

I just stood there, looking at my savior.

"Come on, baby," Frank said. "Get dressed and let's get out of here."

"I love you, Frank," I said in a little voice.

He pulled me close to him, then let me go.

Randall had asked me if Frank was in love with me in the same way I was in love with him. It didn't matter. All that mattered was that I loved him. And he was going to take care of me. That was enough.

I got dressed. I didn't tell Frank what Gregory Montague had tried. To do so would have spoiled the moment. And that, too, didn't matter. Not anymore. Frank might carry the torch for him, but it was *me* he had chosen. Me he had just rescued from a life that was destroying me, a little bit more each day. That was all that mattered.

In two months, Edgar was dead from AIDS. The bar closed down. A year later it reopened under new management. Sometimes Frank and I would go in and watch the dancers there. I looked around the place but didn't recognize it. It was almost as if I'd never been there at all.

PALM SPRINGS

"So what makes you think you're in love with him?"

Randall was playing devil's advocate in the way only he could do. We were in my Jeep, Hassan in the back, heading over to the tram that would take us two and a half miles up the sheer cliffs of Chino Canyon. Kelly was meeting us there. I wanted him to meet my friends.

"Because I think about him all the time," I said. "Believe me, I've tried to forget him, but it's impossible. He's just so special. He makes me laugh. And he reminds me of myself at that age."

"And what does Frank think about you being in love with someone else?" Hassan asked from the backseat.

I sighed. "I haven't used those exact words with Frank. I've only begun admitting them to myself in the last couple of days."

The night I'd left Kelly's apartment after our sexual encounter, I had never wanted to see him again. Truthfully, in that moment, I'd wanted nothing more than to push him out of my mind. My fascination with him had become a terrible burden, and I hadn't realized just how heavy it was until that moment. He had disappointed me, shattered my fantasy, and now I wanted to shake off my burden. I wanted to be free of him.

I hadn't told Frank I was out with Kelly that night, but when I came home, I revealed all. Or almost all. "He's a cokehead," I said, cruelly. I wanted to be cruel in that moment.

"Well, you don't want to get mixed up in that again," Frank said.

"Definitely not," I said. "And sex with him was just a big waste of time. No intimacy. He barely let me kiss him."

Frank sighed, sitting with a cup of tea on the deck under the stars. "He seems wounded. Very guarded. He's not going to let you in, because he doesn't want to get hurt."

I was in no mood just then for sympathy. "Well, it's certainly not worth it for me to spend any more energy on him."

Frank smiled. "I wasn't aware that you were spending that much energy on him."

"Well, I wasn't, really." For a second time, I had just lied to Frank. "I guess I just wanted to get him into bed, and now I have, and it was a big bust."

"Are you sure that's all you wanted from him? To get him into bed?"

I couldn't lie again. Instead, I evaded answering. "All I know is, it's over," I said.

"Well, clearly, Danny, you really like the boy."

That was all I needed to hear. I did indeed really like the boy, and hearing Frank say it, recognize it, affirm it, made it all too real once again. My anger and disappointment dissipated. Suddenly I wanted to hurry back across town to be with him, to give it another try, to take him in my arms and erase whatever hurt had caused him to fear intimacy. I wanted to change his life. I wanted to *save* him. I wanted to take him apart and rebuild him from scratch.

Of course, I couldn't continue the conversation with Frank, not now, not with the way I was suddenly thinking. So I took off my clothes and dove into the pool. We didn't speak of Kelly again.

But I dreamed about him all night long.

And in the morning, I felt desperate. My stomach hurt; my eyes teared up. At my computer, I couldn't work. I wanted to take a drug to counteract the pheromones or whatever chemicals the brain releases when one falls in love. I could feel them coursing through my body, and I was helpless against their power. I knew the outcome could only be misery and discontent. The situation was hopeless. I wanted him still—it was a physical ache—but I argued to myself that if I couldn't hold him, if I couldn't kiss him, what good would it be? I truly wished for a magic drug that would allow me to forget him. Whoever could invent such a product would make millions. I would have paid any amount to get my hands on it.

All day long I tried to push Kelly out of my mind. I'd alternate between anger and tears. But then I couldn't stand it anymore. My will shattered, and I texted him. HEY HOW R U? As if nothing had happened.

For more than an hour, I waited for a response, my phone at my elbow. Finally, the blessed chirp of an incoming text message. GOOD. WHATS UP?

I immediately texted back. DINNER THIS WEEK? He replied, GREAT, and all my despair evaporated. I would see him again. *I would see him again!*

And so we had dinner, and again he made me laugh, and again he drew some pictures of people at the other tables. And again we did some coke, rushing off to the bathroom in repeated intervals, with a little plastic Baggie in our pockets and a pen cap in our hands, using it as a scoop to deliver the delectable white powder to our nostrils. Beaming and giggling, I'd return to the table, a kid again, running around as I had in my twenties in West Hollywood. And I loved Kelly for making me feel this way.

We didn't speak of the sex until I took him home. When I went to kiss him good-bye, he pulled back and said, "No. We can't. Not after the other night."

"Forget about that. We can do better."

"No," he said, getting out of the car. "We can't go there anymore."

"Why not? What are you so scared of?"

"I'm not scared!" he shouted, defensive.

"Who hurt you? Who made you so afraid?"

"I'm not afraid!"

"Then why won't you try again with me?"

"Because I don't want to ruin a good thing," he said, staring at me through the open window. "After the other night, I didn't think I'd ever hear from you again. I'm so glad you texted me. Let's not ruin things."

I would not beg. "Fine," I said, starting the ignition.

"Don't be mad," he said.

"I'm not mad," I told him, but I didn't say good-bye, just drove off.

Yet even before I got home, he had texted me. IM JUST NOT READY 4 IT. PLEASE DONT HATE ME.

I COULD NEVER HATE U, I texted back, my heart melting like ice cream, dripping down inside me, all over my lungs and my guts.

And so we made a plan for today, to ride the tram to the top of the mountain. I wanted Randall to meet Kelly. I wanted someone to understand how special he was to me. And I wanted to admit to someone, to speak the words out loud, that I was in love.

We parked the Jeep and took the shuttle up to the tram station. As we stepped off, I spotted Kelly waiting outside. I was deliriously, disproportionately happy to see him. I practically ran to him, Randall and Hassan following more slowly behind.

I made introductions. Kelly pretended he remembered them from the Parker. We hurried inside to buy our tickets, then stood in line to wait for the next tram.

"What would we do," Kelly asked, his eyes as wide as a kid's, "if one of the cables broke and we were left hanging there, suspended over the canyon, for hours? What if they said the only way we could survive, to keep the last remaining cable from snapping, was to throw some weight overboard? We'd have to toss the fattest people off the tram, or else *all* of us would plummet into the canyon and die. What would we do?"

Hassan looked at him, his heavy brows knitting together. "What a strange, cruel question to ask."

Kelly laughed. I was used to his offbeat questions, his quirky scenarios, his outrageous what-ifs. But Hassan and Randall didn't quite know what to make of him.

"I'd jump," I offered, "and take my chances."

"That's more than ten thousand feet," Kelly replied. "Look, it says so right here." He waved a brochure about the tram in my face. "This is so cool. I've never gone up the mountain before. This is excellent." His dimples were deep as he smiled. I was glad I'd suggested doing this, since it seemed to make him so happy.

When the tram arrived, Kelly pushed through a knot of kids so he could be first in line. "He is quite the impatient one," Hassan said in my ear as we followed along.

Kelly was far enough ahead not to hear us. "Tell me something," I said to Hassan. "When you look at him, what do you see? If you were to take his picture, what would you be photographing?"

"A blur," Hassan said, without hesitation.

We were crowding onto the tram. Kelly was waving us over to one side, against the window. "I didn't want to get stuck in the middle," he said. "I wanted to be right up front so I could have a great view." His nose was literally pressed against the glass. "The tram turns, you know, so you get three-hundred-sixty-degree views."

"Yes, I know," I told him.

Frank and I had taken the tram many times. Back when we first started coming out to Palm Springs, we often made the trip to the top of the mountain so we could hike the trails. As always, our goal was to spot a bighorn sheep. But sightings of the famous creatures with their gorgeous curved horns so prized by hunters were rare. The sheep, dwindling in number, stayed mostly far from the trails. The Crow Indians had believed the bighorns possessed supernatural powers, and if you spotted them, they could grant wisdom and strength to worthy men. Yet in all that time, we never saw a single bighorn—though we did run into mule deer and rattlesnakes, and we watched red-tailed hawks arc across the blue sky.

Sometimes, during the winter, Frank and I would go up on the tram so we could see some snow. Being an East Coast boy, I missed snow. I had fond memories of tobogganing with Becky down the small hill behind our house, into Flo Armstrong's yard next door. In the beginning, Frank and I would go cross-country skiing at the top of the mountain. Our cheeks would be hard and cold, our hearts pumping fast, our breathing deep and clear. But it had been years now, maybe even a decade, since we'd done that.

The tram began to rise, and the canyon floor dropped away from us. Very quickly we were very high up, and I noticed Kelly take a step backward away from the glass.

"Amazing view, huh?" I asked.

"Yeah," he said. But I noticed him take another step back.

"Hey," I said, "those kids are getting in front of you. Thought you wanted the up-close view."

"They're kids. They should have the view."

I realized he was getting scared. I smiled.

"What did you say about the cables breaking?" I teased.

His face was white. "Stop it." He turned away, facing the inside of the tram, no longer looking out.

As the tram passed each of its supporting posts, it rocked, sending a collective shriek from the passengers each time. Even Hassan, so unflappable, let out a small yelp. I was prepared for it, so I didn't make a sound. I kept my eyes on Kelly. The jolt had left him trembling.

"You okay?" I asked quietly.

"Do you think," he asked, equally as quiet, "we could *walk* back down?"

I shook my head. "That's more than two miles of sheer cliff."

"Fuck," he whispered and closed his eyes.

I reached over and put my arm around him. The tram was filled with straight couples and their chattering kids, but I didn't care. I pulled Kelly in tightly toward me. "It's gonna be fine, baby. Don't worry. I've ridden this thing dozens of—"

The tram rocked harshly again, and I reached out to steady myself. Kelly gripped me so tightly, I felt his fingernails through my sweater.

"How long is this fucking ride?" he asked, near tears.

"We're almost at the top," I assured him.

When we docked, Kelly was the first one off. I noticed Randall and Hassan exchange small smiles, and I glared at them not to say anything.

Once we were on the trail, Kelly was calm again. He had his guidebook, and was telling us the best routes to take. I allowed him to lead the way, even though I'd been up there so many times, I could have led us around with my eyes closed. But I knew that the best way to see a familiar place was to take someone who'd never been there before and experience it again through his eyes. Already I was thinking of places I could take Kelly and see afresh. Joshua Tree. Big Sur. Disneyland.

He was up ahead, walking with Hassan. Randall was huffing along at my side.

"So what do you think of him?" I asked.

"He's very attractive."

"Well, yes, obviously. But what do you think of him as a person?"

Randall shrugged. "Hard to say. All I've shared with him is one tram ride, and he was too terrified to say much then."

"But, come on. You can see how sweet he is. He's like a big kid. Look how eager he is."

Up ahead Kelly was pointing up into the trees, pausing to stoop down and examine rocks. He turned around to us at that point and shouted, "The book says there's a clearing up here where we can see the whole valley. Maybe we can see our houses!"

"See what I mean?" I said to Randall.

"Danny," he said to me, "I'm a little worried about you."

I stopped walking and looked at him. "What?"

"I'm worried about you," he said again. "You're head over heels for this kid."

"And what's the problem with that?"

Randall looked at me as if I were crazy. "The problem has a name. *Frank*."

I laughed and started walking again. "Why is Frank a problem? We have an open relationship."

"Danny, this kid isn't just a trick. He's not what's-his-name from Sherman Oaks."

"I know he's not just a trick. I love him. And I can't pretend I don't."

"Bully for you. But what does that mean for Frank?"

I scoffed. "It doesn't have to mean anything. Frank doesn't mind when I pursue relationships on my own. In fact, he hasn't really participated with Ollie and me in a while, and the other night, with Kelly, he just said go ahead and do what we wanted on our own. He was fine with it."

"And you think he'll have the same blasé kind of reaction when he hears you say you're in love with another man?"

I stopped walking again. "I don't know," I admitted. "I don't know what he'd say about that."

"I don't think he'd be happy." Randall sighed. "Danny, the whole reason your nonmonogamy has worked for so long is that, deep down, Frank has always been number one in your heart."

"Well, maybe I just got tired of never having that be reciprocal," I grumbled.

"Oh, cut that out, Danny. Gregory Montague has been dead for a long time. Even if Frank did carry a torch for him all those years, about which you seem so certain, it was *you* he's always been devoted to, *you* he's loved for the past two decades."

"I *know* that, Randall," I said, becoming more annoyed by the second. "But I can't deny the way Kelly makes me feel. I feel *alive* again—for the first time in a very long while. When I'm with him, I feel *young*. With Frank, it's all about aches and pains and being too tired to do things."

"He's jogging. He's trying."

I made a face. Yes, Frank was jogging. And he always came back in red and panting, and completely dehydrated. I told him he ought to take a bottle of water with him on his runs, so he wouldn't dry out so much. I told him one of these days he'd pass out, and if that happened when he was running on the road, he could get hit by a car. I felt as if I was giving advice to my grandfather.

"Danny," Randall was asking, "how does Kelly feel about *you?*"

"I don't know," I admitted.

"You don't know?"

"He's resistant. I don't know why."

"But of course you know why! Danny, once again, it's Frank! Of course Kelly would resist you. Who would want to fall in love with someone who already has a husband?"

I shook my head. "I wish it were that simple."

"It *is* that simple! I can see it plainly. He's trying very hard not to fall in love with you."

I wished that were so. I wished so much that Randall was right. But guys I liked never liked me back, not with the same passion. Why should I have expected it would be any different with Kelly?

Randall leveled his eyes at me. "Do you know what Kelly is for you, Danny?"

"What?"

"A midlife crisis."

"Hey, you guys!" Kelly's voice suddenly cut through the mountain air at that very moment. He and Hassan were quite far ahead of us now on the trail, having been unaware that we'd stopped walking. "What's holding you slowpokes up?"

"We're coming," I said and resumed walking. But I was steaming mad. I could feel my cheeks and neck burning. "How *dare* you?" I hissed at Randall from the corner of my mouth. "I tell you something really profound about how I'm feeling, and you trivialize it as a midlife crisis."

"Danny, I don't mean to trivialize your feelings. But it would seem to me—"

"Stick to orthodontics, buddy," I told him. "You stink at psychotherapy."

I walked on ahead, catching up with Kelly and Hassan just as they reached the crest of the hill and an enormous vista of the valley below opened up before us.

"Wow," Kelly gushed.

The desert floor stretched for miles across the lush greenery of the Coachella Valley towns and the arid sweep of tawny wasteland that ended at the Little San Bernardino Mountains some fifteen miles away.

"You see down there?" I asked Kelly, pointing off to my right. "You can get a tiny glimpse of the Salton Sea. Over there is Indio, and across the way, you can spot Desert Hot Springs."

"And look!" Kelly said, his excitement apparent. "I can see the windmills. The ones north of Palm Springs by the 10."

"Yeah, looks like a garden of them, doesn't it?"

"Yeah." His eyes were soaking up the view. "It's so beautiful up here. You look down and you think of all the people down there, going about their jobs and their lives, and we're up here, looking down at them. Except that we can't see them, and they can't see us. But they're all down there."

I smiled. "Yes, they are."

"It's just so beautiful," he said again.

I moved closer and slipped an arm around his waist. We stood there silent for a while. Randall and Hassan had moved on down the path, leaving us to ourselves. I tightened my hold around Kelly's waist.

"Are you going to take the class at CalArts?" I asked him.

"I can't afford it."

"Then let me pay for it for you."

He pulled away. "No. I can't let you do that."

"I want to."

He looked at me as if he didn't understand what I was saying. "Why," he asked, "are you so nice to me?"

"Because I care about you."

"*Why?*"

"Because you . . . you make me laugh. Because I like being with you."

He smiled. "I like being with you, too."

We were quiet, just looking at each other. I thought my heart was going to break out of my rib cage.

"So I'll call the guy at CalArts," I said. "Let me arrange it for you."

He was hesitant. He looked away.

"Okay?" I asked.

He looked back at me. "I just want to be clear that we are *friends*. Nothing more."

That hurt, but I didn't let myself show it. "Fine," I said. "I promise I'm not going to expect anything for helping you."

Kelly looked at me again with that strange expression. "Why would someone like you care about someone like me?"

"We're not so different, baby."

He looked back out across the valley. "Don't call me baby."

"Sorry."

"It's okay."

We stood silently for a few more minutes. Then Kelly turned and kissed me. For the first time, he took the lead and kissed me. I responded hungrily, grabbing his head in my hands. We kissed for a long time, and the entire world got swallowed up in it, every sight and sound and emotion—until I heard the snap of a twig. We broke apart and turned to look.

For a moment, hope flickered inside me that the creature emerging from the woods might be a bighorn sheep. But instead, a small brown fawn came crunching through the leaves, coming to a stop about three yards away from us, its black, glassy eyes staring in wonder. For a moment nothing moved, not us, not the fawn, not the wind in the trees. Then a crow called, and the startled fawn bolted away on its fragile, tremulous legs.

EAST HARTFORD

The thing that troubled me most, even more than the fact that Dad had lost his job and that our house was up for sale, was the leather jacket I found hanging in Mom's closet. I couldn't stop thinking about it all day at school, wondering why she had bought it, and when she wore it, and who she wore it with.

Brother Pop was passing back our tests. He paused after handing me mine, his doughy hand splayed on my desk.

"You failed, Danny," he said quietly. "Your grades are falling way off this year. I'd like you to start staying after school on Wednesdays for extra help."

"I can't," I said. "I have play practice on Wednesdays."

"You won't be in the play if you can't bring your grades up."

I panicked. I couldn't get kicked out of the play. I absolutely *couldn't.* I had landed the part of Mr. Brownlow, just as I'd been planning to do since last year. All summer long I'd practiced for that part. When I walked into the audition, I knew every line of the part. I didn't even need a script. Brother Connolly, the director, had been very impressed. He gave me the part right there on the spot. I was ecstatic.

Now there was a chance I'd lose the one bright spot in my miserable, dreary existence at St. Francis Xavier, and all because of Brother Pop and his fucking American lit class. The test had been on *The Scarlet Letter,* and while it was true I'd read only the Cliffs

Notes, I thought I knew enough about stupid old Hester Prynne and that crazy reverend who'd fucked her to pass the thing. Clearly, I was wrong.

At lunch I slammed down my tray, almost upsetting my paper cup of Coke.

"What's eating your ass?" Troy asked.

I told him. Troy listened, nodding as he ate his bologna sandwich on white Wonder bread, which his maid had prepared for him.

"Well, looks like you're gonna have to actually start reading your books," he said.

For a while, I'd tried to distance myself from Troy. I knew Chipper thought Troy was a big fag, and I didn't want him getting the same idea about me. But I hadn't seen much of Chipper lately—it was football season—and there really wasn't anybody else to sit with at lunch. Besides, I got horny a lot, and I liked the blow jobs Troy gave me in his car. A couple of months earlier, Troy had turned sixteen, which meant he could drive legally now. So he gave me rides to and from school, happily putting an end to my schlepping home on foot. So I realized pretty quickly that I couldn't completely discard Troy as a friend. And, perhaps most important, he was still pretty useful to Mom.

In the last few weeks, Troy had taken us all over the place, from New York to Boston to New Hampshire. And just a couple of days previous, we'd driven up to see the Rubberman again, who told us the "bitch" with Bruno was indeed Becky. But he didn't dare let her or anyone else know that we were looking for them. We'd have to get to Becky by ourselves. Problem was, every time the Rubberman found out exactly where Bruno had gone, he'd skipped on to somewhere else. Mom began to worry that Bruno had begun to suspect that someone was looking for him and was determined not to be caught.

The Rubberman had admitted she might be right. "He may have a sense someone's after him," he told us, still in the same chair, still smoking like a fiend, looking even more frail than before. This time, however, the television was dark; in fact, all the power in his little house seemed shut off. "And I'll bet he knows it has something to do with his bitch."

Mom no longer recoiled when she heard Becky described as

such. "I just don't want him thinking I'm bringing the heat down on him," she said. "Then he'll go on the lam."

"Did you bring me my communication fee?" the Rubberman rasped. "I need to pay my electric bill."

"Yes," Mom said, handing him another envelope of cash.

The Rubberman took it and peered inside. "All right. I'll send word through a couple of guys that we could maybe make a deal with Bruno that would prove beneficial for him. But like I said, lady, money talks. You understand that."

"I do," Mom said. "And Bruno needs to know he'll get a lot of dough in exchange for Becky."

I frowned. Just where that "dough" would be coming from was not obvious to me. Dad was out of work, fired for showing up drunk too many times. Father McKenna had taken pity and given him a part-time job as a handyman at the church. But even though Dad had told Mom that he'd quit drinking, I'd seen the empty bottles in the basement, and I still smelled whisky on his breath. I knew it was only a matter of time before he lost this job as well. Meanwhile, the brothers of St. Francis Xavier had deferred my tuition for a year, though they couldn't promise anything indefinite.

Faced with all this financial uncertainty, Mom had decided to sell the house. Dad made no protest; he knew his part-time job wouldn't cover the mortgage payments. I think Mom also hoped that we might make a little money in the sale—money she could use in her hunt for Becky.

It had now been a little over a year since my sister had disappeared. My fifteenth birthday had come and gone without comment. It was, after all, the anniversary of Becky's disappearance, too, and that, quite understandably, took precedence. Mom had sobbed from morning to night. Sitting up on my bed in my room, watching *Doctor Who*, I imagined I was explaining the story line to my little boy, Joey. "The Doctor is actually the *fourth* doctor," I told Joey, "having been regenerated into existence after the third doctor contracted radiation poisoning on the planet Metebelis 3." I liked imagining Joey in my room, safe from all the chaos downstairs. "Don't worry," I told the boy. "You don't have to go down there." I would keep him safe, and that made me glad.

But as engrossing as we both found the Doctor's search for the Key to Time, I couldn't forget that it was still my birthday.

I was continually drawn back to that day a year ago, the party with the cake and the M&M's and the friends I no longer had. I remembered what I had seen that morning at the pond, and I knew I could never reveal it. What importance did the memory hold, anyway? That Becky disappeared an hour or so later than what the official report claimed? What possible good would it do to know that little nugget of information?

Of course, the thing that worried Mom most about selling the house was that Becky might come back and find us gone and not know where we were. She might escape from Bruno and make her way back to our house, only to discover a different family living there. Whoever bought the house, Mom insisted, would need to have our new number and address, and would need to keep a sign posted on the door at all times. Without such conditions, Mom said, she wouldn't agree to the sale.

Just where we'd live after the house sold, however, was unclear; Father McKenna assured us he'd help us find something. But the decision to put the house on the market did make one aspect of Mom's life easier: Nana was placed in a nursing home. It broke my heart the day we dropped her off there. We packed up her clothes filling two little suitcases. She sat in the backseat of the car with me, Mom and Dad up front. "Where are we going?" she kept asking, and Dad kept telling her that we'd found her a good place to live, a place where she'd be happy, where she'd be taken care of, and where she'd have many, many friends. But all she'd say in response was, "Where are we going?" And when we finally got there, the place depressed the hell out of me. Old people in wheelchairs sat in the lobby, their necks crooked, their eyes staring vacantly. We didn't even get to see Nana's room. Two nurse's aides greeted us, one taking Nana, the other taking her suitcases. The last thing I heard was Nana asking them, "Can you take me home?" I think even Mom cried a little bit on the way back in the car.

I was thinking about Nana in that place, and I was worrying about having to drop out of the play, so I never even unwrapped the Ring Ding I had bought for lunch. I just sat there, staring off into the cafeteria. Troy noticed.

"You gotta eat something," he said. "You still have geometry class to get through."

"I'm not hungry."

"Do you want pizza? I'm going to go get a slice. I'll get you one if you want."

"No, thanks."

He shrugged and headed off to the cashier.

My eyes spied his book bag. I knew what he kept inside. I knew exactly in which inside pocket he kept his pot. If I was going to do this, I had to act fast. I made sure Troy was far enough away, then I pulled a plastic Baggie out of my pocket. I'd stuffed it in there this morning. Quick as a flash, I yanked Troy's book bag off the chair and got it onto the floor, and in almost the same motion, I unzipped the top. It was a good thing no one sat with us at lunch to see what I was doing. Inside the book bag, my hand felt for the interior zipper and pulled it open. Gripping the bag of pot, hidden by the tabletop, I shook about half of it into my own Baggie. Then I replaced it, zipped up, and returned the bookbag to the chair.

Troy was such a stoner that even if he noticed he had less pot than he had this morning, he'd probably just chalk it up to having smoked a doob and forgotten about it. I'd performed this little sleight of hand before; I knew I could get away with it. I didn't really consider it stealing. Troy always shared his pot with me. I could smoke as much of it as I wanted. I was just taking my share now, instead of waiting until after school. Besides, he was a rich kid with a prodigious allowance. I didn't know where he got his pot, but I knew he didn't have any trouble paying for it. It wasn't like I was taking it from some poor kid who had to save his pennies to buy his weekly dime bag.

I finally ate my Ring Ding just as the bell sounded for my next class. Riding the wave of a sugar buzz—I'd washed the Ring Ding down with Coca-Cola—I made it through geometry, chemistry, and French. And then the last bell of the day rang, and we all scrambled to our lockers. I told Troy to wait for me, that I'd meet him at his car in fifteen minutes; there was something I had to do first.

Out on the field, the football team was in their helmets, shoulder pads, and cleats, gathering for their afternoon practice. They were either running in place or doing push-ups on the grass. I gripped the chain-link fence with my fingers and called across the field. "Hey, Paguni!" I knew it wasn't cool to call the football players by their first names in public. "Hey, Paguni! Come here!"

Chipper lifted his helmeted head and came jogging over to me. The sight made me very happy indeed. I'd been to every one of his games this year, just as I'd promised. It hadn't been a good season; the team had yet to win a single game. Chipper mostly sat on the bench, but the couple times he'd been called in to play, I'd rushed out of the bleachers and come to the fence, just as I had right now, calling, "Go, Paguni!" One time I'd seen a flash of his white teeth from inside his helmet when he heard the words, and that had thrilled me. To think that I, Danny Fortunato, had encouraged Chipper Paguni. There was nothing like the feeling. Nothing at all.

I think I love you. Isn't that what life is made of? Though it worries me to say, I've never felt this way.

"What's going on?" Chipper asked as he reached the other side of the fence.

"Is your car unlocked?"

"Yeah."

"I got you something."

He pulled in closer to the fence. The chin of the helmet actually dinged against the chain-link. "Shut up," he said. "Don't say anything else."

"Okay, okay. Nobody heard."

"Just put it way down under the seat mat."

"Will do."

I could see his eyes moving like brown spotlights within the helmet. "Sure you don't want me to pay you?"

"No. It's cool."

"Why are you so nice to me, man?"

I shrugged. "'Cause you're nice to me."

"Whatever. Come over later."

"I will."

He ran back to the team, and I headed out to the parking lot, where Troy was waiting for me. But first I stopped at Chipper's car and slipped the bag of pot under the mat in the front seat. I couldn't wait for tonight, when I could sit on Chipper's red shag floor, our feet stretched out and toes touching. The shades would be drawn, and it would be all dark, and we'd smoke and get really high, and then he'd ask me to walk on his back again. Lately he'd been taking off his shirt when I did it. He said it was better that way. I'd walk on his naked back, his tight, hard shoulder muscles flexing, and I'd have the biggest boner in my pants I'd ever got. I think he knew. How could he not see it?

"You wanta come over?" Troy asked as I slid into his car.

"No, we can just go to my house. Mom is out with Warren today. Dad's at the church. Nobody will be home."

"Where's your Mom going with Warren?"

Troy was bugging me. I didn't like how much he knew about Mom and her crazy schemes.

"I don't know," I told him. "Going to various biker hangouts, asking about Becky. What else does she do with her life?"

We rode in silence. When we got home, the real estate agent—Dad's old secretary, Phyllis, in fact—was just finishing showing the house to a young couple. The woman was pregnant. It felt odd to think of a new family living there.

"Tell your mom these folks are *very* interested," Phyllis whispered to me, the smell of her orange hard candy on her breath.

Troy and I flopped down on the couch and switched on the TV. I flicked through the channels until I found a rerun of *Gilligan's Island*. It was the one where Mrs. Howell dreams she's Cinderella. I had always liked that one. Troy was rolling a joint. He didn't seem to notice any pot was missing from the bag. I told him to hurry, that I didn't know when Mom would come walking in. We had the Lysol can ready.

We smoked and kissed at the same time, keeping our eyes on the TV. Mrs. Howell dreamed of going to the ball and the Skipper, in drag as her stepmother, laughed at her and called her ugly. I had a nice buzz on, and Troy was a good kisser. I had to give him that. Almost as good as he was a cocksucker, and my pants were already tenting in anticipation. But this time he didn't immediately drop into my lap, but instead moved his lips to my ear, and then down my neck. His tongue left me tingling. He returned his lips to my ear.

"Danny," he whispered. "I love you."

I didn't know what to make of the words. I was high. They seemed unreal. They seemed to have some sort of meaning, but I wasn't sure what. I didn't reply.

Then the phone rang.

I never answered the phone anymore. Mom still did, of course, convinced every time it was Becky. But when Mom wasn't home, I just let the answering machine pick up. If it was about Becky, then it was better to have the message left on the machine than to put myself in a situation where I might screw it up or not ask the right questions, as I had done before. I had never forgotten the slap Mom had given me across the face.

"Danny," Troy said again in my ear, ignoring the ring. Perhaps he thought I hadn't heard him the first time. "I love you."

The answering machine clicked on. Mom's voice sliced between us: "This is Peggy Fortunato. If you are calling about my daughter, Rebecca Ann Fortunato, please leave a message and please, please, *please* leave a phone number. Thank you and God bless you." Then came the long beep.

"Listen good." A deep growl resonated through the living room. "You keep going after Bruno, and you are a dead woman. One warning. That's all." There was the sound of a phone hanging up hard.

My blood froze. I stood up, knocking Troy off me. "Jesus Christ!"

"What was that?" Troy asked.

"Didn't you hear it?" Now my face was hot as I hurried over to the answering machine, the little red light blinking. "It was Bruno! And he wants to kill my mother!"

"You don't know that was Bruno. Maybe it was somebody else."

"Who cares? Bruno wants my mother dead! He'll kill her if she doesn't stop!"

I started to cry. I couldn't help it.

Troy stood up and put his hands on my shoulders. "It's okay, Danny. Just tell her and she'll stop."

"No, she won't! She'll never stop!" My tears were flying off my face as I pushed Troy away. "They're going to kill my mother!"

Troy didn't know what to do or say. He just stood there, looking hopelessly clueless as he replaced his dumb-ass blue-tinted aviator glasses on his face. I wanted him out of the house.

"You gotta go," I told him. "Mom is going to be upset when she gets back."

"Maybe she'll want me to drive her somewhere. . . ."

"No!" I screamed. "No more driving anywhere anymore! They'll kill her!"

"Well, I'll stay until she gets back. . . ."

"No!" I screamed even louder. "You've got to go *now!*"

"Okay, okay."

I turned my back on him and didn't look around until I heard the front door slam. Then, from the living room, I heard Troy start his car and squeal out of the driveway.

I cried harder then.

I didn't move off the couch for an hour. I just sat there, bawling like a little baby. I hoped Dad wouldn't come home, because there was no way I could keep this from him. He'd want to know why I was crying, and I'd tell him, and then he'd confront Mom, and they'd have a huge fight, and then he'd get drunk. Mom needed to come home first, so I could tell her, and we could keep Dad out of it. It was up to me, and me alone, to get her to agree to stop looking for Bruno. We'd just have to let the police handle it. I knew she didn't trust the police, but there was no other way now.

Then I began to worry that she was already dead, that they'd already gotten her. Maybe that was why she still wasn't home even as the sun began to set. I was freaking out. I rushed from window to window, hoping, praying, that I'd hear the sound of Warren's motorcycle. And finally, thank God, I did. I watched as the bike rounded the corner, Mom on the back. She was wearing her leather jacket, emblazoned with a Harley Davidson patch that I didn't remember seeing before. Warren pulled into the driveway, and Mom got off the bike. She reached over and put her arms around Warren and kissed him. On the mouth.

I turned away from the window, sickened.

She came through the front door as Warren roared off down the street. She saw my tears. "What's wrong?" she asked sharply.

"They're going to kill you!" I blurted out. "Please stop! Please, Mommy, stop!"

"Jesus Christ," she said, and I saw her notice the red blinking light on the answering machine. She'd moved swiftly across the room, this little lady in her heavy black motorcycle jacket, a lady who'd just kissed a biker in our driveway and who looked nothing like my mother, Peggy Fortunato. She pressed PLAY and listened to the message. I started to cry all over again.

"That doesn't scare me," Mom said, even though I could tell it did. "We've got to tell the Rubberman."

"No, no more!" I cried.

"No one is going to intimidate me into giving up on Becky!"

"But if you get killed, who will I *have?*" I could barely speak; my tears were choking my throat.

She paused, looking at me. For a moment, she softened. She actually reached over and touched my cheek.

"Oh, Danny," she said. "I know it's been hard on you. But if it were you who had gone missing, I'd be looking for you just as hard. You wouldn't want me to give up on you, would you?"

I wasn't sure if she'd be looking for me just as hard. In fact, I was pretty sure she wouldn't be. "I just don't want you to get killed," I told her.

"I'm not going to get killed, Danny," she said. "You don't have to worry about being alone. I promise."

"If you died, *I'd* die." I blubbered.

"Danny." She placed her hand on the back of my head and brought me close to her. Not a full hug, but it was something. "No more talk of dying, okay?"

I nodded.

She went to the phone and dialed. "Lee Ann," she said, "it's Peggy. When Warren gets home, tell him I need to speak with him. *Pronto.*"

"Mom," I begged after she'd hung up, "please don't go with the bikers anymore."

"Danny, drop it."

She took off her jacket and walked down the hall. I followed her.

"Mom, please promise me you'll stop."

I watched as she hung the jacket carefully in her closet.

"I don't want you to get killed," I said again.

"Oh, Danny." She looked at me with impatience. "I *told* you. I'm not going to get killed."

That was it. I knew if I asked again, she'd get angry. She headed to the kitchen.

"Say nothing of this to your father," she called over her shoulder. "We must be getting close if Bruno is getting worried."

I headed up the stairs to my room. Taking Chipper's underwear out of my drawer, I held them in my hands. They were stiff now, hardened by more than a year of breathing on them and from being fondled by my sweaty hands. But still they were my talisman, my protection. I sat holding the underwear on my bed, my eyes trained through the window to watch for the headlights of Chipper's car to come swinging down the street. I couldn't wait to see him. I couldn't wait to walk on his back.

At least if they killed Mom, I consoled myself, I'd still have Chipper.

PALM SPRINGS

It was the eagerness on Ollie's face, his undisguised happiness at seeing me again, that made me feel like a real shit.

"Hey, Danny!" he said, his smile lighting up his face as I opened the door to let him inside.

"Hey, Ollie," I said in reply, but as usual that was where the conversation pretty much ended. I asked him if he wanted a drink, and he said no, and so I told him to have a seat and that I'd go get Frank.

"He's here," I said, peeking around the corner into Frank's office.

"Okay, I'll be in shortly," Frank said, his glasses down on his nose as he graded papers.

"You sure?" I asked. "Or should I take him out to the casita?"

He lifted a watery eye in my direction. "No. Take him to the bedroom. I'll be there in a moment."

Frank was doing it for me, I knew. Too often he'd begged off from sex in the last several months, and I'd been annoyed. Now, ironically, I really didn't care if he joined in or not. In fact, I wasn't all that psyched about having sex with Ollie myself—no matter how much I tried to concentrate on his delectable ass. I knew very well that poor Ollie was merely a stand-in for someone else, someone I couldn't get. Ollie had driven all the way down here from Sherman Oaks on a pretense, on a terrible lie that was eating away at my conscience. "I've missed you," I'd e-mailed him this morning. Immediately he'd replied that he could be here by tonight. And now he was.

I headed back into the living room. Ollie was just sitting there. He wasn't even reading a magazine. He was just sitting there, with his hands in his lap, waiting for me.

"Sure you don't want a drink?" I asked.

"No, I'm good."

"Not even some water?"

"Oh, okay. I'll have some water."

I went into the kitchen and filled him a glass. This was wrong. This was so terribly wrong. I didn't want to have sex with Ollie. I especially didn't want to have sex with Ollie and Frank. There was only one person I wanted to be having sex with.

But that could never happen again.

That day, after coming back down from the mountain, I let Randall and Hassan take the Jeep, and I went with Kelly in his car back to his place. The kiss we'd shared in the sky had left me reeling. I wanted more. We spoke no words as we fell down onto his mattress. I took off my shirt. This time, I insisted, there *would* be something more. I told Kelly to lick my chest, to play with my nipples. He bit them, far more roughly than I liked. It hurt. I told him to ease up. He didn't. I finally pushed him away and took down his pants. His cock wasn't hard. I felt rejected; he felt embarrassed. He suggested we do a line. I wasn't sure. He got up and did one, anyway. I finally agreed to join in.

But instead of making me horny this time, the coke made me crazy. "Kiss me," I ordered him. "Kiss me like you did on the mountain."

"I can't," Kelly protested. He was pulling his pants back on.

"Why not?"

His face twisted in rage. "Because I'm no good at it! I'm not going to fail again!"

"You won't fail! I won't let you fail!"

But he turned his back and refused to say anything else.

I went home soon after that.

For an hour or so, it was similar to the first time. I wanted nothing more to do with him. I wanted to lay down my burden and savor the bliss of weightlessness. But it was impossible. I was soon texting him that I was sorry. He texted back, asking me not to give up on him. I texted, NEVER.

But the ache was so great. I couldn't sleep. After Frank left for school, I couldn't work. I cried like a baby. I was a big, old, melodramatic queen, listening to sad love songs on my iPod and imagining they were all written about Kelly and me. I took the image he had sketched of me and scanned it into my computer, then sat there, staring at it, for an absurdly long time. I wanted a companion image of him so I could set them together. I'd take down that stupid green daisy over the mantel and replace it with a new, beautiful portrait of Kelly and me, created by a fusion of his talents and mine, together.

Then Frank came home, and I had to dry my tears and pretend nothing was wrong.

What did it mean, this promise I'd made to Kelly never to give up on him? I had an inkling, and it wasn't pretty. It meant a lifetime of love deferred, unfulfilled, unrequited. It was no longer possible, I believed, to win him over, to break him down. I had seen the rage in his eyes. *I'm no good at it! I'm not going to fail again!* I wasn't willing to face that kind of rejection again. I had to forget him. I had to peel my emotions away from him, as hard as that might be, and layer them onto something else.

That was when I e-mailed Ollie and told him that I'd missed him.

We went into the bedroom, and I took off his shirt. I kissed the skin that tasted like salty ham. He lay back on the bed, and I undid my pants. Frank came in then and switched off the light.

"Hi, Ollie," he whispered.

"Hi, Frank."

For the past year, Frank had seemed to prefer doing it in the dark. I didn't care one way or the other. There was enough moonlight cutting across the bed to allow me to see. I dropped my pants into a heap on the floor and stepped out of them, pulling my polo shirt over my head. Frank was naked now, too, and we climbed onto the bed on either side of Ollie. We began licking his ears.

"Mmm," Ollie moaned, and I saw his cock instantly spring up. I felt a momentary pulse of pleasure knowing I could still have that effect on someone. Certainly, I hadn't been successful in that regard with Kelly. I reached down and gripped Ollie's cock in my left hand. "Mmm," Ollie said again. That was the extent of his vocabulary during sex.

But Frank was a bit more vocal. "Baby," he said, whispering to me over Ollie's chest. I looked at him and our eyes locked. "Baby," he repeated. "Kiss me."

I hesitated, but only slightly. So slightly I was sure he didn't notice. But then again, Frank noticed everything about me. Twenty years of sexual relations meant there was little he didn't spot, pick up on, recognize. Still, he gave no indication and took my lips to his with the delicacy that had always been his hallmark. Frank knew how to kiss. I felt his tongue slip inside my mouth. It had been a long time since Frank and I had had sex, and suddenly I realized I couldn't remember *how* long. Since the last time with Ollie? But the last time with Ollie, Frank hadn't joined in. So the time before that? I was stunned to realize that I could not remember.

Of course, every night we slept in each other's arms. For twenty years, our spooning had gotten us through every crisis in our lives. Financial worries. Frank's struggles with grad school. Randall's diagnosis. Gregory's death. Pixie's death. My mother's death. My fears about changing careers. Our move to Palm Springs. The spooning seemed eternal, indestructible. Nothing would change it. Nothing except—

How many nights over the last few weeks had I been unable to sleep? Maybe it was even longer than that, now that I thought about it. Maybe it had been a couple of months. Maybe—possibly—it had been much of the past *year*. Things had started to change over the last twelve months. Frank and I always used to fall asleep at the same time, but now he conked out as soon as he hit the pillow, snoring like a bear. Sometimes I'd crawl into bed, and in the back of my mind I'd be hoping for something a little more than spooning, but Frank would be out cold. Literally. He suffered from bad circulation in his legs, which, I supposed, his jogging might help. Bad circulation, his doctor had told him, was common for guys in their fifties. On some nights, there was just no way I could cuddle up next to those ice-cold feet. And so, more and more this past year, I'd been getting out of bed, dragging my pillow and a blanket behind me, and sleeping by myself on the couch in the office.

Suddenly the image of my father heading down into the basement to sleep crossed my mind.

"Aw, yeah," Ollie murmured, startling me back to the present. I was still stroking his hard cock. And Frank was still kissing me, though my mind was everywhere and anywhere except in that bed.

And then my phone chirped with a text message.

I broke contact with Frank's lips and released my grip on Ollie's cock. "Be right back," I whispered.

I could feel, even if I didn't see, Frank's disapproving look. Grabbing my pants from the floor, I catapulted out into the hallway, where I dug out my phone and flipped open its cover. The text was from Kelly.

I MIGHT AS WELL JUST END IT ALL RIGHT NOW.

"Fuck," I said, rushing into the kitchen and calling him. He didn't pick up. It just went to voice mail. So I texted back: WTF? R U OK?

Thirty seconds, forty seconds passed. What did he mean? Finally, he texted back: I AM SO DEPRESSED.

My thumbs were typing as fast as they could. R U HOME?

YES.

STAY THERE.

I was pulling on my pants as I peered back into the bedroom. "Frank, can I talk to you a minute?" I whispered.

He came out into the hall. "What's wrong?"

"It's Kelly. He's saying he wants to kill himself."

"*What?*"

"He just texted it to me."

Frank made a face. "These kids text everything."

"I've got to go over there and make sure he's okay."

"Did he actually say he was going to kill himself?"

"Yes." I was rushing into the bedroom to grab a shirt and my flip-flops. "Don't say anything to Ollie. Just carry on."

"I don't want to carry on without you," Frank said, sighing. "And I suspect neither does Ollie."

"Oh, Frank, *please.*" I had no time for drama. "I'll be back as soon as I can."

He said nothing more. I hurried out to my Jeep and sped across town. I was wondering if I should call 911. But at this point I figured I could probably get to Kelly's place before they could. I ran three lights on Indian Canyon. Luckily, the Palm Springs police force wasn't the most vigilant in the world.

Outside Kelly's complex, the HAPPY PALMS sign was swinging in the wind. I screeched the Jeep to a stop and bounded up the steps to his apartment. I threw open the door. I had no idea what to expect.

What I saw made my jaw drop.

There was a party going on.

Here I'd thought I'd find Kelly with his head in the gas oven or with a bottle of pills in his hand . . . and there was a party going on!

Eight people, seven guys and a girl, were either flopped on Kelly's mattress or sitting against the wall, with their knees pulled up to their chests. Open bags of Cheetos and Doritos littered the floor, and an empty bottle of wine lay on its side. Most everyone was puffing away on cigarettes, and a hazy gray cloud hung in the room. I glanced around at the faces, a few of which I recognized from around town. One was Jake Jones, the blond kid Randall had wanted to trick with. But where was Kelly?

Turning around, I saw him against the wall behind me, deep in conversation with a gorilla of a man, all shoulders and hairy biceps and standing at least six foot three.

"What's going on?" I asked Kelly.

"Hey, Danny," he said, utterly blasé. "Do you know Damian?"

The gorilla looked at me and extended his hand. "Hey, dude."

I shook his hand but kept my eyes squarely on Kelly. "What the fuck was up with those texts?" I asked him.

He smiled. "What texts?"

I knew right away that he had done a lot of coke, and had probably drunk a lot of wine, and had ingested who knows what else.

"Are you okay?" I asked.

Jake Jones was suddenly at my shoulder. "Hey, Ishmael," he said. "When you gonna use that number I put in your phone?"

"I'd forgotten you had," I admitted, not turning around to look at him.

"*What* did you just call him?" Kelly asked Jake.

The kid smirked. "It's a private joke. He probably doesn't think I'm literate enough to get it, but I do." He moved off.

Kelly laughed. "So you have private jokes with *Jake?* And you have his number in your phone?" He made a face. "I didn't think he was your type."

Damian the gorilla moved in a step closer to Kelly, but his eyes were trained on me. I understood the gesture. He was staking his territory. And though I knew my odds against a gorilla were not good, I was not about to back off.

"I rushed over here because I was worried about you," I said to Kelly.

Kelly seemed genuinely puzzled. "Why?"

I was getting angry now. "Would you come outside with me for a moment?"

"We were in the middle of a conversation," Damian said threateningly.

"Yeah, well, we were in the middle of what I took to be a crisis," I replied. "Kelly, please? For a minute? Outside?"

"I'll be right back," Kelly said to Damian.

We walked outside, onto the landing. There was a breeze, and the fronds of the palm trees were rustling. "Your text said you were going to end it all," I said. "I thought you were suicidal."

"Oh, Danny, don't be such a drama queen."

I was ready to throttle him. "Kelly, I was so worried about you that I left someone who had driven all the way down here from Sherman Fucking Oaks just to be with me. To have *sex with me,* in fact. Who *likes* to have sex with me. Who thinks I'm good enough to kiss and hold and make love to."

"Well," he asked, his eyes suddenly blazing, his voice oozing with sarcasm, "what are you doing *here,* then?"

"I came here because I was worried about you. Because I care about you."

The words shattered his hardness. He broke like a plate-glass window under a well-aimed baseball. All the pieces shimmered and shook, then collapsed to the ground. He looked as if he would cry.

"Oh, Danny," he said.

"What's going on?" I asked.

He looked away, sighed, then returned his eyes at me. "I was out at the bar tonight and ran into some of these guys, and we decided to come back here. One person invited another, and soon there was a party. And all of a sudden I looked around at them, and I just got so depressed. I looked at them and said to myself, 'If this is my life, I might as well just end it now.'"

"And you texted that thought to me."

He smiled a little. "You're the only one I can admit such things to."

I sighed. "Are these people that bad?"

"You saw them." He paused, seeming to remember something. "And apparently you *know* Jake."

"I barely know him."

"Yeah, right. You don't have private little love names with someone you barely know."

"Kelly . . ."

His eyes flashed. "You know, it's all your fault I was feeling so depressed!"

"My fault?"

"Yes, your fault! I was just going on with my life when I met you. Everything was fine until you started telling me I could be something more than I am. That I could take classes at freaking CalArts! That I had talent and potential!"

"But you do."

"Oh, fuck you, Danny."

I gripped him by the shoulders. "Kelly, the reason you're acting this way, the reason you got depressed, was that you did too much coke. And then you drank too much on top of it. You've got to stop it."

He laughed. "No. The reason I got depressed was that I looked around at the losers in my life. They're all gypsies like me. Gypsies who spend a season in Palm Springs, bartending or waitering, and then leave here when too many bridges get burned. Then it's a season in West Hollywood or San Francisco or Miami or Lauderdale or Provincetown . . . and that's it. That's what we call our lives. Moving from shit-bag apartment to shit-bag apartment."

"That doesn't have to be your life, Kelly."

"Well, it's *not* going to be." He looked at me smugly, defiantly. "Because I've found myself a boyfriend."

"What?"

"Damian. He's my boyfriend now. Hot, don't you think? I've had my eye on him ever since I first got out here. He's a massage therapist. And so sexy. I like my men big and dark and hairy."

He had just used three adjectives that emphatically did not describe me. "You're *dating* him? Since when?"

"Since the other day."

"Since *what* other day?"

"We're moving to New York," Kelly said, ignoring my question. "Damian lived in Manhattan for a couple of years. He worked for all the big promoters. He knows everybody there. I've always wanted to live in New York."

"I thought you didn't want a boyfriend."

"Now, Danny." He smiled at me like a grand duchess. "Don't think that I'm not appreciative of everything you tried to do for me. I'm very grateful for your confidence in me. When I'm a big, successful artist in Manhattan, you'll have to come to the opening of my first show."

I looked at him. "Why are you saying all this?"

"Saying all what?"

"You're deliberately trying to push me away."

"I have no idea what you're talking about."

Just then the door opened. Jake Jones stood outlined by the dim light from within. "You guys want to do another line?"

"Yeah," Kelly said, brightening. "I need to come up a little."

I reached out and grabbed Kelly's forearm, stopping him from going inside. "No, you don't. You've had enough."

He made a face. "Since when are you a prude?"

"Since I've seen how your emotions can go up and down like a roller coaster."

"Come on, Ishmael," Jake said, his voice all syrupy, folding his thin arms across his chest and leaning up against the doorjamb. "Come in and have some fun with us."

"No, thank you," I said.

Kelly looked at me intensely. "Yeah, *Ishmael*. Why don't you come on inside? Or do you need to run back to the little twink you've got waiting for you at home?"

"Maybe I shouldn't have left him," I said.

"Guess not." Kelly broke free of my arm and hurried back inside. I could hear him calling, "Damian! Want to do a line with me?"

Jake was still in the doorway, watching me. "So, tell me," he said, once Kelly was gone. "Why did you come to the party if you won't come inside?"

"I guess I wasn't really invited," I said.

"You can be my date."

"Thanks, but I do need to get home."

Jake smirked. "You really have a twink waiting for you there?"

"I don't know." I started down the steps. "But I know my husband will be."

Reaching my Jeep, I gripped the wheel and closed my eyes. What I wanted to do, of course, was rush back up those stairs and burst through the door and carry Kelly off, like Richard Gere did to Debra Winger in *An Officer and a Gentleman*. But I steadied myself and started the ignition, even if I still sat there, not driving away quite yet.

I don't have time for any of this, I thought. The old fiction that we have an unlimited amount of time to do what we want to do, so necessary when we are young, no longer functioned for me. For all Kelly's despair, he still had time, but mine was running out. Every day, a little bit more.

I pulled away from Kelly's apartment. I hated the fact that tears were in my eyes. I hated the fact that I had cried more in the last few weeks than I had in years. *Decades,* in fact. Not since those first couple of years in high school had I cried so much, those days when I lived in constant terror of some biker showing up at our front door and shooting my mother through the chest. I hated that Kelly had turned me once more into that blubbering, stupid kid.

But I wasn't a kid. That was terribly obvious to me now.

"There's no fool like an old fool!" I shouted as I drove. "No fool like an old man chasing after a boy who doesn't want him!"

Driving home, running red lights again with brazen impunity, I realized there was one other adjective that Kelly might have used to differentiate Damian from me.

Young.

Damian was *young.*

He was under thirty. Twenty-nine, tops.

And I was a blubbering old fool of forty-one, who had just burst into a party of kids and made an ass of himself. To think that I'd ever had the gall, the hubris, to think I could make a beautiful young man like Kelly fall in love with me. No one had ever loved me first—no one had ever loved me more than they loved someone else. Why had I ever thought that this time it would be any different?

Ollie had left by the time I got home. I wasn't surprised.

"I knew it wasn't going to work," Frank said, already in bed, waiting for me. "I could tell he wasn't into it after you left, and then, of course, neither was I. So we had a cup of hot chocolate and sat talking by the pool for a while, but you know he's really not the best conversationalist. After a couple of stretches of awkward silence, he went home."

"I'm sorry," I said, crawling into bed beside him and shutting off the light.

"So Kelly's okay?"

"I wouldn't use that word to describe him." I sighed. "But he's not going to kill himself. At least not tonight."

"You care about that boy a great deal," Frank said from the dark.

"I don't want to talk about it."

"Okay."

I turned to him. "Frank, maybe you and I could—"

"I can't, Danny. I'm sorry. I'm just too tired now."

"Okay."

We lay there for a few moments, both of us on our backs. Then, silently, I turned on my side as Frank, in unison, turned on his. His nose nuzzled the back of my head and his arm reached around to pull me close. I took his hand. I held it tight.

"Sleep well, baby," Frank whispered in my ear.

And despite my worries of a sleepless night, I did.

WEST HOLLYWOOD

Pixie had just piddled on the carpet.

"The landlord's going to *freak!*" I shouted, rushing over with Windex and paper towels, the only cleaning tools I could find in the place. We had just moved in, and I hadn't yet gone shopping.

"She's marking her territory," Frank said, unperturbed. "It was just a little piddle."

"You're always making excuses for this dog," I said, trying to soak up the liquid from the carpet with the paper towels. "She knows better than that."

But those black button eyes refused to allow me to stay angry with her. I rubbed my head against hers, and she rubbed me back.

"Danny, come here. Look at this." Frank was in the bathroom, standing at the window. "I told you this place had a view."

"A view of what? A brick wall?"

"No, come here. Look."

He had just gotten out of the shower. That was the moment when I always thought Frank looked the most beautiful, before he'd combed his hair and shaved his face. He was wearing only a towel wrapped around his waist, but his hard, round ass still made itself known. His hair had that vibrant, shiny aliveness that a good shower and a vigorous towel drying always gave it; even the light hair on his chest was alert and electric. As I passed him, I ran my hand across his torso and purred.

"You see there?" Frank was saying. "Look this way out the window. No, this way. Turn your head. What do you see?"

I peered out and turned my head in the direction he was indicating. Yes, indeed, a brick wall—but just over there, almost out of view but not quite, was a glimpse down the hill of Santa Monica Boulevard and the valley beyond.

"Well, I wouldn't put it in the description, like they did in the newspaper ad," I said, laughing, "but I'll grant you, it's a view."

Frank laughed, too. "So you want to take a walk down to our new neighborhood for dinner?"

I shook my head. "Nope. It's our first night in our first place together. And it's not going to be a home until I've made dinner here for the first time."

Frank smirked. "You? Danny Fortunato? You're going to *cook?*"

"Shut up, smarty-pants. It's not like you're Julia Child, either."

Frank followed me into the kitchen. "Well, what are you going to make?"

"My grandmother's recipe for baked macaroni and cheese. I'm going out now to buy the ingredients. There's a little macaroni and a little cheese—but a whole hell of a lot of butter."

"Mmm," Frank said. "Just what I need." He patted his stomach.

I made a face. "Like you have to worry, Mr. Thirty Waist, Mr. I Bike Everywhere Even If It Is Los Angeles." I glanced at myself in the mirror. I was still just a twig, the way I'd been all my life. "I really need to start going to the gym and building some muscle."

"Baby, you're perfect just the way you are."

I hooded my eyes at him. "Keep saying that, stud, and you'll get a lot more tonight than macaroni and cheese."

"That's what I'm counting on."

I smiled, grabbing Pixie's leash from the hook on the wall. She immediately came dashing toward me. "That's right, puffin," I cooed as I hooked the leash to the collar. "That's right. We're going for a walk."

The grocery store was only a few blocks over, but down a very steep hill. Pixie loved to run down the hill, so I had to keep a strong grip on her. It was one of those unexpectedly windy days, when the palm trees rustling overhead sounded like rain. The sky was a sharp blue, so sharp it hurt my eyes. I slipped on my sunglasses and plugged in the earphones of my Walkman, grooving out to Tina Turner's latest album *Break Every Rule*. I had become a huge Tina Turner freak. No more punk for me; Tina ruled. Tina was how I wanted to be: bold and brassy, a survivor, sexy as fuck, despite all the odds being stacked against it. I kind of imagined myself as a younger, whiter, male version of Tina Turner. Heading down Holloway, I sang along. "All I want is a little reaction, just e-nuh-huff to tip the scales. . . ."

A red Porsche 944 Turbo was slowing down alongside me. I kept walking, ignoring it.

"Oh, they say that you match your wits with the best of them," I sang, "but I know when I'm close you're just like the rest of them. . . ."

I glanced over at the driver of the Porsche, dropping my sunglasses down my nose. "Hello, Donovan," I called through the open window.

"Where you going, angel puss?"

"Grocery store."

"Wanta ride?"

"I don't mind walking."

"I don't mind driving."

I sighed.

"You can even bring your little ball of fluff with you."

I smiled. Scooping Pixie up under my arm, I ran around to the passenger side of the Porsche and hopped in.

"Nice car," I said, inhaling the fragrance of the leather seats.

Donovan flashed me his perfect white smile. "I've been offering to take you for a ride for months now."

"Guess I've been otherwise engaged," I quipped, settling Pixie on my lap. She remained still, like a well-behaved little girl. But her eyes watched Donovan with a glint of distrust. I gave her a little squeeze to show her she had nothing to worry about.

I liked Donovan Hunt. Well, I liked flirting with him, anyway. He was rich. Richer than even Gregory Montague. And Donovan was no withered old Katharine Hepburn clone in male drag. He was tall, handsome, successful—and only a few years older than I was. "Quite the catch," Randall kept pointing out to me after I'd met Donovan one night at a club. "But I already *have* quite the catch," I'd tell Randall each and every time he said it. Frank might not have had Donovan's money, but at least he was devoted to me. Donovan Hunt, however, seemed to have a different boyfriend every time I saw him.

"So what are you doing riding around town?" I asked.

He sighed. "I just had to get out of the house. I had a huge fight with my father on the phone. He told me he should never have allowed me to come out here to L.A."

Donovan's family was old money. I think he liked the fact that we both hailed from Connecticut, though East Hartford was a world and several broken-down factories away from Greenwich. I asked him why his father was being so pissy.

"Because I want to invest some money in a film that he thinks is going to be a huge flop," he told me. "But I think it's going to pay off really well."

"What film is it?"

"It's this action-adventure thing with Bruce Willis."

"You mean the guy from *Moonlighting?*"

"Yeah. That's the one."

I laughed. "Somehow I can't see him as an action-movie star."

"It's an exciting project. He plays a cop who fights back against terrorists."

I rolled my eyes. "As an actor, Donovan, let me tell you, these special-effects movies are killing Hollywood's artistic soul."

We had reached the grocery store. He pulled into a parking space and switched off the ignition.

"Danny, I've told you I'd love to fund a serious movie with you starring in it."

"Great. So find me a script and a director."

"Sure. Let's have dinner, and then we can talk about it over breakfast."

"Oh, you're a funny, funny man," I said, my hand on the door.

"Please don't go yet," he said. "I really am kind of down about the fight with my father. Talk to me for a while."

I looked at him. "Okay, what do you want to talk about?"

"You and me."

I laughed. "You're someone who gets what he wants all the time, don't you?"

"No. But seems *you* are."

"Me?"

"Yeah. The boyfriend, the dog . . ."

I laughed again, louder this time. "Oh, Donovan, you have no idea about my life."

"Nor you mine."

I narrowed my eyes at him.

"When I told my father I was gay, he told me he hoped I got AIDS."

"Wow," I said.

"Yeah. So here I am in L.A., and all I want to do is make more money than my father so I can call him up and say, 'Hey, Dad. Fuck you.' "

I was quiet for a moment, looking off at the sky. "Well, Donovan, we live in very different worlds, but I suppose I can understand the whole parental thing."

"Really? What's your relationship with your family?"

"None."

"None at all?"

"None at all."

My parents had no idea where I was. When I first got to L.A. more than two years ago, I called my father as I'd promised. I told him I was okay, that I'd gotten here in one piece. He seemed happy to hear from me and asked for my phone number. I replied that I'd just moved in, and didn't know the number. That was a lie. I still felt the need for a safe distance. A little fear lingered that my mother would somehow come barging across the country for me and drag me back home. Dad asked me to send my address when I got settled, then he turned to my mother and asked her if she had anything she wanted to say to me. I heard her say no. Dad came back to the phone and said Mom was asleep. I was glad then I hadn't given the phone number. And I never sent the address or called them again.

But I didn't tell Donovan any of this. I just kept looking at the sky through his green-tinted windshield. The wind was picking up. The fronds of the palm trees were all blowing in one direction. "I guess that's what Los Angeles is all about," I finally said. "All of us gypsies can come here and try to start over."

"Yeah, but it's a hard city in which to get a foothold."

I shrugged. "And why *shouldn't* it be hard? It's a city founded on illusion and make-believe. Everything's artificial here. And so we go along and invent scenarios for ourselves, and we try to live them out, just like they do on the screen. Our scenarios might not be any more real than the ones in the movies, but they're better than nothing." I laughed, a little hard. "And if we expect anything more than that, we're going to be disappointed."

Donovan looked over at me. "You're really content to live with that?"

"It's not so bad," I said, stroking Pixie.

"You're really something, Danny. You know that? I can talk to you like no one else out here."

"Oh, go on. You have a thousand boys hotter and hipper than I am."

"Not really."

I laughed. "Thanks for the ride, Donovan." I opened the car door.

He smiled. "Thanks for the talk."

Pixie and I hurried over to the store. Soon my basket was filled with two boxes of elbow macaroni, three hunks of sharp cheddar cheese, a half gallon of milk, salt, pepper, paprika, bread crumbs, and a pound of butter. "This is going to be so tasty," I told Pixie as we walked back home, the wind whipping my hair, Tina Turner blaring in my ears.

Frank, bless his heart, had found a couple of candles and had lit them by the time I came back in through the door. The little apartment flickered with soft candlelight as the sun set through our windows. He'd also gone out and bought a bottle of champagne and two plastic glasses. We had glasses somewhere, but they were in one of the boxes stacked against the wall. We had no furniture yet, so we set out paper plates on the floor of the living room, careful to put down a sheet first to cover any remnants of Pixie's piddle. I boiled the macaroni, recalling Nana's recipe from memory as best I could. After it had cooked, I poured it into a glass baking dish and added the cheese, milk, butter, bread crumbs, and spices.

Nana had been such a good cook, far better than Mom. When Becky and I would stay at Nana's when we were little, we loved what she made for us. Orange-marmalade chicken and the mac and cheese. Cinnamon streusel cake and strawberry-rhubarb pie. We'd eat and eat, and then we'd head outside to run around the field behind Nana's house, ignorant of, and indifferent toward, the world beyond those yellow hills. All that mattered back then was the full, happy, exhausted feeling I had at the end of the day, falling asleep in Dad's old room, Nana tucking me in, saying, "Good night my sweet Danny off the pickle boat," and kissing me on my forehead.

"Danny," Frank was saying. "Baby, what's wrong?"

I was crying. "Oh, nothing," I said. "How stupid of me." I shrugged my shoulder to wipe my tears as I placed the baking dish of macaroni and cheese into the oven.

"It's not stupid, baby."

"Yes, it is." I noted the time on the oven. The macaroni and cheese needed to bake for at least an hour.

"Baby, I can only imagine what it was like to lose your sister like that, how it turned everything upside down."

"Oh, no, that's not the way it happened out here," I told him. "See, that's what's great about L.A. Here the movie can end happily. I can imagine that Becky came home. It was all just a big misunderstanding, a big farce. She got a loving cup stuck on her head. So she couldn't see and got on the wrong bus. But then Ricky and Fred found her and brought her home in time for the fade-out. You know, big laugh track, the end." I tried to smile. "Really, Frank, I'm fine."

"You were thinking about her," he said.

"No, actually I was thinking about my grandmother. She's the one I feel the worst about. I used to dream that I'd make a lot of money, and I'd bring Nana out here to live. She must be dead by now, and Dad wouldn't have had any way of letting me know." I let out a long breath. "But in a way, if she's still alive, that would be even worse. To live so long in that state. In that half-light of existence. In that netherworld. Oh, poor Nana."

"Come here, baby."

"No, I'm done crying. Come on. We've got to toast our new home. Where's the champagne?"

Frank held the bottle over the sink and popped the cork. It hit the ceiling. The bubbly flowed into our two plastic glasses.

"Let's take a picture," Frank said and dug out his camera from his bag, placing it on one of our unpacked boxes of clothes. I squatted on the floor with Pixie as he set the timer. "Okay!" he called, hurrying over to squat beside me. We both held up our glasses and grinned. The camera flashed.

And the macaroni and cheese exploded in the oven.

Thirty minutes of wiping down cheese and picking up shards of broken glass later, ripping the blaring smoke alarms down from the ceilings, we called out for Chinese. Frank and I were laughing so hard when our sweet-and-sour chicken arrived that we could barely pay the delivery boy.

"Well," I said, "I should just accept there are some things I can't do."

"Cooking is an overrated talent," Frank said, shoveling some rice onto his plate.

I smiled.

But in fact I felt horrible. My laughter was a ruse. It wasn't just cooking that I couldn't do. I couldn't act, either. If I could, I'd have landed a job by now. I couldn't cook; I couldn't act; I couldn't find my sister.

I was such a failure any way you looked at it. I had come all the way out here to get away from everything I had done wrong. Three thousand miles! And if the only way to escape my failure was to live in a dream, in a half-lit netherworld not unlike Nana's, where nothing was what it seemed, then I was content to do that.

But perhaps even that wasn't attainable. Frank had no idea how miserable I was for the rest of the night, how devastated I felt at being unable to make a simple dinner for him, to turn our little apartment into a home. Such a foolish dream.

Everything's artificial here. We go along and invent scenarios for ourselves, and we try to live them out. Our scenarios might not be any more real than the ones in the movies, but they're better than nothing.

My own words. Yet even as I had spoken them, I had secretly

hoped I might somehow, someday be proven wrong. I had allowed myself to hope that maybe, just maybe, I *could* expect a little bit more.

But now, with the stink of burned cheese permeating the house, that hope was gone. Even as I lay back in Frank's arms against the wall, buzzy with champagne, Pixie nosing the empty bottle around the floor, I knew that none of this was real. It was all an illusion. If Frank could have instantly transposed me with Gregory Montague, he would have. That he cared for me was obvious; that he would make good his pledge of support and devotion was unquestioned. I'd landed a fantastic deal, better than any Gregory could have gotten for me, and more than I had a right to expect. I'd never told Frank about Gregory's perfidy, the way he'd tried to buy me right out from under his nose, and I never would. That would have been cruel, and I could never be cruel to Frank. Likewise, I knew Frank would never be unkind or disloyal to me. But still, I knew that his love—his true love—would never be fully mine. Of this, I was not in doubt.

"Shall we go to bed?" I asked in his ear.

"Mmm," he said.

I helped him stand. As I did so, he caught me, and he placed his hands on either side of my face and kissed me. We made love passionately on the mattress in the bedroom. He filled me up, brought me to the top, left me breathless and panting, hanging over the side.

Yes, indeed. Much more than I had a right to expect.

PALM SPRINGS

The text messages had started early the next day. IM SORRY. DONT HATE ME. DONT GIVE UP ON ME. Not until the sixth or seventh one did I finally respond.

I COULD NEVER HATE U.

But still I resisted seeing him. The texts continued, becoming increasingly vulnerable.

I MISS U TERRIBLY.

I NEED U TO HOLD ME.

I CANT STOP THINKING ABOUT U.

They were texts I might have sent myself, and with each one, my spirit soared a little higher. Was it happening at last? Was Kelly finally starting to admit that he felt for me the same as I did for him?

We met for coffee. The day was gorgeous. It was the kind of day that reminded people why they had come to Palm Springs, where the air was warm and dry and soothing, where a simple walk outside could feel as good as a full-body massage. The mountains were changing from the dull, flat grays of summer to soft amber browns, with even the occasional hint of green. But not even their majesty could eclipse the stunning beauty of the young man who walked through the courtyard toward me, his dark eyes shining even from a distance of several feet. As usual, he was dressed simply, in a black shirt and olive corduroys. He smiled when he saw me, melting me once again with his dimples. We embraced. He smelled like blue sky.

"I never told you," he was saying, his voice choking. "Maybe it will explain some things for you."

"What is it?" I asked.

"All this time," he said, "I've been in therapy."

I looked him deep in the eyes. "You have?"

He nodded. "I've been trying to work out all my issues, all the reasons why I do the terrible things I do."

"They're not terrible, Kelly," I said. "They're just—"

"No, they're terrible. And I've been trying so hard to figure out why I am the way I am. For five long years now, I've been seeing this therapist, and I've been spilling out my guts to him, telling him everything. And he always just sat there, taking notes, nodding his head. He never said a word to me until finally the other night. And what he said crushed me."

I looked at him. "What did he say?"

"No hablo inglés."

It took me several seconds to realize it was a joke.

"You will pay for that," I said, a smile blooming on my face despite myself.

Kelly laughed. We sat down on the grass. We picked up as if the other night had never happened. We laughed and joked all afternoon. I spied a couple of guys I recognized from around town, guys my age, sitting with their friends or lovers at the little tables, sipping their lattes, watching Kelly and me giggling, sprawled out on the grass. I was glad they could see me. I knew they envied me. I liked the feeling.

"So I got fired," Kelly told me.

"Fired?"

"Yeah, I went into work last night, and they told me I had to take the back bar. They are always giving me the back bar and giving somebody else the front. The front bar makes at least fifty percent more a night. And I was like, 'I will not take the back bar again.' And they said to me, 'If you don't, you're fired.' And so I said, 'Fire me.' They said to get out, and on my way I picked up a pitcher of water and threw it in the asshole's face. He said he's going to charge me with assault. For throwing water!"

"Oh, Kelly."

"I mean, have you ever heard of anything so stupid? Charged with assault for throwing water?"

"Let's hope he doesn't."

He stretched out on his back, his hands behind his head. "I don't care. I've already got a line on another job. Thad Urquhart said he'd put in a word for me at this new restaurant they're opening over near the post office. It's going to be really fabulous."

"So you plan on sticking around," I said. "Aren't you and Damian moving to New York?"

"Oh, no way." He sat back up, his eyes level with mine. "Let me tell you about Damian. He's a *massage therapist.*" He said the words with hand quotes. "You know, which really means escort. That's right. He advertises in the back of *Frontiers* as a massage therapist, but he's really just a whore."

"I see."

"I mean, I don't care if people are whores. But the thing is, he is so *used up.* He's going to be thirty next year. *Thirty.* And he's been doing this for like twelve years. He used to be the most beautiful guy in West Hollywood, or so I'm told."

"Really now?"

"Yeah. But now just look at him, and you can see he's been around the track a few too many times. Let me tell you, he is *not* getting the clients he used to get. In a couple more years, he will be really tragic."

"I thought you considered him hot."

He shrugged. "There's nothing sadder than an old whore."

He lay back down on the grass. I just sat there, staring up at the mountains, which were turning a golden pink from the sun. I would have thought that learning that Kelly and Damian were not, in fact, boyfriends would have made me happy. But somehow it didn't. Somehow the course of our conversation had taken me from feeling giddy to feeling uncertain and uneasy.

What was I doing? Why was I sitting in the grass with this con-fused young man, as pretty as he might be? In my mind the clouds were retreating as if after a rainstorm. I felt as if I were sitting with someone I knew from long ago, though I couldn't place quite who— but someone who didn't understand what was happening. It was my job to explain it to him as best as I could.

We sat there in silence, however, beause I didn't know what to say. The sun began edging behind the mountains. The courtyard filled up with purple shadows. One by one everyone else left, and we were alone.

"Want to go back to my place and do a line?" Kelly asked, suddenly standing up.

"No," I said.

"No?"

"Look, Kelly, I shouldn't have done coke with you. See, I had a little bit of a problem with it once. When I first came out here to the West Coast, I was doing way too much of it. I shouldn't have started up again with you. And I don't want it becoming a problem for you like it did with me."

"It's not a problem," he said. "I just do it once in a while."

I remained seated on the grass. "I think you do it more often than that."

He frowned. "Well, what do you want to do then?"

Finally, I got to my feet. I took his hands in mine. "Kelly, I don't fully understand my feelings for you. All I know is I care about you very much."

His body stiffened.

"Kelly, those texts you sent me . . ." My words trailed off. "They made me very happy. You said you wanted me to hold you . . ."

"Danny," he said. "I've told you before. I don't want to ruin a good thing."

"Why would it have to ruin it?"

"You have a husband!" he suddenly shouted at me.

"You are using that as a cop-out. You know it's an open relationship—"

His black eyes were flashing. "You just don't get it! *You have a husband!* Why can't you understand that? What that *means?*"

"I love you, Kelly. Maybe I shouldn't. But I do."

"You can't say that to me."

"I love you."

"Shut up!"

His temper was quick. I imagined it was just as quick—or even quicker—on the job. No wonder he had lost so many of them.

"I will not allow myself," he said, "to fall in love with you."

"Well, bully for you," I replied. "I guess I don't quite have that much self-control."

"You have a *husband*," he said to me, one more time.

"Yes. I do. And for the first time in twenty years, for some crazy notion, I have actually allowed myself to imagine what it might be like to—"

"Don't say it."

I was damned if he was going to silence me. "What it might be like to fall in love again, while there still was a little time. To consider the idea that maybe, *maybe,* I could finally find someone who loved me the way I loved him. And if that meant leaving Frank, then—"

"Stop it! All my life I've gone from place to place. Nothing ever permanent. But seeing you and Frank made me think something permanent was possible. Don't ruin that for me!"

"It's just that you've made me feel things I haven't felt in so long—"

"Stop talking this way!" Kelly actually put his hands over his ears. "You're old enough to be my father!"

That stopped me. That shut me right up. I stood there, reeling.

When I found the words to respond, they were pitiful. "No, I'm not," I said. "Not unless I knocked up my girlfriend in high school."

Kelly had fallen into silence, too, and kept his gaze away from me. "I'm sorry if I misled you with my texts," he said quietly. "I just missed you, that's all."

I realized that a couple of guys had wandered out of the coffee shop and had overheard parts of our conversation. I wanted to get out of there. I suddenly wanted a lot of distance between Kelly and myself. I told him I had to go.

"Fine," he said. "Walk off again, like you did the other night."

I didn't respond, didn't take the bait. I just headed to my Jeep and drove as fast out of town as I could. Before I knew it, I was on Interstate 10, heading toward Los Angeles. I passed the gigantic windmill farm, those mammoth, oddly birdlike structures that generated millions of watts of electricity for communities far beyond our little valley. I kept driving, not thinking about where I was going, just heading west, as if pursuing the setting sun. When I saw a sign that read LOS ANGELES 60 MILES, I realized that I was actually traveling back into time, driving through a time warp, and if I kept going, I'd end up in West Hollywood circa 1985. I'd be a kid again, not much younger than Kelly. I'd report to work at the bar, snapping on my yellow thong and climbing up on my box and shaking my ass to the hoots and squeals of the crowd. The most beautiful guy in West Hollywood. That gorilla Damian had no claim to the title.

But before I could make it there, I turned around and drove back to Palm Springs. It was dark now, but I had no desire to go home. Frank was at the college; I was free to do whatever I wanted. And there was only one thing on my mind.

Some called the bars on one side of Arenas Road the Lairs of the Living Dead. In those places, men in their fifties were considered fresh meat. Inside, the lights always bewildered me with their brightness. Maybe, I thought, stepping through the door, with all illusions gone, shadows were finally dispensable, and the light was actually liberating. I sat at the bar and ordered my vodka straight. No olives, no twist. Just pure alcohol. I drank it fast, avoiding eye contact with anyone. I ordered a second, and a third, all the while watching out the window as young men filed into Hunters across the street, the one place in town where young men might find others of their own kind. After my third vodka, I felt fortified enough to cross the street and follow them inside.

There was a stripper, naturally, a boy buffer than I'd been at his age, but still not nearly as buff as I was now. It didn't matter, of course: he was pretty and lithe and barely twenty-one, oblivious to anyone but himself. Or maybe he just *seemed* oblivious. After all, I had experience to draw on. When I'd been up there, I'd been very aware of all those who walked past me, those who gawked and those who pretended not to see me. Sometimes I'd felt very silly swishing around up on a box, nearly naked, while others, fully clothed, engaged in conversations with friends. Sometimes I'd seen someone come in who I thought was cute, and I'd hoped he might look up at me; other times I'd seen someone horrendous and prayed he wouldn't come by for a feel. So maybe this boy on this box was just as aware of his surroundings as I had once been. Maybe he spotted me the moment I walked in. Or maybe, in fact, times really had changed beyond my recognition of them, and he really was as oblivious as he seemed, and I was really as invisible as I felt.

I ordered another drink. A hand came to rest on my shoulder.

"Well, hello, Ishmael."

I turned. "Jake Jones," I said, and as soon as I heard my slurry voice, I knew how drunk I was.

"Let me get that for you," he said, gesturing to the bartender that my drink was on him. "So have I finally found you out alone?"

"You have," I said, sipping my vodka as if I were parched. "Indeed, you *have* found me out alone."

"You know, of course, Ishmael, that I think you're very hot," he said, sidling closer to me.

"Oh, do you?" I asked. But playing coy was always difficult when I was this drunk.

"Yeah, I do." His small blue eyes held mine. "But you have a husband."

"Yes, I do. I have a husband."

He smiled accusingly. "But it seems Kelly Nelson found his way around that particular obstacle."

"Kelly Nelson?" I asked. "Who's that?"

Jake laughed. He put his head back and let out a whoop, and as he did so, his Hollister shirt lifted up, so I could see his tight stomach, smooth except for a blondish happy trail that crept down past the waistline of his aussieBum briefs. I wanted him. I wanted him more than I'd ever wanted anyone.

"Dance with me," he said suddenly. The DJ was mixing in the Pussycat Dolls. Tugging me by the hand, Jake led me out onto the dance floor. I gave him no resistance. We shouldered our way into the middle of the floor, finding ourselves among a mix of tourists and young Latino boys, probably from Redlands or Indio. It had been a while since I'd been out dancing, but I figured I could still keep up.

That was, until Jake latched on to me with his eyes and gave me a show, peeling his shirt off over his head. "Don't cha wish your boyfriend had abs like me?" he sang, changing the lyrics to suit the occasion at hand. And suit the occasion they certainly did. Turn-of-the-century housewives would have paid good money for washboards as rippled as Jake's stomach. For a second or two, I stood unable to move, a combination of the vodka and an unexpected, overpowering lust. But then I moved in, my hands on his small waist, my lips on his neck.

"Come on, Ishmael!" Jake shouted, pushing me back. "I've been waiting to see this body for a long time! Off with the shirt!"

He yanked at my tee. I happily obliged, confident I could impress these little children. Jake growled, leaning in to lick my chest. I was beaming.

I wanted him. I wanted to fuck Jake Jones right there in the middle of the dance floor. Not just because I'd suddenly realized how gorgeous he was, but for the simple reason that *he wasn't Kelly.* He was blond and bright-eyed, without an ounce of body fat. As different from Kelly as he could be. And he wanted me. That was different from Kelly, too.

And—this was significant—Jake was even younger than Kelly was. *I don't need you,* I was thinking. *I can get better.*

My lips made a sloppy landing onto Jake's mouth. The boy laughed, gently moving away and grabbing my hand. "Come on!" he urged. "Let's show them!"

The stripper was off his box. It sat there vacant. Jake hopped up, pulling me along with him. I almost fell getting up there, but I managed. I found my balance and looked around. Twenty years. It had been twenty years since I'd had this vantage point.

"Let's show them!" Jake cried again.

And so we did. We made everyone wish their boyfriends had abs like us. We banged each other's crotches; we humped each other from behind; we twisted and we turned and we spun around. It was exhilarating. I had forgotten how liberating, how magnificent, this felt. All eyes were on me. *Me!* I soaked up their stares, wolfed down their desire. Me! They were looking at me!

There was only one flicker of embarrassment: when I looked out and spotted Thad Urquhart and Jimmy Carlisle across the room, watching me, with surprise on their faces. I shook off the feeling. For the evening, I wasn't Danny Fortunato, the artist. I was Danny, the kid on the box, even if my yellow thong had long ago been discarded.

"Kiss me," I said to Jake, pulling him in. "Let's give 'em a show!"

"I gotta go pee," he said, hopping down off the box.

For a second, I turned and faced the crowd alone. Were they looking at me? Or had they been looking at Jake all along? I was suddenly mortified. I hopped off the box—and as I did so, I stumbled. I was immediately up on my feet. No one had seemed to notice. Or maybe I was too drunk to notice if they had noticed.

I made my way over to Thad and Jimmy. "Well, well, quite the show," Thad was saying as I approached.

I laughed. "Your little friend Jake dragged me up there."

"Darling, you seemed like a pro," Thad said.

"I am," I said. "Or I was." I looked around for Jake. "Is he out of the bathroom yet?"

Thad looked at me oddly. "Oh, no, darling, Jake said good night. He left with some friends."

"What? No. He said he had to go pee," I replied.

Thad gave me a sympathetic smile. "Perhaps he did, but then he left. We just said good night to him."

I didn't know what to say. The kid had been after me for weeks. Then he got me, and he—*he walks away?*

It was the same old thing that I'd dealt with all my life. As soon as I showed interest in a guy, he wasn't interested in me.

I mumbled something to Thad about needing to pee myself and hurried away through the crowd. More mortifying than dancing on the box—or falling off of it as I got down—was giving the appearance that I'd been dumped. I was pissed. I pulled my phone out of my jeans and scrolled through my contacts. Sure enough, there was Jake's number where he'd placed it. I was about to call when I saw I had a voice mail. I could see it was from Frank. I figured I ought to listen to that first, so I entered the code to hear it. But the noise in the club was too loud for me to make anything out, so I saved the message for later. I decided to text Jake.

WHATS UP? U COULDVE SAID GOODBYE.

Almost instantly: SORRY. MY PEEPS WERE LEAVING. FUN DANCING WITH YA.

I was fuming. THOUGHT WE MIGHT HAVE DONE A LITTLE MORE THAN DANCE.

Again, almost instantly: SORRY. DIDNT MEAN TO MISLEAD U.

I staggered a little. That was what Kelly had said earlier.

I looked around. The stripper was back up on the box, pretending he didn't see me. I realized that no one in this place saw me. No one was looking at me. They had never been, not even when I was dancing, except to maybe glance at me with pity. I was vanishing—as surely as Becky had vanished all those years ago. Suddenly I felt so utterly foolish. An old man trapped in a warehouse of children. Once again, I was an old man who'd made an ass of himself by pretending he still had what it took, that he could still play the game. My vision was spinning. It was time for me to go home.

I slid into my Jeep and steadied my hand before inserting the key into the ignition. It had been a long time since I'd been drunk behind the wheel of a car. Back in the day, I thought nothing of driving around West Hollywood drunk or high. And never once did I have an accident or get pinched. But now I actually felt a little apprehensive about driving home the few blocks from the bar. I supposed it was a sign that I was starting to sober up.

But just how drunk I remained became obvious when I banged my leg as I came through the front door. Frank was sitting in a chair, waiting for me. He said nothing, just looked up at me with a blank expression. Immediately, I was on the defensive.

"Okay, okay, I'm sorry I didn't call."

"I was getting worried."

"So I went out. I went dancing. Big deal. Is that a crime on a Saturday night?" I was aware that my voice was slurring, but I couldn't stop now. I was on a roll. "We used to go out dancing on Saturday nights. Remember that, Frank? We used to go out, you and me. But tonight you had a function on campus, and lo and behold, I wanted to go dancing. Is that such a crime?"

Frank said nothing. I went into the kitchen and poured myself a glass of water. I drank it down without stopping for breath.

"No, Danny, it's not a crime." Frank had gotten up and followed me into the kitchen. "It's just that you usually call me to let me know where you are."

"I'm sorry," I said, wiping my mouth with the back of my hand. "It was spur of the moment. I lost track of the time."

"And when I called you, you didn't call back."

"I was in a *club,* Frank. Clubs are *loud,* in case you no longer remember. I couldn't hear your message." I leveled my eyes at him. "You should have texted me."

"Danny, you know I don't know how to text."

I laughed. "Okay, well, if you're done grilling me, I'm going to bed."

He put his hand on my shoulder as I tried to pass him. "Danny, you're drunk and you're angry. What's going on?"

"I'm *bored,* Frank!" I suddenly shouted, shaking his hand off me. "I'm fucking *bored.* That's what's wrong!"

He just looked at me. I couldn't have stopped now even if I'd been sober and completely in control of my emotions.

"*You* got boring, Frank. Yes, *you!* You sit around here, drinking coffee and grading papers and watching television. That's your life. When was the last time we went hiking? Huh? Took a canoe up to Arrowhead? When was it that we officially gave up our goal of finally spotting a bighorn sheep?"

"I wasn't aware we gave it up, Danny. I just—"

"When was the last time we went dancing? When was the last time we had *fun,* Frank? *When?*"

His face remained expressionless. He took a long breath and seemed to think about what he should say. "I'm sorry, Danny," he finally replied. "I know I've become sedentary. That's why I've started jogging again. I hope it will help me. . . ." He stopped, and for a moment, I thought he might cry. "I'm sorry that you're bored."

I made a noise of exasperation and continued down the hall.

"Danny, wait," Frank said. "We still have fun. Ollie comes down and—"

I spun around. "And you sit at the end of the bed and *watch,* Frank! Or you don't participate at all!"

"I tried last time," he said quietly. "You walked out on us."

I waved him away as if his point was irrelevant. "All I know is, Frank, I'm not ready to get old like you are. I've still got some life left in me. I'm not ready to go gently into that good night quite yet. I want to have some fun before it's too late."

"I've never stopped you from having fun, Danny."

I didn't know what to say to that, or why his words pissed me off so much. At the moment, it felt as if he was the obstacle to *all* my fun, to *everything* I wanted, but I wasn't sure how to express that idea, or if it, in fact, made any sense at all. I started to say something, stopped, then turned and headed down the hall toward the bedroom.

"Danny," Frank called after me. "Does any of this have to do with Kelly?"

I turned back to face him. "Yes," I said forcefully. It was as if the dam suddenly burst. "Yes, indeed, it has everything to do with Kelly. I love him, Frank. I can't deny it. I'm *in love* with him."

"I see," Frank said.

We were silent. I didn't regret my words. I was glad I had spoken them. But I had no idea what to say next. We just stood there, in the hallway, looking at each other.

Frank broke the silence. "And does he feel the same way about you?"

"I don't know how he feels," I admitted.

Frank just nodded slowly.

"For once in my life," I said, less agitated now, "I want to know what it feels like to be loved by somebody the way I loved *you,* Frank. I want *so bad* to know how that feels."

"Do you think Kelly can give that to you?" Frank asked, his voice thick.

"I don't know," I admitted again.

Frank turned away. "I'm sorry I've failed you, Danny."

My instinct was to reassure him, to tell him he hadn't failed me. But he had. We had failed each other. We'd stopped honoring that bargain we'd made twenty years ago, when we'd tacitly accepted that the deal between us was the best either of us would ever get. Neither if us had entered into this partnership with rosy misconceptions. Even as recently as three years ago, when we'd exchanged vows in front of that Unitarian minister in Vancouver, I'd known what I was pledging myself to. I'd understood the marriage's limits, its lines of demarcation. But such limitations no longer served. To reassure Frank now would be disingenuous and wrong. I would not do it.

"I'll sleep in the casita tonight," Frank said, moving down the hall.

"No, Frank, that's not necessary. . . ."

"Yes, it is," he said. "For me."

"Frank, then you take our bed. I'll sleep on the couch. . . ."

He didn't look back at me. "I don't want be under the same roof as you tonight, Danny," he said, his voice sharp. The anger in his words surprised, even reproached, me.

He walked out the kitchen door. I watched him through the windows as he moved like a ghost across the deck and then down the path to the casita.

In that moment I felt as if I'd never see him again.

My cell phone chirped. I dug it out of my jeans and flipped it open.

A text from Kelly.

IM SORRY. PLEASE DONT GIVE UP ON ME.

I covered my face with my hands.

EAST HARTFORD

The Swan Convalescent Home smelled of Lysol, which was bad enough, but it was the smell lurking under the Lysol, the one you knew was there but couldn't quite detect, that was even worse. Down the corridor I walked past doors that opened onto the small, shriveled occupants within, like creatures in a zoo. Old women sat making repetitious hand circles on the trays in front of them. Old men with crooked necks and open mouths stared unblinking up at the ceiling. Occasionally, one of these souls would call to me, a guttural sound accompanied by a pleading of hands. I tried not to look at them. I kept my eyes straight ahead of me, my terror threatening to surge into my throat. I quickened my pace and rounded the corner to Nana's room.

As usual, she was adorned with a big red bow in her hair. She had never worn bows before coming here, but some nurse's aide had apparently decided "Adele"—what they called her, never "Mrs. Fortunato"—looked good with a bow. I thought she looked silly. The lipstick they put on her was even worse. As red as her bow, it was perfectly applied, unlike Nana's clumsy attempts at Aunt Patsy's funeral. But the worst part was the striped sash that tied her to the chair she sat in. "It's the only way to keep her from wandering off," a nurse had explained when I asked her about the sash a few weeks before. "She keeps saying she's going home.

We found her out in the street once. She's tied down for her own safety."

"Hi, Nana," I said, sitting down opposite her, setting my schoolbooks on the floor.

As usual, her old eyes found me but registered nothing.

"Danny off the pickle boat," I said.

"Can you help me?" she asked.

"Did you just finish your lunch?" I asked. The remains of a tuna sandwich on white bread sat on a tray off to the side.

A visit to Nana was all about questions. The two of us sat there, asking each other questions to which the answers were either pointless or impossible. She'd ask me to help her or to take her home, and I'd ask her if she'd enjoyed her lunch. Never an answer for either of us. It was always just questions.

"Nana, I don't like that red bow, do you?" I asked, standing up. "I'm going to take it out of your hair, okay?"

I reached up to her gray head and pulled the ribbon. The bow came undone.

"It makes you look like Baby Jane. Did you ever see that movie? With Bette Davis?" I crumpled the ribbon and threw it in the trash. "Believe me, you don't want to look like Baby Jane."

I sat back down and looked at her.

"Can you take me home?" she asked.

I sighed.

Every Monday I came to see Nana. Dad and Mom never came. It was too hard on them. I didn't blame them. I figured since they couldn't do it, I needed to come, even if Nana never seemed to know who I was or to appreciate my visits. It was just an endless repetition of "Can you take me home?" and "Can you help me?" I think her brain had frozen on those two questions, the last fragments of her conscious mind, the last words on her lips as she went under for the final time. Now they'd been placed in endless rotation by a brain that was no longer functioning properly, like a needle stuck forever on an old 45 record. On most of my visits, I'd sit opposite Nana and just listen to her ask those same questions, over and over, interrupting her now and then with my own futile queries, and that would be how the whole hour passed. Her roommate, an old black woman with a large purple growth on her forehead, would occasionally look over at me from her chair and smile sympathetically. She'd be watching television—*Guiding Light* usually—and she'd never utter a word.

But this time I wanted to tell Nana something. Something that had been building up inside me for weeks, getting stronger and stronger. The pressure was becoming so strong that I felt as if my chest would split open if I didn't speak the words out loud. I *had* to tell someone, and since there was no way I could tell Mom or Dad or anybody at school, not even Troy, I figured I could tell Nana.

I waited until her roommate's head was nodding down onto her chest. She often fell asleep, sometimes even snoring so long that even Nana seemed to notice. Once I was sure she was asleep, I pulled my chair as close to Nana as possible.

"Nana," I told her, "I'm in love."

"Can you help me?"

"You remember Chipper," I said. "He lived across the street."

I decided not to remind her of the Becky connection. If she was following my words somehow, I thought it was best not to muddy up my story with the fact that Chipper used to be Becky's boyfriend.

"He's a great guy, Nana. He's on the football team. They've had a real bad season this year. They haven't won a single game yet. And it's because the coach won't let Chipper play enough. He hardly plays at all. He's really angry about that. He tells me how he feels. I'm the only one he confides in. We sit in his room and—"

Again, I left out some details, like the pot and the way I'd walk on Chipper's back. "And we *talk*," I said. "He's really opened up to me these last couple of weeks. It's been great. It's really a great feeling, you know, to be in love."

"Can you help me?"

I sat back in my chair and smiled. It felt great to be talking out loud about Chipper, even if Nana didn't understand a word I was saying. I was aglow. I'd walked to the convalescent home from school, but Chipper was picking me up here after football practice. He told me he thought it was a good thing that I came to see my grandmother every Monday. "You're a good guy, Danny," he'd told me. I had nearly cried.

At every game, I was there, cheering him on from the bleachers. I'd force Troy to join me in chanting: "Send in Paguni! Send in Paguni!" Sometimes we'd get everyone around us chanting. The coach never listened, however. So it was *his* fault that the team never won. If he'd only send in Paguni, the team would win.

I sighed. "I don't expect that Chipper feels the same way for me," I told Nana. "He likes girls. So do I. I'm not gay. I'm bisexual. And see, here's the thing. Maybe Chipper is, too, deep down. Elton John says *everybody* is deep down. Maybe even you, Nana!" I laughed. "Sometimes I get the sense that Chipper knows how I feel, and that it's okay with him. Though I'll never ask him. It's fine if he doesn't like me that way. I can live with that. I just like being with him. It's enough."

"Can you help me?"

"Oh, Nana." I shifted in my chair. "You know what? I've got to read this book for school. If I don't pass the next test, I might get kicked out of the play. And that can't happen. I have a real part this year. I wish you could come see me. I think Mom and Dad are going to come. I told them about it, anyway."

I reached down and lifted my latest assignment from Brother Pop's class.

"*Moby Dick,*" I said to Nana. "Did you ever read this? It's a huge book. How about if I read it to you? Then I can visit you and get my homework done at the same time. How's that sound?"

"Can you help me?"

I opened the book to the first chapter. "Call me Ishmael," I said.

"Can you help me?"

"Some years ago—never mind how long precisely—"

"Can you help me?"

"—having little or no money in my purse, and nothing particular to interest me on shore, I thought I would sail about a little and see the watery part of the world."

I waited, expecting to hear Nana chime in, but she didn't. So I went on. I read to her, and for the whole time, she was quiet. No more of her anguished routine questions. She just locked her eyes on me and seemed to listen. I didn't think she actually understood what I was saying, but somehow the sound of my voice lulled her. I read her the entire first chapter of *Moby Dick*. I had even started on the second—"Chapter Two, The Carpet-Bag"—when a hard rapping on the open door startled me. I looked up.

"Troy!" I said. "What are you doing here?"

"Your mom called me." He stood in the doorway, looking at me with his blue glasses. "She needs me to take her to some bar."

"Oh, Jesus."

"I knew you were here. I want you to come with us."

"No way. I'm tired of her craziness."

"Well, I don't want to go alone with her. She's *your* mother."

"Well, you should have told her no."

"I couldn't do that." He gave me a plaintive frown. "I told her I'd pick her up in fifteen minutes. Please come, Danny, okay?"

"Oh, *man*." I stood, gathering my books. Leaning over, I kissed Nana on the forehead. "I'll come back and read again to you, Nana. Thanks for listening to me today."

"Can you take me home?" she asked, the record once more spinning under its broken needle.

I smiled sadly. At least that hideous bow was gone from her hair.

In Troy's car, I threw my books into the backseat and folded my arms across my chest. "My mother shouldn't be calling you," I grumbled. "She's out of her mind."

"She says she got a lead."

"She's always getting leads. Which take her fucking nowhere."

"She says the Rubberman told Warren that Bruno is back in the state, and that he spends most of this time at this bar in Naugatuck."

"Naugatuck? Where the fuck is that?"

"I don't know. Down near Waterbury. Your mom has directions."

"Jesus Christ," I said.

The thing that pissed me off the most was that Chipper was going to show up at the convalescent home to pick me up and I wouldn't be there. And there was no way to get word to him that

I was taking off. I'd have to explain to him later tonight. Hopefully, he'd understand. He knew how crazy Mom was, after all.

Troy drove across town to the apartment complex to which Mom, Dad, and I had moved a few weeks earlier. It was a boxy, orange-brick place, with four apartments per unit, two up and two down. We were downstairs on the right. There were only two bedrooms—one for Mom and Dad, and one for me—but Mom had insisted that Becky, when she came home, should not feel that she'd lost her place in the family. So my room, which was small enough to start with, had been summarily divided in two. Mom had actually hung a sheet from the ceiling. On one side was Becky's bed, made up in pink and lace; her teddy bears still sat waiting for her against the wall, and her easel waited for her to finish the painting of the white house. On the other side of the sheet was my bed. The dresser was so close that I couldn't get out of bed except by climbing over the footboard.

I hated that apartment. It was horrible. Oh, it was clean enough. Mom had been worried about bugs, but so far there hadn't been any. I think if there had been, I would have run away. The apartment was just so small, so plain. I missed our yard. I missed Chipper being across the street. We'd had to sell most of our furniture, and what was left was crammed into the living room of the apartment: the stereo system balanced on top of the television, which sat on top of Mom's hope chest. For the size of the room, our old couch was way too big, but it served its purpose: Dad slept there most nights. The walls of the apartment were so thin that I could hear him pouring whiskey in the middle of the night from my room.

Mom was waiting outside of the apartment when Troy and I pulled up, her leather jacket draped over her arm. I got out of the car and let her get in front. "I think this is our lucky break," she said as I slid into the backseat. "This time I really think we're onto something."

I didn't reply. In fact, I didn't say a word for the whole hour it took for us to get to Naugatuck, all the way down on Interstate 84 and then onto Route 8. I pressed my face against the window and watched as giant tractor-trailers rattled past us. A Buick LeSabre driven by a harried-looking woman and filled with screaming little boys passed us on the left. As it did so, one of the brats stuck his tongue out at me through the back window. I gave him the finger.

We pulled onto a side road. "That's it," Mom said, yanking on her leather jacket. "That place up ahead."

The sign out front said THE BLUE DOG. There was nothing blue, however, that I could see. It was a dark shingled building with a red awning over the front door, the only wooden structure on a street of concrete warehouses. Motorcycles were parked out front, and there were broken bottles everywhere, but still it wasn't as desolate as that place in Yonkers, the one with the three *x*'s on its roof. I'd had nightmares about that place.

Troy parked the Jaguar on the street, and Mom immediately opened the door. "You boys can wait here," she said.

"No," I said. "I'm going with you."

And since I was going, that meant Troy was coming along, too. The three of us crossed the street and walked up the steps under the awning.

"Please God," Mom prayed in a little voice before opening the door.

It took a few moments for my eyes to adjust to the darkness inside. When they did, the first thing I noticed was the men staring at us from the bar. Big men, in black shirts and with long hair and fuzzy arms. Across the room, two other men had paused in front of the dartboard, darts in hand, to look our way. Mom fooled herself that she could pass for a biker babe in that leather jacket; that was why she wore it, she said, so she could get into these places. But few biker babes wore Keds sneakers or walked around with two teenaged boys still wearing their dorky school pants and white button-down shirts.

Mom leaned up against the bar. "Warren here?"

The bartender, a fat, bald man with a full gray beard, shook his head.

"He told me to meet him here," she said, trying to sound tough.

No one said a word. The men sitting at the bar continued to stare at us. At least the guys playing darts resumed their game.

The place reeked of beer and piss. Some drunk had pissed on

the floor once, I suspected, and that smell was never going away. The jukebox was playing Lynyrd Skynyrd. *Sweet home Alabama, where the skies are so blue* . . . I'd been in enough of these places to wonder why these Yankee bikers seemed to have such a love for Southern rock. I had a pretty strong hunch that their counterparts down in Alabama didn't harbor a lot of love and good feeling for Connecticut boys, whether they rode Harleys or not.

"Hey, Peg," came a voice from the darkness. Some guy was coming out of the bathroom. I squinted my eyes, expecting it to be Warren. But it was his friend Lenny. He recognized me. "Hey, buckaroo."

"Lenny, where's Warren?" Mom asked. "He told me to meet him here. He said Bruno might be—"

Lenny motioned for her to be silent. Dropping a leathered arm around her, he led us over to a corner where we could speak more privately. "Warren's in the hospital," Lenny told us. "He got some infection."

"Oh, dear!" Mom seemed genuinely alarmed. "Is it serious?"

"I dunno. But listen. I know where Bruno's living. I been there. It's not far from here. And he's got a coupla bitches living with him. Maybe one's your daughter."

"Take me to him!"

Lenny shook his head. "Nope. Bruno's onto the fact that somebody's looking for him. I don't know if he knows why, but I think we can't trust the Rubberman anymore. I think he gave Bruno your name. That's why you've gotten those threats."

"Then he must know we're looking for Becky!"

"Maybe. All I know is I can't be showing up at his house with some old lady, even if she *is* wearing a leather jacket."

Mom didn't seem to take offense at being called an old lady. "So how do we find out if Becky's with him?"

"You know, I've never said this before, and I can't quite believe I'm suggesting it now," Lenny said, giving us a little smile, "but maybe you should just call the cops."

Mom's face hardened. "They'll never go. They don't even take my calls anymore."

"Then I don't know what to say," Lenny told her.

Mom had turned to look at me. "Danny," she said, "you go with him."

"*Me?*"

The idea terrified me. I had heard the voice on our answering machine. It was the voice of a killer. A crazed demon who would snap my neck without a second thought. The Rubberman had killed men with his bare hands; I was sure Bruno was just as capable of doing so.

"Yes," Mom said, turning from me back to Lenny. "Take Danny!"

There was something about her words that cut right through me. *Take Danny. Take Danny, and bring me back Becky.* As if she would have been glad to make the exchange if it might actually work.

"I don't know," Lenny said. "You know, Warren's in charge of this. I shouldn't be stepping in here."

Mom pulled out an envelope from her jacket pocket. "I brought the money he asked for," she told Lenny. "Please. We can't delay."

I had no idea where she'd got more money to give these guys. Dad's hours had been cut back at the church. We had no more savings. But there she was, thrusting a crumpled white envelope filled with cash into Lenny's hands.

He looked down at her and frowned. "I didn't know Warren was asking you for more money," he said.

"It's okay. It's not for him. It's for the Rubberman, so he can keep feeding us tips."

"We're cut off from the Rubberman now," Lenny said, "and Warren knows that." He pushed the envelope away. "I don't want your money, Peg."

"Please," she cried, near tears. "My daughter may be at that house!"

Lenny turned to me. "What about it, buckaroo? Want to go for a ride?"

"Please, Danny," Mom begged, her eyes wide and moist in the darkness of that bar. "Please, Danny, you must! Go find Becky, and bring her home to me!"

I looked at her. My insides turned to mush.

"What do I have to do?" I asked Lenny, though I kept my eyes on my mother.

"We'll just take a ride up to the house. Bruno knows I got some young friends that I teach how to ride. We'll just ride up there and see who comes out. You keep your helmet on, and if it's your sister, she won't recognize you."

"Oh yes, Danny, go!" Mom screeched. "Go, *please!*"

I saw the wildness in her eyes. I realized how much she had stopped looking like the mother I remembered from a long time ago. She was skinny and drawn, and she wore a leather jacket. Her voice was different, too. Everything about her was different. My mother, the one who used to make me drink ten glasses of milk a day, the one who worried that I'd catch poison ivy again like that time in seventh grade, would never have asked me to do what this woman was asking me to do now. My mother would never have allowed me to get on a motorcycle and ride away with a guy we hardly knew. It hurt me far more than that slap she had given me across the face.

"Okay," I said quietly.

She wrapped her arms around me in gratitude. I didn't hug her back.

Outside the bar, Lenny tugged at my shirt. "This will have to go."

I removed my white collar shirt, standing there in just my undershirt. Lenny reached down and pressed his hands on the street, gathering up grime. Then he wiped them all over my beige school pants. "That's better," he said. Mom made not a word of protest.

Lenny handed me his helmet, and I slipped it on. It was way too big for me, but he secured it with the strap. I liked the smell inside the helmet, a deep musk that reminded me of the pile of dirty clothes in the corner of Chipper's room. In fact, I kind of felt like Chipper in that moment, since Chipper also wore a helmet, albeit one of a very different kind. I couldn't deny a certain thrill in straddling Lenny's bike again, wrapping my arms around the giant ribs in front of me, my face pressed into the back of Lenny's leather jacket.

But that didn't chase away the feeling that Mom was trading me for Becky, that the chance of finding my sister was worth the risk to my life.

"Hang on, Danny!" Mom shouted as Lenny's motorcycle roared into gear. Troy echoed her, "Hang on, Danny! Hang on!"

In moments I was sucked into a cyclone of sound. With a squeal of rubber, the bike bolted forward onto the road. We didn't go far. After just a few minutes of whizzing along the winding lane, we were slowing down, veering to our left, and rumbling over a cracked pavement road. We stopped in front of a row of dilapidated Victorian houses. "Keep your helmet on," Lenny whispered as he dismounted the bike. "Stay here and keep an eye out. If you recognize her, don't say anything. We can't tip them off. Just be cool, okay?"

"Okay," I said in a small voice.

He sauntered up the broken front stairs of one house and rapped on the door.

I got off the bike and leaned against it, trying as best as I could to see through the helmet. Someone had come to the door of the house. I thought I heard a female voice. "Have Bruno come out," Lenny was saying. "I want to show him my bike."

I started to panic. *Bruno is going to come out here.* He would see me, and he'd know who I was. He'd slit my throat without asking any questions. I forced myself to calm down. Lenny was still at the front door of the house, talking. Laughing, even.

"What's your name?" he was asking someone.

"Mary Beth," came the answer.

But it sounded like Becky's voice.

Dear God, it sounded like Becky's voice.

I strained to see. Lenny was in the way, but there were two girls on the steps now. One was a blonde. The other was dark. I couldn't see them clearly.

But the dark girl. She might have been Becky.

She might actually be Becky.

All of a sudden my heart was beating wildly in my chest. It seemed to have come alive like a bird and was attempting to fly its way up my throat.

On the steps of the house, a man had joined them. He was bald, with a big black beard, standing not more than five-five. He barely came to Lenny's chest. *I* was taller than he was, for God's sake. *This* was Bruno?

I steadied myself. The four of them were walking toward the bike now.

Please let it be Becky, I prayed—even though most of the time I wasn't sure if I believed in God anymore. But in that moment, I did. *Please, God, let it be Becky. Let me go back and tell Mom I've found her. We can call the cops, and I'll tell them I saw her with my own eyes.*

I imagined the joy on Mom's face when I brought her back the news. I imagined our lives returning to what they had been. I imagined how grateful to me Mom would be.

But then a crazy, unexpected thought intruded.

If it *was* Becky, and if Becky came home . . . what would that mean for me and Chipper?

"Yep," Lenny was saying as the four of them gathered around the bike. "It's a brand new motherfucker. An FLT, with a rubber-isolated drivetrain." I stepped aside so he could caress the motorcycle's chrome. "The engine and transmission are hard bolted together."

Bruno was looking it over closely. The girls hung back a bit. Nobody paid any attention to me. Which allowed me to check out the dark-haired girl. She had her shoulder to me, preventing me from getting a full look at her face. From the back, she could definitely be Becky. I took a step forward, trying to get a better glimpse.

"And who's this?" Bruno suddenly asked, and I felt his black eyes on mine. Instinctively, I looked at the ground.

"This is my latest buckaroo," Lenny said. "Teaching him how to ride."

Bruno was studying me. "Well, he ain't riding now," he said, and I recognized the voice from the answering machine. "What's he got his helmet still on for?"

My eyes swung around and latched onto the face of the dark girl. If it was Becky, I was prepared to run. If not—

My eyes found hers. She was looking straight at me.

And she wasn't my sister.

I took off the helmet. "Hey," I said casually.

Bruno immediately lost interest. He examined the bike a bit more, then exchanged a few words with Lenny on the sidewalk. The girls wandered back inside. Then Lenny told Bruno he'd see him around and nodded for me to hop back on the bike. I replaced the helmet and once again gripped him around the middle. We roared off.

"Not her, huh?" he shouted over the sound of the engine.

"No," I said.

Waiting for us outside the Blue Dog, standing beside Troy's car, Mom was furious with the news. She acted as if somehow I'd made a mistake.

"It's been a year!" she shrilled. "You might not have recognized her. She could have changed. She could have lost weight, put on weight . . ."

"It wasn't her," I said.

"What about *inside?*" Mom demanded. "There could've been another girl inside."

"The word is that Bruno's living with two girls right now," Lenny replied. "And we saw both of 'em."

"*Up close,*" I told her. "It wasn't Becky."

Mom went on. "But Warren said the Rubberman said—"

"The Rubberman was wrong," Lenny told her. "And frankly, Peg, I think he's been wrong all along."

Mom's face was so red, the vein in her forehead pulsing so prominently, that I thought, quite truthfully, that her head was about to explode. Clenching her fists at her side, she leaned back and looked up the darkening gray sky and screamed at the top of her lungs. One long howl. Lenny rushed over and put his hands on her shoulders.

"Listen to me, Peg!" he shouted. "I don't know where your daughter is, but she's not with Bruno! Maybe she was at one time, but she's not anymore! Stop giving money to Warren! You're just pissing it away."

She yanked herself away from him and threw herself into the car, slamming the door behind her. "I'll talk to Warren myself!" she yelled through the window. "You don't know what the fuck you're talking about! I won't listen to you! Just wait till I call Warren! Warren will know what to do!"

I slipped into the backseat as Troy started up the car. Mom was angry and sputtering all the way home. I kept trying to tell her that I'd done my best, but she just barked at me to shut up. "I can't think," she said. "I just need to talk to Warren."

I settled back against the seat and closed my eyes, realizing I'd probably never see Lenny again, and that made me sad for an odd reason. I liked how he'd called me buckaroo.

Back at our apartment, Mom stormed inside, leaving Troy and me to lean against his car and watch the sun drop behind the trees. The sky was stained pink and orange.

"You think she'll ever find her?" Troy asked, pink light on his face.

I just shook my head.

"So what do you think happened to Becky?"

I shrugged. "Guess you were right in the beginning. She's probably dead."

I felt no emotion speaking the words.

Troy pressed his shoulder against mine. "You know, I was worried about you when you took off on that bike. I didn't know what might happen to you at Bruno's house."

"Well, nothing did," I said.

"Still, I was worried."

At that moment, a car came screeching into our complex, a car I recognized. It was Chipper's Mach 1. My heart quickened. He slammed to a stop on the other side of the parking lot so that Mom wouldn't see him. He saw us and got out of the car, motioning us over. I could tell by his movements that he was pissed.

"Oh, man," I said and ran toward him, Troy at my heels.

"Where the *fuck* were you?" Chipper was asking, wearing a football jersey with the number eleven on the front and a pair of faded blue jeans. "I waited for you at that fucking nursing home for a fucking hour."

"I'm so sorry, Chipper. It was my Mom. She—"

I noticed the look he threw at Troy.

"Oh, I see," he said. "You had a meeting of Fags Anonymous."

"Fuck you, Chipper," Troy said.

Chipper lunged forward, grabbing the front of Troy's shirt. Troy's face was terrified.

"Stop!" I shouted, pushing my hands between them. Chipper let go, and Troy backed off a couple of feet. "Chipper, you know that Troy hauls Mom and me around when she's out hunting for Becky. She had another crazy scheme today, and I had to leave my grandmother. I'm sorry. There was no way to let you know."

Chipper folded his arms across his chest and looked away. "Whatever. I just had a really shitty day, and I didn't appreciate waiting around at that frigging nursing home, feeling all stood up—especially after I'd been good enough to offer to give you a ride home."

I stood in front of him, feeling horrible. "You're right. I am *so* sorry, Chipper."

Chipper moved his eyes suddenly to meet mine, and the intensity of them startled me. Chipper had beautiful eyes. So dark. So reflective. I could almost see myself in them.

"Let's go for a ride," he said in a low voice. "Just us."

I turned to Troy. "I gotta go with Chipper now."

I could see the hurt on Troy's face. Troy had shown courage in standing up to Chipper, but it was stupid, too. Chipper was right. Troy *was* a fag. A stupid fag. At least I was bisexual. That little bit of straightness in me made the difference between us, I thought.

Troy looked at me through his tinted glasses. "You want me to come by tomorrow and pick you up for school?"

"No," I said. I realized I needed to redeem myself in front of Chipper. "You know, Troy, the only reason I still hang out with you is that my mom makes me. She needs you to drive her around. But that's over now, after what happened today. I think from now on you should just keep your distance."

Troy took a step back, as if I'd punched him. "Fuck you, too, then," he finally said.

"Okay, whatever," I said.

He turned to Chipper. "Hope you continue to enjoy playing tailback on the team. Every time you get out to play, Coach says to get your *tail back* on that bench."

Chipper's eyes went wild. He made another mad lunge at Troy, but Troy sprinted away too fast.

Hopping into his Jaguar, he sped off.

"Get in," Chipper said, swearing under his breath. I ran around to the passenger side of the Mach 1. In moments we were squealing out of the parking lot. Chipper drove with one hand and dug out his marijuana pipe from under the seat with the other. He handed it to me to light.

"You know, it pisses me off to come over here and find you hanging out with that fag Kitchenette again," he said.

"His name is Kitchens."

"Whatever," Chipper said. "He's still a fag."

I lit the pipe and took a hit. It was the last of the pot I had stolen from Troy. I was feeling pretty bad about what I'd said to him. It would be hard to be in the play together and not be friends. When I saw him the next day, I'd have to apologize.

"He's really not so bad," I told Chipper, handing him the pipe. "He gets good weed, you gotta give him that. Plus he puts up with Mom's crap." I laughed. "She got this tip that Becky was living with Bruno down in Naugatuck."

"Naugatuck? Where the fuck is that?"

"Down near Waterbury. So we drove down there, and it wasn't her." Chipper handed me back the pipe. "I'm starting to think she's not with Bruno at all."

"I coulda told you that."

I looked over at him. "How could you have told me that?"

He scoffed. "All that talk about Becky running off with bikers. That's bullshit. She wasn't into bikers. That's not why she disappeared."

He had never been quite so definitive before. "Then why *did* she disappear?" I asked.

He didn't answer.

"Chipper," I said, pressing, "do you know why Becky disappeared?"

"All I know is," he told me, taking another hit off the pipe, "I had one fucking long, shitty day."

"Why? What happened?"

We turned into Eagle Hill Cemetery. The Mach 1 jostled over a dirt road, climbing the hill to the summit of the old graveyard.

"That little fucker Kitchenette was right." The car dropped down into a rut, knocking us around a bit, but Chipper didn't comment, just drove on. "Coach O'Brian says I'm not big enough to play against St. Thomas. All the guys are frigging brutes on that team."

"Well, he's making a big mistake," I told him.

"Damn straight he is. I think I'm *plenty* big enough." He came to a stop and shut off the ignition behind a large tree. Only a few orange leaves still clung to its branches. "Okay," Chipper acknowledged, "so maybe I'm not as big as that dickhead Tommy Masters, the coach's kiss-ass quarterback, but Masters hasn't won a single game for us all season. He's the clumsiest player on the team."

"He's terrible," I agreed.

"And if I'm not as big as some of those freaks, I'm *strong*. I'm stronger than any of them." Chipper suddenly popped open his car door and jumped outside. "I'll show you how strong I am."

I got out of the car as well, watching him. The sun had set, but there was still enough blue light to see as Chipper made his way to an overturned gravestone. Bending over, he struggled with it, getting his fingers underneath, digging into the moist earth. Finally, he budged the stone and lifted it up toward his chest, grunting. He managed to get it up off the ground by about five inches; then he let it drop. I think he was disappointed that he couldn't lift it over his head, but I decided to cheer, anyway.

"Aw right!" I said. "That was awesome!"

There was a hint of a smile on his face. "Fucking coach," he muttered under his breath. "I'm plenty strong."

"You *are*. You have an amazing body, Chipper."

Shadows crept across his face. From the top of the tree, a crow cawed several times. "I've been going to the gym every day," he said, cocky now. "I've been getting really ripped up. You wanna see?"

I could barely answer. "Yeah . . ."

He pulled his football jersey over his head and tossed it to the ground. His torso was leaner than those of most football players, but he'd developed a nice set of round shoulders. His pectorals were defined but flat against his body. A six-pack of abdominals dropped down into his jeans. He flexed me the classic double-bicep pose.

"Wow," I said, and I meant it.

Suddenly he sat, plopping down on the gravestone he'd attempted to lift, and covered his face with his hands. I thought he might be crying. "I've waited four years to make a name for myself on the team," he muttered. "And now that fucking asshole won't let me play! All four years of high school *down the fucking drain!*"

I sat down beside him and placed my arm around his naked shoulders. "You're a great player, Chipper. He's *got* to see that."

He looked at me. "Do you have any idea what I'm going through? All my life was leading up to this year. *This year!* My senior year! I was supposed to be the big star of the school! My dad always told me I'd be the top guy. He said I had everything going for me. And now he acts like it's somehow my fault that I'm not playing, that the coach keeps me on the bench. He blames me!"

"Well, he doesn't know what he's talking about. . . ."

Chipper leaned his head back, his face contorted, the veins on his neck standing out. "I was supposed to be the star, not that asshole Tommy Masters! It was supposed to be *me!*"

"If you were the star, we'd be undefeated. Masters sucks!"

He put his face in his hands again and moaned. "Everything started going wrong for me the day Becky left," he said in a muffled voice. "From that day on, I was cursed."

"Why?" I asked, drawing in a little closer. "What happened that day?"

Chipper stood up. "I am *fucking strong!* Nobody can say otherwise! Come here! Feel my bicep!"

I stood and obeyed, cupping my hand over his left bicep. A jolt of electricity shivered through my body.

"Wow," I said again, and once again meant it. Even more this time.

"Okay, that's enough," Chipper said and pulled his jersey back on.

Without saying another word, he got back into the car. I followed.

For much of the ride home, we didn't speak. When the apartment complex was in sight, Chipper turned to me and said, "You liked that, huh?"

"Liked what?"

"Feeling my muscle."

I shrugged. "I liked it okay."

"Then maybe you *are* a fag."

I was silent.

"If you keep hanging out with that Kitchenette kid, mark my words, Danny, you *will* turn into a fag," Chipper told me. He pulled the car into the lot outside my apartment, making sure to park far enough way so that Mom wouldn't see us. "And if you turn into a fag, we can't hang out anymore."

"I'm not a fag," I said.

"Hard not to think so the way you jumped on my muscle."

"You asked me to."

"I was just testing you."

I sighed.

"You're the only one who understands me," Chipper wailed suddenly. "My father is on my ass all the time. And Coach O'Brian is an asshole." He turned and looked at me hard. "So I don't want you hanging out with Troy anymore. Okay?"

"Okay."

"See you tomorrow, then."

"Okay, Chipper."

I got out of the car, and he sped off.

Inside the apartment, Mom was already in bed. I imagined she'd cried herself to sleep again. Dad was sitting on the couch, drunk, watching *Match Game PM*. There was nothing in the refrigerator to eat, so I just went to my room. I couldn't get Chipper's words out of my head. He had felt cursed since the day Becky disappeared. Why? What had happened that day?

He drowned her.

The idea hit me like a freight train.

He drowned her in the pond.

But I was sure the police had dragged the pond in their search for her. I was being crazy. Chipper would never do such a thing. Why would such a crazy idea come into my mind?

I pulled out my scrapbook of Beautiful Men. I turned each page, gazing into their eyes, caressing the glossy magazine images, no matter that they were bumpy and scarred from the paste underneath. Recently I'd added Erik Estrada, John Schneider, and David Naughton to the collection—the last of whom hailed from Hartford, so he was my current favorite. David Naughton was proof that somebody from here could grow up and make it.

But none of them, I decided, were as beautiful as Chipper, whose shirtless torso in that dark cemetery remained burned into my mind.

PALM SPRINGS

It was Penelope Sue's annual Halloween party. Everybody who was anybody—or at least everybody Penelope Sue had decided was anybody—was there. My invitation, I was certain, had come courtesy of Donovan, since his wife seemed determined to cling to her complete and utter oblivion of my existence. It had always been Donovan who'd made sure Frank and I got invited to these soirees at his house.

This time, however, Frank had indicated by a slow turn of his head that he wasn't interested in attending; since our contretemps the other night, he was still sleeping in the casita, and most of our communication had become similarly nonverbal. So I was obliged to ask Randall to accompany me. When I apprised Donovan of this change to the guest list, he insisted that Randall bring along his "hunky new Arab boyfriend." So it was three of us who gathered on Saturday night at Hassan's to put on our costumes.

"I am less an authentic sheik," Hassan said, slipping into an Arab headdress, "than I am Rudolph Valentino playing one in a silent movie." He admired himself in the mirror. "Just so that it's clear."

"Well," said Randall, "I'm less an authentic drag queen than I am a Century City orthodontist playing one for a pretentious Palm Springs party."

I laughed. Randall had wanted to go as Cher, during her "If I

Could Turn Back Time" period. Black fishnet stockings stretched across the round tree trunks he called thighs, while a wig of black ringlets cascaded from his head. But when the look failed to come together, he came up with the idea of going as Cher playing Baby Jane Hudson in a remake of *What Ever Happened to Baby Jane?* Rouging his lips, caking on face powder, Randall strode around the room, swinging his hips and waving a cigarette—Cher doing Bette Davis doing Baby Jane. "You are the gayest man ever to live," I told him.

As for me, I couldn't decide what to wear. I wasn't really in the mood for a party. But it was the prospect of seeing Donovan that had finally convinced me to accept the invitation. Now, even I had to admit *that* was a first. Donovan Hunt was usually the very *last* reason I ever went to one of his (or his wife's) parties. But this time, I needed to talk with him. He was the only one I could talk to, in fact. Besides, another night of sitting alone in the house, with Frank watching television out in the casita, neither of us speaking, was just too depressing to consider.

"Does this look okay?" I asked the boys.

Randall made a face. "What are you supposed to be? A matador?"

"No, silly," Hassan interjected. "He's a pirate."

I scoffed. "You're both wrong. If I were a matador, I'd have a red cape. If I were a pirate, I'd have an eye patch."

"Then what *are* you?" Randall asked.

"I'm a gypsy." I turned and looked back in the mirror. I thought I looked pretty good. Okay, so the short little black vest I was wearing, picked up at a vintage costume shop, probably did come from a matador costume originally. And the single large gold loop hanging from my left ear might well have been more appropriate for a pirate than a gypsy. But only a gypsy wore this many rings. From every finger of both of my hands, including my thumbs, sparkled fake amethysts and rubies and diamonds. And only a gypsy would wear a pentagram around his neck, its sharp points occasionally stabbing his bare chest, in order to ward off were-wolves. I thought it was obvious that I was a gypsy.

Piling into the Jeep, we headed out to Rancho Mirage. The house Donovan shared with Penelope Sue was perched as high up the mountain as city code allowed. It was a slick and stream-lined concoction of steel and stone and glass. An elongated swim-ming pool wrapped around three sides of the place like a moat, crossed at strategic points by stone bridges that led from various rooms into the terraced gardens. In the sunken living room, one wall was made entirely of glass, through which we could view those in the pool like sea creatures displayed in an aquarium. This night, as shirtless waiters in Mardi Gras masks passed out hors d'oeuvres, Donovan had arranged a show of sleek-limbed boys and girls to swim gracefully past us like so many trained dol-phins.

In one corner, Penelope Sue held court. She was dressed as Marie Antoinette—a rather tone-deaf costume, I thought, given her reputation as the richest and most elitist woman in the Coach-ella Valley. But maybe she rather liked the reference and had de-cided to embrace it rather than run away from it. In any event, she stood there in her enormous white wig and glittering pink hoop skirt—looking more, Randall thought, like Glinda the Good Witch than Marie Antoinette—and grandly received the air kisses of her guests. I watched. After each one, she rolled her eyes. Suddenly I missed Kelly terribly.

From across the room, Thad and Jimmy waved animatedly. They were dressed as Musketeers, complete with hats and feath-ers and ruffled shirts. "Only two Musketeers?" I asked, approach-ing them. "Where's your third?"

Thad gave me a sly grin. "You must have tired him out the other night, dancing on top of that box."

I groaned, not wanting to be reminded of that night.

"*These* are what so transfixed the entire bar," Thad said grandly, running his palm down my abdominals. "Believe me, I dreamt about them all night long."

"He did," Jimmy spoke up, a rare utterance from his corner. "He told me so the next morning."

I blushed.

"And *you*, darling," Thad said, turning to Randall. "Who are you trying to be? Michael Jackson in *Thriller?*"

"I'm Cher playing Baby Jane Hudson," Randall explained.

Thad shivered. "Brilliant concept. I'll give you an A for effort."

He leaned in to give Randall a kiss. I could see Randall tense up as he did so. I realized my friend hadn't told Hassan about his little encounter with Thad and Jimmy. Clearly, he was hoping for some discretion, and except for the kiss, Thad complied, giving away none of their intimacy as he shook Hassan's hand.

"And *you*," Thad said, apprising Hassan up and down. "You can slip into my tent any time you want."

Hassan smiled. "I thank you for the offer," he said courteously.

Thad laughed. "Don't thank me. Just take me up on it." He knocked back the last of his drink. "Fabulous party, don't you think? My dear Penelope certainly knows how to throw them."

"That she does," I said.

"But my dear Danny," Thad said, leaning his head in toward me. "I can't help but notice there are no Fortunatos hanging on the walls. I mean, I know there are a couple of Renoirs and a Picasso or two or three, but nothing by *you*? And here I thought Donovan was an old friend of yours."

I laughed. Thad had bought a print of mine just last week, so he apparently expected others to follow. "I think it's *Mrs.* Hunt who makes the decisions about what art goes on the walls," I told him. "And she's never seemed able to remember my name."

"Hmm," Thad said.

"Speaking of Donovan," I asked, "where is he?"

"Oh, he's around," Thad replied. "With a new boy on his arm. And in my humble opinion, the most stunning one in a long time. For a change, he's a blond."

"Well, you know, blonds were Donovan's first love," Randall quipped, his eyes turning to me.

I ignored him. "It's amazing what Penelope puts up with."

"You are assuming," Hassan interjected, "that marriages are only successful if they are based on passion. Perhaps Mr. and Mrs. Hunt have founded their union on things other than romantic bliss."

I laughed. "Well, I'd have to agree with you there. *Definitely* other things than romantic bliss."

"I need a refill," Thad said. "Jimmy and I will mosey on over to the bar. Can we bring you back anything?"

I asked for a Grey Goose martini, up, with a twist. Hassan requested a club soda. Randall said he'd accompany Thad and

Jimmy so he could help carry back the drinks. Off they headed across the room. That left Hassan and me to scope out the crowd by ourselves.

"It's a strange but fascinating custom, this Halloween," said Hassan.

"The gay national holiday," I told him.

Not all the guests were gay, of course, but certainly more than half were of the lavender persuasion. And nearly everyone present considered themselves *fops:* friends of Penelope, a designation taken very seriously in the desert. Some of the costumes they'd put together were extraordinary. Clearly, many of the fops had spent the better part of the year planning for this night. One guy came as a Christmas tree, complete with balsam branches and a star on top of his head. One woman was dressed as a butterfly, with gigantic gossamer wings, which she kept folded behind her, except for those moments when she spread them, five yards wide, to the astonishment of the room. Hassan and I stood off to one side, gazing out across the great oval-shaped room, with its tan suede walls. An assortment of witches and soldiers, vampires and harlequins, cowboys and ballerinas mingled and sipped their drinks under the magnificent chandelier.

"I think if I were to take your picture tonight," Hassan said suddenly, apropos of nothing, "it would be a portrait of grief."

It took me by surprise, and I looked over at him. "Excuse me?"

"It has changed. Your image. The emptiness has been filled in with grief."

I said nothing, just nodded my head slightly.

Hassan leaned in close. "Feeling grief is better than being empty."

I thought of Frank, alone in the casita.

"You know, Hassan," I said, pushing the thought away, "this whole Yoda thing is getting a bit weird."

He frowned. "Yoda? I don't know the reference."

"He was the cuddly little oracle in the *Star Wars* series. He was always spouting off words of wisdom, seeing things in the characters that nobody else saw."

His frown turned into a smile. "So are you calling me cuddly?"

I smiled back. "If I could take a picture of *you*," I said, moving my face close to his, "I'd take a portrait of somebody in love."

His eyes flickered away. "Do you mean Randall? I am not in love with Randall."

"Well, then, I'm sorry to hear that."

"I am very fond of him," Hassan said. "But, no, I am not in love."

"How do you know?" I asked, and the question was genuine. "How do you know when you're in love and when you're not?"

Hassan laughed. "I think the concept of being 'in love' is much overused in this country."

"Perhaps," I said—and even as the word was still on my lips, I turned and saw him. *Kelly.* Across the room. Dressed as himself, no costume, just his usual dark shirt and corduroy pants. He looked like a homeless man, hovering on the sidelines. Then the crowd shifted, and I lost sight of him.

"Here you go, Mr. Chippendale," Thad said, suddenly at my side, handing me my drink. My heart was thudding in my chest, and for a moment, I didn't respond. "Well, do you want me to *drink* it for you, too?"

"Oh, thanks," I said, accepting the drink and taking a big sip.

My eyes returned to the crowd, searching. It had occurred to me that Donovan might invite Kelly, but I hadn't dared to ask. Since the other day, when Kelly had told me he wouldn't allow himself to fall in love with me, I hadn't replied to his texts. They'd come in fairly frequently that night and the next day. Then, gradually, they began tapering off. Finally, the last one had said: I GUESS BEING MY FRIEND IS TOO MUCH WORK. SORRY THEN. GOOD-BYE.

He was right. It *was* a lot of work. For too little gain. Yet still I missed him fiercely. It was agony not texting him back. I was miserable not seeing him. I'd tried to hold my ground and put him out of my mind. I tried to distract myself with a trip up to Sherman Oaks, where I took Ollie out to dinner to make up for running out on him. Driving into Los Angeles for the first time in many, many months, I realized I no longer thought of the city as home. I hated the traffic and the congestion and the noise and the commotion and couldn't wait to get out of there. But Ollie was so grateful, so touched, by the fact that I had come to see him that the long stretches of silence over dinner were almost worthwhile. Still, I couldn't help but compare the experience to the dinners I'd shared with Kelly, who'd kept me in stitches with laughter and ensured there was never an awkward, quiet moment. That night, driving back into Palm Springs, passing the windmills on my right and glimpsing the lights of the city in front of me, I felt for the first time as if I was coming home. It had taken me this long—and meeting Kelly, I realized—to feel that way.

It was then that the chain around my neck broke, and my pentagram dropped to the floor.

"So much for protection from werewolves," I said as Randall bent down to retrieve it.

"What did you and Hassan talk about while I was gone?" he whispered in my ear as he pressed forward to hand me the pentagram.

"Grief," I said.

"Grief?"

I nodded. "Apparently I'm grieving."

"Of course, you are," Randall said.

I shook my head. I felt *guilt* about Frank, not grief. In fact, as much as it pained me to think that I had hurt Frank, our separation felt right. Appropriate. How could I continue spooning with Frank in our bed every night when my mind was fixed on someone else? It wasn't fair to Frank; it wasn't fair to *us*, to the "us" that we had been. As long as I felt this way about Kelly, it was better to be apart. How long that would last, I didn't know. But glimpsing Kelly again tonight, and the tumble of emotions that followed, suggested my feelings for him weren't quite over yet.

"Danny," Randall was saying, pulling still closer to me. "I told Hassan I loved him today."

I turned my head to him sharply. "And what did he say?"

"In his typical, formal way, he thanked me for it." Randall laughed. "I think that's his way of saying he loves me, too."

I gripped Randall by the shoulders. "Be careful, buddy," I said. "I don't want you getting hurt. Not so soon after Ike."

Randall laughed again. "Ike? Who's that?"

I gripped his shoulders tighter. "*Please*, Randall. Falling in love can hurt. It can be the worst thing in the world."

"Or the greatest," he said.

I felt a hand on my shoulder. I turned. It was Thad, with Marie Antoinette.

"*This* is the man I was telling you about," Thad said to Penelope.

"Hello," I managed to say.

She extended her white-gloved hand. "Penelope Sue Hunt," she said.

"Yes," I said. "We've met."

"Darling," Thad said to her, "you must see Danny's work. He will soon be all the rage. I just bought a print, and I understand Bette Midler has commissioned something. And the rumors are that Gwyneth Paltrow has ordered up a whole series. And you know Geffen has a Fortunato in his house on Fire Island."

"Really?" Penelope asked, her collagen-injected lips curving into a small smile.

None of this was true, except for the fact of his own purchase. I glared at Thad.

"Well, of course, Danny has a policy of never confirming rumors about who he does work for," Thad continued. "But that's what they say."

"You do lithographs?" Penelope asked, not entirely with admiration.

"Various kinds of prints. Photographs, digitally manipulated," I said.

"I see." She adjusted her enormous white beaded wig, probably to keep it from falling over. "I'd like to see some of your work. I trust Thad's opinion."

"Well, I'd be happy to bring some by," I told her.

"Mmm," she said—and then she did it.

She rolled her eyes.

"Thank you," I said. But she was already moving off into the crowd.

"You're *in*, baby," Thad whispered to me. "If Penelope buys from you, *everyone* will follow."

I smiled. "Thank you."

"Don't mention it," Thad said, hurrying to follow Penelope Sue. "We working-class kids need to stick together to get what we can out of the fat cats."

I laughed.

"That's fabulous, Danny," Randall said. "Frank will be so happy when he hears."

"Well, you'll have to tell him. He's not speaking to me," I said.

Randall shook his head. "This is crazy. Danny, you can't let this go on much longer. You and Frank, you're like the same person. You complete each other. You can't throw away twenty years."

I turned, not wanting to have this conversation. I was in luck. I finally spotted the other half of the Hunts. Donovan was approaching me through the crowd.

"Did I just see my wife speaking with you?" he asked.

"Indeed. She wants to see my work."

Donovan made a face of surprise. He was dressed as an army general, his chest resplendent with ribbons. And on his arm, as Thad had prepared us for, was the most spectacular blond specimen I had seen in a very long time, dressed as a sailor in his formal whites. Tall and broad-shouldered, the young man couldn't have been more than twenty-five, and he possessed eyes as blue—and as cold—as the North Sea.

"I guess my wife listens to Thad Urquhart more than she listens to me," Donovan said. "I've been telling her about you for years." He sighed. "Then again, who am I? Just her husband. Thad is going to be the mayor of Palm Springs."

"She hasn't bought anything yet," I said. "She just said she wants to see my work."

"Oh, she'll buy something," Donovan said. "If you've gotten this far with her, she'll buy something." He seemed to remember the young man on his arm. "Oh. This is Sven." The boy nodded, unsmiling, not offering his hand for us to shake. "Sven, this is Randall and Hassan and Danny." Donovan's eyes, stretched so tightly from so many cosmetic surgeries, clamped onto me. "Danny is one of the first friends I met when I first came out to L.A. a hundred years ago."

I smiled. An image of Donovan from those days flashed in my mind. Back then, he hadn't needed cosmetic surgeons to stretch his eyelids, to tighten up his cheeks. None of us had. We'd been the boys then, the young prizes on older men's arms. How fast the time had gone. I remembered a day, sitting in Donovan's old Porsche—long discarded, since he'd upgraded to Bentleys—and listening to him talk about his father, the father who'd expected so much from his only son, the father who'd only truly been satisfied when Donovan married the even wealthier Penelope Sue.

"Not quite a hundred years," I gently corrected him. "But close enough to it."

Donovan laughed. "So are you all having fun?"

"Brilliant party as usual," Randall said.

"And *you?*" Donovan purred to Hassan. "Are *you* having fun, my hunky Arab?" I saw Sven frown slightly.

"I am honored to have been asked to your beautiful house," Hassan told him.

"Well, I hope you'll come back another time," Donovan said, winking, as he and Sven began to move away. It was the same old Donovan, flirting with someone no matter who else was around.

Before he could get too far, however, I reached out and grabbed his arm. "Donovan," I said, "might I speak with you a moment?"

He threw an eye back over his shoulder. "Sure. What's up?"

"In private. Just for a moment."

"All right." He turned to Sven. "Run along and keep Penelope company for a while, okay, sugarplum?"

Sven said nothing, just frowned again and slunk away.

"Swedes can be so sullen," Donovan grumbled as we moved off in the opposite direction. "Sometimes I feel like he just stepped out of a Bergman movie."

I smiled. "I remember when you didn't know what a Bergman movie *was*. It took me to show you, to take you to the AFI screenings." Of course, it was Randall who'd introduce *me* to classic film, teaching me there was more to see than just *Doctor Who* and *Monty Python* and *Star Wars*.

Donovan threw his arm round me, grinning wide. "Oh yes, I remember those days well. You would argue with me about the need to make movies that actually *said* something." He opened the door to his private study, which opened onto his bedroom, and gestured for me to enter. Enormous picture windows looked out onto the mountains and down into the valley, sparkling with lights from the city below. "And I would say to you," Donovan continued, "'Danny, I'll only make those kinds of pictures if you will star in them for me.'"

I smirked. "You were just blowing smoke up my ass so you could get up there yourself."

Donovan closed the door behind us and looked over at me slyly. "So why didn't the good husband accompany you tonight? Why did you show up with a posse of girlfriends?"

"Frank . . . he had a . . . school thing."

Donovan's smile showed he didn't believe me. "I see."

I let out a breath awkwardly.

"So what did you want to talk to me about?" he asked.

"I don't know. It's silly, really. I . . ."

Donovan folded his arms across his chest and leaned against his desk, a big old mahogany piece that had been his father's, which he'd shipped out here from Connecticut after the old man finally died.

"Danny, what is it?" He seemed to find my discomfort amusing. "What's on your mind?"

"Kelly," I blurted out.

Donovan looked at me oddly for several seconds. "Kelly?" he finally repeated.

"Yes."

"Kelly . . . Nelson?"

I nodded.

He laughed. "You want to talk about *Kelly?*"

"We've been . . . seeing each other."

Donovan made a face as if I were speaking a language he didn't understand.

"L-look," I stammered, "I don't know what kind of relationship you had with him, and I don't mean to pry. But I can't really talk to anyone else about this . . ."

"About *what?*"

"About how I'm feeling about him."

"About Kelly?"

"*Yes!*"

Donovan looked at me intently for a moment, then threw his

head back and laughed loudly. Not a mean laugh, just one that seemed genuinely amused.

"What?" I asked. "What is so funny?"

"Danny Fortunato," Donovan said, composing himself, "are you in love with Kelly Nelson?"

I swallowed. "Yes. Yes, I am."

"I don't know what to say."

"You're the only person I know who really knows him," I said. "And I know that if someone isn't worth it, you don't keep them in your life. So Kelly was obviously worth it, since you had him to your party at the Parker." I paused. "And I saw him here tonight, too."

Donovan stood and walked over to the window. "Yes," he said. "He's worth it."

"Well, I can't figure him out." I sighed, feeling foolish. "I've been trying to help him, but he's so hard to reach. And I can't figure out how he feels about me. He seems to want me, but then he . . ."

"Did you get him into bed?" Donovan asked, not turning around to look at me.

"If you can call it that."

Donovan turned, a small smile on his lips. "Then you got more than I did."

I looked at him. "Did you . . . fall in love with him, too?"

He sighed. "I wouldn't go that far. But I *was* fascinated. I met him in L.A. He was working at the Abbey. One night I saw him get into a fight with the manager, and he got fired. I suggested he move out here. I hoped . . ." His voice trailed off.

"You hoped what?"

"That something might blossom between us. But it never did, though I sure as hell tried. He wasn't interested in all the sparkly things other boys are interested in. He wouldn't let me buy him a damn thing."

"Didn't you get him that old Mercedes he drives?"

"Nope. He bought that himself with money he saved." Donovan sighed. "God, he's beautiful."

I nodded. "Don't I know that all too well."

"Funny what beauty does to a man," Donovan said, moving back toward me now, lifting a bottle of brandy from his desk and pouring two snifters. He handed one to me. "I've kept him in my life chiefly because of his beauty, but also because—and this I *will* grant you, Danny—there is something rather special about him, down deep." He smiled. "It all rather reminds me of the way I felt for you, Danny, all those years ago."

"Oh, come *on*," I said as we toasted each other and sipped the brandy. It tasted good. Warm and thick and sweet.

Donovan shook his head, smiling as he looked at me. "You've never trusted your own appeal, have you?" he asked. "I could never understand that. I still can't. You were the hottest boy in West Hollywood in those days. Everyone wanted you."

"I was not and, no, they didn't."

He smiled. "Perhaps that was part of your appeal. You were oblivious to it."

"I wasn't oblivious. I was just realistic. Any twenty-year-old boy who gets up and shakes his ass in a thong is going to get a crowd of horny older men wanting him."

"But I didn't know you then," Donovan said. "Remember I only met you *after* you gave all that up, and *after* you'd hooked up with Frank." He made a face. "To my eternal regret."

"Oh, Donovan," I said.

"I'm being totally serious. I know I can come on strong. I know I can be a real smooth talker. But I liked you, Danny. I liked you a lot."

I was touched. "Thank you, Donovan."

"And now here we are. To think, all those years I hoped that *I* might be the one who could break you and Frank up. But no. Along comes a drifter like Kelly Nelson to succeed where I failed."

I said nothing, just shook my head.

"Is it true, then, Danny?" Donovan asked. "You really *would* leave Frank if Kelly seemed available to you?"

"I don't know," I admitted.

He laughed. "I should be *furious*. I should throw you out of my house right now." He poured himself some more brandy without offering me a refill. "I mean, all these years I've allowed myself to believe that the only reason you turned me down was because what you shared with Frank was so special, so profound, so rare. I contented myself that, in the face of such a profound love, even I—Donovan Hunt—stood no chance." He shrugged. "I could live with that. But to think that you might so easily give up that special and profound love for a measly little trifle like Kelly Nelson—"

"Kelly is not a trifle!" I actually took a step forward in my defense of him. "Maybe you didn't take the time, Donovan, to really see him for what he is. Kelly is a smart, talented person who—"

"Oh, come on, Danny. He's a wanderer. A vagabond."

"Yeah, well, maybe I like vagabonds."

"Maybe you just wish you'd been one a little longer than you were." He smirked. "You know, you're shattering all my illusions tonight, Danny. Here I was, envying you—"

I laughed out loud. "*You* envied *me?* Donovan, for Christ's sake, my whole house could practically fit inside this study. I drive a beat-up 1999 Jeep Wrangler. And when was the last time you had to worry about paying your monthly bills?"

Donovan's eyes popped with such sudden fury that they startled me. "As if money is worth envying! When was the last time *you*, Mr. Danny Fortunato, felt like a *fraud?*"

"Oh, many times," I assured him.

"Then you're being even more foolish." Donovan got up close in my face. "Every morning, Danny, you wake up and look into the eyes of a man who loves you. A man with whom you have spent *twenty years of your life*. Whose eyes do I look into? My wife's? A woman who, when I married her, understood this was going to be a union of convenience, but who has nonetheless come to hate me, more and more each day, with every fiber of her being." He paused. "Maybe, you say, I could look into the eyes of my revolving series of boyfriends? Boys who come to me not for who I am, but for what I can *give* them. The truth is, Danny, I look into no one's eyes. *No one's!* Imagine for a moment what it's like to go through life without ever being able to look someone in the eyes and know those eyes are looking back at you."

I didn't know how to respond. I just let out a sigh and leaned back against Donovan's desk, the empty snifter in my hand.

"Hang on a second, Danny," Donovan said, moving toward the door. "Just wait here a moment, okay?"

I nodded. He went out, back into the party, probably to check on the wife who hated him or the boy who was hoping to get something from him. I set the snifter down on the desk and covered my face with my hands.

In a few moments I heard the door open again. I uncovered my face, intending to apologize to Donovan, and I saw Kelly standing there instead.

"What are you doing here?" I asked.

"Donovan said you wanted to see me."

I stared at him. He was so beautiful, he took my breath away.

"No," I managed to say. "I didn't say that."

"Then I'll leave."

"No!" I moved forward, my arm outstretched. "Don't go."

Kelly's black eyes burned into my own. "He also said that we needed to figure out what was going on between us."

"Would that I could," I said.

"Well, if you have nothing to say, then I'm heading back to the party."

"Wait." I looked at him. "I know I've been unfair, asking you to love me. I had no right, being married and all."

He just gave me those eyes.

"It's just that—I can't be sure if you resist me because of Frank, or because you simply don't feel for me what I feel for you."

Kelly sneered. "You're too much, you know that? You're crazy."

"Why am I crazy?"

He took a step toward me. "You go through life letting people love you but you don't see it. You just don't see it!"

He was angry. I reached out to touch him but he pulled away.

"What's wrong with you, Danny? Why are you so fucking blind? Did Mommy not love you enough?"

"Okay," I said. "Stop there."

"No, I won't! You asked me when we first met if I'd ever been in love. I didn't know. You said I would have known if I had been." His eyes shone over at me. "Well, now I know! Now I know I have been."

Whether he made the first move or it came from me, I didn't know. But somehow, we came together. Our arms encircled each other. We kissed. It was a good kiss, like the one on the mountain.

We could have been anywhere, been anyone. It was only with tremendous effort that I forced myself to remember where we were, and that Donovan could come striding back through the door at any time.

"We shouldn't," I murmured. "Not here."

"I think he wanted this to happen," Kelly said.

I looked at him. "Do you?"

He hesitated, then nodded slowly.

I gripped his hand and led him through the door at the back of the room. Donovan's bedroom. A California king–size bed sat on a pedestal, the only major piece of furniture in the stark, spare white room. Kicking the door shut with my foot, I maneuvered Kelly toward the bed, where we fell down on our sides, kissing all the time. My erection threatened to pierce my underwear as my world tumbled over itself. Everything I had longed for was coming true. Nothing would ever be the same again.

I peeled off his shirt, kissing his neck. Unbuckling his belt, I slid off his pants, kissing his inner thigh as I did so. I was determined to make love to him the way I'd always wanted to, slowly and affectionately at first, building to a crescendo. I would banish all his fears, penetrate his heart and his soul. I straddled him now, still dressed in my silly gypsy costume, my one earring dangling above his face as I pinned his hands down with my own. The rings on my fingers sparkled in the light.

"You are so beautiful," I told him.

His black eyes reflected my face.

I lowered my lips to his chest. Hundreds of tiny kisses rained down on his torso, sprinkling his stomach and ending at his belly button, which I filled up with my tongue.

"There is so little time," I said. "It's running out. So little time."

"What do you mean?" he asked.

"Let's go away," I said. "You and me. Go away."

"Where?"

"I don't know. Somewhere."

"You'd leave Frank? For me?"

"Yes," I said.

I kissed his side, fluttering my lips into his pit, over his shoulder, down his inner arm. . . .

And then I stopped.

I saw it.

I saw what the sparseness of our previous intimacy had prevented me from seeing before.

The birthmark.

The birthmark shaped like a crescent moon.

Like . . .

Becky's.

No.

More like Mom's.

The birthmark that had linked Mom to her daughter forever, and forever excluded me from their special bond.

For several seconds, I just sat there, unmoving, straddling Kelly's chest, my erection shriveling in my pants.

"Danny?"

I got off the bed in a quick, jerky movement.

"Danny, what's wrong?"

I stood at the far side of the room, not looking at him.

What was I thinking?

"Danny, what's wrong?"

There is so little time.

An avalanche of images. That girl dancing in the bar in Yonkers, New York. Sitting on Troy's bed, smoking weed. Riding on the back of Lenny's motorcycle. Mom pulling me into her and telling me she would love me if only I could find Becky. And finally Becky and Chipper swimming in the pond.

"Your mother," I managed to say in a low, slow voice, still unable to look at him. "Your birth mother . . ."

"What?"

"Your birth mother!" I shouted, turning now to face him at last. "You said you remembered her a little!"

He sat up on the bed, looking like a frightened little child in his underpants. "What are you *talking* about?"

"Just answer me! What do you remember about your birth mother?"

"You're freaking me out," Kelly said, swinging his legs off the bed and pulling on his pants. "I knew we shouldn't have tried this. I knew it would ruin everything."

"Kelly, listen to me! Trust me! Just for a minute! What do you remember about your birth mother? Please tell me! And no jokes this time."

He was buckling his belt. "I hardly remember anything about her!" he shouted back at me. "I was five years old the last time I saw her."

"But you said she tried to get you back a number of times."

"Yes, but I never saw her again." He clearly resented talking about this. "She was a drug addict. They were never going to let me go back to her. Why are you asking me all this shit?"

"What did she look like?"

"I don't know . . . She had dark hair . . ."

"Would you recognize a picture of her?"

"No! I was five years old!"

"What was her name?"

He didn't want to answer, but he did. "Ann," he said.

"Dear God."

"Danny, what the *fuck* is going on?"

"Where was she from?"

"I told you. I was born in San Francisco."

"I mean *originally*. Where was your mother from *originally?*"

"I don't know." There was just the slightest pause. "Back East somewhere. That's all I know."

Back East somewhere.

"And your father?" I asked, my voice cracking.

"I don't know. My mother wasn't married to him when she had me."

The information was rushing at me like lava from a volcano, and it was all I could do to keep from falling under. "And your birthday . . ." I was struggling to do the math in my head. "You were born in April, right? And you're twenty-six now?"

"I'm getting out of here," Kelly said. "Did you and Donovan do some coke or something? Because you are acting *so* weird, Danny, and it's freaking me out!"

The math figured perfectly.

I couldn't speak. I just stood there, staring at Kelly.

And I realized the dark eyes looking back at me weren't his.

They belonged to Chipper Paguni.

EAST HARTFORD

My old friend Katie was applying the gray whiskers to my face for the dress rehearsal for *Oliver!* With so much time having passed, we hardly knew what to talk about. If we weren't both in the same play—I as Mr. Brownlow and she as part of the makeup crew—we'd probably have sat there in silence. We talked about Brother Connolly and the lighting crew and the costumes. Anything but the old days, those ancient times at St. John's. That would have been childish and silly. We were different people now, practically adults, sophomores in our prestigious school play. There was only one reference made to what used to be as Katie carefully applied the whiskers to the epoxy on my cheeks. She asked softly, "Did you ever find any clue to what happened to Becky?"

"No," I told her.

All those escapades, all those explorations of motorcycle bars and strip clubs, and it boiled down to one word.

No.

I didn't know if Mom and Dad would come to the see the play. Dad had made vague assurances that he would, and promised he'd convince Mom to come along, too. But Dad had a tendency to get drunk on Saturday nights and be hung over through the next afternoon, which severely dimmed the chances that he'd show up for either the Saturday night presentation or the Sunday matinee. So I didn't feel I could hold him to it. Mom, of course,

I'd never even asked. I knew better than to bother Mom with stuff as trivial as school plays. So I just left a flyer for the show secured to the refrigerator with a magnet—one of the Becky magnets, with her photo and a number to call. On the flyer for the play, I'd highlighted my name in yellow among the cast. I hoped Mom or Dad would see it, take the hint, and come.

But all that really mattered was that Chipper would be there.

"I went to every one of your games," I reminded him. "You owe me this."

Chipper had grunted. "I can't believe I have to go see a faggot-ass play," he'd said, but I could tell he was really glad to do it. We had been sitting in his room, on his shag carpet, leaning against opposite walls, the soles of our bare feet pressed together. I must have grown in the past year, because when we'd first started sitting this way, my legs hadn't reached far enough to touch his. Now I'd watched as Chipper's black eyes danced and his face lit up with a smile. "I'm gonna stand up when you come out on the stage," he said, "and yell, 'Go Fortunato!' the way you used to yell for me at my games."

It was good to see Chipper smile when he mentioned his games. The season had ended with him barely having played, and his team not winning a single game. His dreams of being a big senior-class hero had evaporated. He'd never got Mary Kay Suwicki or anybody else to be his girlfriend, either, so he rode out his last, anticlimactic months in high school hanging out with me, smoking pot in his room, listening to Aerosmith, playing footsie, and sometimes letting me walk on his back. I was content. I knew Chipper wasn't bisexual like I was. So this was the best deal I was going to get.

Sometimes I'd glance over at our old house across the street and watch the family that had moved in there. A mother, a father, a girl, and a boy. Just like we had been. The girl was younger and the boy was older, but otherwise, it was the same setup. The boy was a towhead like me; the girl dark like Becky. The mother even had big tits like Mom. I didn't hate those people for taking our house. They seemed to belong there, better than we had, at least at the end. When I watched the boy shoot basketballs into the net they'd installed over the garage door, I felt nothing, really. It was a place I didn't recognize anymore. I couldn't even remember living there—at least not before Becky disappeared. That part of my life, all those years leading up to my fourteenth birthday, seemed gone, almost as if they had never really happened at all.

But, of course, they had. Because here I was, fifteen, almost sixteen. You don't just get to be that age without going through everything that had come before. It was hard to believe I was almost at the end of my second year in high school. In some ways, it felt as if I had always been in exactly this same spot, been exactly this age, and always would be.

My life had fallen into a kind of pattern. Every day after school, except on days when I had play practice, Chipper would drop me off at the convalescent home, and I would read to Nana. I'd read *Moby Dick, The Grapes of Wrath,* even *The Catcher in the Rye,* blushing as I'd utter the swear words in front of her. This semester it had been British lit, so Nana got to hear *Wuthering Heights* and *Jane Eyre* and *Great Expectations.* I'd enjoyed them all, especially *Jane Eyre,* with that creepy lady running around in the walls. Nana always seemed so content when I read to her, the only time she wasn't agitated, the nurses said. They called my father and told him I was such a good grandson to Nana. One night Dad came in and sat down on the edge of my bed and thanked me for spending so much time with his mother, since he rarely did. He was drunk, so his words were slurred, and he was a little more teary than usual. But still, I appreciated his effort.

I was doing so well in literature that Brother Pop thought I should become a teacher or a writer—but I had my heart set on something else. I wanted to be an actor. The dress rehearsal for *Oliver!* had only confirmed that ambition for me. It was so cool to act with upperclassmen: except for mine, all the parts were played by juniors and seniors, and I'd been accepted by them as if I were one of their own. No more spitballs tossed at the back of my head. Danny Fortunato finally had his clique. For the first time since leaving St. John's, I was enjoying school. Rehearsing for the play filled me up with an energy I hadn't known for more than two years. I loved being there in the auditorium: the smell of the wax and polish on the shiny wooden stage, the heaviness of the red velvet curtains, which creaked when they went up and down, the heat of the spotlights, the echo of our voices in the empty hall. I'm not sure I'd have described my life as happy, but it wasn't bad. Not bad at all.

"All right now, Danny!" Brother Connolly was clapping his hands. "Take your place onstage, next to Jane Marie."

I hurried up to stand beside Jane Marie Schuster, who was playing the part of Nancy. Jane Marie was a senior and absolutely the coolest girl at St. Clare's. "I got you the brochure," she whispered. "I'll give it to you later."

"What brochure?"

"The UConn theater program brochure." Jane Marie was planning to major in theater at the University of Connecticut next year. "If you want to study theater, Danny, you should really start planning now."

"Oh, I do!" I replied. "Thank you so much!"

"No problem." Jane Marie's green eyes twinkled. "Maybe we'll act in more plays together in college."

"And then on Broadway!"

She laughed. "And then in movies!"

I let out a whoop.

"What was that?" Brother Connolly asked, spinning around.

"Sorry, Brother," I told him. "I just burped."

All my friends laughed.

My eyes caught those of Troy in the wings. Troy was in the chorus. He was in costume, too, that of a beggar boy. He gave me the thumbs-up sign, and I flashed it back to him. Then Brother Connolly called for Jane Marie and me to act out the scene.

If I'd thought play practice had been fun, dress rehearsal was amazing. The costumes, the lighting, the sound effects. This was how it was going to be on opening night—except that the auditorium would be filled with people. People who would applaud for us, for *me*. I'd look out into the empty seats and imagine the crowd that would come. They'd sit there, with their programs in their laps, their faces raised to the stage. I couldn't wait. All my dreams were coming true. From the time I woke up in the morning until the time I went to sleep at night, my heart was constantly

racing in my chest in anticipation of opening night. I sensed
nothing would be the same after that moment. Everything in my
life would be different.

After Jane Marie and I had finished our scene, Brother called
out, "Perfecto!" I raced off backstage, beaming. Troy caught up
with me and slapped me five.

"You never mess up your lines, *ever!*" he exclaimed.

"Well, I've had them memorized for over a year."

Troy drew close to me. "You know, you look kind of sexy with
those whiskers."

I laughed. "Oh, right."

"You do."

I smiled. Troy had forgiven me. He always did. He blamed my
cruel words on Chipper. He said he understood that I needed to
act tough around Chipper so that he wouldn't suspect what was
going on between us. I felt like a schmuck. But at least it meant
that Troy and I could continue our secret little trysts, which had
become as much a part of my life as play practice and reading to
Nana. But it was a fact that, when I kissed Troy, I would close my
eyes and visualize Chipper. I knew Troy would feel bad if he knew
this. But as much as I felt guilty about it, I couldn't help it. Every
time Troy touched me, I imagined it was Chipper's hand. Every
time he kissed me, I imagined it was Chipper's lips. It just happened automatically. I couldn't have stopped it if I'd tried.

I'd somehow managed to keep Chipper in my life, too. What a
balancing act. One couldn't know about the other. But today
Chipper was picking me up after dress rehearsal. I planned to
sneak away at the last moment and meet him in the back parking
lot. Part of me was torn: the cast had plans to go to Giovanni's
Pizza afterward, where we'd all hang out together for the last
time before the show. I really wanted to hang out with Jane Marie
and Paul, who played the Artful Dodger; and Lance, who played
Bill Sikes; and Greg, who played the nasty old Fagin; and especially Eddie, who was our impish Oliver Twist. And, of course,
with Troy, too, and all the chorus and crew members. We were
like one big family. I'd never had so many friends at one time before.

But Chipper had been insistent. "I had a *huge* fight with my father last night," he'd told me in the corridor earlier that day. "I need to go out tonight and just get totally wasted. And I need you to come with me. There's nobody else I trust enough."

Words like that always had the power to sway me. "Okay," I'd replied.

I figured I'd just slip out when dress rehearsal was over, not saying anything to anybody. I'd meet Chipper at his car, and we'd take off. Nobody would know. I'd give explanations the next day.

But Troy seemed to suspect something. "You *are* coming out with us tonight, aren't you?" he asked a couple of times.

"Yeah, why wouldn't I be?"

He just watched me with wary eyes.

Mr. Brownlow didn't have another scene for a while. So I sat backstage, cross-legged, watching the action onstage through a space in the dusty red velvet curtains. Troy was sitting beside me. He kept nudging his knee into mine.

"Stop it," I whispered. "You're gonna distract Lance and Jane Marie."

"I'd like to distract *you*," he said in a low voice.

"Stop it."

But my dick was getting hard nonetheless.

What was it with my dick? Sometimes all it took was a look, or a single word, to make it go all hard and raging. And at that moment, Troy's word *distract* was enough to fire me up and completely take my mind off the play.

"We could go into the men's room in the back," Troy was whispering. "Nobody goes in there."

"No," I said, but my voice betrayed my ambivalence.

"I want to clamp my mouth around your cock," Troy told me. "Suck it so hard for you. I'll even swallow."

I started breathing heavily. A minute and a half before, sex had been the furthest thing from my mind. Now I was panting for it, my cock threatening to pierce my underwear. "Okay," I said, and we both stood.

Tiptoeing out the side door and into the corridor, we broke into a run, our footsteps echoing against the brick walls.

Troy was right. The men's room at the far end of the school was never used during play practice. We'd be safe there. "But we have to be fast," I insisted as we came inside and Troy flipped on the fluorescent overhead lights. "I need to go back onstage in twenty minutes or less."

Troy looked at his watch and nodded. "I promise we'll be done by then."

The janitor had already been through here today; the place smelled strongly of bleach and cleaning fluids. A line of five ceramic sinks sparkled against one wall; opposite stood five brown metal stalls, each with its door latched. Troy opened the last stall and practically pushed me inside. I closed the lid on the toilet and sat down. Dropping quickly to his knees, Troy began pulling down my pants—Mr. Brownlow's felt trousers with the satin lining. His fingers slipped under the waistband of my Fruit-of-the-Loom underwear.

"Oh yeah," I moaned, closing my eyes and leaning my head back.

Troy's warm, wet lips slid over my erection. It felt good. Awesomely good.

For about thirty seconds.

That was when the chaos began. I heard a shout: "What the fuck?" I felt Troy's lips leave my cock. I heard the bang of the stall door opening and closing, and the thud of a body being thrown against the sinks. Above the stall, I caught a glimpse of an enraged face.

It was Chipper.

"What the fuck? What the fuck?" he kept repeating "What the *fuuuuuck*?"

I yanked up my pants and burst out of the stall. Chipper had pulled Troy off me and tossed him against the sinks. Troy had come down hard on his butt. He was struggling to stand up.

"Faggots!" Chipper was screaming now. "I should've known! You really are a couple of faggots!"

"Shut up," I said to Chipper. "Please, shut up! They'll hear you!"

Chipper's hands were in his hair. His face was scrunched up, and his mouth was opening and closing, sometime spewing forth a word, sometimes just silent. It looked almost as if he were having a heart attack.

"Faggots!" he shouted again. "You're both a couple of dirty faggots!"

"Chipper, please be quiet! Let's just get out of here!"

He turned his crazy black eyes on me. "He told me to meet you guys in here! He told me to be here on time, and so I was! He told me we'd smoke a joint together, that he had some good pot! And this is what I find! *Faggots!*"

I spun on Troy. "You . . . set this up?"

There was no time for Troy to respond. Chipper screamed at the top of his lungs like an Indian warrior going into battle and lunged at Troy again.

"Help me, Danny!" Troy screamed.

"Shut up," I told him now. "They'll *hear!*"

And they did hear. Brother Connolly came bursting through the door then, just in time to grab Chipper by the shoulders and throw him off of Troy. Chipper staggered backward, catching himself on a sink.

"What the *hell* is going on here?" Brother demanded.

"They're faggots!" Chipper bellowed. "I caught them in the stall—*doing it!*"

Brother's eyes widened as he looked from Troy over to me.

"It's not true," I said, my voice shaking terribly. "We were just in there talking . . . I wanted to go over my lines. Troy was just listening to me go over my lines!"

"Troy was sucking his faggot dick!" Chipper screamed, his black eyes accusing me of everything—of lying, of depravity, of loving Troy more than I loved him.

"No, no." I still tried to bluff my way out of this. "He *thinks* he saw that because I was taking a piss. I mean, I was urinating, Brother. I was going over my lines while I was—"

"Chipper's right," Troy interrupted, his voice as calm and reasonable as could be. "I was sucking Danny's dick." He smiled at me, then over at Brother. "And enjoying every moment of it, I might add."

"Sweet Jesus," Brother managed to say.

"Sorry, Danny," Troy said, looking back at me. "Really I am. But when I saw Chipper's car in the parking lot and realized you were planning to cut out on me again, I decided to take matters into my own hands for a change. I thought Chipper would come in here and see us and just storm off." He threw a disdainful glance in Chipper's direction. "I didn't realize what a hissy fit the stupid closet case would throw."

"You fucking little—," Chipper roared, but Brother held him off with one hand and a look that told him his entire graduation was on the line.

"And *this* is what lured him in," Troy said, producing from his pocket a Baggie filled with pot. "I know he's got more in his car. I was out there only a few minutes ago. I told him that I had better stuff than he had, and he should really come in and smoke with me and Danny here in the bathroom. If I were *you,* Brother, I'd go out there and search his car before he has a chance to clean it up."

Brother snatched the pot from Troy and turned to face Chipper. "Is this true, Chipper? Have you been smoking pot with these boys?"

"These *faggots,* you mean," Chipper sputtered.

"Please, Brother," I cut in. My hand was caressing the whiskers that were glued to my face. "This doesn't mean I can't be in the play, does it?"

Brother turned his eyes on me. "Oh, it does indeed mean that, Danny. I'm afraid it's going to mean a great many things." He looked around at the three of us. "For all of you."

A small smile ghosted across Troy's face. He could have cared less what was in store for him. He seemed pleased, in fact, by the way the whole thing had turned out.

"Okay, move your asses," Brother commanded. "You first, Chipper. Straight to the principal's suite. Danny, you go to my office. Troy, you go to Brother Finnerty's."

Chipper and Troy walked out ahead of me. I stopped in the doorway and turned back to look into Brother's face.

"*Please,*" I said, tears now rolling down my cheeks and into my fake whiskers. "Please don't kick me out of the play, Brother."

"I'm afraid you kicked yourself out, Danny," he said coldly.

On my way to Brother's office, I walked past the door to the auditorium. The whole cast and crew had gathered there to see what all the commotion was about. I couldn't bear to lift my eyes from the floor to look at them, to see the way they must have been looking at me. Jane Marie and Lance and Greg and Eddie and Katie.

I never saw any of them again.

PALM SPRINGS

"Danny, this is crazy."

I sat there, facing him, my eyes bleary from lack of sleep and too many hours spent staring at my computer screen. We were out by the pool. The sun was directly overhead, a white fluorescent ball. The reflections of palm trees wavered across the azure surface of the pool.

"Danny," Randall said, "there must be *millions* of people on the planet with similar birthmarks. And you don't even know for sure that your sister *had* a child."

"But it all makes sense finally." My head throbbed, and I massaged it with my fingers. A headache had blossomed behind my eyes a day ago and had yet to release its grip, no matter how much Motrin I swallowed. "Everything makes sense. My feelings for Kelly. Why I was so drawn to him. And why Becky disappeared. Finally I know the answer. Becky left home because she was pregnant."

Randall shook his head. "But how did she get to San Francisco? More importantly, why? Why would she go there if she had no connections there?"

"Why did I go to Los Angeles when I had no connections there?" I sat back in my chair, still rubbing my head. "Maybe Becky just wanted to get far away from the scene of all her problems—just as I would want to do a few years later. So she hopped on a bus and went to San Francisco and gave birth to her baby far away from any condemnation from my mother or the church."

"And then got addicted to drugs." Randall shook his head. "From what you've told me, that doesn't sound like your sister."

"Randall, nobody could have predicted that little Danny Fortunato of St. John's School would become a pothead at St. Francis Xavier or a coke fiend in West Hollywood."

"Still, I think the odds are so unlikely—"

"The dates match up exactly! If Becky left home when she found out she was pregnant, she would probably have been about a month or two along. So she would have given birth the following April or May." I leaned across the table to make my points, ticking them off on my fingers. "Kelly was born in April of that same year. He's Italian. His mother was from somewhere 'back East.' She wasn't married to Kelly's father. Her name was Ann—Becky's middle name. And, to cap it off, Kelly has a birthmark very much like the one both my sister and my mother had, and in exactly the same place." I glared at Randall. "*And* he has Chipper's eyes."

"I still think you're seeing what you want to see." He folded his arms across his chest. "The only way you could prove it is through a DNA test."

"I'm aware of that." I leaned back in my chair and looked across the deck. A hummingbird was flitting around the red bougainvillea that climbed over the fence. "And I can't go that route. Not yet. I can't let Kelly know what I think."

"Why not?"

I stood and watched the hummingbird, the way its tiny wings beat so fast. I'd read where a hummingbird beats its wings fifty times *a second*. That was *three thousand* times a minute. Once, a hummingbird had gotten into the house. Try as we might, neither Frank nor I could guide it out. The poor thing flew against windows and darted in and out of rooms for an entire day. Exhausted, it finally perched on our ceiling fan. It was the first time I'd ever seen a hummingbird sit still. I stared at its long, slender beak, at the frenetic wings that were finally stilled, folded back against its body just like those of any other bird. But a hummingbird is not like any other bird. I felt terribly sad seeing it sit there on the ceiling fan. It was almost as if a hummingbird at rest was not something we were meant to see. Finally, Frank managed to swing a paper bag and catch the tired little creature inside. Outside, in the garden, we released it—and I cheered as the hummingbird flew out of the bag, landed once on a rosebush, then buzzed off into the night.

I turned back to Randall. "I can't let Kelly know until I'm *sure*. It might only drive him away if he has an idea of what I'm thinking."

"Danny, why do you want this so much?"

"I just want the truth."

"I would think you'd recoil from the idea." Randall was studying me, his eyes narrowing. "Danny, you said you were in love with this boy—this boy who you now think might be your nephew."

"I know." I looked around for the hummingbird, but it was gone. "But it just feels *right* somehow. As if it explains everything. As if it explains . . ." My voice trailed off before I came back to finishing the thought. "As if it explains my entire life."

"You had *sex* with him," Randall said, dropping his voice to a whisper. "If what you believe is true, then aren't you a little freaked out?"

"No. Not at all."

He made a face. "Danny, surely if this *is* true, you wouldn't still want to be . . ."

"If this is true, then Kelly has a place in my life. We'll be connected forever."

Randall stared at me. "So *that's* why you want it to be true."

"Yes. Is that so wrong?"

He looked away.

"Is that so wrong?" I asked again, more urgently now.

"I don't know," Randall said impatiently, looking back at me. "I just think you can't go planning Kelly's place in your life, planning on being connected to him forever, while the man with whom you've spent the past twenty years of your life is still sleeping in the casita."

My headache pulsed against my eyes, and I sat down, pressing my thumbs to my temples. "I know," I said. "I know."

"Before you resolve anything with Kelly," Randall said, "you need to resolve what's going on with Frank."

I just rubbed my temples, not wanting to think.

The past couple of days had been lived entirely in my head. No doubt that was why it ached so much. I had plotted out, over and over again, every scenario that could possibly link Becky to Kelly. I'd written down everything I could remember, everything Detective Peter Guthrie had said about Becky's disappearance. All those trips with my mother to see the Rubberman and all those visits to New York's seedy underworld now seemed even more pathetic. Becky had never been there, had never known those people. She'd been three thousand miles away all that time, living in some flophouse in San Francisco, where she gave birth to Chipper's baby.

At my computer, I'd purchased access to various public records sites, scrolling through hundreds and hundreds of California vital records, looking for the name Rebecca Fortunato or Ann Fortunato. I knew it was highly unlikely that Becky would have used her real name, but I had to check to be sure. There was nothing. Next, I'd searched the Social Security Death Index. No one fit under that name. Of course, Becky had probably given up Fortunato as soon as she boarded the bus for the West Coast. So I'd looked for a Rebecca Paguni, reasoning she might have used Chipper's name, and then a Rebecca Cronin, thinking she might have used Mom's maiden name. I'd even checked under Horgan, Nana's maiden name. Nothing fit positively. But maybe my futile quest suggested something else. Maybe Becky was still alive.

The thought made the hair on my arms stand up. I'd long ago accepted the fact that my sister was dead. But maybe, in fact, she was still out there. And maybe I could reunite her with her son, and Kelly with his mother. Together, Kelly and I could uncover the secrets of our shared past, of the heritage that bound us. We'd petition the court for access to his birth records. We'd take a DNA test. We'd find the answers. Together.

But before all that, there was one test I could take myself. Before we could track down Kelly's mother, I planned to track down his father.

Online, I'd found an address for Chipper, under his real name, Charles. He was still living in East Hartford.

There was a phone number, too. But I wouldn't call him. He'd hang up the phone the moment he realized who was on the line. Or if he chose to listen to me for a moment, he'd never admit over the phone what I suspected.

That he'd made Becky pregnant, and then told her he wouldn't support her and her baby. *Their* baby. Maybe he really *had* felt like drowning her in the pond.

What else could I believe? Becky had been in love with Chipper. She wouldn't have left if he had promised to stand beside her. I suspected she'd gone to the pond that day to tell him the news. Probably soon after I'd left, she'd revealed to Chipper that she was carrying his child. No doubt he'd exploded, telling her it would ruin him, destroy his great dreams of being the senior-class football hero. For a couple of kids in Catholic high schools, the situation was untenable. They would've had to drop out of school and get married. Or—as Chipper had no doubt urged—Becky would need to slip away for an abortion. That way, no one would ever have to learn about their little mistake—a "mistake" I now knew as Kelly. But my sister, no doubt, had balked at the idea. She had been determined to have her baby. And so there had been no choice left but to say good-bye to all of us.

I used to think sometimes that I had ruined Chipper's life. But in fact, he had ruined Becky's by refusing to support her, and by extension, he'd ruined the lives of my parents and come damn close to ruining mine. Not to mention what he had done to the son he'd left adrift by his lack of responsibility.

And now here I was, positioned to take care of Chipper's son.

Randall and I were walking out to his car.

"Call me later if you need to talk," he said. "You need to really take the time to think all this through, Danny. You are too emotional right now to think clearly."

"I'm thinking more clearly than I have in twenty-five years," I told him.

Randall hugged me. "I love you, Danny. You're my oldest friend in the world."

I hugged him back.

"Please don't act rashly," he said. "And please talk to Frank."

After he was gone, I went back and sat by the pool. My laptop was in front of me on the table, and I heard the little click indicating a new e-mail. Confirmation of my travel itinerary. I sat back in my chair and sighed. I would need to tell Frank about my plans when he got home tonight. I'd need to open up a dialogue with him after a week of mostly silence. I didn't look forward to it. I imagined it would only lead to more hurt. But it had to be done.

He came home earlier than usual. He was carrying a bouquet of daisies, dyed green. He'd obviously decided on a thaw.

"You gave me a green daisy once," he said, handing me the flowers. "Thought I'd return the gesture."

"They're very pretty, Frank. Thank you."

He gave a small, awkward laugh. "The florist couldn't understand why I wanted them green. She said that St. Patrick's Day was months away."

"They're very pretty," I said again, cutting the stems and placing them, one at a time, in a vase filled with water.

"Danny, I'm sorry I pulled away," Frank said.

Hearing him apologize only made me feel guiltier. "Frank, it's okay. I'm the one who should apologize. I wish I hadn't chosen to express my feelings when I was drunk. The conversation might have gone very differently."

Frank was leaning against the counter, watching me arrange the flowers. His eyes looked old and tired. "Danny," he said, "I've missed you. Every morning and every night."

"I've missed you, too, Frank."

"Really?" He looked at me with genuine puzzlement. "Have you really?"

"Yes, of course."

Of course, I'd missed him. It was no fun sleeping alone. It was sad and lonely, especially after twenty years. The bed was cold, and the room disconcertingly silent without Frank's snoring to keep me awake. Of course, I missed him.

He took a long breath. "I need to know what you want to do, Danny."

"About what?"

"About us."

I closed my eyes. My headache still throbbed. "I don't know, Frank," I admitted.

"Do you want to be with him?" he asked. "With Kelly?"

I opened my eyes. I had no answer for that. Not now.

"Because if you do, I can't stand in your way. I'm fifty-five years old, almost fifty-six. Sure, I'm running these days. Jogging. I'm trying to get back in shape. But I'm not ever going to be able to turn back time to the kind of springtime beauty that Kelly possesses. In less than five years, I'll be sixty. And you'll still be a young forty-something, looking as good as you do, looking even younger than you are, able to attract beautiful young men, like Ollie or Kelly or anybody else." He paused. "I can't keep up with you, Danny. That's just a cold, hard fact."

"Frank," I said, but then I couldn't find the words to continue. I just sighed and sat down at the kitchen table. He joined me, taking a chair opposite.

"Danny," he told me, "I look back across our twenty years, and I cherish every moment. We've been through so much. So much happiness, so much heartache, but always together. From the days on Venice Beach, running with Pixie, to our walks in Griffith Park and our trips up the coast to Big Sur . . ." His voice trailed off. "I miss those days. I miss how athletic I was. I'm trying to get back some of that—"

"Frank, don't do it for me," I said. "If you want to jog, if you want to run—do it for yourself."

"I *want* to do it for you."

Our eyes met. His were bloodshot and moist. I felt that mine were hard and brittle. I tried to smile at him, but I was afraid I would cry. Maybe it would have been all right if I cried. But I didn't want to. I looked away.

"Danny, when we took our vows, I told you I would be there forever—"

I stood up abruptly. "I knew you'd bring up our vows. Frank! I'm not trying to back out on our vows! I'm just being honest with you about how I feel. I can't pretend that I don't have these feelings."

"Of course not, Danny. Of course, you can't pretend."

"And let's face it, Frank. When you took that vow, you did so knowing if things had been different, if you'd had your choice—"

Now Frank stood up as well. "Don't say it, Danny! I am so tired of you saying that!"

"Well, it's true."

"It is *not!*" His face was red. "Why have you always believed that my heart was elsewhere? Why have you never been able to believe that *you are worth loving?*"

"Frank, you don't need to justify your love to me." I took a moment to compose myself, then continued. "You have more than lived up to your end of our bargain. You were there for me when I was a scared young kid, making no money, struggling with my career. You paid my bills and gave me the confidence I needed to change careers. You have been my rock, Frank, and I will be eternally grateful to you for that." I took a deep breath. "Just don't feel you need to pretend that I was your first and only love, Frank. Because there's no cause for that. None at all."

He was quiet. I moved across the room, smelling the daisies he had given me.

"I'm going on a short trip," I said.

Frank looked at me strangely. "Where?"

"Home."

He seemed bewildered. "Home?"

"Connecticut."

"But your father isn't there anymore."

"No." I paused. "But someone else is."

I told him the story. The whole crazy story, a story that seemed even crazier as I relayed it to him. But that didn't make me doubt it. Frank listened calmly as I spoke, making no response, offering no reaction. Not a nod, not a question, not a single lift of his eyebrows.

"The only way I can know for sure," I finished, "is to confront Chipper."

Still, Frank said nothing. He just sat down at the table.

"I leave tomorrow," I told him. "I fly from here to Dallas, then Dallas to Hartford. I've rented a car."

"What if Chipper's not there?" Frank finally asked.

"Then I wait until he gets back."

"Danny, the odds are—"

"I know." I ran my hands through my hair. "Randall has already drilled into my head that the odds are stacked against me. That millions of people with unwed mothers from the East Coast might have birthmarks like crescent moons on their upper arms."

"But millions of people don't also have eyes like Chipper Paguni," Frank said.

I looked over at him. "That's right. They don't."

"At least, eyes like you *remember* Chipper Paguni's." He paused. "That was a long time ago, Danny."

"I'm aware of that."

Frank stood and walked into the living room. I watched him from the kitchen.

"And what if Chipper won't see you? What if you go all that way and he—"

"He *will* see me," I said, my voice set.

"Danny," Frank said, turning around to look at me. "You're aware of what's happened here, aren't you?"

"What?" I asked.

"You've become your mother."

I didn't have a response to that.

"All these years you've believed you failed her," Frank said. "Now you can finally make it up to her. You can pick up her quest where she left off. Maybe *she* could never find Becky, but *you* will." He smiled compassionately. "You know, I don't think you want Kelly as much for yourself as you want him for your mother. If you can turn him into Becky's son, then you can finally say to your mother, wherever she is, 'Look, Mom. I did what you asked. I found Becky! Now you can love me again!' "

I laughed. "You're an English professor, Frank. Not a psychologist."

"Danny, it's just plainly obvious."

"Okay, fine. You've made your point. You think I shouldn't go."

"Oh, no, not all. I think you *should* go. By all means. It's the only way for you to get any kind of resolution with this."

I sighed. "Thank you, Frank."

I came into the living room and sat down on the couch.

"Danny," Frank said, looking down at me kindly. "I've never been good at telling you how much I love you. I suppose that's been my fault. I'm just not all that good at showing how I feel."

"You show it fine, Frank."

He sat down beside me. "I need to say this. I need you to hear it."

I looked at him.

"At night," he said, "when you crawl in next to me in bed, I feel as if my whole world is complete. As if there's no need ever to get up again. I have felt that way for twenty years, and I feel that way just as strongly now."

I looked over at him. "Frank . . ."

"You were *never* second to me, Danny. How could you believe that for so long? What can I do to prove to you that you're wrong to think that way?"

"Frank, there's no need . . ."

"Yes, there *is* a need, Danny!" His face was red again, as if he'd just come in from running. "You have *always* been first in my heart! Always! Since that day I picked you up on Mulholland Drive and you broke down in tears in my car. I fell in love with you in that moment, and for every day since, every *hour,* it's always been you, Danny, always *you!*"

I looked at him. I couldn't respond. Couldn't even think.

He gently pulled me into his embrace. "Always you, baby," he said in my ear. "Always you."

The words seemed wrong to me. Unreal. To absorb them, to believe them, was impossible, foolish to attempt. I hadn't gotten through my life believing words such as those. I'd survived by letting words like that bounce off me, ricochet away, never breaking the skin. I'd survived by being too smart to fall for them. I knew Frank didn't love me first. How was such a thing possible? No one had ever loved me first.

Still, I let him take me to bed and undress me and kiss me and hold me close, my head on his warm, furry chest, listening to his heart beating all night long.

WEST HOLLYWOOD

We sat holding hands as we waited for the results. Opposite us, a young, straight Latino couple sat stiff-backed in their chairs, watching us. We didn't care what they thought. Frank and I just sat there, with our eyes looking straight ahead. We didn't speak; we didn't read a magazine. We just sat there, holding hands.

Finally, a nurse approached us and told us we should follow her.

"I'm terrified," I said in a little voice as we stood.

"It'll be all right, baby," Frank whispered, his lips on my ear.

Two weeks ago, Randall had tested HIV-positive. Suddenly we knew dozens of people whose test results had been the same. Three guys in our neighborhood were sick. I'd seen the sarcomas on their necks and arms. Edgar, my old boss, had died of AIDS. I'd seen him a few weeks before he died, a skeleton walking on the street, all the bones in his face visible. Once I had kissed that man, even had sex with him. And now he was dead.

"I'm terrified," I said again as the nurse closed the door on us in the small inner office. The room was entirely white, from walls to curtains to plastic chairs to the crinkly paper that covered the examining table. Frank and I gripped each other's hands even tighter, still not saying a word to each other.

I thought about Randall. I prayed that he wouldn't get sick. I couldn't imagine my handsome young friend with sunken cheeks and protruding teeth. He'd started immediately on some antiviral drugs, none of which had proven all that effective in other people. I'd seen people with AIDS around town, their beepers going off in the middle of movies. I'd seen them at sidewalk cafés, swallowing their pills. I'd seen them crossing La Cienega at Santa Monica, looking like the cast of *Night of the Living Dead.* Was that going to be our future, too? Taking those horrible pills every day, pills that made you sick, that gave you diarrhea, that caused your body to waste away? I didn't understand the good of them if, even after all that, they didn't stop you from dying.

But why should any of it surprise me? Didn't it all make sense in a terrible kind of way? Did I really think I could get away, that hopping on a Peter Pan bus would really save my life?

It was worse for Frank. Frank was a teacher. We'd heard the stories from all over the country of teachers with AIDS being fired. I was just an actor, after all. Sure, it would be an issue if I had to kiss someone in a scene: people were still clucking over the way Rock Hudson had kissed Linda Evans on *Dynasty.* I'd have to deal with such talk, of course, and I'd probably lose out on some roles. But still, it was worse for Frank. Much worse. He'd dedicated years of his life to studying to be a teacher. I squeezed his hand, and he squeezed mine back.

If the results were positive, I wondered if I'd tell my parents. Frank's parents were dead, so it wasn't an issue, but mine were still out there in the world, at least as far as I knew. I hadn't been in touch with them now for a few years. I imagined picking up the phone and telling them that I had AIDS, and Mom breaking down in tears and saying, "Oh, my little Danny" and rushing out here to take care of me. But then I laughed to myself. In what universe might that happen? No, I didn't think I'd tell my parents. Mom would just see it as confirmation of her frequently expressed belief that I'd chosen a sick, degrading, and sinful lifestyle. No. I wouldn't give her that satisfaction.

Of course, a positive result was far more likely for me than it was for Frank. I'd been the hooker, after all. I'd been the one to take it up the ass from strangers and allow them to shoot jizz into my colon for a hundred bucks a pop. I wasn't proud of it, but there it was. Still, Frank was older than I was, he'd been having sex for a lot longer, and he'd had sex with a lot more people than I. Probably, I figured, we were both positive. Everybody we knew was. Why should we be any different?

"Danny," Frank said finally, breaking the silence in that little white room. "You know it's going to be all right, one way or other, don't you?"

"No," I admitted. "I don't know that."

"It will be. Trust me." His bright eyes found mine. "Do you trust me, Danny?"

I smiled. "More than anybody ever."

Frank's green eyes smiled back at me. He was so beautiful. Even after two years, he was still the most beautiful man I'd ever seen. On his strong shoulders, Frank seemed able to carry the world, and that included me. His eyes were so alive, so bright, so filled with a sense of what was right and what was possible. As I sat there, looking at him, I thought that I'd never really known what beauty was until I met Frank. All those men in my scrapbook, with their pretty eyes and pearly white teeth, were nothing compared to Frank. With my free hand, I reached over and touched his cheek and his strong jaw. There was no man in the world more beautiful than Frank Wilson.

"If we're positive," he was telling me, "we'll find the meds that work. There are new ones, much more effective ones, on the horizon. And there are alternative treatments, too. We'll find the ones that work best for us."

"But what if only one of us is positive?" I asked.

"Then we'll deal with that, too. Together."

Suddenly the terror rose up in my throat like bile. "Will you stay with me, Frank?" I blurted out. "Will you?"

I knew that hadn't been part of the bargain. But I needed to know.

"Of course, I will, Danny," Frank said, without missing a beat. "Of course, I will stay with you."

I didn't believe him, but the words were good to hear nonetheless.

But then he asked softly, "Will you stay with *me*?"

"Of course," I echoed. "Of course."

The door opened, and the doctor came in. He was a young man, quite handsome, with dark hair and blue eyes. He nodded and sat down opposite us in a white plastic chair. He opened the file he held in his hands.

"Okay, Frank," he said, scanning the results inside. "Your test came back negative."

"Oh," I heard Frank say, more a shudder of relief passing through his chest and out of his mouth than any authentic word. I grabbed his hand as tightly as I could.

"And you, Danny," the doctor said, his eyes moving down the page, "your test came back—"

There was a moment's pause. I teetered at the edge of a cliff.

"—negative as well."

"Oh, God!" I started to cry. "Are you sure it's not a mistake?"

"It's not a mistake, Danny," the doctor said, smiling. "You don't have HIV. Neither of you do."

I broke hands with Frank to make the sign of the cross. I hadn't made that gesture in years. It was something left over from my mother, perhaps the only thing I still had of hers.

"Now continue practicing safe sex," the doctor said, standing. "I don't want to see these results change."

We smiled at him, still seated, as he left the room.

"I don't believe it," I said to Frank. "Just like that. Our worries are gone."

He was beaming. "Believe it, baby."

"I was so *certain* I was going to be positive," I said, as much to myself as to him. "After all the things I did. I was so certain."

Frank stroked my hair. "We're incredibly lucky, baby."

"It's just so odd," I said. "It felt as if testing positive would make sense. That *of course*, I'd die young, probably in a couple of years. I was certain that was the way my life would go, and it wouldn't have surprised me in the least."

"No, baby," Frank said, still stroking my hair. "That's *not* the way it will go."

"So odd . . ."

Frank leaned forward to rest his forehead against mine. "We're going to have long lives, baby. We are going to last and last and last. We are going to grow *old*."

"How wonderful," I whispered, scarcely able to believe it still.

Our eyes locked as our noses rubbed together. My mother used to get up close to Becky and me like this. She'd call it "seeing the owl." I smiled at Frank.

"That doctor just gave us a blank check, baby," he told me. "The road is stretching out in front of us. We can take it anywhere."

"But why were our tests negative when Randall's was positive? Why are we so lucky when so many others aren't?"

"That I don't know, Danny."

The door opened again, and the nurse reappeared, seeming surprised to find us still inside. "Oh, I'm sorry," she said.

"It's okay," Frank told her. "We were just leaving."

We stood and made room for the next people to sit in these chairs, whose news might not be nearly as good as ours. But for us, the joy was unbound. Taking each other's hand again, we headed out into the rest of our lives.

EAST HARTFORD

The principal of St. Francis Xavier High School was a small, elfish, red-faced Irishman named Brother Doyle, whom I had never liked, and who, I was sure, had never liked me, either. Certainly he didn't like me that day in his office, his red hands folded on his highly polished desk, Mom, Dad, and I seated in straight-back chairs in front of him. Above his head was the motto of the school—BE A MAN—something I appeared to have failed miserably at, and above that hung an enormous crucifix, with a near-naked Jesus writhing in the throes of his last human agonies. At that moment, I could definitely relate.

"But it is the other matter that is even more distressing than the marijuana," Brother Doyle was saying.

Neither he nor Mom nor Dad would look at me.

Brother Doyle continued. "Troy Kitchens has admitted to us in rather graphic detail the sins he and Danny committed on a weekly basis for much of the last two years."

Mom made the sign of the cross.

"Of course," said Brother Doyle, "we have compassion for these two boys, both of whom have suffered terrible family tragedies, losing beloved family members—"

"We haven't lost Becky," Mom interrupted. "We're going to find her."

"Of course." Brother Doyle cleared his throat. "But still the

trauma of her disappearance has clearly pushed Danny into perverse behaviors."

I saw Dad rub his forehead.

"I am certain that the use of that drug caused it," Mom said,
leaning forward, her big, manly hands opening and closing into
fists. "And I believe that Chipper Paguni is the real criminal here,
for he introduced my daughter to that drug as well. I believe he
started Danny on it, and his mind was corrupted from there."

"Well," said Brother Doyle, "it's clear that Chipper partook of
the drug with Danny, but Troy has admitted it was he who introduced your son to the drug."

His eyes flickered briefly over to me but then looked away.

I had fallen into silence. While Troy seemed happy to sing, to
spill his guts, I said nothing. No longer did I try to deny it, to bluff
my way out of it, as I had in the men's room the day before. But
neither did I confirm anything, either. As Brother Doyle read the
charges against me, I sat expressionless, immobile. When he
asked me if I had anything to say, I simply shook my head. Mom
and Dad had so far said nothing to me. There had been no angry
words, no confrontations. Only silence.

"All I know is," Mom said, "Chipper Paguni has been an evil influence on my children. I expect any punishment he faces will be
as severe as Danny's."

Brother Doyle nodded. "Of course, Mrs. Fortunato. But remember that Chipper was not involved in the perversities. . . ."

"He has *plenty* of perversities!" Mom retorted. "He knows more
about my daughter's disappearance than he has ever admitted!"

"Be that as it may, Mrs. Fortunato, that is not the matter at
hand here."

"He shouldn't be allowed to graduate," Mom said. "Are you
going to let him graduate?"

Brother Doyle sighed. "We haven't yet decided the course we
will take with Chipper. But we do know that we cannot allow
Danny or Troy to continue at St. Francis Xavier."

Mom cocked her head. "Are you saying . . . that you're expelling Danny but possibly not Chipper?"

"Mrs. Fortunato, we do not tolerate such perverted behavior in
our school."

"Danny's not going to do it again!" she shouted. "I'll see to that!"

"I'm sorry, Mrs. Fortunato. We have essentially been giving Danny a free ride here. We haven't asked you to repay the tuition you've missed." He gave her a sanctimonious smile. "And *this* is how we are thanked."

"So you're kicking my son out?" Mom asked. "Just like that?"

Brother Doyle sighed. "I'm afraid we can see no other way."

Finally, there was life from Dad's chair. He stood up abruptly. "And you call yourself a Christian," Dad said thickly, striding out of the office.

Mom paid him no heed. "Brother," she said sternly, "I do not want my son educated in a public school. If he has these perverse tendencies, only a good Catholic education can wipe his mind clean."

I closed my eyes. The room was starting to spin.

"I'm sorry, Mrs. Fortunato, our decision is final."

She was outraged. "Is Troy Kitchens being expelled as well?"

"We haven't decided about Troy yet."

My eyes opened to see Mom suddenly leap from her chair and press her hands down on Brother Doyle's desk, her nose only inches from his. "So only Danny! You're only expelling Danny!"

"Danny is the only one we've been subsidizing," Brother Doyle spit back.

"And the Kitchens money probably comes in real handy now that you're building a new gymnasium, doesn't it?"

"Mrs. Fortunato, I will pray for you and Danny and your family. That is all I can offer you at this time."

"You can go to hell," Mom said, turning on her heel and storming out of the room.

That left me sitting alone in front of Brother Doyle. I looked at him.

I smiled.

"You may go, Danny," he said uncomfortably.

I laughed. "Oh, I'm going," I assured him, my first words all day.

Outside in the corridor, Mom and Dad were nowhere to be found. Maybe they'd left me behind. Maybe I was on my own now. But when I headed out into the parking lot, I saw them waiting for me in the car. I trudged over and slipped into the backseat. Not a word was spoken all the way back to our apartment.

But once inside, the volcano of Mom's emotions erupted. For two hours, she railed at me. I was sick, she said. I was depraved. I had done all this to hurt her. I was selfish. I had caused her so much shame and anguish that she feared she'd lose the energy to look for Becky. I was, she said, the ruin of everything.

Throughout it all, I remained silent. I sat on the couch, with my hands in my lap, my eyes on the floor. Dad poured himself a drink and paced from room to room. Mom's shrill voice filled up that tiny apartment. I was certain the people next to us and above us must have heard her every word.

"It is a filthy thing!" she cried. "No son of mine will be a homosexual!"

I closed my eyes.

"I've lost two children now! I've lost both my babies!"

I heard the front door slam. Dad had gone out. He couldn't take any more. I doubted we'd see him for a couple of days.

Mom stopped ranting after Dad left. She down at the kitchen table. A thousand things seemed to be going through her mind. Her silence disturbed me far more than her rants.

At that moment, the doorbell rang. With tremendous effort Mom stood to open the door.

It was Detective Peter Guthrie. He had come, he said, because he had information.

"Come in, come in!" Mom said, suddenly animated again, ushering him inside, fluttering around him like a giant moth. He sat at the kitchen table and looked grim.

"The man you call Bruno," he told her, "has been arrested on a narcotics charge. I suspect he will go to jail for a long time."

"Then he can tell us where Becky is!"

"Mrs. Fortunato," the detective said, his thin, reedy face expressing annoyance. They'd clearly had this conversation many times.

It occurred to me sitting there that I had never witnessed any real discussion between Mom and Guthrie before. She had usually spoken to him on the phone. But now, from across the room, I listened closely.

"There has never been any evidence that Becky was with Bruno or any other biker," Guthrie said. "I have followed up this lead of yours only because you have insisted, and that is why I am here today." He paused for emphasis. "Bruno knows nothing about your daughter. He says he has no idea who she is or where she is. He admits he called you, because he learned you were following him. He thought you were a private detective and you were onto his drug ring."

"He's lying!"

Guthrie shook his head. "Even when offered a possible reduction of the charges against him, he could offer us no information." The detective looked at Mom with stern eyes. "Mrs. Fortunato, your daughter was *never* with Bruno. Those bikers were bilking you for cash. That's all."

"I won't believe it!" Mom shouted. "Warren is my friend! There have been too many sightings of her for it all to be a lie. Too many bikers have seen Becky!"

"Mrs. Fortunato." Detective Guthrie stood. "It is time that you faced facts. Your daughter left home because she was unhappy."

"She was not! My daughter was very happy! We were very close!"

"Not according to her friends. You know that I interviewed all of them immediately after Becky's disappearance. I spoke with Karen Mulgrew. I spoke with Pam Antolini. I spoke with Carol Fleisher. I spoke with dozens of girls. They all told me of the arguments the two of you had been having. They all told me that Becky felt you were pressuring her about her relationship with her boyfriend."

I had never known this. I had had little contact with Becky's friends. They were all over at St. Clare's, and all were older than I was. Becky's life and my life had become so separate. I knew that she and Mom had been arguing a lot, but I'd been unaware that her unhappiness had grown so great that she'd told all her friends.

"If Becky was unhappy," Mom was saying, "it was because of him, because of that Chipper Paguni, not me!"

"Whatever the reason," Guthrie replied, standing from his chair, "she was unhappy at home. I believe you need to face the fact that Becky *ran away*, Mrs. Fortunato. The evidence is there. Her missing clothes. The money that was taken from your cookie jar."

My eyes widened. More information that I hadn't known. Missing clothes. Money from the cookie jar. Mom had never spoken of such things in front of me.

"Becky wasn't kidnapped, Mrs. Fortunato," Detective Guthrie said, trying to sound kind, but years of frustration seeped through in his voice. "Certainly not by bikers."

Mom's lips had gone white with rage. "So you will continue overlooking leads, then! You will force me to continue searching on my own!"

Guthrie sighed, his hand on the door to leave. "We will investigate every viable lead, Mrs. Fortunato. Trust me, I would like to find Becky very much. It's just that I still believe she will come home on her own eventually."

"Get out," Mom said contemptuously.

Guthrie said good-bye and left.

Mom picked up a plate from the table and tossed it against the wall. Miraculously, it didn't break. It just bounced like a Frisbee and landed on the couch, beside me. I jumped, but only a little.

I looked over at my mother. "You never told me about any of that," I said, my words hard and accusatory.

"Listen to me, Danny," Mom said. "Your sister wasn't unhappy. Your sister was a good girl!"

I stood now, taking a couple of steps toward her. I even managed a small laugh. "She took *clothes* with her? And *money*?"

"Becky did *not* run away!"

"Why are you so sure?"

Mom's eyes were wild. She rushed at me, as if she might try to tackle me. I tensed. Let her try. She stopped immediately in front of me, her finger wagging in my face. I did not back away.

"You listen to me, Danny! Your sister was a good girl! She wouldn't leave me! She and I had so many plans!"

Mom's face was pitiful. I stared at her.

"Ever since Becky was born, I knew what a bright future awaited her." The tears sprang into Mom's eyes. "She was such a good baby. She never cried. I held her in my arms. I changed her little diapers. I put her in for her naps. I held her, my baby, in my arms. . . ." Her voice broke.

I was melting, despite myself.

"It's not natural!" Mom cried. "It's not natural for her to be gone! Parents aren't supposed to lose children! I watched over both of you, wanting to keep both of you safe. I failed you! I failed both you and Becky."

The tears began flowing from her eyes. "I'm sorry, Danny. I stopped looking out for you the way I should have, and that's why you did what you did. When a mother fails, this is what happens. It's my fault."

I stood there, not wanting to feel anything. But I was.

"I remember when Becky went off to kindergarten," Mom was saying. "She was so pretty and smart and talented. All the nuns said so. And she was going to go to Salve Regina College and major in art. She was going to marry a wonderful boy, a boy as smart and talented as she was, and I was going to give her a big wedding, the kind of wedding I never got, and she'd wear a beautiful gown, and I'd watch her walk down the aisle and listen to everyone say how beautiful she was." Mom's eyes were imploring me to understand. "That's what a mother dreams about for her daughter. Don't you see? That's what a mother dreams about!" She burst into tears.

"Mom," I said, my hand reaching out to her.

But she willed away her tears, seemed to suction them right back up into her eyes. Drawing herself tall, she ignored my outstretched hand. "It's not *right*," she said angrily. "This isn't how it was supposed to be. All along, I've thought, she can *still* come back! We can still go on, still follow through with our plans. But every day that she's gone, it becomes harder. Don't you see? It gets harder the longer she's gone."

Her voice hiccupped with emotion, and I wanted so much to hold her, to comfort her. But she remained tight, coiled into herself.

"If Becky had been gone only a few months," she said, "she might have still come back, and we could still have picked up where we left off. Every day I'd think, 'If she comes back today, we can still make it all happen.' But now it's been two years! If she doesn't come home soon, it might be too late. Time is running out! How can you pick up after two years?"

Her eyes remained fastened to mine.

"So many dreams. So many dreams for Becky—and for you, Danny! A mother has *plans* for her children. She expects to see them through the rituals. School and graduation and weddings and babies. It's not right when that doesn't happen! It's not natural! A mother has such dreams!"

"I know," I said.

"I expected that you would get married someday, too. Don't you understand what I'm grieving, Danny? You were supposed to be my fine, upstanding son, a son who would make me proud. But now everything, everything I dreamed about . . ." She began to cry again, turning her face away from me.

"Mom, you can't control everything. You can't always make it be just what you want it to be. I'm not a kid anymore that you can protect from the poison ivy, or make drink extra glasses of milk to make sure everything turns out fine. Life is more complicated than that."

She looked at me with eyes like a little girl's. It was as if all this was my responsibility to explain to her.

"I'm a simple woman, Danny," she said, brushing aside any attempt to understand. "Brought up to believe that if you play by the rules, go to church, teach your children right from wrong, that you'll be rewarded, that it will all work out. Maybe it's all a crock. But I can't be any other way. I can't change, Danny, and I'm sorry for that."

"Mom," I said, my own tears falling. "We can still find a way. . . ."

"You're right about that, Danny," she said. "You'll be sixteen in a few months, and you'll get your driver's license. You can make it all up to me!"

I took a breath.

"You can take me where I need to go." Her face was no more than a couple inches away from mine. It was almost like the game she used to play with us, when she'd tell us to "see the owl."

"Yes, indeed!" Mom was saying. "We can continue to look for

Becky, you and I. You can make it all up to me, Danny! All of it! I'll forgive everything if you help me find Becky!"

I sat back down on the couch, my emotions shutting down, hardening once more.

"We still have time," Mom was muttering, more to herself than to me. "We can still find her. We can still get back to the way things were. All of us. We can all go back and do it right. We can still make our dreams come true."

I said nothing.

And through my silence, I entered into a pact with her. A pact I knew I was not yet strong enough to break. But I would be, one day.

That night, in my bed, I thought about Chipper, about the look in his eyes when he found Troy and me. I tried to remember how I'd felt about him just twenty-four hours earlier, but I couldn't. I had loved him, I knew that much, but I could no longer recall how it had felt to love him. Part of me wanted finally to reveal that I'd seen Chipper with Becky on the day she disappeared. But even that felt pointless. I simply didn't care anymore. All I cared about was the little boy, the little son, I'd someday have. Joey, I would name him. And I would love and protect Joey with all my heart for as long as I lived.

EAST HARTFORD

Twenty-Five Years Later

Could it have been that my memory was wrong? That this wasn't the block where I had lived for the first fifteen years of my life? But, of course, it was. That was Flo Armstrong's house down the hill to my left. And across the street was the house that had been Chipper's. Even though the place had been extensively remodeled, I recognized it. For fifteen years, I'd looked out my bedroom window at that house.

But where, then, was my own?

I stood on a vast empty lot. A half acre of grass, covered with yellow leaves blown from the trees next door. Out behind me there should have been a cornfield, but instead, there was a new subdivision of houses.

"Hello," came a voice.

I turned. A young woman stood on the sidewalk out front, dressed in a green plaid pantsuit. She waved.

"Are you interested in the property?" she asked.

"I . . . I used to live here."

She approached me. "I'm Kathy Singer." She handed me a card. "Century 21 Real Estate. The lot is for sale, if you're interested."

"I used to live here," I said again.

She flashed me a wide, insincere smile. "Really? When was that?"

My eyes were still flickering around the yard. "Another lifetime."

I'm not sure what had brought me here. This hadn't been part of the plan. But as the plane had circled over Bradley Airport and I'd looked down on the long blue snake of the Connecticut River and the rolling yellow hills of the surrounding countryside, I'd known I'd had to come. After checking in at my hotel, I'd driven around the town. So many new buildings, so much steel where there used to be green. I'd driven here to my old neighborhood without even thinking about it, almost as if from habit.

I looked at the woman in front of me. "What happened to the house?"

She smiled sympathetically, more sincere this time. "Oh, it burned down about six years ago. The property was in escrow for a while, with the various heirs of Mrs. Hernandez trying to decide what to do with it."

Hernandez. I tried to remember if that was the name of the family who had bought the house from us. I didn't think so.

"How did it burn down?"

"It was an old house. Bad electrical wiring. It hadn't been updated in over thirty years." She sighed. "Fortunately, no one was living there at the time. Mrs. Hernandez was in a convalescent home. But she'd left many appliances plugged in." The real estate agent made a face, lifting perfectly shaped brows over her pale blue eyes. "Let that be a lesson. Always unplug major appliances when you're not using them."

I glanced around the yard. "But what happened to all the trees? We had lots of trees here. There were maples and a big oak and at least two elms. . . ." My voice caught in my throat. "My sister and I built a fort in a tree that used to stand over there." My eyes scanned the grass. There wasn't even a stump.

"Well," said the realtor, "at first the Hernandez family was going to rebuild. So everything was razed. The house was going to be magnificent, much larger than the old one. But then the city wouldn't approve the plans, so everything was off, and they decided to sell."

"The house burned down . . . ," I said, almost in awe.

"I'm sorry," the woman said, and although she probably meant it, I had the distinct sense that she was done with me, that she thought it was time for me to leave, that, no matter my history with the place, I was still trespassing.

But I wasn't ready to leave. "I slept right *here,*" I told her, moving a few feet to my left. "Right here was my room."

She just continued smiling.

"My sister used to paint that house up there, on the hill. You see? She'd stand right over there at her easel, and she'd paint those houses up on the hill."

Kathy Singer extended her hand. "Well, you have my card. Perhaps you'd like to own the old family homestead again."

I shook her hand. "Oh, no. I'd never want to own this again."

She gave me one last small smile and headed back to her car.

After she was gone, I walked around the property some more. Down the hill, little children jumped in piles of leaves in Flo Armstrong's backyard. Except it wasn't Flo's backyard anymore. I was sure Flo was dead, like nearly everyone else from here. The smell of autumn was in the air: apples and burning leaves, a smell I'd forgotten, having lived so long among the sagebrush and date palms of California. Walking across the grass, I breathed in the crisp air, stumbling upon a concrete slab. A relic from the foundation of our house.

I headed back to my rental car. I supposed it was only right that the house should be gone. All that was left of that time were fragments as fleeting and as fragile as the yellow leaves tumbling across the lawn. I started the ignition, trying to feel something. But there was nothing. Just a powerful, overarching self-awareness, which I didn't like. Not at all.

I looked at the address on the printout in my folder. The street I was looking for hadn't existed when I'd lived here as a kid. MapQuest placed it smack in the middle of what I remembered as a tobacco field, where Dad's father had worked when he first came over from Italy. I think Nana had worked there, too, not in the field, but in the office. I think that was where she met her future husband, my grandfather. So I was heading to a place that if not for what it once was, I would never have been.

The field had been subdivided into quarter-acre lots, each with well-manicured lawns and carefully tended trees. The houses were all of the same design, either colonials with one-car garages or ranches with no garage at all. It wasn't an upscale neighborhood, but neither was it working class; the cars in the driveways were Toyotas and Hondas and the occasional VW Bug. Leaves had been raked into careful piles along the street, awaiting pickup by the city. The bare trees looked no more than five or six years old. All of the streets were named after flowers: Poinsettia Place, Azalea Avenue, Rose of Sharon Road. I was looking for 64 Carnation Court.

It turned out to be a colonial, with a redbrick front facade and cranberry-colored aluminum siding. A motorcycle rested on its kickstand in the driveway, a fact I found vaguely ironic. Inside the open garage, I spied a green SUV of some kind. On the lawn, an overturned tricycle rested among the blades of grass. At the start of the walkway, one of those little ceramic men holding a lantern waited to greet visitors. On the metal mailbox near the street, elaborate calligraphy spelled out the name Paguni.

According to the online records, Chipper worked for a contracting company, building shopping malls and office complexes. Maybe he'd even helped build the housing development he now lived in. I remembered hearing that, after high school, he had gone on to Central Connecticut State College, though whether he'd graduated I was never sure. After the incident in the men's room, I had no further contact with Chipper. Mom was always pissed that the brothers had consented to give Chipper his diploma. She didn't consider the fact that he was barred from graduating with his class as sufficient punishment, even though I knew that, for Chipper, it must have been one final humiliation heaped on a year filled with so many of them. I doubted if Chipper ever fully recovered from it all. Oh, from the looks of it, he had found a decent job and a decent house; he had a wife and a family, too, and even a motorcycle, which he probably drove on weekends very fast, breaking the speed limit, up Interstate 91 or east on I-84, the wind in his face. But I doubted he ever really got over what had happened.

I pulled up in front of the house and parked the car. I contemplated whether I should just go up and ring the doorbell. I supposed I could take out my cell phone and call him, and explain that I'd come all this way to see him, and ask him to please come out and speak to me for ten minutes. But I didn't want to ask Chipper to do me any favors. I just wanted to see him, ask him what I'd come for, and then leave.

A woman, dark and plump and about my age, eventually came out of the door and, never glancing my way, walked around the front of the house and entered the garage. In a few moments, the green SUV was backing down the driveway. I wondered why she hadn't entered the garage from inside the house. In my mind's eye, I saw construction in the family room, barring the way to the garage. Chipper was putting down a new floor or paneling the walls. He might even be building an addition onto the back.

I waited a few more moments. It was a Saturday. Clearly, there were children in the house; the tricycle told me that, and occasionally, I could hear hoots and laughter from upstairs. It was a warm day; the windows were open. How many children did Chipper have? Besides Kelly, that was.

I was just about to get out of the car and walk up to the door, scolding myself for behaving like a stalker, when Chipper sauntered out through the garage, wearing faded jeans and a gray hoodie sweatshirt. He bent down to inspect a tire on the motorcycle. I quickly got out of my car.

"That your bike?" I asked.

He stood up, looking my way. The late afternoon sun must have obscured my face, or perhaps he just didn't recognize me, because he replied cheerfully, "Sure is."

I walked toward him. "How are you, Chipper?"

"Chipper?" He laughed. I remembered that laugh. It was the same laugh I'd heard so many nights, when we'd sit in his room, our feet touching, my heart racing. "Nobody's called me Chipper in years," he said. "Who are—"

Then either the light shifted or my face registered for him. He fell silent.

"I just need to ask you one thing, Chipper," I said calmly. "Then I'll be off."

He stared at me. I could see him clearly now. He had gotten

heavy—not fat, but big around the waist, with a belly and a wide, flat butt. His hair was still thick and dark, and it looked as if he had never changed his hairstyle. It was still parted on the side, with bangs feathered back. Not so different from the hair of those pretty boys I'd pasted in my scrapbook, none of whom could match, in my teenage opinion, Chipper Paguni.

"What do you want?" Chipper stood in his driveway, his back suddenly stiff, his feet planted firmly apart on the pavement. It looked as if he was protecting his house, his entire life, from me.

I kept my voice level. "Just the answer to one question. When Becky disappeared, is it possible that she may have been pregnant?"

He didn't reply.

"Might that be why she ran away?" I asked.

"Listen." He was angry. "All that was a long time ago. I told the police and your mother everything that I knew."

"I'm not accusing you of anything, Chipper. I just want to know if it was possible Becky was pregnant."

He made a face. "I don't have to talk to you."

"No, you don't, but I think you should. You owe it to me, Chipper."

"Daddy!" a little girl's voice called from the front door. "Are you making us SpaghettiOs?"

I couldn't see her face. It was getting too dark. But I could see her pudgy little hand on the door handle.

"No, Jamie Lynn," Chipper called over to her. "Mommy will be back in a little while. She'll make supper."

I heard the front door click shut.

Chipper took a step closer to me. I saw his eyes, those black holes that seemed to bore deep down into his brain. "How dare you come here," he seethed in a whisper, "and say I owe you *anything* after what happened?"

"Well, what *did* exactly happen, Chipper? Isn't it just possible that my sister came to you the day she disappeared and told you that she was pregnant?"

"No," he said. "I didn't see her on the day she disappeared."

"Yes, you did." My voice was calm. "Because I saw the two of you at the pond that day. I never told anyone what I saw, because I didn't want you to be accused of anything. But maybe I *should* have told. Maybe I should have told what I had seen."

"You don't know what you're talking about."

"Tell me the truth, Chipper!" I was aware that I had raised my voice. In that quiet little subdivision, voices floated quickly over the manicured lawns. "I saw you and Becky that day at the pond!"

"Okay! So what! We had a swim, and that was it!"

"No, it wasn't. I'll tell you what I think happened. I think Becky took off because she was pregnant and you wouldn't support her. You were a big football star. Or you *wanted* to be, anyway. It would have ruined all your big dreams if it came out that you'd made your girlfriend pregnant. Isn't that right, Chipper?"

"No!" His black eyes blazed. "That's not what happened! I don't know where Becky went! I don't know what happened to her! Why won't you fucking believe me?"

"Daddy!" The little girl was at the front door again. "We want our SpaghettiOs now!"

"Just a *minute,* Jamie Lynn!"

"Just tell me, Chipper. Is it possible that Becky was pregnant that day?"

"I don't know if she was!"

I narrowed my eyes at him, angry that I wasn't getting the confession I'd expected. "She didn't come to you that day at the pond and tell you she was pregnant?"

"No! She did not!"

"But is it possible? *Might* she have been pregnant, and by you?"

Chipper moved in very close to me. Once, such close proximity would have thrilled me. But Chipper was no longer the young football player, with the strong, taut muscles. Instead, he was overweight and had bad breath. Beer and Doritos. "Look," he said forcefully. "I have a family. I have *three daughters* inside that house."

"All right." My voice was barely a whisper. "Just tell me if it's possible that Becky may have been pregnant, by *you,* on the day she disappeared. Tell me if that's possible, and then I'll go away."

He hesitated just a moment. "Yes," he admitted. "It's possible."

"Daddy!"

Chipper looked at me. Our eyes held for several seconds.

"Thank you," I said quietly.

He hurried inside the house. I got in my car and drove away.

My brain was shutting down. I couldn't think clearly. I wasn't sure what it meant. But I'd done what I'd come here to do.

I headed out of the subdivision and drove back through the old part of town. I passed the church in which I'd been baptized, where Mom had spent so much time praying for Becky's safe return. I turned into the cemetery.

I knew where the grave was located, because I'd been there many times when I was a boy. On every Memorial Day before I turned fourteen, Dad would bring Nana, Becky, and me there, and we'd lay flowers on my grandfather's grave. Grandpa was buried at the back of the cemetery, where the water table was high, and marble headstones routinely toppled over onto the grass. Many times I had struggled to help Dad right Grandpa's stone. I wondered if by now it would be permanently embedded facedown into the ground.

It was not. New concrete had been laid around the stone to secure its foundation. I wondered when that had been done. Probably when Nana had died and been buried next to her husband. I got out of the car and walked across the grass to the stone. Nana's name was etched into the marble, right below Grandpa's and right above Aunt Patsy's. ADELE HORGAN FORTUNATO. Dead these past twenty-one years. She had passed away just months after I'd left home.

But it was the stone beside Nana's, a flat marble slab nearly covered by long grass, that I had really come to see. I bent down to read the name closely. MARGARET CRONIN FORTUNATO. A woman better known to the world as Peggy, lionized by the local media as Becky Fortunato's indefatigable mother.

She was my mother, too.

Was she looking down at me now? That's what the nuns at St. John's used to teach, that the dead looked down from heaven upon the living. I wasn't sure what I believed anymore. So little of my Catholic school education had stayed with me, except for sentence construction. Still, enough of the catechism had lingered that I had come here to the cemetery, wondering if I might feel some kind of connection, if I might sense my mother's presence at her grave.

I did not. The air was still. A couple of birds called from the trees. The sun was low in the sky, and the shadows of the grave-stones were long against the grass. My mother was not here. But I spoke to her, anyway.

"I believe him," I said. "I believe Chipper. If Becky was preg-nant, she didn't leave because he wouldn't support her. She left for other reasons. Reasons I guess we'll never know. That maybe we aren't meant to know."

I bent down and cleared away the grass that obscured my mother's name.

"I came back because I thought I'd finally learned the truth about what happened to Becky," I told her. "I thought I'd finally figured it out." I laughed at myself. "Frank and Randall warned me I was grasping at straws, but I didn't want to believe them. I wanted so much to know what happened. I wanted to know why everything changed for us. For you and me and Dad."

I stood up, letting out a long breath.

"But I don't know. Sorry to report, Mom, but I was still unable to find Becky for you. I believe Chipper when he says Becky didn't tell him she was pregnant." I stared down at her name. "Now, it's still possible she *may* have been. Maybe she was. Maybe she wasn't. Every scenario is possible, Mom, as I'm sure you realized many times since I'm sure you thought of them all."

I looked over at the setting sun, the swirl of pinks and golds.

"Maybe you were right, Mom. Maybe sometime after her swim in the pond, Becky met up with a kidnapper who took her away. Or maybe, in fact, it was Guthrie who was right, and the truth is that Becky decided to leave on her own. Maybe it had something to do with her being pregnant, and maybe she wasn't pregnant at all. Maybe it was a spontaneous decision. Maybe it was premedi-tated. The missing clothes and money make me think it was pre-meditated, but who knows? Maybe she gave the clothes away. Maybe she took the money to buy me a birthday gift. Any sce-nario is possible."

I felt tears well up behind my eyes. "I wish I could remember Becky's face that day at the pond," I said, staring down again at my mother's stone. "I can't picture her. Only her back, and her long, wet hair. Was she anxious? Sad? I don't know." The first tears squeezed themselves out of my eyes. "Sorry not to be bring-ing you better news, Mom. But the truth is, we won't ever know."

I looked around, conscious suddenly of talking out loud in a cemetery. I was relieved to see that I was still completely alone, with only the dead and the birds in the trees as company. Still, I dropped my voice to a whisper.

"That was the worst part of it, wasn't it, Mom?" I asked. "The not knowing? The constant feeling in your gut that you had somehow caused Becky to leave? It was easier, wasn't it, to believe that she'd been taken by bikers, that she was living under some pier in New York or stripping in a club in Boston? That was easier to bear, wasn't it, Mom? That she had been *taken* from you, rather than the idea that she had *left* you?"

I stared down at her name. Margaret Cronin Fortunato. The tears began dropping to the ground, one by one.

"Did you feel anything when *I* left you, Mom? I know you were angry. But did you feel anything more?"

It was one more thing I would never know.

I gazed down at the date of her death. It was eight years ago. I remembered the morning I woke up and just knew it was time to call home. There had been no mulling over the idea. It was just there, present and certain when I opened my eyes. I picked up the phone and called my parents' number. After thirteen years, it was still in service. Thirteen years since I'd had any contact with them. My father answered the phone.

"How did you know?" he asked as soon as he heard my voice.

"Know what?"

"Your mother died this morning."

It had been breast cancer, like Aunt Patsy, and Mom had gone almost as fast. He'd tried to find me, Dad said, but he'd been un-successful. I wasn't sure I believed him. I wondered if Mom had forbidden him to do so, insistent to the very end that she had no children, that she'd lost both her daughter and her son. But maybe it hadn't been that way. Maybe Dad had tried to find me. The Internet wasn't that big yet, and Dad surely had had little knowledge of how to search it. Maybe, in fact, Mom really had hoped I'd come at the end. But I hadn't. I'd called exactly five hours after she died.

I chose not to return home for the funeral. There would be too many questions, too much awkwardness. Instead, I lay in Frank's arms. I cried once, a big, heavy, gut-wrenching sound, as Frank stroked my hair and whispered, "It's okay, baby," over and over in my ear. But mostly I was silent, kept from shattering into a million fragments by Frank's strong arms.

I longed for those arms now.

What had I come here expecting to find? What was it that I was really looking for, not just here, but in everything that I'd been through these last several months? They seemed a foolish, childish blur. What had I been hoping to find?

I turned and walked out of the cemetery, not looking back, knowing I'd never return. My father was not going to be buried there. After Mom's death, I'd stayed in touch with Dad, talking occasionally with him on the phone. I was pleased to learn that Father McKenna had gotten him into AA and that he'd stopped drinking, getting some of his life back. Toward my mother, he bore no ill will for all their years of conflict. He hoped it might be the same for me.

"Don't hate her, Danny," Dad had said over the phone.

"I don't hate her," I'd assured him.

"She loved you. I know it didn't feel that way. But she did. Her grief destroyed her, and it nearly destroyed me."

"Why didn't you ever leave her?" I'd asked.

"I loved her," Dad had said simply. "When you're with someone that long, when you've been through so much together, you become part of each other. The love doesn't go away." He'd paused. "I'm not sure if you can understand what I mean."

I hadn't then. But now, walking out of the cemetery, longing for Frank's arms, I understood very well.

A few years after Mom's death, Dad had moved to Florida with a lady friend. Her name was Angela. I was happy for him. Vague plans were made about seeing each other again someday, but I doubted if it would happen. Perhaps our occasional phone calls would be enough.

I sat for a moment behind the wheel of my rental car. If I could have, I would have driven to the airport right then and there and gotten on a plane back to California. That was where I belonged.

I missed Frank desperately. I wanted Frank to hold me, to whisper in my ear that everything was okay. My entire body ached for him.

Every morning, Danny, you wake up and look into the eyes of a man who loves you. Imagine for a moment what it's like to go through life without ever being able to look someone in the eyes and know those eyes are looking back at you.

Popping open my cell phone, I speed-dialed Frank and got his voice mail. "I'm done here," I told him simply. "I'm coming home."

Heading back to my hotel, I drove along the same route the bus had taken when I left this place so long ago. I'd looked out of the bus window then as the buildings of my childhood rushed past, dropping out of my frame of vision one after another. I'd carried with me as many questions then as I did that day in the cemetery.

Two decades later, I'd discovered the answers were no answers at all.

EAST HARTFORD

Twenty-One Years Earlier

"I've come to say good-bye, Nana."
"Can you help me?"

I set my suitcase down by the door and smiled down at her. They'd stopped putting the bows in her hair, but her face was still painted with too much lipstick and rouge. I took a tissue from the box on the side of her bed and began to gently wipe it off.

"I'm moving to California," I told her. "I'm going to become an actor."

"Can you help me?"

"I've got my bus ticket," I said. "It's going to be a long ride across the country. Almost a week. But I'm up for it."

"Can you help me?"

I kissed her forehead. She smelled of disinfectant. I remembered her sweet, spicy perfume and missed it very much.

"Can you help me?"

I sat in the chair opposite her. "Okay, okay, Nana. I hear you. I'll read to you for a little bit. I know how much you like it."

I pulled a battered old paperback from the inside of my denim jacket.

"I'm reading a wonderful play right now. It's called *The Glass Menagerie*. Tennessee Williams wrote it. You know, the same guy who wrote *The Night of the Iguana* and *Suddenly Last Summer.*" I smiled broadly. "I like this one best of all. I'd love to play the part of Tom."

I began to read, from Tom's opening monologue: "Yes, I have tricks in my pocket, I have things up my sleeve. But I am the opposite of a stage magician. He gives you illusion that has the appearance of truth. I give you truth in the pleasant disguise of illusion."

As always, Nana became serene as I read to her.

I understood the power of great words. For the last three years, books and plays had been my escape. Forced out of St. Francis Xavier, I'd been sent to East Hartford High—which in some ways wasn't so bad. I'd thought maybe I'd run into my old friend Desmond, but his family had moved away. Which was just as well. No one at East Hartford High knew who I was or what I had done in the men's room. They'd even largely forgotten about the Becky Fortunato case by now, so I was able to just slip into a corner and stay there, pretty much out of sight, for my junior and senior year. For me, the myriad teenage dramas that were enacted around me held no interest. Nor did I risk involvement in another school play, though I was tempted. Instead, I lost myself in books, both those assigned in class and those I'd take out from the library. During the summer, literature was an especially boon companion, since, through my own choice, I had no friends with whom to hang out. Williams and Poe and Faulkner and Fitzgerald and Jane Austen and Eugene O'Neill proved more than satisfactory comrades.

I became, once again, the good student I had been at St. John's, though my grades weren't so extraordinary that I drew any special attention—except in my American theater class during the first semester of my senior year, where my teacher had written on one paper: "You show such a passion for drama that you could become either a major actor or playwright." That one line had convinced me to seriously pursue acting upon graduation—a decision not received well by my parents.

With Mom and Dad, I had settled into a routine of wary coexistence. My father remained an intermittent ghost in my life. My mother alternated between bouts of manic activity and long stretches of solitary depression. She never let go of the idea that Becky was still out there somewhere, just waiting to be found, and that everything Warren had told her had been the gospel truth.

And as she'd warned me, she expected that I would pay off my sins when I got my driver's license. My penance was accepted without argument. I drove her wherever she wanted to go. Once I drove her to Somers State Prison so she could meet with Bruno himself face-to-face. I didn't go in with her, passing the time instead in an airless, small outer room. I watched the clock in utter terror of a prison break. When Mom came out, nothing had changed. Bruno's repeated denials of knowing anything about Becky had failed to convince her; she remained certain that he was lying, and that some day she'd get him to divulge what he knew. When he was murdered in a prison brawl a month later, she was convinced it had something to do with Becky, and rued that my sister's whereabouts had gone with Bruno to the grave.

Other times, I drove her to New York, where we searched for Becky under piers and among the hard faces of the hookers in Times Square. Once there was a trip to Boston's north shore, where a tipster had said Becky was working in a beachside dive that sold fried clams and onion rings. It wasn't her. A psychic placed her on Cape Cod, advice my mother insisted *must* be true, since that was where Becky and Bruno had supposedly first been spotted years before. But a trek up the long arm of the Cape in the dead of winter had proven, yet again, fruitless. All we got was stuck in an ice storm.

On these trips, Mom and I spoke only the most necessary of words to each other. "Turn here." "Slow down." "Do you want to use the bathroom?" "Look at that girl over there." By now, I'd given up all hope of finding my sister, but I chauffeured Mom everywhere without complaint, serving my sentence for longer than Bruno served his.

Even after high school graduation, I continued schlepping Mom around. But I was also now working two jobs, at Friendly's Ice Cream and Bob's Big Boy, so her trips had to be planned around my schedule. I was also saving my money for my escape. The first time I announced that I was going into New York to audition for a play, my mother hit the roof. "New York is filled with perverts!" she told me. But still I went. Though I didn't get the part, I was glad I'd gone into the city to read for it, anyway, because it allowed me the chance to flout my mother's opposition.

I managed to land some small roles in regional New England theater. The greasepaint and spotlights and applause convinced me that I had indeed found my calling. I became fixated on the idea of Los Angeles—*Hollywood*—which meant, of course, television or movies instead of the stage. That was fine by me. At night I'd lie in bed, imagining myself the star of a television series. What would Mom do then? The star of his own TV show didn't haul his mother around to smelly biker bars. As a star, I'd be able to do whatever I wanted, without conditions from her. It would be heaven.

And finally the day came. I had just driven Mom all the way up to the border of Canada in Maine, where she'd met with one of the Rubberman's old girlfriends, a hag who lived in a fishing shack and kept farting as we talked to her. She didn't know a damn thing, but when Mom pushed some cash across the table, she conveniently remembered seeing a girl who fit Becky's description at some biker rally or another. That did it for me. I vowed this would be the last excursion I'd ever make with Mom. The next day, I bought a bus ticket to Los Angeles, packed my bags, and headed over to the Swan Convalescent Home to say good-bye to Nana.

"I'm going to miss you, Nana," I told her, putting down *The Glass Menagerie*. She looked at me with her round, peaceful blue eyes. "Now, don't go thinking that I'm forgetting about you just because I'm moving to California." I knew my words were nothing more than white noise to her, but still, I felt the need to say them. "When I make it big, I'll send for you. I'll get you round-the-clock care in a gorgeous house with a beautiful garden, like the kind of garden you used to have. I'll read to you every day. Or if I can't read myself, I'll hire someone to do it. So don't worry that I'll forget you."

She continued looking at me with those round eyes.

I reached over and unzipped my suitcase, rummaging inside

among my clothes. "This morning, when I was packing, I took only the most necessary things, like underwear and socks and jeans," I told her. "But I did take this."

I produced the four-generation family photo.

"See, Nana? You gave this to me on my fourteenth birthday. I'll always keep it. And maybe someday I can come back here, and we can take a photo of you and Dad and me and my son." Just because I was gay—I had stopped saying "bisexual"—didn't mean I'd never have a son.

I placed the photo in Nana's hands. She looked down at it, saying nothing.

"You see, Nana? There's your grandparents, who came from County Cork. And your parents. I was named after your father. Daniel Horgan. And there's you and Grandpa and then my dad, in the christening robe."

She just kept looking silently at the photo.

I hated leaving behind so much of my stuff. But there was no way I could take all my comics or all my records, or more than a few books. I spent the morning going through my room. Mom was with Father McKenna at a prayer service; various ladies from the parish gathered regularly to sit, holding hands, in a circle and pray together for Becky's safe return. I had no idea where Dad was. But having the apartment to myself to pack was important; I didn't want to answer any questions until I was ready to leave. I took one good shirt and one nice pair of pants; the rest of my wardrobe would have to consist of jeans and T-shirts.

Digging through the back of my dresser drawer, I came upon a crumpled wad of worn cotton. Chipper's underwear. Without much regret, I tossed them into the trash.

But something else in my drawer gave me greater pause, compelling me to sit on the edge of my bed for a moment. In my hands I held my Beautiful Men scrapbook. It had been a couple of years since I'd pasted anything in there: the last photo, clipped from *People* magazine, was of Tom Selleck in a flowered Hawaiian shirt. I leafed through the pages one last time, vaguely worried that if I left the scrapbook behind, Mom might find it. But I no longer cared. I replaced it in my drawer, imagining that someday some little gay boy might clip *my* photograph out of a magazine, once I, too, was a big star.

I was heading outside when I saw Father McKenna drive up and Mom get out of his car. I frowned. So I hadn't made it scot-free, after all.

Mom saw my suitcase as she came through the door.

"Where are you going?" she asked sharply.

"I'm leaving," I said.

"What do you mean, leaving? Are you going down to New York again?"

"No," I told her, struggling to keep my voice level. "I'm leaving for good. I'm moving to Los Angeles."

"Los Angeles?" She didn't blow her top, as I'd expected. Instead, her voice echoed the evenness of my own. "What's in Los Angeles?"

"The film and television industry."

"Danny." She took a step toward me. I tightened my grip on my suitcase. "You just can't go waltzing off to Los Angeles like that. You know no one there."

"I'm aware of that. But I'm still going."

She took another step. I kept my eyes on her, waiting for her to lash out and try to hold me down. But I was bigger than she was now. If she tried to slap me again, I could block her. I could hold her off.

"Danny, you're talking nonsense," she said, her voice still calm and steady. There was even a flicker of a smile on her lips, as if she was mocking me. "How would you get there? It's a long, long way."

"I'm taking the bus. I already have my ticket."

That seemed to shake her. I was serious.

"Danny, you just can't get on a bus to Los Angeles!" Her voice was rising just a bit now. I noticed her big hands were shaking as she made the sign of the cross.

"Why not?"

"Because I need you!" Now her eyes were wide and terrified. Her voice trembled. "You can't just walk out on me! I need you, Danny!"

Part of me was breaking. Part of me, even still, never wanted to leave her. But another part, a stronger part, the part that lived in the front of my brain and had nothing to do with my heart, could have cared less what she needed. It was that part of myself that took a step toward the door.

"You can't just *leave!*" Mom shouted.

"Yes, I can."

Now she was apoplectic. "If you walk through that door, don't think you can just come wandering back whenever you feel like it!"

"I won't."

"*Danny!!*"

I headed outside, the screen door slamming shut behind me.

"Danny!" she shouted from inside the apartment. "Don't leave me!"

I refused to cry as I headed out onto the street.

Heading to the convalescent home, I kept my mind focused on my dream. On those few trips I'd taken into New York on my own, I'd met other actors. People like me, who were daring to take leaps into the unknown. "The artist never truly knows," one director had said at one audition, quoting Agnes de Mille. "He guesses and takes leap after leap into the dark."

One time, I'd run into Troy Kitchens in Greenwich Village. I hadn't seen Troy since that day in the men's room. Like me, Troy had been expelled over the incident, even if the good brothers had surely rued the loss of Mr. Kitchens's financial endowments. Yet, no doubt, they'd considered the possibility of an uppity, unapologetic homosexual continuing under their roof a far worse outcome. For Troy, of course, there would be no East Hartford High: he was trundled off to some prep school in upstate New York. Now, he told me with tremendous satisfaction, he was living with his older brother and taking courses at NYU.

"And I'm a musician," he added over coffee and cigarettes in a joint frequented by bohemian types wearing long sideburns and leather pants. "I learned how to play guitar my senior year in high school. And six months ago, I formed a punk-rock band with some other guys." He beamed. "We're Troy Kitchens and the

Utensils." He laughed, and I laughed with him. It was good to see Troy laugh. "We've already headlined a couple gigs in the city," he told me. "You watch, Danny. We're gonna be big."

We didn't talk about that day in the men's room. All I said was, "I'm sorry, Troy," and he said, "No, man, I'm sorry," and we let it drop there. I didn't blame Troy for what happened. In some ways, it had been more my fault than his. I'd treated him pretty badly at times, and I supposed I deserved what I got. I told Troy I was glad for his success and that I, too, would make it big. We shook hands, then gave each other a quick kiss on the lips. I was heading west soon, I told him. If he ever made it there, he should look me up.

"Where west?" he asked.

"Hollywood," I told him.

I was heading to Hollywood.

"I've got to get going, Nana," I said suddenly. "My bus leaves in ninety minutes, and I have to walk downtown."

"Can you help me?"

I stood, replacing the photograph in my suitcase.

"Can you help me?"

I put my arms around her. "I love you, Nana," I said, kissing her cheek. "Danny off the pickle boat will always love you."

"Can you help me?"

I picked up my suitcase and headed out into the hall. And as I turned, I saw my father walking briskly toward me.

"Your mother told me you were taking a bus," he said, out of breath.

I nodded.

"But I knew you'd come here first to say good-bye to Nana."

I nodded again.

"Danny," Dad said, and his words were accompanied, as always, by whiffs of whiskey, "you can't just go get on a bus and move to Los Angeles."

"Why not?"

It was the same question I'd asked Mom, and Dad had no better answer. He just put his hand on my shoulder. He gestured that I should follow him into an empty reception room across the hall.

We entered and sat in chairs opposite each other. I placed my suitcase between my knees. On the wall a television aired *The Price is Right*.

"You don't have any connections in Los Angeles, Danny," Dad tried arguing. "To be an actor, you need an agent or something like that."

"I'll get one."

He sighed. "There are a lot of people out there who will take advantage of an inexperienced kid from Connecticut just off the bus."

"I can take care of myself."

"Danny, I . . ." His voice quavered, and I saw tears form in the corners of his eyes. "I know I haven't been very good to you these last few years. I know—"

"Dad, it's okay. Look, I'm going to be late. I need to head downtown to get my bus."

"Danny, this lifestyle of yours . . ."

I stiffened. "What lifestyle?"

"You know what I mean."

I laughed. "My lifestyle is working at Big Boy and hauling Mom all over hell and creation. That's the only lifestyle I have. I can't go on that way anymore, Dad. And you know I can't."

His eyes, previously elusive, met mine. He seemed to understand.

"I just want you to be safe," he said to me. "You know, after losing Becky, I just can't . . . I mean, I think about you in some back room somewhere. . . ."

"Dad, I'm not going to be in any *back room*," I replied. "I'm going to find an apartment and go to the television studios and audition for parts."

"You have no money."

"Yes, I do. I've saved quite a bit. And I took it all out and turned it into traveler's checks. You see? I'm responsible. I knew I shouldn't travel with cash."

"Oh, Danny."

That was it. The end of his argument. He knew it; I knew it. I stood to leave.

"Danny, wait."

"I can't," I told him. "I've got to make my bus."

He stood now, too. "You may need *some* cash." He reached around to his back pocket and produced his wallet. With trembling hands, he pulled out five twenties—probably all that was in there—and handed them over to me. "Don't tell your mother I gave it to you."

"I can't take it," I said.

His face twisted into a mix of outrage and grief. "You've *got* to take it, Danny! It's all I have to give you, and I've got to give you something. After all this time, I've got to give you something."

I put out my hand and accepted the money, folding it into my pocket. "Thank you," I said quietly.

Dad and I faced each other for several moments, not saying anything.

"I have to go," I said finally.

"Call us, will you?" he asked. "When you get settled?"

I nodded. Then I turned and walked quickly out through the front lobby of the Swan Convalescent Home. From their wheelchairs, old women stretched out their withered arms, beckoning to me. My vision began to blur.

Outside, in the bright sunlight, I finally allowed myself to cry. I cried for several blocks, not caring who saw me. But by the time I reached the bus station, my tears had dried. I boarded the bus, taking a seat far in back. First stop, Middletown, then New Haven, Bridgeport, Stamford, and New York. I'd transfer there for a Chicago-bound bus, where I'd sleep straight through the Midwest. From there it would be on to Omaha, Wichita, Amarillo, Albuquerque, and Phoenix. And finally, after a journey of nearly a week, Los Angeles. The City of Angels. The Land of Dreams.

Pressing my forehead against the window, I watched East Hartford fall behind me, along with everything I had ever been and everything I had hoped to be. Eventually, all that was familiar was far out of sight.

PALM SPRINGS

My plane landed a few minutes early into the delightful Palm Springs airport, with its open-air terminals and tentlike roofs. The smell of dry sage and dusty earth struck me, and I knew that I was home. The wonderful thing about flying east to west was, if you left early enough, you could arrive before noon and have the whole day ahead of you. Heading out of the airport, I felt good, filled with the possibilities of the day.

My phone chirped with a message when I turned it back on. I assumed it would be from Frank, since he'd never responded to the message I'd left the night before, and I'd called him again during my layover in Dallas. But it was a text, and it was from Kelly. LEAVING TODAY. MOVING TO PUERTO VALLARTA. WANTED TO SAY GOODBYE AND THANKS 4 EVERYTHING.

I called him immediately, and he answered. I told him not to go anywhere, that I'd be right over. I drove directly to his apartment from the airport. The slanting rays of the morning sun had turned the mountains violet and sapphire. Along the way, the clusters of annuals planted along the sides of the road made me smile. Yellow snapdragons, red and white petunias, pink and purple poppies. And the pear trees, once again in bloom, suffused the air with a tart fragrance that smelled unmistakably like semen. Only in Palm Springs, I thought, would the air smell like cum.

I found Kelly packing his old Mercedes with his few possessions: his clothes, his sketch pads, his milk crates, his cinder blocks. His print of Jackie O had been laid carefully on the ledge beneath the back window. He looked up a little warily when I arrived.

"Puerto Vallarta?" I asked, getting out of the Jeep and approaching him. "How'd this come about?"

"Damian got a job down there at a resort, and he suggested I go along." He shrugged. "Vallarta is a big gay tourist destination, you know. I figure there are lots of places where I can get a job bartending."

I decided not to ask if he and Damian were dating each other again. "You have a work visa?"

"Damian's taking care of all that."

"I see. How long will you stay?"

He was shoving a backpack behind the front seat. With the cinder blocks and milk crates taking up most of the back, there wasn't much room left in the car.

"I don't know," Kelly replied, not looking at me. "Maybe just for the season. Maybe longer. Anyway, there's nothing here for me."

"There's the course at CalArts."

He rolled his eyes, not unlike Penelope Sue. "Danny, I'm not an artist."

"I think you are."

"Well, you can think what you want." He succeeded in stuffing the backpack into the car and slammed the door. Finally, he looked over at me. "Will you help me carry down my mattress?"

"Sure."

We headed up the stairs. I wasn't sure how I was feeling. Kelly was moving to Mexico; I had no idea when I might see him again. A couple of weeks ago, I would have felt desperate to stop such a plan. I'd have been cajoling and arguing, trying to find a way to get him to stay. But I had no energy for such an effort today. I just followed him back into his apartment.

It was empty, save for the bare mattress sitting in the middle of the floor. "Do you have a place to live yet?" I asked.

"Damian knows a guy there. He's another massage therapist. He has a place not far from the gay beach, and he said we could stay in his guest room."

I nodded. So they'd be staying in the same room. Again, I felt nothing.

Kelly bent down and lifted an end of the mattress. "Will you get the other side?" he asked.

I hesitated. "Listen, Kelly, I want to apologize for the other night, for acting so weird."

He set the mattress back down and put his hands on his hips. "Weird doesn't even begin to describe it."

"I know," I said. "It was just some stuff that was going on for me. My mind was all over the place."

He grimaced. "But why did you ask those questions about my birth mother?"

I sighed, running a hand through my hair. "I was being crazy. I'd been thinking about my family. About my sister."

"What about your sister?"

"You see, my sister disappeared when she was sixteen. She just vanished without a trace. We never found out what happened to her. I just got back from a trip to my hometown in Connecticut, in fact. The first time in more than twenty years."

"Why did you go?"

I sighed. "I thought I had found out what happened to her."

"And did you?"

I looked into his eyes. They did indeed resemble the eyes of the man I had confronted in his driveway the day before. Was that the reason they had beguiled me from the start?

It was *possible*, Chipper had said. It was possible Becky had been pregnant.

"No," I said. "I didn't find out."

"But what did my mother have to do with it?"

"Probably nothing," I told him.

His head tilted in sudden understanding. "You thought . . . oh my God! You thought maybe she and your sister . . ."

"It was craziness. Just grasping at straws."

I didn't mention the birthmark.

"Well, that would have been really weird, huh?" he asked, dropping the idea as quickly as he had thought of it and picking up the end of the mattress again.

"Oh yeah," I agreed. "Really weird."

I lifted my end of the mattress, and we hauled it down the stairs, carefully taking one step at a time, our floppy load balanced over our heads. Onto the top of the Mercedes, we slid the mattress, and Kelly began securing it with rope.

"So what do you think happened to her?" he asked. "Your sister?"

"I don't know. I've come to the conclusion that I'll never know."

"But what do you *think*?"

"I think she left home because she wanted to. My sister was a lot like me. Or at least, I became a lot like her. I wasn't always that way. But Becky wanted to see the world ever since she was a kid. I was thinking about her on the plane this morning. So many things I had forgotten about her. Becky wanted to see the world, to find her place in it, way before I ever did. I think that's why she left home. I don't think she meant to stay away forever. But then something happened, and she was never able to come back."

"What do you think happened?"

I smiled wanly. "I don't know. But life gets messy some times."

He was tying the rope in a messy knot inside the car. "Do you think she's dead?"

I took a breath. "Yes," I said. "I think Becky died a long time ago."

"That's sad."

I nodded. Sad—but liberating, too. I remembered one of my conversations with my father a few years ago. He'd told me that it wasn't until after my mother had died that he was finally able to accept that Becky was gone and never coming back. "Your mother had carried that torch for so long," Dad said, "that to reach such a conclusion while she was still living would have felt like a betrayal in some way." He'd paused. "But once Peggy was gone, I took Becky's easel and that last, unfinished painting of hers and buried them in the ground. I said a prayer and hoped my little girl rested in peace. After that, I never took another drink. It was just like that. Oh, AA helped, but it was burying Becky's things that really did it. After that, I never had the urge to drink again. Finally, everything felt done."

I looked over at Kelly. He had finished securing the mattress.

"Well," he said, looking at me with those black eyes. "I guess this is it."

"Yeah," I said. "I guess so."

He laughed. "You're not going to try to convince me not to go?"

I shook my head. It was indeed surprising, but I wasn't going to make any attempt to stop him. So this was how it would end. After all the high drama, all the emotion, all the great, big romantic dreams, I would say good-bye to him on the street, in front of an old apartment complex with a sign that read HAPPY PALMS. This was it.

"You're heading to Mexico today?" I asked, my voice thick.

He nodded. "I'm meeting Damian in L.A., and then we drive down tonight."

How long had I known him? Just a matter of months. I had dreamed about him; I had lain awake thinking about him. He had filled up every available space in my mind. And now, as I stood across from him, it all felt so meager. So small and insignificant. As if I had spent all that time and energy on something that, in the end, amounted only to this: a ratty mattress strapped to the top of an old car. And a boy looking at me with his incomprehensible black eyes and saying good-bye.

But it had been worth it. I walked over to him and placed my hands on his shoulders. Yes, indeed, he could be Becky's son. Becky and Chipper's son. Chipper had said it was possible. A day or so ago, I wouldn't have let him leave without a DNA test. I would have told him what I thought—no, what I *hoped:* that he was my nephew, that we were inextricably bound together forever. I knew that without my establishing that link, he might leave today and never again cross into my life.

But I chose to say nothing. Maybe I didn't want to know for sure what a DNA test might reveal. Maybe it was better to always just believe in the possibility. Maybe knowing for sure would cause too many other problems. Maybe it was enough just to have this much. I reached out and pulled him close, feeling his arms wrap around my back and his head rest against my chest.

"I'm sorry," I told him. "I'm sorry for pushing you, promising things I shouldn't have . . ."

"No, don't be sorry. You're the first person who cared enough to fight for me, the first person since my mother, my real mother, who fought so hard to get me back from the state." He gripped me tighter. "That means a lot."

In my mind, I was seeing the photograph Nana had given me.

"Here," I said, breaking our embrace and reaching around to my wallet. "Let me give you something for your trip."

"No," he told me, raising his hands as if to ward off a blow. "I have money. I went to the bank this morning and got traveler's checks."

I smiled. "American dollars can come in handy in Mexico." I took five twenties from my wallet and handed them over to him. "Please. I've got to give you something."

Kelly shook his head. "No, Danny."

"Please," I said. "Take it."

He grimaced, but he accepted the money, tucking it into his front pocket. "Thank you," he said in a small voice. He looked as if he might cry. His face twisted; his eyes hooded over. "I'm sorry, Danny," he said. "I'm sorry I couldn't love you the way you loved me."

"That's okay," I said. "You've loved me as much as you could. That's enough for me."

I placed my hands on his cheeks and kissed the top of his head.

"Just be happy, okay, Danny? You and Frank? Be happy, be together. I'll like knowing that."

"What if," Kelly asked, looking up at me, "I get to Mexico, and one day, as I'm exploring the ruins of a Mayan pyramid, I find an ancient Indian amulet, and I cause an international incident when I try to steal it?"

"Just tell some of your really bad jokes and they'll be glad to release you," I told him.

He smiled as we broke apart. I stepped back to watch him go.

"I'll let you know when we get there," he said.

I nodded. "Yes. Please do. Let me know when you get settled."

He got into the car.

"Hey, Kelly," I called out.

He turned from behind the wheel to look at me. I saw his eagle tattoo peeking out above his T-shirt.

"What did the man with five penises say?" I asked.

There was a flicker of a smile in the rearview mirror.

I didn't give him the chance to figure it out. "'These pants fit like a glove.'"

He turned around, flashing me an eye. "You're good."

"Finally stumped you."

He started the car. "Except shouldn't it have been peni, not penises?"

I laughed.

He drove off, waving at me with his left hand as the Mercedes headed down Arenas Road, the mattress flopping around on the roof. I watched as he took a right onto Palm Canyon, then the car was gone.

I got back into my Jeep. Opening my suitcase, I took out something I had brought with me. Kelly's drawing of me. I looked at it again, at the lines he'd drawn with his hand. I ran my finger along the contours of my face. At first, I had thought the drawing looked like me, but now I wasn't so sure. I replaced it in my suitcase. I started the Jeep and drove home.

I was heading past the pool when my phone rang. I smiled, thinking it was Kelly calling with one last joke, but as I fumbled the phone out of my pocket, I saw it was from a local number that I didn't recognize. I flipped it open and said hello.

"Danny Fortunato?" came a woman's crisp, efficient voice.

"Yes."

"Penelope Sue Hunt. Thanks for dropping off your portfolio. Sorry I wasn't here when you came by."

"That's okay." I peered through the sliding-glass doors and saw Frank sitting in his chair. "Did you find anything you liked?" I asked Penelope Sue.

"No, I did not." Her words were clipped, brusque, and my heart sank. "But I like what you do," she added. "I want to commission a series. Portraits of myself and my husband. A whole series. I want to line the passageway leading out to the solarium with alternating images of Donovan and myself. I want you to do something Warholian with them. Like what Andy did with Liz Taylor and Marilyn."

Or the Campbell's soup cans, I thought, my lips curling into a smile. I tapped on the glass, trying to get Frank's attention. He was sitting with his head back, his running shoes kicked off beside him. He must have just come in from jogging.

"I would *love* to do that," I told Penelope Sue. "I can come by and take the photos and then see what I can do with them digitally."

"Perfect. I'd like you to come next Wednesday afternoon. At three."

I wasn't about to haggle over the time. "Certainly," I said.

"Good. We'll see you then."

"Since this is a commission, I'll have to come up with a fee. . . ."

She made a sound of impatience. I was certain she was rolling her eyes. "I don't care what the fee is. Just give me an invoice when it's done, and I'll pay you."

"Okay," I said.

"See you Wednesday."

"Yes, Wednesday."

She hung up without saying good-bye.

I slid open the door and let out a whoop. "Guess who that was, Frank! Penelope Sue! She doesn't want to buy any of my work. She wants to commission *a whole series*! We are *in*, Frank! Everyone will want to commission me now. This is going to be the most money I've ever made!"

I dropped my suitcase onto the floor and headed into the kitchen, pulling open the refrigerator to pour myself a tall glass of lemonade. It was a hot day, and I'd worked up a sweat helping Kelly haul down that mattress.

"So wait until I tell you about my visit to the old homestead," I said, wiping my mouth after my first swig of lemonade. "What a trip it was. It was eye-opening, Frank. I feel like I've been sleep-walking these last couple of months. Everything now seems so clear."

I looked over at Frank in the living room. He was still in his chair, his head back. He hadn't changed position or said a word about any of my news.

"Frank?"

I set down the lemonade and headed out of the kitchen.

"Frank, are you asleep?"

His eyes were closed; his mouth was slightly open. His phone was in his lap. One arm hung limply over the side of the chair.

"Frank!"

Suddenly I knew. My hand flew out to touch his forehead. It was cold.

"No!" I screamed.

He didn't appear to be breathing.

I gripped his hand, tried to feel for a pulse, but my own hands were shaking so much, it was impossible.

"Frank!" I shouted, shaking him. "Frank! For God's sake, answer me!"

I turned and bolted back into the kitchen, frantically looking for my phone. It was nowhere to be seen. I had just spoken with Penelope. Where the fuck was it? I was just about to run back and grab Frank's phone off his lap when I whipped open the refrigerator door and saw my phone inside, next to the jug of lemonade. A crazy thought at a crazy time: *I'm getting forgetful. I'm getting old.* I grabbed the phone and pressed 911.

"Please!" I shouted at the operator. "You've got to get here! My partner—my husband—he's not responding! I think maybe he's had a heart attack!"

I gave the address. The operator assured me help was on the way. In the meantime, she asked me if I knew CPR. "No," I said pitifully.

"Tell me what his condition is now, sir," the operator was saying.

I hurried back into the living room to stand over him. "He's just lying there," I said, looking down at him. "He won't open his eyes."

What she said next I couldn't hear. Suddenly Frank's face filled up every corner of my consciousness. I had called him last night. And he hadn't answered. And he hadn't called me back. *Had he been like this all the time?* Had my phone rung in his lap as he lay there, unable to answer? Had he been in this condition all night, and all morning? Had he taken his last breath as I'd hurried one last time to see Kelly? Or had it been earlier, when I'd faced Chipper Paguni in his driveway?

"No, please God, no!"

I fell to my knees, holding Frank's hand to my mouth. My phone went sliding across the black-and-white tiled floor. Any advice the 911 operator might be trying to give me was worthless now. I just pressed my face to Frank's hand, calling to him.

"You have always been first, Frank! Always!" I was sobbing. "How could I ever have thought anything else?"

A cavalcade of memories tumbled out of my brain. A hike down a steep cliff at Big Sur. Holding Frank's hand in the clinic as we awaited our results. The reflection of the setting sun in his eyes as he slipped a titanium band onto my finger on a beach in Vancouver. A run with Pixie along the sand. Getting into his old Duster that dark night on Mulholland Drive. The crowd applauding as he walked up to accept a plaque as Teacher of the Year. The look on his face when I'd presented him with the print of his "green daisy." The way he had called me, plainly and simply, an artist. And the words he had said not so long ago, when he'd told me that when he looked at the mountains, he, too, saw Becky.

"No one," I whimpered, kissing his hand, "no one but you, Frank. No one ever but you."

Too late. It was all too late. My sleep walking had gone on too long. This was my punishment. But of course. Why should I have thought that it would all end happily for me?

This was only right. This was what I deserved.

But then . . .

His pinkie moved.

Or had I imagined it?

Maybe I had moved it myself . . .

No.

It moved again.

"Frank!" I screamed, standing up just as the paramedics were at the door. I ran to let them in. "He's alive! You've got to save him!"

I retreated into a corner, my hands at my mouth, as they began their work on him.

"You've got to save him!" I cried again. "You've got to! Please! He's my entire life! Don't let him die!"

EAST HARTFORD

It was my thirteenth birthday, the day before starting eighth grade, and my last year at St. John's. Already I was freaking myself out about what I might face this time next year as I headed off to high school, but Mom just smiled and told me to stop worrying. "You have a whole *year* to get ready for that, Danny," she said. "Just enjoy this last year at St. John's. Just be a kid. After that, you grow up so fast."

We were in the backyard. Dad was barbecuing some hamburgers and hot dogs, and Nana and Aunt Patsy were husking corn on the cob. Between two trees dangled a string of cardboard letters that spelled out HAPPY BIRTHDAY, which later Mom planned to move inside for the party tonight with my friends Katie and Desmond and Joanne and the Theresas. On the picnic table she'd placed my birthday cake—my favorite, of course, yellow Duncan Hines with chocolate frosting—and she was busy spelling out my name across the top with M&M's. Becky stood off to the side, near the rusted old swing set, doing her best to ignore all of us. She was painting at her easel, intent on capturing some scene or another. We knew better than to interrupt Becky when she was painting.

"Danny off the pickle boat," Nana chirped. "Tomorrow you're coming to my house, and I'm making you my homemade macaroni and cheese."

"I love your mac and cheese," I told her.

"Well, today you've got to settle for burgers and dogs," Dad said, flipping them onto a platter. "Dig in."

"I've made *two* cakes," Mom told me. "One for the family and one for your friends for later."

"Thanks, Mom!"

"Becky!" she called. "Come have a hot dog and a piece of Danny's birthday cake."

Even from across the yard, I could see my sister heave a sigh of annoyance. She didn't reply, just went on painting.

Mom made a face. "She's angry because I didn't allow that Paguni boy from across the street to join us."

"Aren't they dating?" Aunt Patsy asked.

Mom shrugged. "I suppose. But she's far too young to be getting serious with anyone."

Dad was lining up the corn on the grill now. "Peggy, would you bring out the butter?"

Nana hopped to her feet. "I'll get it! You eat, Peggy." She hurried off into the house.

I settled down at the picnic table and took a bite of my burger. I loved the way Dad grilled them, really burned and crispy. Mom sat opposite me. Aunt Patsy stayed where she was, since it was hard for her to get up and down after the operation. But at least she was better now. The doctors said she was cancer free.

Nana came back out of the house. "What did I go inside for?"

"The *butter*, Ma," Dad said. "That's okay. Go sit down. I'll get it."

Aunt Patsy looked sadly over at Mom. "She's been getting so forgetful," she whispered.

Nana came and sat down next to me, giving me a big, wet kiss on the cheek.

"Becky!" Mom shouted over her shoulder. "Come eat! It's your brother's birthday, for crying out loud!"

"I am in the middle of *painting!*" Becky shouted back in a voice that imparted her conviction that we could never possibly understand what she went through as an artist. The muse, she had told me once, didn't always sing at opportune times. Certainly, a hot dog or a hamburger was not going to distract her from her art.

Dad came out with the butter and slobbered it over the grilled corn. I loved grilled corn. It tasted like popcorn, only better.

Sweeter. Moister. Soon my lips and cheeks and chin were covered with butter and salt and kernels. Mom laughed, reaching across the picnic table with a paper napkin.

"Oh, Danny," she said. "You do enjoy yourself, don't you?"

They were clearing away the plates when Becky finally wandered over and sat down beside me.

"Maybe there's nothing left now, Miss Georgia O'Keeffe," Mom said to her.

"I see *plenty* of food left," Becky replied in that superior teenage-girl voice of hers. She tossed her long brown hair back over her shoulder with a sigh as Mom fixed her a plate. She looked at me. "Gross," she said. She meant my butter-covered face. Mom hadn't gotten it all.

"How are you *not* supposed to make a mess eating corn on the cob?" I asked.

"Normal people seem to manage fine," she said, sitting down next to me.

Mom set Becky's plate in front of her. With a plastic knife, my sister began cutting her corn away from the cob.

"That's no fun!" I declared. "It doesn't taste as good that way!"

"Of course, it tastes as good," Becky said, shoveling some into her mouth.

Nana and Mom were walking around, picking up dirty paper plates and cups. Aunt Patsy struggled to her feet and began placing the candles in my birthday cake.

"Do we have to *sing?*" Becky asked, rolling her eyes.

"Yes, of course, we have to sing," Mom told her. "It is your brother's birthday! We sing on birthdays, Miss Smarty-pants!"

Becky just sighed.

Dad lit the candles with his lighter. There were thirteen of them, stuck in between the M&M's that spelled out my name. As everyone—minus Becky—launched into a heartfelt chorus of "Happy Birthday," I couldn't quite believe I was now a teenager. Thirteen felt so old, so mature.

"And many morrrrrrre," Nana trilled at the end.

Mom was kissing my cheek hard, with a lot of exaggerated noise. "Happy birthday, honey!" she cooed.

"Happy birthday, Danny," Aunt Patsy said, smiling over at me.

"Happy birthday, son," Dad said, dropping a hand onto my shoulder.

I turned to look at Becky.

"Happy birthday," she said, without a lot of enthusiasm.

Mom passed a piece of cake to each of us. The adults ate theirs standing up, except for Aunt Patsy, who sat in her own folding chair. Becky and I were alone at the picnic table.

"So now that you're a teenager," my sister said in between forkfuls of cake, "you should start thinking about what you want to do with your life."

"What do you mean, with my life?"

"You know. Like what are you going to be?"

I was puzzled. "You mean like when I grow up?"

"Exactly, Professor."

I hadn't really thought about it. When I was a little kid, I'd liked the dogs and cats in the neighborhood, and I'd said I wanted to be a veterinarian. Then, for a while, like in second grade, I'd thought being a fireman might be cool. But Mom had me promise not to be a fireman, because, she said, she'd worry too much about me. For a while I'd thought about being an astronaut, but I thought that was just Desmond talking; I'd never really been all that keen about getting stuck inside a space capsule and shot out into orbit. After that, nothing else had ever come to me.

"You'll be in high school next year," Becky said, "and by the time you're a sophomore, which is what I am now, you should really make a decision."

"How come?"

"Because that's when you start thinking about colleges."

"Are you going away to college?" I asked her.

"Of course, I am. Do you think I want to stay in East Hartford all my life?"

"Why not?"

She made a face. "You are so pathetic, Danny. You really want to live in this crummy town for the rest of your life?"

"I like this town," I said.

She scrunched up her face even more.

"I guess I'll be a business guy or something," I told her. "Maybe a real estate agent like Dad. I'll build a big house in that cornfield behind us, and I'll put in an inground pool so you and Mom and Dad and Katie and all my friends can come over and use it."

Becky laughed. "*That's* your dream? *That's* what you want to be? How pathetic. You think I'll still be around to come in your pool? Well, think again, Danny."

"Why? Where are you going?"

"I don't know yet. But I'm going somewhere." She leaned in close to me. "I'm going to be an artist. And being an artist means you have to be willing to do things differently than everybody else. Chipper understands that."

"Is he going to be an artist, too?"

"No. Well, maybe. If he can get away from his father, who only wants him to play football." Becky shuddered; then she smiled, exhibiting a row of perfectly white teeth unmarred by any butter or corn kernels. "You watch. Whatever Chipper does, he's going to be *very* successful. We'll live in a big penthouse somewhere, like in Manhattan or Boston."

"Cool," I said.

Nana was behind us, collecting our empty plates.

"Beckadee, Beckadoo," she said in her singsongy voice.

"You know what, Nana?" Becky asked. "Danny says he wants to build a house in that cornfield over there so he can live next to Mom and Dad all his life."

"That's a nice thought," Nana said.

Becky laughed. "I think it's foolish."

Nana smiled as her hand patted my head. "The man who is a fool none of the time is a fool all of the time," she said, one of her sayings.

I, of course, had no idea what she meant.

Later, I wandered off into the cornfield. Most of the stalks were broken now, their fruit harvested, their leaves turning brown. I could envision a very nice house rising up from this field, a house where I could live, where I could be an adult. I'd have a room just for my comic books, arranged and catalogued on shelves, and another that housed a giant television and pillows strewn all over the floor. I imagined the house and the pool and the parties I'd have, with Mom and Dad and Nana and Aunt Patsy and all my friends being there. Maybe I'd even have a son by then. Imagining my future like that made all those worries about high school seem very far away, indeed. I didn't need to be afraid, I told myself.

Everything was going to turn out just fine.

PALM SPRINGS

The day was orange. Even though the sky was blue, and the hospital shone starkly in white and chrome, the day itself was so orange, it seemed that everything around me had caught on fire, and I was living in its reflection. Thankfully, Randall and Hassan were with me. I couldn't have gotten through any of this without them.

"Is it time?" I asked.

Randall nodded. "We're all set to go."

I turned and looked at Frank. He looked so handsome, so at peace. I knelt down and kissed his cheek.

"You ready to go home, baby?" I asked.

He gripped my hand tightly. "More than ready," he replied.

I beamed.

Pushing the wheelchair toward the elevator, I bid good-bye to all the nurses and thanked them for all their good care. Frank blew them kisses. Behind us, Randall and Hassan each carried a vase of flowers, the only two of the dozens that Frank had received that we weren't leaving for other patients to enjoy. One vase was filled with the latest spray of green daisies that I'd had arranged to be delivered every day for the entire week of Frank's hospitalization. The other bouquet was from my father, a collection of yellow lilies, white roses and baby's breath that bore a card reading LOVE DAD AND ANGELA.

I'd called him to tell him about Frank's heart attack, and Dad had seemed genuinely concerned, asking me if I wanted him to fly out. I said no, but his offer meant more to me than he could possibly realize. Or maybe, in fact, he did know how much it meant. Maybe that was why he'd offered.

"After seven days of hospital food," Frank was saying as I wheeled him down the corridor, "I'm actually looking forward to Danny's cooking."

"Watch it," I warned, "or I might lose control of this wheel-chair, and it'll go flying straight through that window at the end of the hall."

"*We're* cooking tonight," Randall told us as I maneuvered Frank into the elevator. "Hassan and I are making a very healthy meal of leafy greens and vegetables."

"I'm going to miss my ice cream," Frank said, pouting.

I hit the L button for lobby, and the doors slid shut. "Listen, mister," I told him, "you had three arteries clogged up. No more ice cream. No more red meat."

"And always lots and lots of water," Hassan reminded him.

"Indeed," I echoed.

It had been dehydration that had left Frank unable to call for help. He'd slipped into a state of unconsciousness as he lay there in his chair all night and most of the morning. The heart attack itself was not severe; if not for the dehydration from running three miles on a wickedly hot day without any water, he might have been able to even drive himself to the hospital.

The pain had come, Frank told me later, during his run. He'd thought he was suffering from heartburn, so he'd sat down in his chair when he got back home, kicking off his shoes, intending to rest for a moment. He'd been dizzy and light-headed, and in a few moments, he had passed out, with only the dimmest aware-ness of his condition.

"I wasn't entirely out of it," he told me. "I'd go in and out of consciousness. I knew I needed to get up, but I couldn't. I just couldn't move."

He'd had the sensation of falling, he told me. "It was a lot of work not to fall down the rabbit hole," he explained after the op-eration, when he was able to sit up in his hospital bed. His doctors told us he'd come through the bypass surgery with flying colors. "What kept me going," Frank insisted, "was the memory of your phone call, Danny."

He was referring to the call I'd made from the cemetery in Connecticut. He'd gotten the message when he'd come in from his run, right before he'd sat down in his chair and passed out. "I'm done here," I'd told Frank. "I'm coming home."

"That's why I hung on," Frank said, looking over at me with green eyes that seemed rekindled, sharper than they had been in a very long time. "Part of me wanted to slip away. It would have been easier than to keep hanging on. It was very, very tempting. But you were coming home. I kept telling myself, 'Don't go anywhere. Danny's coming home.' "

I had cried when he told me the story, pressing his hand to my lips, kissing his palm. Now I reached down and squeezed his hand again. With a chime, the elevator doors opened onto the lobby. The orange sunlight of the day streamed in.

Randall hurried on ahead to bring the car around to meet us. We waited for him just past the front doors. I watched Frank's eyes flicker up to take in the mountains, awash in vermillion. As always, his mountains restored him. He smiled.

Randall's SUV rolled up in front of us. "Here, I'll help Frank get in on this side," Randall said, hurrying around to take the wheelchair from me. "You put the flowers in the back."

Hassan had already opened the hatch and was placing my father's bouquet inside. I slid the green daisies in next to it.

"You have been quite the inspiration," Hassan said to me.

I looked at him. "What do you mean?"

"I watched you as you tended to Frank over the last week. And what I saw changed not only how I saw you, Danny, but how I saw myself."

I lifted an eye to make sure Frank was okay as he got out of the wheelchair and took his seat on the passenger's side of the car. Randall was holding him securely. I returned my attention to Hassan.

"What change are you talking about?" I asked.

"I saw a man no longer in conflict, no longer grieving for something that is missing. Rather, I saw a man in love."

I smiled. "So is that what you would be photographing, then, if you photographed me? Love?"

"Nothing so simple as that. I would be photographing love and commitment and determination and promise. And success. I think success most of all."

I laughed. "It's not a word I've ever used to describe myself."

"With Penelope Sue's commission, you might start using it more." His dark eyes sparkled. "Danny, I cannot begin to thank you for your generosity in that regard."

"Oh, please." I shrugged. "I'm just a hack photographer. My art comes in when I get the images onto the computer. You're the real shutterbug. So it made sense for you to take the photos of Penelope and Donovan. Then I can do my thing digitally."

"I have not done collaborations before. I am looking forward to it."

"As am I."

Hassan smiled. "To share the money with me is most magnanimous on your part."

I winked at him. "We need to stick together if we're going to get what we can out of the fat cats."

He laughed and slammed the hatch shut.

We were starting to head around to the other side of the car when I stopped him. "But what did you mean when you said that you'd changed your view of yourself?"

Hassan's voice dropped to a whisper. "You remember my doubts, no?"

I nodded.

"Danny, I come from a culture where a man does not love another man like this. Certainly not a man who has a virus in his body that might take him away before his time. But then I witnessed you sitting on the edge of Frank's hospital bed, holding his hand, willing him to live. I realized then that love knows no boundaries, abides by no rules. Yes, it sometimes becomes confused, sidetracked. But I watched you sitting there, and I saw on your face that you knew your journey with Frank was not over. That in many ways, it was just beginning, or perhaps it was starting over. I saw that, and I was not afraid anymore to admit that I loved Randall."

"What are you two whispering about back here?" Randall said, suddenly poking his head around the side of the car.

"You," I told him.

Randall smirked. "All good things, I'm sure."

"I was just saying that your Halloween costume was actually your secret fetish, that you dress up as Cher in the privacy of your room all the time." I winked at Hassan. "I figured he should know the truth."

Randall grinned. "See, that's the problem when you've known someone for as long as I've known Danny. They learn all your secrets."

We got in the car. Frank was in the front seat, next to Randall, his eyes wide as we headed out of the parking lot and down Indian Canyon. A water bottle sat next to him, and every few minutes he took a sip. It was a bright day, glorious. The mountains off to our right looked like papier-mâché, folded in various and intricate patterns. Frank couldn't take his eyes off them. I had the feeling that at some point during his crisis, he'd feared he'd never see his mountains again.

I had my own rush of emotions somersaulting in my head. Gratitude, most of all, that Frank was coming home. It felt incredibly generous, more than I could have, or should have, expected. And yet there was a certain odd sadness, too: an ache for a boy I had known for so long, a boy who had finally and permanently gone away. I had liked him well enough, even if he'd been riddled with fear and diffidence and uncertainty, traits that had sometimes made him hard to live with. But he'd been young and cute and occasionally rather witty, and he could often be a lot of fun to have around. But finally, in the end, all his anxiety, all his self-doubt, had proven too much, both for him and for me, and so he had gone away. I would miss him. But he had to go.

"The desert has been very good to you," Hassan had once told me. Indeed it had. Suddenly I forgave the place all the little faults I had found so egregious before. I reached forward in my seat and stroked the back of Frank's hair.

Hassan was right about another thing, too. My journey with Frank was not yet over. Might there even be a second twenty years